METADATA MURDERS

METADATA MURDERS

A Novel

by

William Fietzer

iUniverse, Inc.
New York Lincoln Shanghai

METADATA MURDERS

Copyright © 2005 by William Fietzer

iUniverse books may be ordered through booksellers or by contacting:

iUniverse
2021 Pine Lake Road, Suite 100
Lincoln, NE 68512
www.iuniverse.com
1-800-Authors (1-800-288-4677)

ISBN-13: 978-0-595-36822-8 (pbk)
ISBN-13: 978-0-595-81236-3 (ebk)
ISBN-10: 0-595-36822-0 (pbk)
ISBN-10: 0-595-81236-8 (ebk)

Printed in the United States of America

"Metadata is a cloud of collateral information around a data object...[and] a tool to accomplish various processes."
—Clifford Lynch from his 1998 keynote address at the institute, "Managing Metadata for the Digital Library: Crosswalks or Chaos?"

"Memory is like a shop in the window of which is exposed now one, now another photograph of the same person. And, as a rule, the most recent exhibit remains for some time the only one to be seen."
—Marcel Proust. *Within a Budding Grove.*

CHAPTER 1

▼

Memory can be a harsh mistress. The data we associate with our loved ones can warm our hearts or chill our souls.

Even kill.

The memory Benjamin Hackwell wanted to rekindle this hoary Minneapolis evening was the warmth of family relationship, even if the heat generated from that contact emanated from the heart of his personal computer.

He had received a pop-up message on his work computer from his daughter, Caitline. Her first e-mail to him in months and only her third since Ben's divorce, he had forwarded it to his home address to savor without administrative interference.

Ben unlocked the door to his basement bedroom, tossed his motorcycle jacket on the bed, and pressed the On button at the top of his computer-processing unit. In the moment it took his late model Gateway to awaken from sleep mode, Ben slapped three slices of baloney between the halves of an onion bagel, flung his silvering, blond ponytail over his shoulder, and hunkered down before the image of Farrah Fawcett on his screen saver.

He stuffed the bagel down his throat in three huge gulps and opened his pop-mail connection. Five new messages appeared at the bottom of his Inbox index. Caitline's appeared second from last. Ben double-clicked the address and watched the forwarded header data pop onscreen. Below it, he read

Dear Dad,

Here is the graduation picture you requested. For the video, try Caitline.com.

XOXOX,

Catiline

Ben grimaced. He'd hoped for something more. After ten months of enforced separation, she hadn't even bothered to correct misspelling her name. Caitline always seemed to be involved in eight things at once, but he had hoped her programming courses at the University would cause her to appreciate the value of such details. Obviously, it hadn't.

He clicked the attachment icon and his face softened. A cropped photo of a rangy girl of sixteen with a burgundy mortarboard clamped over honey-blonde hair laughed into the camera lens.

Ben studied her full mouth, high cheeks, and aquiline nose that looked so much like her mother's. Like Jennifer, too, was Caitline's ability to become the focal point of any gathering. Only Caitline's blond hair and cleft chin were his as was her ability to stand up for herself.

He smiled with pride at his recollection of her eleventh birthday. Caitline had insisted they go shopping at the Mall of America that afternoon. As his first trip shopping with her, Ben assumed they were scouting for toys, but Caitline headed straight to the perfume section at Nordstrom's. After directing the sales clerk to pull the purple vial on the second shelf of the case, Caitline handed her two twenties and dabbed the glass stopper behind both of her earlobes.

"Where did you get the money for that, young lady?" Ben asked.

"From my savings," Caitline replied.

"I thought we had decided you were too young to wear perfume," Ben said.

"You decided, not me," Caitline replied.

Nonplussed, Ben sniffed the bottle rim and inspected the label.

"Evening primrose?" Ben said.

"It's inexpensive, smells good, and I like it," Caitline replied.

"What am I supposed to tell your mother?" Ben asked.

"That's your problem," Caitline declared.

Jennifer never brought it up. Neither did he. Ben chuckled. That resolve still lurked in Caitline's eyes whose lavender color always reminded him of winter storm clouds. Intelligent, impetuous, independent, Caitline was more than able to take care of herself. That much of him he'd managed to instill in her before Jennifer took her away.

Something nudged Ben's pant leg. He ignored it. A more insistent rub prompted him to peer down into the emerald eyes of Desdemona, his 3-year-old gray tabby. She glanced toward the refrigerator and mewed. Ben felt the sudden urge to pee, but Desdemona rubbed against his leg again, took a few steps toward her food dish, and turned. When she was satisfied that Ben was following, Desdemona proceeded to her dish and supervised as Ben replenished her dish, checked her water bowl, and poured a new layer of litter in her box.

Ben rose stiffly from his kneeling position and entered the bathroom where he relieved himself in a steaming hiss. Such self-restraint hardly could be the brutish behavior of the self-indulgent animal that his wife had claimed in court.

He emerged from the bathroom and surveyed the room's Spartan interior with approval. The military tuck of his bed sheets could bounce a quarter. The title-alphabetized technical manuals on the bookshelf testified to his self-reliance and discipline.

Above him one of his two tenants thumped across the kitchen floor. The whine of the electric can opener indicated that Tyler Olson was getting dinner for his pet ferret. Ben frowned at the notion of having any rat-like creature for a pet. Yet, renting out the upper two bedrooms of his side of the duplex would enable him to meet his support payments and pay off his mortgage in ten years. Not too shabby, he thought.

His wall phone rang. He had made it his new personal rule never to bring work home. He had completed upgrading the security software before he left the office. Anyone calling at this hour wanted to repair his roof or sell a new long-distance rate.

The call switched over to Jennifer's voice mail.

"This is Jennifer. Answer the phone. We need to talk."

Ben's heart leapt as it always did at the sound of her voice.

Careful, he reminded himself. He had been hurt enough already. The last time Jennifer called resulted in his restraining order. He checked his watch. Ten seconds elapsed.

"Answer the phone, Ben," Jennifer said. "I know you're there."

He let five more seconds tick off.

"Dammit," Jennifer said. "This is exactly the behavior the judge warned you about. Stop what you're doing and answer me."

Ben sighed. Having a practicing lawyer for an ex-wife rendered evasion or escape virtually impossible. He cleared his throat and made a mental note to curtail the duration of the message file on his answering machine as he lifted the receiver.

"Hello?" Ben answered.

"Polishing the brass again?" Jennifer asked.

"Just reading e-mail from work," Ben replied.

"Your commitment to work remains consistent," Jennifer said.

"It comes with the territory if you care about what you do," Ben replied. "You should know."

"Touché." Jennifer chuckled. "I never did understand your fascination with computers."

Ben knew that. He also knew that it didn't bear repeating.

"Computer security constitutes what I do for a living," Ben explained. "It's hardly a fascination."

"What is?" Jennifer asked.

"Oh, I don't know," Ben replied, uncomfortable with trying to explain his predilections. "Lots of things."

"Like what?" Jennifer asked.

"Oh, the usual things," Ben said tried to sound noncommittal. "You know."

"No, I don't," Jennifer retorted.

"Okay. Spring rain, Keats' poetry, the roar from a big Harley," Ben said. He glanced around his room and spotted Desdemona under his feet. "Cats, too, I guess."

Ben smiled and rubbed behind Desdemona's ears.

"No people?" Jennifer asked.

"Caitline, of course," Ben replied and paused. "You."

"I didn't know you still felt that way," Jennifer said.

Of course, you, Ben thought. He felt the hardness between them beginning to melt.

"All part of the complex of metadata that surrounds me," Ben added.

"I never understood that, either," Jennifer replied.

"Metadata?" Ben asked.

"No, the flippancy," Jennifer explained. "Your need for the smart remark."

"It's not a need," Ben responded.

"It bordered on obsessive before," Jennifer replied.

"You never seemed to mind when my obsessions focused on you," Ben said.

"And just like that they didn't," Jennifer responded. "Why was that?"

Ben squirmed in his chair. His disaffection didn't happen "just like that." He glanced at his watch.

"Is this why you called?" Ben asked. "I'd rather we didn't go through my shortcomings again, especially at 10 P.M. on a work night."

"I'll try to be more civil," Jennifer promised. "Let's begin with formal introductions."

"Hello, Jennifer," Ben said.

"Hello, Benjamin," Jennifer replied.

"What do you want?" Ben asked.

"Aren't you going to ask how I am first?" Jennifer asked.

"It's late and I'm tired, Jennifer," Ben replied.

"You never were one for foreplay, were you," Jennifer taunted.

Ben gritted his teeth. He did not appreciate her sexual innuendo.

"How are you then?" Ben asked.

"Funny you should ask," Jennifer said with a giggle and paused. "Your support payment was late again."

Ben sat erect. Jennifer's true reason for calling was coming out.

"You know what my cash flow's like," Ben replied.

"I know your obligation to your daughter," Jennifer responded.

"I can't do anything until my renters' checks clear," Ben said, the anger rising in his voice. "You know that takes a while, sometimes."

"I know what you can fool a divorce judge with," Jennifer said.

"You agreed to the payment structure," Ben responded.

"I don't want to get ugly about this," Jennifer said. "You were supposed to take care of Caitline's college expenses. That's the only thing I asked for in the settlement."

"I told you I pay them in as timely a fashion as my cash flow allows," Ben replied.

"Then why is the University dunning me for her unpaid bills?" Jennifer declared.

Ben puffed the air from his cheeks. Jennifer wasn't going to get the better of him this time.

"Because you have her permanent address," Ben said. "If the University sends the bills to your address and you forward them to mine, it takes that much longer for them to receive my check."

Jennifer became silent.

"And you pay them on time?" Jennifer asked.

"As soon as I receive them," Ben replied.

"Has Caitline said anything to you about this?" Jennifer asked.

"I haven't talked to her in months," Ben replied with a mirthless chuckle. "Your restraining order, remember?"

"It wouldn't be the first time you lied to me," Jennifer's said. Her voice sounded flat, wooden. "I wouldn't be surprised if she's there right now."

"Is that what you're worried about?" Ben cried and jumped to his feet. Desdemona scurried under the bed. Stay in control, he reminded himself.

"Even if Caitline did want to see me, the restraining order prevents it," Ben said evenly. "You're the one who saw to that."

"That's because you can't be trusted," Jennifer replied.

"But you can trust me to supply the money, is that it?" Ben asked.

"It was your choice," Jennifer said.

"A choice I never agreed to," Ben replied.

"Look, get the payment to the bursar in the next two days," Jennifer warned. "Or I'll be forced to take the appropriate legal action!"

She slammed down the receiver.

Ben did the same.

So what if the University didn't get its money on time, he reasoned as he scanned the room for moral reinforcement. If Jennifer and her judges cut him off from his daughter like a crazed bull, hemmed in at every turn by support payments and monitored visits, that gave him license to act like one. They could expect nothing else. He reseated himself before his monitor and nudged the Enter key on his keyboard. Farrah's banal invitation disappeared. If you believed Jennifer, Ben obsessed over the Internet. If you listened to Ben's side, securing Web sites demanded a great deal of his time. As a masculine response to a failing marriage, Ben's withdrawal only mimicked obsessive behavior, but the judge sided with Jennifer's interpretation.

Ben entered the Web address Caitline had sent him and received a "The page cannot be displayed" response. He clicked the Refresh icon on his Tool bar. A sex site with links to a dozen more popped up. He clicked his Close icon. Another sex site appeared. With increasing alarm, he escaped five more sites that disabled his Back button or threatened fatal operation failure and landed in a bondage and fetish site with a western theme. All the women wore boots and chaps; the dominant one or two wielded whips. Its advertisements promised a greater feeling of superiority than they could deliver.

Ben frowned as he tried to make sense of what he saw. Why should the Web address Caitline had sent him be ensnared in a tangle of pornographic Web sites?

He clicked several of the links listed at the bottom of the page. None proved active. He tried the last one entitled VISAs. Despite the speed of his cable link, the response time was slow. The site contained either an enormous file or an amateur loading mechanism—or both.

Ben decided to abort.

A lavender and gray panel descended from the top of his screen. The banner read **XXXSURPRISE!** Under it:

VIRTUAL RAPTURE/TRUE LOVE
EXTREME SEX!
AT YOUR FINGERTIPS!
(Or wherever else feels good! And BAD!)
CUM INSIDE!

Ben smiled ruefully. Instant physical gratification was just a mouse click away—the old come-on. Most sex sites promised sexual satisfaction. Few promised love, true or otherwise. Or seemed so confident they could deliver.

Ben clicked the underlined link. The download again ran slow.

A gray panel ascended from the bottom of his screen. At the top the banner read:

EXTREME SEX!

Below it were two sets of downloading instructions. The one to the left read:

Download the girls who make your fantasies real!
Click to put this Love icon on your desktop.

The tiny icon was a winking scarlet heart with an arrow through it.
The second set of instructions contained a three-step process:

1. Click download button—Save lovemefree.exe to your desktop
2. Look for Love icon and open by double-clicking on it
3. You're ready to begin!

A narrow dialog box ran below with two sets of explanations of the user's rights and obligations once the user clicked the set of instructions. Ben clicked on the right hand scroll bar. The box contained an extended download icon; the software sent a credit of $49.95 to the user's phone bill.

Ben pressed his Back button. The screen jumped to an image taken from a video clip. A swarthy, naked man holding a whip in his right hand straddled the bloodied and busty dominatrix lying bound and gagged on the hardwood floor.

His screen went blank. Enormous red letters zoomed in from the left.

**HOW DOES IT FEEL
WHEN IT'S GOOD BUY?
FOREVER?**

That message dissolved into:

HOW *BAD* DO YOU WANT TO KNOW?

The letters revolved to:

**FIND OUT!
WITH TOUCHSCREEN
AND OUR HAPTIC INTERFACE!
ONLY $99.95!**

The screen flashed ADIOS! And went blank. It stayed that way for ten seconds before it returned to the opening panel.

Ben stared at his monitor. The experience recalled his ogling the science fiction covers of his youth. Like then his heart raced. He checked his hands and wiped the palms on the knees of his jeans.

It was foolish to follow their advice. You had to be pretty desperate to pay $100 when you could experience the same thing in the Warehouse District for half that.

Ben decided to leave and clicked his mouse.

The opening screen disappeared. A gauzy picture of a woman with incandescent strawberry hair and collagen lips beckoned him inside. She had a cleft chin.

The image faded to the Extreme Sex banner and its twin download icons.

Ben re-wiped his palms. The incandescent hair had to be a wig. That couldn't be Caitline under the wig. Many women had cleft chins. It certainly wasn't worth a $100 debit on his credit card to find out.

He clicked his Back button. The screen jumped to another video-captured image. The scene and setting remained the same. The swarthy man stood with his back to the camera, but in extreme close-up. The camera focused on the black .38 pointed at the left breast of the bound and bloodied woman lying on the floor.

Three shots erupted.

"HOW DOES THAT FEEL, BITCH!" the swarthy man declared.

Ben's screen went blank.

The woman on the floor was Caitline.

CHAPTER 2

▼

Early the next day Ben steered his Harley Dyna Glide motorcycle onto the acceleration lane by the Mall of America exit. He turned off the Beltway at the I-94 exit and headed west. Despite the potholes, the raw March wind, and the lingering snow piles the consistency of granite, his drive away from the Twin Cities eased his frenzied state. He needed to relax. Try as he might for the rest of the night, he had been unable to retrieve the video he'd witnessed the previous evening. Every attempt to reach the ExtremeSex Web site resulted in a 404 error or "The page you requested is no longer available" message.

He tried enough times until he thought he had imagined the entire incident. He lay on his bed and tried to fall asleep, but the intense image of three pistol shots fired at point blank range refused to leave his head. If the video was a stage-managed incident, he wondered why Caitline had gotten involved. If the video recorded a real murder, he needed to know how it had happened. More important, he needed to know who did it.

He considered calling some of Caitline's friends, but he could not recall the names of any. She had made the requisite number of friends and acquaintances during her years growing up in Washington, D.C. and later on in Minneapolis, but as Caitline raced through high school in three years, the friends she had made seemed to melt away. He had no idea about the nature of her acquaintances during her two plus semesters at the University of Minnesota.

Ben's alarm increased the next morning when he checked Caitline's bank accounts. They had been inactive for months. He fought the urge to drive straight to Caitline's apartment. Jennifer's restraining order permitted him to come no closer than 200 yards of Caitline or of her. When he tried phoning

Caitline's number, her security system blocked his calls; those to Jennifer's phone went unanswered.

He considered going to the police, but dismissed the idea. He had no real proof Caitline was missing. She could have transferred her funds to another bank. The police never would believe his story given such circumstantial evidence and his inability to retrieve the incriminating video. And when they discovered Jennifer's restraining order, they'd consider his story a ploy to circumvent the order and put him back in jail.

That's why Ben needed to get to work early. The pop-up screen at the Extreme Sex site stated that the customer needed to purchase a touch screen interface to access the site. That indicated the server at the site recognized only those computers whose metadata contained the correct security information. Though the commands from a keyboard or a touch screen would be the same, the server at the Web site accepted only those commands sent from an Internet address identified as having a touch screen interface. He knew that PHD's Public Services Department possessed a computer with a touch screen monitor that they used to provide directions and locate the offices of physicians in the building. He could adapt it to discover whether his nightmare from the previous evening proved true.

True or not, Jennifer had a lot of explaining to do. How could she let Caitline get involved in a sex site? Did she know?

Ben shook his head. He supposed not. But the court had entrusted Jennifer with the well being of their daughter. She was the one who had argued that riding on the back of a cycle with a pack of grown men was no place for a four-teen-year-old girl. If moral rectitude formed the basis of proper behavior, Caitline's involvement as a sex slave in a virtual reality video did not seem to Ben a step in the right direction.

He decelerated his bike from the down ramp onto the gravel frontage road that led to Professional Health Delivery headquarters. It loomed a half a mile ahead like a pile of tan brick Legos some colossal infant had stuck together in the middle of the prairie before being distracted by a prettier toy. Ben parked his bike in the crowded public lot. He could have parked in an underground space reserved with his own nameplate, but he preferred the anonymity and egalitarian-ism a motorcycle provided. He also fancied its potential for a quick getaway should he need it.

Ben opened the leather saddlebags slung over the back fender of his cycle, pulled out a rolled-up, red plastic case that contained pliers and screwdrivers he'd collected over the years, and stuck it inside his jacket. You never knew with every new job how much adaptation might be necessary. He liked to be prepared.

Ben strode through the revolving door, nodded to the yawning, young security guard, and surveyed the inside. PHD's offices faced out upon a central atrium that was three stories high covered by a glass ceiling. Though obscured by the bamboo tree and Savannah grass of the cement planter in front of it, a small, rectangular sign with black letters on a white background indicated the information desk that was located under it.

Ben squatted before the monitor seated in a rollaway stand at the other end of the counter whose continuous tape loop displayed the invitation "TOUCH ME TO BEGIN." Touching the screen displayed a directory of doctor's names and office numbers that lasted 15 seconds before the tape resumed displaying advertisements for local businesses.

A Dell processing unit hummed on top of the counter. Ben pulled out the keyboard shoved behind the CPU and shut down the looped display showing on the monitor. He spotted the icon for a Netscape connection in the Control Panel, double-clicked onto the Internet, and typed the address for the sex site.

Ben scanned the atrium and checked his watch: 6:10 A.M. Many employees started to arrive by 6:30. He needed to finish his investigation before they came.

He typed in the address to the ExtremeSex Web site. The Home screen that Ben had seen the previous evening appeared. He swiveled the monitor toward his side of the counter and repeated the entry process.

The twin pierced heart icons displayed onscreen with their respective sets of instructions. Ben nudged his cursor. The screen went blank.

Another video image materialized. The same saturnine, swarthy man wielding a whip and pistol straddled a woman lying bound and gagged on the floor. Beneath the shimmering bangs of her strawberry hair, Caitline stared at the man in wild-eyed terror.

Ben's stomach knotted, as if he were being forced to witness a train wreck. His immediate question remained unanswered: where was she? He was reluctant to witness her demise again to find out.

It's only a video, he reminded himself.

The screen displayed its haptic interface offer. Ben touched the pierced heart icon on the monitor. The icon bled red tears. The cool, firm, fleshy sensation in his fingertips recalled fingering a pound of well-marbled steak in a butcher shop.

The screen returned to the video image of the same cheap hotel room. The camera peered through the iron spokes of the headboard toward the door in the opposite corner. Ben touched the screen. The image froze. The curve of the bed frame felt cool and gritty as if it had not been dusted for some time.

Ben removed his fingertips from the screen. The video resumed. Caitline squirmed against the ropes that constrained her wrists and ankles. Ben touched the screen again. The intertwining weave of the hemp rasped his fingertips.

Ben lifted his fingers. The door of hotel room flung open. A lithe, male silhouette stood framed against the gelid light of the hallway. The door slammed shut behind him.

Caitline stopped squirming. A clammy bead of sweat trickled past her left ear toward the downward curve of her jaw. Ben froze the image with the tip of his finger.

His fingertip felt cool and hard like the surface of the TV monitor. That indicated tactile sensations did not accompany every image.

Ben removed his fingertip. The droplet continued its wayward descent until it disappeared under Caitline's chin.

The man stripped to the waist and secured the whip and gun from the rack on the wall behind him. Caitline shuddered. She turned away and covered her face with her trussed-up arms.

Ben brushed the crook of her trembling left arm with his fingertips. It felt moist, feverish, like flesh during a panic attack. His palms felt sweaty. He was experiencing every sensation that Caitline did.

Ben wiped his hands on the sides of his pants legs. The man on the monitor approached the foot of the cot. His somber, hazel eyes traversed the length of Caitline's body as if he was calculating her weight for market.

He stepped around the foot of the cot, grabbed her right shoulder, ripped away her bra, and spun her over to face him.

Cowering behind her upraised arms, Caitline did not look up. The man inserted his left hand through the red wristband, stuck the knob of the whip handle under her chin, thrust the handle upward, and slapped her right cheek. Hard.

Caitline's eyes popped open in surprise. The imprint of his hand faded underneath her makeup.

The man drew her face to his and puckered his lips.

Caitline spat in his face.

The glob of spittle trickled down the bridge of his nose and plopped onto his thin upper lip. His pale tongue protruded onto his upper lip and caressed the globule. Swabbing it dry, his tongue disappeared back inside his mouth.

He grinned.

Flinging her back onto the bed, he uncurled his whip and cracked it once beside the bed. Caitline gazed at the lash trailing down the length of his right leg. Her lips parted in expectation, her tongue poised at the corner of her mouth.

The man returned to the wall rack and exchanged the double leather lash for one of pale nylon. Caitline's eyes widened in terror as he inserted the new lash into the haft and turned round.

Ben's right hand remained poised above surface of the monitor. The line of his jaw hardened. What he witnessed involved neither sex nor love. Nor twisted rapture.

The man turned her over so Caitline faced away from him. He flicked his whip across her arms and legs. Once, twice, three times. Caitline shuddered each time.

Ben wanted to turn away, but forced himself to watch every detail. One of them might reveal where Caitline was.

Three scarlet creases the width of paper cuts flared across Caitline's lower thighs. A drop of blood oozed from her upper leg and plopped onto the bed.

The man grabbed her shoulder and turned Caitline to face him. She pulled away. He flung her onto the floor and raised his whip.

Ben's palm covered the screen at the first retort. He could watch no more. The nerve endings in his fingertips pulsed to the spasms of her mortified flesh. He shared her terror and her excitement.

"What are you doing?" a voice asked.

It was a woman's voice. Ben peered at the screen. The end of the lash remained frozen in impact on Caitline's thigh.

"Behind you, Mr. Hackwell," the woman directed.

Ben peered over his left shoulder. Constance Ordway's watery blue eyes peered up at him from behind the iron rims of her glasses perched on a nose pinched orange-red by the March wind. Bundled in her wool cardigan and matching black cap, she regarded him with the inquisitive detachment of an emperor penguin.

"I'm checking the output of this touch-screen monitor," Ben answered.

"And what output are you checking?" Constance asked and peered around him. "Looks like a dirty movie. Raise your hand from the screen."

"This doesn't concern you," Ben said.

"Mr. Davidson might feel differently," Constance replied.

She spun on her heel, picked up her bags, and waddled across the atrium toward the elevator.

Ben gathered his tools from the counter, stuck his equipment case inside his jacket, and shut down the computer. He needed to learn more about the Extreme Sex Web site. It seemed unlikely, but the coding on its Source page might contain information on where the site originated.

Ben tramped up the stairwell to the second floor. The cubicle that served as his office lay on the other side of a row of metal filing cabinets. With the wall of Davidson's office, they formed a hallway into the vast rectangular room that housed technical services for the consortium. Automated systems occupied this one corner; technical processing and the biochemical lab occupied the rest.

Ben entered his cubicle, stripped off his jacket and tossed it onto the metal coat rack beside his battered oak desk. Except for its size and utility, Ben regarded his desk as an organic anachronism in an office where every piece of equipment was modular and interchangeable.

The plastic cushion on his swivel chair chuffed its displeasure as Ben plopped into it and spun toward the monitor seated on the typewriter tray beside him. Ben turned on his monitor with three keystrokes; three more retrieved the sex site home page. He clicked on the "View Source" option and skimmed the few lines of HTML code on the page, most of which had been written in Frames. Outside of its title header and the placement of the pierced heart logos, the page contained little information.

Ben rubbed his chin with his index finger. The sophistication of the best sex sites never ceased to amaze him. They were sure to have a model up and running within days of the announcement of the latest audio or video innovation in the most advanced trade journals. In the survival of the fittest ethic that characterized Internet commerce, theirs proved one of the most cutthroat.

He scanned the source pages of the other few pages that constituted the site. They contained little information outside of the scrolling script used to secure the user's credit card number. He needed either to crack the security code that authorized financial transactions or secure its list of users.

Ben heard the rapid rap of someone's knuckles against the side of his filing cabinet. Mavis Portillo, Davidson's middle-aged secretary, stuck her head around the entrance.

"Mr. Davidson would like to see you in his office," Mavis announced.

"Right now?" Ben asked.

"If it's convenient," Mavis responded.

It never was convenient, but refusing never was an option, especially after PHD's first wave of corporate downsizing. Ben exited his Netscape connection and followed Mavis around the line of filing cabinets to the entrance of Davidson's office.

A tall, taciturn man who once had played a season with the Washington Generals, Brian Davidson stood behind his desk and gazed at his e-mail while stretching his arms above his head until his fingertips grazed the ceiling.

Ben rapped his knuckles on the doorframe.

Davidson beckoned him inside with a wave of his right hand.

"Close the door," Davidson ordered, finished stretching, and resumed his seat in his ergonomic office chair. "I won't waste our time. I've received a complaint from Ms. Ordway. Since you know the policy of this company about non-work related Internet use, I'm authorizing your taking a leave without pay."

"But—" Ben said.

"No buts," Davidson cut Ben short.

Ben blinked. No explanation? No request for his side of the incident?

"For how long?" Ben asked.

"Until the board of inquiry meets to make its decision," Davidson replied.

"That could take months," Ben exclaimed.

"Not nearly so long as that," Davidson replied.

Ben eyed Davidson with chagrin. It had been Davidson's idea to limit Internet access to the administrative staff of each department. When Ben complained, he had been relocated to the unused office at the end of the hallway. When he took his case to the administration, the upgrade scheduled for his computer went to the one in the atrium. Davidson had sought to get rid of him ever since. Ben had handed Davidson the excuse he needed on a silver platter.

"What about the security installation?" Ben asked.

"There are others in this organization who can finish it," Davidson replied.

"I wouldn't have needed to access the computer in the atrium if my own had been fully authorized to begin with," Ben said.

"So you could use it to view porn?" Davidson retorted.

"So I could find my daughter," Ben replied.

Davidson shook his head.

"Your personal affairs don't concern me," Davidson said. "Your security responsibilities do. And those are secondary to the well-being of our employees."

"While I have to safeguard the company Intranet with one hand behind my back," Ben said.

Davidson sat back in his chair and folded his hands.

"This company will not tolerate offensive behavior," Davidson declared.

"The only way not to offend someone is to do nothing," Ben replied. "Is that what you want?"

"You don't get it, do you?" Davidson said and leaned forward across his desk. "With these security alerts and our government contracts, everybody's on edge. Your viewing a sex site doesn't just offend our female employees; it violates their right to enjoy a safe working environment. You might as well place a burning cross on the desks of our black employees or paint swastikas on the monitors of our Jewish ones."

"And where are my rights?" Ben cried. "Just because I happened to access a sex site one time, I'm guilty?"

"I won't argue this any further," Davidson declared. He leaned across the desk and pressed a button on his telephone console. "Security? Send one of your men to my office."

Davidson stared at Ben as if he relished the thought of his departure.

"Security is sending someone to insure you and your equipment are out of the building by the end of the workday," Davidson announced. "Is that clear?"

"Very clear," Ben replied. He knew when he was outflanked. He pivoted on his heels and marched to the doorway.

"Stay at the door until they arrive," Davidson ordered.

Ben halted at the doorway. The lanky security guard he'd seen at the building entrance arrived a moment later.

"Close the door on your way out," Davidson said and resumed reading his e-mail.

Ben reached around the guard and closed Davidson's door with exaggerated carefulness. He marched to his cubicle with his escort in tow, grabbed his saddle-bags, emptied the contents of his middle desk drawer into the left pocket, and stuffed several technical manuals from the shelf into the other. Slinging the bags across his left shoulder, he picked up his jacket and strode past Ms. Portillo's desk humming "Whistle while you work."

When they reached the elevator, the guard pressed the button for the main floor and motioned Ben inside when the doors opened. Glancing down the hall, Ben spotted Mavis continuing to type at her desk. She did not look up as the guard closed the elevator doors behind them.

CHAPTER 3

▼

Ben felt glad to be leaving PHD headquarters. The security guard escorted him to the front door without a word, which seemed to him typical of their treatment of staff. Though Ben found his work interesting, the power games that Davidson and others in management played distressed him. The same power games had occurred during his career at the Defense Department, but he always found someone to hear out his good idea or different way of doing things. He never had found someone like that at PHD.

Nor anywhere else since he left the military ten years ago, Ben realized as he returned on I-94 toward Minneapolis. He smiled sardonically. Now that PHD had relieved him of the pesky business of earning a living, he had time to reflect on this.

Jennifer once had been there for him. But after they decided to return to her hometown of Minneapolis, she became engrossed in making a name for herself practicing environmental and copyright law. Ben fended for himself by accepting a series of computer-related jobs. None of them ever felt quite right or evolved beyond the term of the contract into a full-time position. He drifted into Internet security because the pay was good and the management interference minimal until his stint at PHD.

Ben pulled in at a wayside that overlooked the Mississippi River. Skirting the chain that blocked the entrance, he parked beside a refuse stand empty of its drum, laid his white helmet on the bike seat and strode down the concrete path toward the historical marker. He skimmed the paragraph about the inconclusive skirmish between settlers and local Indian tribes and turned toward the inky, swirling river. Broken slabs of ice sloshed and crashed against the foot of the granite bluffs and resumed their passage down river. On the other side, a dust devil whipped up dirt from the dormant fields.

Ben had filled the role of stay-at-home parent during those periods between security jobs. He smiled as he recalled the many days he drove Caitline to school and picked her up afterwards. One sunny afternoon in late spring he picked her up on his midnight blue Harley Dyna Glide. Rather than take their usual route home, he drove the winding Mississippi River Road at ever increasing speed until Caitline wrapped her arms around him laughing with exhilaration.

He told Jennifer none of this, of course. Caitline's riding on his cycle was always too dangerous as far as Jennifer was concerned. He wondered whether she ever had approved of anything he did with Caitline. The day they were scheduled to leave for the Harley Davidson convention, Ben had waited all morning as promised for Jennifer's call on the tobacco suit verdict from the state supreme court. When her call didn't come, he straddled his cycle at high noon and drove off with Caitline seated behind him, her aura of primrose perfume enveloping them both. They drove until sunset and all the next day, headwinds sculpting their faces like sandstone, a father and daughter idyll.

That's when their marriage started to disintegrate, Ben decided. Caitline had been caught in the middle. That was almost two years ago. Could that be linked to her disappearance?

Damn the restraining order!

Ben returned to his cycle. He had not spoken face-to-face with Caitline in over a year. She was missing, perhaps dead. A father should know the truth.

He was certain of another thing. Jennifer had caused this information gap. She damn well could fix it now.

Ben called Jennifer's home phone and her office on his cell phone. Both systems had caller identification. A detached, metallic voice announced that it was not programmed to provide access to callers with this identification number.

Ben paced back and forth beside his cycle. If he confronted Jennifer in person, she'd have him sent to jail this time. He was certain of that. That hell was not worth risking after all the time he already had spent in purgatory.

He recalled the sensation of Caitline writhing in terror under his fingertips. Her fear was palpable. Could he let his fear of jail time jeopardize rescuing his daughter?

Ben climbed onto his cycle and sped toward the I-35 Interchange. After navigating the midmorning traffic of downtown, he turned off on University Avenue. Jennifer's law office was located upstairs in a corner brick building across from one of the strip malls located near the 280 by-pass that divided eastern Minneapolis from western St. Paul. When heavy industry pulled out of the area, they took their revenue streams for local businesses with them. The refurbished office spaces failed to lure big businesses back. Or reduce petty crime. That enabled small offices like Jennifer's law firm to afford to rent from the neighborhood landlords.

Ben climbed the oak steps to the second floor. The boldface lettering on Jennifer's door read copyright, patent, and environmental attorney. To Ben that meant she'd represent any politically correct cause that came her way.

He grinned and stepped inside. Jennifer wore her politics on her sleeve only when its silk was paid for first.

The interior contained the same oak wood floors as the steps. The office, once a one-bedroom apartment, was partitioned into a waiting area and Jennifer's office. Her secretary sat behind a huge oak desk located in front of a bay window that overlooked the street. The photocopy and FAX machines stood in an alcove that contained a kitchen sink and a small, gas-fired range.

"Is Ms. Roloson in?" Ben asked.

The middle-aged woman wearing a flower-print, sateen hijab smiled and straightened the vest of her tan work duster. The nameplate on her desk read Mrs. Anouri. She spoke with a clipped British English accent.

"Ms. Roloson is in conference with a client," Mrs. Anouri announced.

"Do you mind if I wait?" Ben asked.

"If you wish, Mr. Hackwell," Mrs. Anouri replied.

"You know who I am?" Ben asked in surprise.

Mrs. Anouri's almond eyes flashed her misgiving.

"Wait as long as you wish," Mrs. Anouri declared. "Ms. Roloson instructed me that you were not to proceed any farther than this waiting room."

Her duster rustled as Mrs. Anouri stood up and sashayed toward the hot plate on the kitchen counter.

"Would you care for some coffee?" Mrs. Anouri asked.

Ben sat on the plastic chair on the other side of the railing.

"Am I special or do all of Jennifer's clients receive this treatment?" Ben asked.

"You are special," Mrs. Anouri replied. "But, yes, all our clients receive this treatment."

She returned with a metal platter that held two small porcelain bowls, one for sugar and one with cream packets. The aroma of almonds wafted up from his cup.

"Sugar or cream?" Mrs. Anouri asked.

Ben shook his head. Holding his cup with both hands, he sipped the steaming brew and watched Mrs. Anouri resume her seat. Sometimes the quickest route to debug a program meant using a workaround. In this case, the route led through Jennifer's secretary.

"What flavor am I tasting?" Ben asked.

"Ethiopian brew with Mocha almond," Mrs. Anouri replied.

"Jennifer wouldn't go to all this trouble," Ben observed. "You buy it yourself?"

Mrs. Anouri ducked her head and smiled.

"We are not a big firm as you know," Mrs. Anouri said. "We cannot help everyone. At those times our clients can depart with some part of a positive experience."

"Leave with a good taste in their mouths, you mean," Ben said.

"Exactly," Mrs. Anouri replied.

Ben set his cup on the counter behind him.

"I'd like that experience, too," Ben said. "If you could just call…"

"Oh, no. I cannot do that," Mrs. Anouri said and waggled her index finger at him. "Ms. Roloson warned how charming you could be. You are not allowed inside."

Ben stood up. At least Jennifer acknowledged that he had some positive qualities, however ill applied. He wrung his hands and approached her desk.

"Look, Mrs…" Ben began.

"You may call me Azeb," Mrs. Anouri replied.

"Do you have children, Azeb?" Ben asked.

"Two sons." Azeb pointed to a small picture frame standing at the corner of her desk. She picked it up and shook her head. "They have families of their own now."

"Here in the states?" Ben asked.

"No, back in my home in Ethiopia," Azeb replied.

"All the same, you'd worry if you learned something had happened to one of them," Ben responded. "Say, one of them was missing?"

Azeb nodded.

"That's my problem, too," Ben confided. "My daughter's missing. I think Jennifer should know that."

Azeb hesitated.

"Wait right here," she ordered. Azeb stood up, glided to the oak door at the end of the aisle, knocked twice, and stepped inside.

A moment later the door flew open. A tall, paunchy man with an owl's beak nose and a mane of sorrel hair emerged from Jennifer's office. With his tapering fingers joined at the palms, he marched to the hallway door with the solemnity of a chaplain at Vespers. Ben did not recognize him.

Jennifer ignored Ben's nod as she emerged from her office and escorted the man to the front door.

Ben watched the sinuous sway of Jennifer's hips under her gray mini-skirt. Trim and taut as a woman half her age, he approved of the renewed, raven luster of her hair and its short, stylish power flip.

Jennifer shook the man's hand for an extended moment before he turned and entered the elevator. When its door slammed shut, she flung the office door open and whirled toward Azeb.

"I told you never to allow him in here," Jennifer exclaimed.

"This is the reception area, Ms. Roloson," Azeb replied. "Is not everyone who enters to feel welcome?"

"He's the exception," Jennifer responded.

Azeb returned to her desk, placed her hands on the keyboard, and started typing.

"Leave her alone," Ben interrupted. "She did her job."

Jennifer spun toward him. Her cobalt eyes sparked.

"You," Jennifer said and motioned toward the door with her thumb. "Out of here."

Ben sat back in his chair. Once upon a time, those energy bolts would have melted his heart.

"I haven't been in this office in ten months," Ben said. "Aren't you interested why I'm here?"

"My only interest is that your appearance is in strict violation of our agreement," Jennifer said.

"I'm quite aware of the provisions of the judge's restraining order," Ben replied. "I'm willing to risk the consequences only because of the importance of what I have to say to you."

Azeb glanced up from her typing.

"Listen to him, Ms. Roloson," Azeb urged. "He has something important to tell you."

Jennifer trained her laser stare on Azeb.

"I'll be the judge of that, if you don't mind," Jennifer said evenly.

Azeb resumed typing. Jennifer turned back to Ben.

"You have one minute," Jennifer said and crossed her arms.

"Last night on the Internet..." Ben began.

"Surfing your usual haunts again?" Jennifer interrupted.

"Not entirely," Ben responded.

"Call the police, Azeb," Jennifer ordered and strode back to her office.

"Caitline's dead, Jennifer," Ben said.

Jennifer halted in front of her door. Ben stood up and repeated his announcement.

Jennifer turned, her porcelain jaw quivering.

"That's a horrible thing to say, even for you," Jennifer responded.

"I saw her," Ben said. "She got killed on one of the sites."

Jennifer reacted as if she had been struck in the belly. She shook her head and closed the door behind her. Wiping a lock of hair away from her eyes, she faced her ex-husband with a wavering smile.

"That's virtual reality. A toy," Jennifer said. "That's your problem. You confuse reality with your fantasies."

"Did I confuse reality when her body took three slugs, one right after the other?" Ben responded, shaking his head. "Or her trembling the instant before it happened?"

Jennifer took a step forward.

"What do you mean?" she asked.

"I felt it," Ben said and glanced at his hands. "I don't know how, but I felt her body on the screen."

Jennifer reared back, defiant.

"You sick, perverted bastard," Jennifer said.

"No, no," Ben pleaded. "It was part of the site."

"It was acting, you fool," Jennifer exclaimed. "You know she takes acting classes."

"No, I didn't," Ben replied. How could he? "When did this happen?"

"Last semester," Jennifer said.

"I thought she was in computer engineering," Ben said.

"She is," Jennifer said. "Caitline said she wanted to do something fun for a change."

"And you just let her," Ben retorted.

"Yes," Jennifer replied. "I did,"

"Without any input from me," Ben said.

"That's not for you to decide any longer," Jennifer responded and whirled toward Azeb. "Make that call. I want this man arrested before he ruins someone else's daughter."

Jennifer opened her office door, slid inside, and locked it.

Ben rushed to her door. He had to convince Jennifer of Caitline's disappearance.

"Her phone's off the hook," Ben exclaimed. "She has no money in her bank accounts. How do you explain that?"

Silence.

"Don't you care that her image appears on a sex site?" Ben asked.

The seven-note sequence of dialing a touch tone phone bleeped behind him. Ben turned. Azeb spoke into the phone and lowered the receiver into its cradle.

"It would be best if you go now," Azeb said and glanced toward the door behind him. "If the police do not find you here, I will tell them that it was a false alarm."

Her eyes entreated his.

"Please?" she asked.

Ben stepped away from the door. A siren wailed outside. The police couldn't respond that fast. Or could they?

The siren faded away.

"Who was the high brow Jennifer saw to the door?" Ben asked.

"That was Mr. Rykert," Azeb said.

Ben's face must have betrayed his bewilderment.

"He is the deacon of Ms. Roloson's church," Azeb explained.

"Church?" Ben asked. "Which one?"

"The one that sponsored our coming to America," Azeb replied proudly.

"Do you know the name?" Ben asked.

"Of that I am not sure," Azeb responded, frowning as she rummaged her mental data banks. "One of the even angels call churches."

"Even angels call?" Ben asked and smiled at Azeb's miscomprehension. "Evangelical, I think is the term. They're so happy with God that they send their missionaries everywhere to spread the word."

"Then you know," Azeb declared.

Ben frowned this time. Once upon a time, the closest thing to religion that he or Jennifer ever got came as a result from a spirited experience in the sack. Then she founded her Women Across Borders Cooperative to promote women's rights. Their marriage started to unravel after that. Now Jennifer had joined forces with a church deacon to rescue women trapped in third world hellholes and bring them to the United States. Part of him felt proud of her achievement. Another part felt more abandoned than ever.

Azeb leaned forward.

"Ms. Roloson devotes all of her time to him these days," Azeb whispered.

"All of her time?" Ben retorted. "With that queer duck?"

"Not so it interferes with her other clients," Azeb added. "But a good deal."

Ben rolled his eyes. He wanted to imagine that their relationship was platonic. "How much of that is off the clock?" Ben asked.

Azeb frowned.

"I am afraid I do not understand," Azeb said.

"Are they in a relationship?" Ben asked.

"They respect one another," Azeb responded.

"Sexually, too?" Ben persisted.

"Really, Mr. Hackwell," Azeb replied with a giggle and ducked her head. "I am sure I do not know that."

Ben noted the earnestness in Azeb's reply. Women always closed ranks to protect each other's reputation, he thought. Of course, Azeb meant sexually. He glanced toward Jennifer's office door and shrugged. Jennifer hadn't been his woman for some time. Seeing her with Rykert underscored the point.

Azeb followed his gaze. She sat upright and folded her hands.

"Ms. Roloson is not a bad person," Azeb said. "You must have hurt her deeply."

Ben grimaced.

"That knife cuts both ways," Ben murmured.

A siren wailed outside. It grew louder this time.

"Go now," Azeb urged. "Before they get here. May Allah accompany you on your journey."

"Thanks," Ben said. He descended the stairs and ducked out the back entrance as the police siren wailed to a stop in front of the building.

CHAPTER 4

▼

Ben turned his cycle onto Chicago Avenue and zoomed down the street. Jennifer had gotten religion. He wondered whether she had gotten Caitline involved. He supposed so, but tried not to think about it. He had made a separate peace with God and country when he left the military.

He revved the accelerator as he approached the street to his house and leaned into the curve. He had no time to worry about Jennifer's entanglements. Their daughter was missing, perhaps dead. Assuming Caitline was alive, It would take more than religion, evangelical or otherwise, to find and get her back.

Ben left his cycle in the driveway beside the birch tree, entered the downstairs hallway, and unlocked the door to his room. Everything remained as he had left it. He checked his phone messages. None were from the company, or his union representative. He had not expected any.

Was reinstatement what he wanted? Did he want more of the same until some punk Caitline's age or younger brought the system down? Before his dismissal from Davidson, his Internet security position already had devolved into stringing code in increasingly elaborate counter measures until the hackers gave up or the system crashed.

Ben brightened. Who better to help him find Caitline than Hoot Gibson, the Roughrider of the Internet? Their relationship went back to electronics school during his Special Forces training. Five years before they met, Hoot had emerged as the hotshot of the squadron, the plebe who instructed the instructors. Whether his exploits involved engines, computers, or women, Hoot bent all of them to his will with the wiles of a necromancer. When the Navy in its mega-anal penchant for security had wanted every rivet in their new submarine indexed, they recruited Hoot Gibson. The U.S.S. Scorpion may have sunk two years later, but every bolt at the bottom of the ocean had been accounted for.

The code they used for that job became SGML, Standard Generalized Markup Language. Hoot had helped create it. The military brought him on when they started ARPANET some years later. That evolved into the backbone of the Internet by the time Ben graduated from advanced training in military intelligence. Spotting a kindred spirit, Hoot took a raw, eager recruit under his wing and instilled military discipline along with his knowledge and appreciation of the intricacies and potential of metadata on the Internet.

Ben clapped on his helmet and stepped into the hallway. Muffled footsteps sounded on the carpeted floor above him. Someone scampered into the kitchen followed by a frenzied scratching on the linoleum.

Kim had her miniature poodle dancing for his supper again. Poor dog.

Ben hesitated and ascended the stairs until his eyes reached floor level.

Dressed in a faded red sweatshirt and hip hugger cutoffs, Kim Jorgenson kneeled on the kitchen floor and scratched her puppy's ears while he ate from his bowl.

When he finished eating, she tore a skein of paper towels from the roller, wadded them into a ball, dampened it, and wiped the floor where the bowl had been.

Ben cleared his throat.

Startled by the pair of bullet eyes probing her from floor level, Kim scooped up her dog and scampered to her bedroom.

Ben mounted the remaining steps as she returned down the hallway and stopped before him. He stared down at the crown of her corn silk head and searched the sparse cloud of data he had associated with her. Outside of her being a nursing student, he knew little. Did he even know her dog's name?

"Look, Kim…" Ben began.

"I know exactly what you're going to say," Kim interrupted. "You're right, Rex and I should have our own place to play in."

Rex? Ben watched the playful toy poodle slurping his water dish. Kim's dog did not resemble the king of anything.

Kim sidled closer to Ben.

"Took care of that this morning," she gushed. "Put the down payment on the old Nickerson place out in the country. We'll be out of your hair by the end of next week."

Kim grinned and skipped back down the hall as though Ben knew all about her financial transactions and the Nickerson place.

"Kim," Ben called. Her leaving sounded so impersonal. Was he at fault?

Kim paused inside her doorway.

"You don't have to leave that soon," Ben said.

"That's all right, I'm ready to go," Kim replied and giggled. An embarrassed blush suffused her neck and shoulders. "I didn't mean that how it sounded. It's just that when I'm ready to do something, I do it. Especially something I've dreamed about my whole life."

"How big a place is it?" Ben asked.

"Three-quarters of an acre," Kim answered and glanced at her wristwatch. "Gosh, look how late it is! Gotta a lotta packing to do before Tuesday. Bye!"

Ben watched her slip inside her room and click the door shut. An acre and a place of your own, he thought. It seemed to be the proverbial dream for everyone. He'd dreamt Minnesota could be that place for he and Jennifer, once upon a time.

If Kim was leaving next week, Ben knew he needed to place an ad in the newspaper right away. He also knew that he needed to see Hoot as soon as possible. If Caitline was missing, he needed Hoot's help before her trail grew cold.

Ben strode out to the driveway, revved his cycle, and headed south on Cedar Avenue. When he reached the Mall of America, he turned west onto the 494 Beltway, zooming past cars as though he was outrunning a herd of stampeding cattle.

At the Chanhassen interchange he turned south, west again, and then zoomed down a straight stretch of asphalt. The spring air slashed at his cheeks and rasped the insides of his lungs. The needle of his speedometer nudged the nether side of 100.

Puddle mirages appeared in the road ahead despite the chill. Ben eased off the accelerator. One might be real, he thought. You never knew which one.

To hell with it.

The needle climbed the bonus side of 100. All his senses zeroed upon the point where road met open sky. This was better than sex. This was freedom, this was life, this was...

A stalled engine.

The cycle floated, slowed, and coasted to a stop on the gravel shoulder between two dwindling mounds of ice-tipped snow. Blue-gray smoke wafted from the manifold. The reek of scalded oil filled his nose and lungs.

Ben scanned the area as he waited for the engine to cool. No gas stations appeared in his sight. He started the engine and let it idle. The smoke turned to vapor. It might be a leak. Or it might be something worse. Without the proper set of tools, he had no way to know for sure.

He checked the sign of the street that intersected Highway 5. Hoot's house lay two miles ahead. He steered his cycle down the roadway inches from the gravel shoulder. Several honking motorists zoomed by close enough for their wind shear to shove him onto the shoulder, but he rallied back, leveled off, stayed on course. Before he had exulted at every digit beyond 100, now he fought to steady the gauge at 30.

Ben reached the turnoff that led to Hoot's house and steered in a sweeping curve onto the country lane. The traffic here was less hectic, but he could not relax his vigilance.

Ben glanced at the sports utility vehicles standing like grazing buffaloes on the winding driveways through these manicured lawns. Hoot Gibson in the land of the soccer moms. It still surprised him that Hoot had wound up here.

Ben turned into a gravel driveway where a heavy-set man wearing a dingy pork-pie hat and cutoffs scoured the tires of his customized, copper-colored Ford Bronco with a garden hose. The man's upper torso jiggled like that of a chorus girl when he turned. Already in the military Hoot had evinced the physical attributes by which he would be nicknamed for the rest of his life. He looked even burlier now.

Hoot's gunmetal eyes crinkled in his gaunt face as Ben coasted to a stop.

"Shane!" Hoot exclaimed. "You're back!"

Ben grinned. "Shane" had been his war room identity.

Hoot extended a meaty right hand around which Ben wrapped his own. Pivoting his hand around Hoot's unresisting thumb, Ben thrust their joined fists up between them in a salute of solidarity.

"Where you been?" Hoot asked. "Haven't seen you since Fido was a pup."

"Don't get out this way much," Ben replied.

"You never did," Hoot said with a grin. "What's the matter? Is Jennifer losing her grip?"

"That's over," Ben declared.

"Yeah, I heard that," Hoot replied as he dropped his thumb over the nozzle. Twin water jets splashed against the Bronco's rear panel. "She never forgave you our little motor trip, huh?"

"Or you either," Ben replied.

"Too bad," Hoot said. "A Harley anniversary celebration should be harmless enough."

"She's a proud woman," Ben said.

"That's what happens when women go into politics," Hoot observed.

"Don't start," Ben advised. Jennifer's political aspirations had driven a wedge between Hoot and himself that caused them to see little of each other though they lived in the same metropolitan area.

Gibson turned his wrist 90 degrees, rinsed the Bronco's undercarriage, and gazed back toward Ben.

"How did what's her name, Caitlin, handle it?" Hoot asked.

"Caitline," Ben corrected.

"Caitlin, Kathleen," Hoot retorted. "Did you and Jennifer ever agree on anything?"

Ben chuckled.

"Only about the conception," Ben replied.

Hoot shut off the hose.

"Your daughter handled it OK, then," Hoot said.

"Well enough," Ben responded and shrugged. Hoot's probing made him feel uncomfortable. He didn't need to know everything. "Every kid acts out in those circumstances."

Hoot shook his massive head.

"Tough break," Hoot agreed.

"Didn't you always say we make our own breaks?" Ben gibed.

Hoot grinned and wrapped his arm around Ben's neck in a bear hug.

"Or they break you," Hoot replied. "Am I right?"

Ben peered into Hoot's steely eyes. Hoot's aggressive joviality threw Ben off guard. Hoot squeezed harder.

"Am I right?" Hoot repeated.

"Cut it out," Ben ordered. Hoot's roughhouse sometimes went too far. Ben grabbed Hoot's wrist across his neck, pivoted, and released himself from Hoot's hold. "Something's come up with Caitline that…"

"Something the matter with your steed?" Hoot asked as he spotted the thin plume of smoke wafting up from the Harley's manifold. "It looks kinda serious."

"Blew a smoke cloud out on Highway 5," Ben explained, nettled by Hoot's change of subject. "I thought maybe you could confirm that it's just a leak."

Hoot grunted and knelt on one knee.

"Start it up," Hoot ordered and listened with his ear next to the engine. His pudgy fingers palpated the folds of the manifold like a doctor sounding for pneumonia. "Rev it."

Ben turned up the accelerator and revved the engine several times.

Hoot nodded and shook his head.

"Turn it off," Hoot ordered. He grunted and stood up. "Sounds like a lifter."

"You sure?" Ben asked.

Hoot rolled up the sprinkler hose and headed toward the garage.

"Bring it back to the shop," Hoot said. "I might have something we can use."

Ben followed, steering his cycle around the bed of lavender crocuses at the corner of the garage. Beds of white and yellow jonquils flanked the walk that led to the breezeway.

Ben surveyed the fresh drywall while Hoot poked through the boxes in the wall of wooden cubbyholes standing against the garage side of the room. Opposite the screen door stood his mother's massive armoire whose drawers contained every wrench and sprocket known to man. An executive desk formed one side of a pathway leading to the inside of the house. A Compaq Presario 1460 computer occupied the corner of the desktop.

"You do your computer work out here now?" Ben asked.

Hoot glanced over his shoulder.

"That old hoss?" Hoot replied and rubbed an index finger under his nose. "That hunk of crap inventories my cycle data. 80 gigs hard drive, 512 RAM."

Ben pressed the Enter key. The monitor flashed the Windows 2000 display.

"Why not use this to find what you need?" Ben asked.

"Tactility, son. I'm a hands-on learner," Hoot replied and waggled his fingers. "I like to get a feel for what I'm pokin' around in.

My real workstation's in the house. You get lucky and I'll show it to you later."

Ben rubbed his index finger across the surface of Hoot's executive oak desk. It contained not a trace of dust.

"If I didn't know better," Ben observed, "I'd say this reflects a woman's touch."

"No such thing," Hoot responded. "Dust and computers don't mix. You know that."

Hoot grunted, pulled open a bottom drawer from the cabinet, and stood up. His fingers held a five-inch metal rod.

"This should do the trick," Hoot said.

Ben examined the rod dubiously.

"That off a Kawasaki?" Ben asked.

"Sure," Hoot replied. "But it'll fit."

Hoot knelt with a grunt beside Ben's cycle in the center of the breezeway and ran his hand along the manifold. He placed the rod alongside it and eyeballed the difference.

"'Bout a quarter of an inch too long," Hoot declared with a wink and stood up. "Don't worry. We got ways around that."

He strode toward the corner of the office where a blue plastic tarpaulin lay discarded in the corner. Hoot pulled off the tarp and revealed a metal lathe.

"Stand back," Hoot ordered. "I got work to do."

Hoot secured the rod in its holder and flipped the power switch. Turning a series of cranks and handles, he nudged the diamond-headed auger close to the rod until they joined in a shower of yellow and blue sparks. An acrid cloud rose above the spinning bore of the lathe as he sight-lined the bore plate with the end of the cylinder rod.

"Couldn't you get the computer to handle that?" Ben shouted.

"Sure," Hoot shouted back. "But we're not fixing the space shuttle here. I don't need precision tolerances, just need a rough and ready feel for how much to grind off."

"Your bathroom still in the same place?" Ben asked. Hoot's patchwork jobs often took a while to complete.

"Yeah," Hoot glanced up and grinned. "That information still in your data banks? Or did Jennifer delete that file, too?"

Ben dismissed Hoot's remark with the upward thrust of his fist, opened the screen door, and passed through the narrow, galley-style kitchen. It remained much as Hoot's mother had left it: avocado Sears refrigerator, matching Tappan stove, walnut-stained cabinets. The musty air of disuse and the stack of pizza boxes beside the cellar door revealed how the current denizen survived.

The dining room continued the ponderous decor with a massive old-country serving board that occupied the kitchen-side wall. Ben opened the first door on the left of the hallway that led to the bedrooms. Long and narrow like the other rooms, the bathroom's fiberglass shower stall lent a modern touch with its frosted glass panels.

Ben urinated in the rose-hued toilet bowl and washed his hands with one of the scented soaps shaped like Tiffany eggs. A faint fragrance of jasmine wafted up from the wicker basket as he wiped his hands on the rose colored towels.

Ben stepped back into the hallway. The scented soap and coordinated towels surprised him. The amenities of living never had mattered much to Hoot before.

The whir of the grinder emanated from the breezeway. Ben sniffed. The odor of singed metal pierced the musty air.

He strode to the end of the hall. If Hoot had pictures, they would be here.

He opened the door to the master bedroom. A metal desk, filing cabinet, swivel chair, and a plastic wastebasket occupied the center of the shadowy room whose chintz drapes were drawn shut. A 23-inch, flat screen monitor, keyboard, and laser-jet printer rested on top of the desk. A blinking green light at the foot of the desk marked the tower-style processing unit residing inside the leg well.

Ben knelt and examined the processing unit's case. Smaller than a standard Pentium computer, the entire outside identifying marks and logos had been removed. As with Hoot's cycle repair, the unmarked case hinted at the contraband nature of the contents inside.

Ben fingered the keys of the ergonomic keyboard and spun the tracking ball in the center. Twin black leather gloves rested on each side. Long as baking mitts, each finger contained three electronic pads connected to the central processing unit. Four more pads covered the expanse of the palm.

Ben turned on the monitor. The back of his hand brushed against a skein of wires that trailed over the back of the desk into the processor. Interlocking hearts appeared on the screensaver. Twin arrows entered from either side of the screen and pierced the hearts, blood dripping like tears down the face of the monitor until the bottom of the screen turned crimson. The screen turned blank, the hearts reappeared, and the process repeated as the arrows entered from the vertical axes of the screen.

Ben tapped the Enter key. The monitor flashed to the desktop image of a busty redhead, her lips slightly parted, wearing a pink peignoir and lavender bustier with her arms wrapped behind her head to enhance the bustier's uplifting effect.

He leaned forward and studied her face. Despite the excessive make-up, her cleft chin and gray eyes hinting on lavender proved the image was Caitline's.

Ben picked up the left-hand glove. The eyes of Caitline's image widened as she dropped her arms. He slipped on the right hand glove. The image smiled as she undid the knot of her peignoir.

Ben felt a smooth, slippery sensation between his fingertips that reminded him of the surface of a satin ribbon. He set the glove back on the desktop. The back of his hand brushed against a skein of wires that trailed over the back of the desk into the processor. They connected to a score of electronic sensors that encrusted a limp, nine-inch rubbery sheath.

A sudden shaft of light from the doorway obscured Caitline's onscreen image. "What're you?" Hoot growled. "The Internet nark?"

CHAPTER 5

▼

Ben returned the electronic condom to its place on the desk and faced Hoot. The mouth of Caitline's onscreen image remained parted and expectant.

"This is what you wanted to show me if I got lucky?" Ben asked as he pointed at the monitor. "Do you have any idea who that is?"

"Would it matter if I did?" Hoot replied.

Ben clenched his right hand into a fist. Caitline was 14 the last time Hoot saw her. That had been in the middle of cyclers' convention. He decided to give Hoot the benefit of the doubt.

"It might since it's my daughter," Ben responded.

"When did you get so virtuous?" Hoot asked. "Isn't Farrah still on your desktop?"

Hoot strode to the desk and turned on the desktop image of program icons set against a wheat field.

"You're a little old to be playing cyber cop," Hoot declared. "Or my mother."

"I didn't expect you to be diddling her virtual image!" Ben said.

"Is that what you think?" Hoot asked. "Get serious. This is research."

"Research," Ben retorted. "On what?"

"HUIs," Hoot replied.

Ben's expression must have betrayed his ignorance.

"Haptic user interfaces," Hoot explained. "You might have heard of them?"

Ben shook his head in chagrin as Hoot slid into the chair. It appeared Hoot was going to enlighten Ben again regardless whether he wanted the information or not.

Hoot rolled his chair behind the desk and opened the lowest drawer on the left-hand side. Producing a flat gray object that resembled a keyboard, he set it in his lap and extended the foot-long mechanical arm from the right side of the board. A metal stylus substituted for fingers at the end of the arm.

"Ever see one of these?" Hoot asked.

"A few," Ben responded. "Graphic pens, aren't they?"

"Computer aided design and manufacturing interfaces, actually," Hoot corrected as he returned the arm to its retracted position and set the interface on the edge of the desk. "Engineers use one of these to model their CAD-CAM designs to specific dimensions and tolerances."

"So?" Ben said. Hoot's pedagogy was growing tiresome.

"So, not every design can be visualized in two dimensions on a computer screen," Hoot replied. "And not just engineers use them."

"Yes, yes," Ben said with a dismissive wave of his arm. "Some of our specialists at PHD use them for heart surgery."

"Not very successfully, I'll bet," Hoot replied.

Hoot spun his chair around and pulled his keyboard to the edge of the desk. Folding his hands around the tracking ball, he nudged the cursor across the screen to a folder icon. On the third attempt, he opened it. A still image of the graphic stylus appeared onscreen with "HAPTIC USER INTERFACE" in white, 48 point Times Roman font written across it.

"Not very impressive, is it?" Hoot asked.

"I've seen more inventive home pages," Ben said dryly.

"No. No. My fumbling attempts to open it," Hoot said. He guided the cursor across the screen to the upper left-hand corner, pressed the left mouse button and closed the screen. "Now watch this."

Hoot reached toward the monitor and touched the tip of his index finger on the folder icon. The screen flashed on the haptic home page.

"What do you think?" Hoot asked.

"You have a touch screen interface," Ben replied. "A pretty sensitive one. So what?"

Hoot grinned and took Ben's wrist. The pressure from his fingers felt no stronger than that of a child's. He extended Ben's wrist toward the monitor and guided it toward the twin bleeding heart icon.

"Press it with your finger and hold it," Hoot ordered.

Ben did as he was told. The image fluttered under the pressure of his finger. It felt as if he were poking a slab of steak, as he expected it would.

"How does that feel?" Hoot asked.

"Squishy," Ben replied.

"Exactly," Hoot said with satisfaction. He pulled Ben's hand away. The icon returned to a stable image. He guided Ben's hand toward a folder icon.

"Press that one and hold it," Hoot instructed.

Ben did so again.

"How does that one feel?" Hoot asked.

"Smooth and dry," Ben replied. "Maybe a little grainy."

"Like manila paper?" Hoot asked.

"That might be too fine a distinction," Ben said.

"Pooh!" Hoot said as he dismissed Ben's reaction with a wave his hand. "You could tell the difference between the two images?"

"Yeah, sure," Ben agreed. "What's the point?"

"The point is that millions of users won't have to limit their use of computers to voice commands," Hoot said. "The blind can move around the Internet by touch alone. Cripples like me won't have to hunch over their tracking balls nudging their cursors like some squirrel trying to roll an acorn away for the winter."

Ben glanced at Hoot's hands. Self-pitying comparisons weren't Hoot's usual style.

"What happened to your hands?" Ben asked.

"The things that usually do when you spend your lifetime at a terminal," Hoot replied as he spread his hands over his knees and wheeled around to face Ben. "In my case an advanced state of carpal tunnel syndrome compounded by rheumatoid arthritis."

"I'm sorry," Ben responded.

"Don't be," Hoot retorted. "The things that don't kill you make your stronger. Am I right? As long as you're still man enough to do something about them."

Hoot spun back to his computer.

"Let me show you something," Hoot said.

With his two index fingers he typed out a lengthy Internet address at the top of the screen and pressed the Enter key. The image of a corporate homepage appeared onscreen with the speed of an exchange of camera shots from a TV studio's line feed.

"Helluva processor you got there, fella," Ben commented.

"It gets me there," Hoot said. "Monster band-width helps."

The page contained little outside of a cherry red Exit button and an apple green Enter button on a white background. The winking black and white camera eye logo at the top contained the word "WEB(W)RIGHTS" written in scarlet Gothic font.

Hoot guided his cursor over the Enter button and pressed the Enter button on his keyboard. A gray warning screen materialized with the declaration that the user was entering a secure area.

He guided his cursor over the Continue button and pressed Enter again.

The screen displayed an index page laid out in Frames format. An Index with miniature corporate logo buttons extended down the left-hand side of the screen. A summary of news flashes and corporate announcements occupied the remaining two-thirds of the screen area.

Hoot guided his cursor over the button inscribed Latest News and produced a list of summaries of the company's latest involvement. He scrolled to the bottom of the page. The update statement was dated from the previous day.

He scrolled back to the Archives section and guided his cursor over the button.

"We'd be reading it by now if they had my interface," Hoot muttered.

"Reading what?" Ben asked.

"Just hang on," Hoot said. "I'm getting there."

Hoot pecked out more commands. The Archives section displayed a long list of newspaper headlines going back the previous three months, all indexed by the first word of the title.

"It's in here somewhere," Hoot said as he scrolled down the list of titles.

"Don't they have a search engine?" Ben asked.

Hoot glanced over his shoulder.

"Sure they do, but it's not worth a damn," Hoot replied. "Just a basic word search. Didn't even pay the contractor enough so you could run a decent Boolean search on it."

Hoot stopped scrolling about a third of the way down the list at a headline printed in purple. He raised his fists in triumph.

"Here it is," Hoot cried and pressed the Enter key. The screen image switched to a lengthy text display. Hoot pushed his chair away from the desk and turned toward Ben.

"Read it," Hoot ordered.

Ben approached the desk and tilted the monitor upward. The headline read:

WEB(W)RIGHTS SEALS DEAL FOR RESEARCHERS

He scanned the opening paragraph dated ten days earlier.

> In a major move certain to affect research and development projects at every level, Web(W)rights announced an agreement with Westinghouse and Bell

Laboratories to secure royalties from all of their electronic and Internet research. Although details of the agreement were not announced, an unidentified spokesperson for Web(W)rights stated that her company would handle all licensing agreements for Westinghouse and Bell Labs. In exchange, Web(W)rights promised to supply and maintain rights management software that manages the access to and remuneration for both companies' patented and/or copyrighted information.

This contract makes Web(W)rights the largest rights management company operating on the Internet today. Wall Street responded favorably to the announcement. Web(W)rights stock on both the Dow Jones and Nasdaq indexes advanced with…

Ben paused. Despite all his work at a computer, he disliked reading documents that extended beyond two screens.

"Forgive me," Ben said. "But company press releases don't excite me all that much. Unless I own stock in the company."

"Don't you see?" Hoot replied. "They're controlling access to all their research information."

"So?" Ben said.

"So," Hoot persisted. "They're making information available only on a pay-by-the gulp basis."

"It's their information, isn't it?" Ben said and glanced back at the screen. "Can't they control it how they like, even if it is just to make a profit?"

"They're limiting access," Hoot declared.

Ben shifted his feet. He knew from past experience that his debates with Hoot seldom went anywhere, but he was annoyed enough not to care.

"What's to stop you from getting the information someplace else?" Ben asked.

"Because often there is no someplace else," Hoot replied.

"Research and development costs money," Ben countered. "They are in business, after all."

"I'd expect one of them to say that," Hoot said.

"Don't polarize me," Ben retorted. "I don't like to make a point of it very often, but corporate profits are what's been paying the bills at my house for the past seven years."

"I know," Hoot said and shook his head. "So little vision."

"And don't patronize me, either," Ben declared.

"You always were easy to rile," Hoot said with a grin. He leaned back in his chair and folded his arms under his chest. "Well, get riled over this. If Web(W)rights gets all the research companies to come on board, which seems likely, what happens to all the independent engineering researchers?"

"Like you," Ben said.

"Yes," Hoot agreed. "Like me."

Ben sat on the corner of the desk. Like most of Hoot's arguments, this one was self-serving. Ben resisted the urge to fold his arms and grabbed the desk edge instead.

"They factor the cost of accessing information as part of their grant application," Ben said.

"Pooh, grants," Hoot retorted and rose to his feet. "Is that what made the Internet? Did grants create interoperative platforming? Or Z39.50 interfaces? Did Westinghouse or Bell Labs or Honeywell take chances? Did Web(W)rights? Are they the ones who figured out how to make it all work?"

"Maybe not," Ben admitted. "But, they want to protect their interests now."

"They want to cash in, you mean," Hoot replied.

"If that's the way you see it, yes," Ben said and shifted his seat. "But, they were subsidized. Somebody paid the bills. Just as we were subsidized when we worked for DARPA on ARPANET and all the other projects right through Mogadishu."

Hoot peered into Ben's face.

"That was then, this is now," Hoot declared. "I haven't been subsidized, as you call it, for the past ten years."

"How do you live?" Ben asked.

"With what's up here!" Hoot replied and pointed to his temple. "And now they want to take that away from me."

"Through Web(W)rights," Ben said.

"Exactly," Hoot said as he returned to his chair and plopped into it. "They want to tame it all and make it pay."

Ben glanced at the monitor screen. The screen saver returned to the parted lips image of Caitline. His chest tightened. He resisted his urge to touch the screen. If that image were of anyone else, he thought. He left the rest of it unfinished.

Hoot lifted his head. His eyes searched Ben's.

"We made the Internet," Hoot said and reached toward the keyboard. "And some of us have balls enough not to stand for it being turned into a damned corporate slot machine."

Ben grabbed Hoot's thick wrist.

"Just a minute," Ben said. He recoiled at the touch of Hoot's skin. The flesh on Hoot's wrist felt flabby, desiccated. Old. "Companies like Web(W)rights don't intervene unless someone tells them to. Just who do they represent in all this?"

"A bunch of different groups," Hoot replied. "Nobody in particular."

Ben studied Hoot's face.

"Now why don't I believe that?" Ben asked. "You know everything about the issue except the identity of your opposition? Is that what we learned in intelligence training?"

Ben picked up the velvet electronic condom lying beside the monitor.

"Maybe you'd like to tell me how you got this," Ben said and shoved the condom into Hoot's hand. "Did this little number come full blown out of the sky? Or did somebody nudge you a little bit with the idea?"

Hoot's hand dropped into his lap. The score of wires hooked to the electrodes of the condom radiated down his legs like the tendrils of a stranded man-o'-war. He returned the condom to its place.

"Nobody nudged me with the idea as you put it. It was all my own," Hoot said as he resumed his seat and re-laid his hands upon his knees. "It was simple. You calculate the force by feeling a sample object, then feed the forces back through the tactile display capabilities of the software. You use large forces to affect the fingers and hands simulating movement, small forces to stretch and pull the skin to simulate texture."

Hoot was good at making everything sound clinical and detached like a good engineer, Ben thought. Yet, he knew Hoot was not an evil man. The time the spent together in military intelligence told him so.

"If you intended your touch device to be used by cripples and the blind, why did you make a condom out of it?" Ben asked.

"Can you think of a better way to promote its potential?" Hoot replied.

"To simulate sex?" Ben protested.

"Sex sells, my man, in case you haven't noticed," Hoot chuckled. "And I'm an independent contractor who needs to make a living."

"That's a rather mercenary attitude," Ben said.

"Maybe you haven't lived in the United States the past 20 years," Hoot replied.

"Maybe some of us still know where to draw the line," Ben responded. "I always thought you were one of them."

"Don't get all noble on me," Hoot protested and held up the palms of his hands in mock terror as if to fend Ben off. "Not everyone resigns their commission over a disagreement in strategy."

"They shouldn't have sent our soldiers in there in the first place," Ben declared. He felt his face getting warm, but ignored it. "Nor the men to rescue them."

"It's standard military policy to rescue injured personnel," Hoot replied.

"Mogadishu was a waste of personnel and time from the beginning," Ben argued.

"Maybe so," Hoot agreed. "But soldiers need to follow orders."

"Even bad ones that will get them killed?" Ben protested.

"The military relies on esprit de corps in order to survive," Hoot replied. "A soldier needs to feel someone will come to rescue him if he's willing to lay his life on the line."

"Mogadishu wasn't worth the risk," Ben declared. "Ten years later and the war lords and their mercenaries are still fighting it out."

"In hindsight, that's true," Hoot admitted. "Perhaps it was a bad decision. But someone had to establish the rule of law over there."

"You'll never have the rule of law over there," Ben declared. "It's in the mercenaries' best interest not to."

Hoot shook his head.

"Maybe so, but we're all mercenaries to some extent. Even you."

Ben recoiled at the certainty in Hoot's reply. They had disagreed deeply over the rescue at Mogadishu, but Hoot's response indicated a deeper cynicism toward people than Ben had realized. Wondering how far it reached into the present, Ben leaned forward and pointed toward the monitor.

"Did you know that your model was Caitline?" Ben asked.

Hoot glanced at the screen.

"Not immediately," Hoot replied.

"Not immediately," Ben retorted. Hoot was not going to wriggle off the hook because he was doing it for research. "When did you figure it out?"

"About the time she introduced herself," Hoot responded as his screen saver turned to a rushing star field. He nudged the space bar with his finger, and Caitline's image returned on the monitor. "You have a very attractive, friendly daughter possessed with an incisive, compassionate intelligence, much like yours."

"Thanks," Ben said though he was not mollified. Compliments were not going to get Hoot off Ben's shit list. "And yet it didn't bother you that the daughter of a friend is willing to come to your home to simulate sex with you?"

"Pooh," Hoot replied. His hand sliced the air in irritation. "How many third world hellholes were we involved in where the families sold their daughters into slavery? Or just plain abandoned them?"

"This isn't the third world," Ben replied.

"The same things happen here," Hoot observed. "More than you know."

"What's that supposed to mean?" Ben asked.

Hoot removed his hat and smoothed his few gray hairs across his forehead in an effort to appear conciliatory.

"Look, I don't have a daughter," Hoot observed. "But, it was pretty clear after talking to her for a while that here was a girl with issues."

"Issues?" Ben said in surprise. "What issues?"

"What teenager caught in the middle of a divorce isn't going to have issues?" Hoot responded. "An attractive girl with an active brain is bound to act out."

Ben recoiled. How much had Caitline confided to Hoot? Why him?

"What do you mean by acting out?" Ben replied.

"You know the old saying, if it looks like a data object and acts like a data object," Hoot said as he studied the brim of his hat in his hands. He peered up at Ben. "Sleeping with the first stranger she met seemed like acting out to me."

"If you think I expected that to happen—" Ben began.

"I don't," Hoot interrupted. "But what kind of a father brings his teenage daughter to a motorcycle convention?"

"What kind—" Ben spluttered. He had wanted someone to share the experience with him. Jennifer was too busy, so he had turned to his daughter. Hoot was sounding just like his ex-wife. What did he know of being a father, or a husband? He knew nothing about family, or love.

"What kind of friend doesn't tell the parent about his underage daughter's sexual activities?" Ben replied.

"I'm telling you now," Hoot declared. "Caitline told me she was tired of being a pawn in of your arguments with Jennifer."

Ben stiffened. Caitline never indicated she was unhappy with him.

"That's ridiculous," he replied. "I never placed her in harm's way."

"That's not how Caitline saw it," Hoot responded.

"And she was so mad at me that she ran out and got involved in the first sex site she could find," Ben said.

"I wanted to tell you, but Caitline wouldn't hear of it," Hoot replied.

"Headline: Teenage girl Prevents Special Forces veteran from revealing sex site experiments," Ben hooted. "Tell me, did she beat you, or just tie you up?"

"Look, all I was looking for was an attractive, capable girl who knew something about computers and was willing to participate in my research on touch screen interfaces," Hoot explained. "There was no way I could know they'd send me Caitline."

"They?" Ben asked. "Who's they?"

"Schariah's," Hoot answered. "They're a sex club in the warehouse district."

"Why them?" Ben asked.

"Their Web site advertises that their dancers are available for parties, gatherings, films, and videos," Hoot said.

"That's interesting," Ben murmured.

"Why?" Hoot asked.

"Because one of the clips Caitline's in is a snuff film," Ben replied.

"And you think…" Hoot paused and sucked air in between his lips. "Those bastards! You can't trust 'em."

"What do you mean?" Ben asked.

"Don't you see?" Hoot said as he rose to his feet. "Schariah's are the people battling me for the intellectual property rights."

He placed his right arm on Ben's shoulder.

"Look, I contacted them to send someone to model, figuring they'd be used to removing their clothes," Hoot confided. "I had no idea they'd send me Caitline."

Ben shook his head. That was the amazing thing about the Internet. You had a universe of data at your fingertips. How you felt and acted upon that data was your own business.

Hoot pushed the cursor to one of his bookmarks. The photographic image of a swarthy man's face in three-quarter profile appeared on the screen.

"Here's the leader of the sex site group," Hoot said as he stepped back from the monitor. "Scott Wilson. His real name is Wilzetsky. He's a Russian-German émigré out of the Ukraine by way of Chechnya. He came here on refugee status after the Soviet collapse in '88. He owns Schariah's gentlemen's club. He's the one's that organized the sex site owners to throw their weight behind Web(W)rights."

Hoot eyed Ben with uncertainty.

"I could use someone who can build a firewall to keep them off my back, maybe crack an encryption code or two," Hoot said. "How'd you feel about working for me?"

Ben studied the narrow, saturnine face on the monitor. Wilson appeared to be about 35, with pockmarked cheeks and a high forehead that detracted from what some people might consider cruelly handsome looks. He refused to speculate whether one of them was Caitline.

Hoot followed Ben's gaze.

"He used to be some kind of a movie star over there," Hoot added. "Porn probably. Hardly looks like a lady killer though, does he."

Hoot rubbed the back of his neck.

"So, how do you feel about it?" Hoot asked. "It'd be like old times."

Ben grimaced as he peered around the distracting sway of Hoot's chest and gazed at Caitline's image on Hoot's screensaver. Her full lips remained parted in the same yearning position. Emotions swirled throughout and about him like conflicting cyclones. Each new data bit fed their intensity until all he wanted was to escape the maelstrom that constituted his feelings.

He glanced toward his cycle.

"You fix my bike?" Ben asked.

"It's ready when you are," Hoot replied.

"I'll be in touch," Ben said with relief. "Don't hold your breath."

Hoot slumped in his chair as Ben slammed the door behind him.

CHAPTER 6

▼

Ben rolled his motorcycle out the breezeway door and down the jonquil-flanked walk to the rear of Gibson's Bronco. It took two pumps before the engine engaged. He revved it to 5000 rpm and throttled back. It idled rough, but all right considering the patchwork nature of the job.

He spun his cycle in a tight arc and drove down the driveway into the street. He glanced over his shoulder as his cycle mounted the crest of the hill and spotted Hoot watching him from the doorway.

Ben turned and focused on the road ahead. Hoot had no right to enlist him in his private Internet war just because they had worked and trained together years ago. He never could trust Hoot again. Whether he did it for the sake of technology, whether it was with Caitline's virtual image, whether he knew it was her or not, Hoot had violated Ben's trust.

A wind-blown tear trickled down Ben's right cheek. Dismissing it as a speck of road dust kicked up by the cycle, Ben flicked it away and noticed his right hand was trembling. It felt weak, enervated. He knotted his hand into a fist until the cords along his arm tingled with strength, with purpose, with the conviction only a father knows protecting his loved ones.

Ben squeezed the throttle. The engine wailed, and his cycle plunged forward.

What did Hoot know of exhilaration? Of frenzied abandon? Of power, or of love? All he had was his limp-wristed little interface, and the pathetic constituency it served. People who had no real life, people who got their kicks second-hand from an engineer's gradient curve, who cowered before real sensation as Caitline had before each crack of the whip.

Caitline.

Ben relaxed his grip on the throttle.

He'd felt Caitline's sweat-glistened shoulder trembling. Her fear was palpable. Real. If not then, if not in real time, it had occurred somewhere else for Hoot to model it.

As had the torture. And the beatings. And…

Why had Caitline confided in Hoot instead of him? Hoot had not married. He had no children. He hadn't sacrificed his career for his family as Ben had. If Caitline had issues about the divorce, she could have come to him. As her father, that would have been the natural thing to do. If Caitline was acting out, why had she chosen this monstrous way to do it?

Ben wiped his cheeks again and peered ahead through the wind shear. The exit ramp to Lyndale Avenue lay a quarter mile beyond. As if on automatic pilot, his cycle had delivered him to the place he needed to go. He calculated that Caitline's apartment was located two miles north off of Lyndale in the Uptown District. A simple visit to her apartment would allay all of his misgivings.

The court injunction? To hell with it, Ben decided. To hell with 'em all.

He steered his cycle onto the exit ramp and maneuvered past a sluggish Volvo onto the street as the access light flashed amber. Ben slowed his cycle to a pedestrian thirty and steered around a road repair barrier. Constant as the equinox, more vivid than the robins, the true harbingers of spring milled about in burnt orange coveralls as they patched a string of potholes.

The aroma of asphalt invaded Ben's nostrils, suffused his lungs. He chuckled as he recalled the old saw about the two seasons that comprised Minnesota's calendar: winter and road repair. He relaxed his grip on the handlebars. In a few minutes, everything would be put right. He'd see Caitline, dismiss her reproaches about the court injunction, and reabsorb himself in finding a better job.

He turned off on Halifax Avenue and parked his cycle in front of a three-story brownstone apartment complex on the next corner. Built like many of the apartment buildings in this area, the wings of each end of the building formed a courtyard. What differentiated this complex was the black, wrought iron fence that enclosed the courtyard.

Two lissome women slightly older than Caitline, perhaps 18 or 19, squeezed through the cumbersome gate and swung it back until it clicked shut. They pivoted on their roller blades, eyed Ben up and down, and skated up the sidewalk.

Ben watched them proceed down the street and climb inside a black Ford minivan. Arms wrapped around each other's shoulders in loose embrace, giggling, sharing each other's secrets, the girls embodied the joie de vivre that attracted upscale mothers like Jennifer to pick a place like this to launch their fledgling daughters into the world.

Ben approached the gate and peered at the brass plate embedded in the bricks at the apex of the arch. The tarnished letters on the plate read:

GRAFTON APTS

He pressed the intercom button bolted against the underside of the arch. A smoky, female voice with a trace of Slavic accent asked what he wanted.

"Could you notify Caitline Hackwell that her father's here?" Ben asked.

After a pause, the smoky voice reported that their records indicated he was barred from associating with his daughter.

"I understand that," Ben answered. He had expected this procedural delay. "I just want to check whether she's all right."

"I can assure you that she is," the doorwoman replied.

"When was the last time you saw her?" Ben asked.

"I can assure you that your daughter is fine," the doorwoman said.

"Have you actually seen her?" Ben persisted.

"Mr. Hackwell, I must insist—"

"Look, whoever you are," Ben interrupted, tiring of the woman's interference. "I have reason to believe that Caitline's well-being may be in jeopardy. I simply want to confirm that those misgivings are not accurate. That is still a father's privilege, is it not?"

"We have a court order signed by the young woman's mother to the—" the woman said.

"Is it not?" Ben repeated.

"Yes," the woman admitted. "But, I am not permitted to allow you inside."

"Do you have any idea whether she's in her room?" Ben asked.

"Yes, I think so," she replied uncertainly.

"Could you ring her room for me, please," Ben asked. "And let me speak to her?"

"I imagine that would be all right," the doorwoman replied.

A lengthy pause ensued. Ben gazed through the iron bars and studied the dormant rose beds laid out in arced rows in the front half of the quadrangle. White, plastic cones encompassed each bush like snoods. Cheesecloth draped over the tops completed the wimpling effect. Behind them, white jonquils danced in the wind.

A metallic click and scrape on the intercom announced that the disembodied doorperson had returned.

"Mr. Hackwell," the doorwoman said. "Your daughter does not appear to be in at this present time."

"That doesn't disturb you?" Ben replied.

"We are dealing with young adults," she responded. "They are free to come and go as they see fit."

Ben glanced up and down the street. He refused to let this gatekeeper's obstinacy throw him into a panic. He had to find some way to get through to her.

"What if I reported this situation to her mother?" Ben replied. "She might not prove as sanguine about the quality of your monitoring, especially given the money she's paying you."

"That is your prerogative," the doorwoman said. "We encourage collaboration between the parents of each of our residents."

That's enough, Ben decided. He grabbed the bars of the iron door and shook them. The door yielded half an inch. He stepped back.

"Look, I believe my daughter may be in jeopardy," Ben cried at the intercom. "Nothing you've told me eases that concern. She hasn't answered my calls, her bank accounts have been closed, and no one has seen her for weeks. If you were her father, wouldn't you be worried?"

The voice on the other end remained silent.

"Are you still there?" Ben asked.

"Yes," the doorwoman replied. "I am still here."

"Well, how about it?" Ben urged. "Can I see my daughter or not?"

"You were informed that she is not in," she replied.

"Could I see her apartment, at least?" Ben asked.

"That would be violating your daughter's privacy," she said.

Ben clenched his hands. Caitline already had been violated to death.

"If she were home, I'd at least check her room occasionally," Ben argued. "Even if only to pick up her dirty clothes."

A brief, throaty chuckle erupted on the other end.

"Your daughter is not at home any more," the doorwoman reasoned. "And she's responsible for her own laundry. What would checking her room accomplish now?"

"At least I'd know if it was lived in," Ben replied.

"You could tell from that?" she asked.

"If that's all the data I had, yes," Ben said.

"There's still the matter of the restraining order," the doorwoman pointed out.

"That only applies if we meet in person," Ben responded. "If she's out as you say, the order won't be violated."

"Very well," the woman answered.

A buzzer sounded followed by a staunch metallic click. The barred iron door nudged forward.

Ben seized the bars of the door and heaved. It halted quivering six inches away from crashing against the bricks that formed the opposite side of the arch.

He strode through the entrance and halted at the corner of the rose bed. The door glided behind him to its original position and clicked shut.

Strolling up the sidewalk on the left-hand side of the quadrangle, Ben found little to see inside the ground floor apartments. Most had their drapes pulled shut.

He mounted three crumbling granite steps to the entrance and peered inside. A battery of bronze mailboxes constituted the right side of the entrance with the end of an apartment desktop curving out of sight beyond that. Crowded groupings of ferns and worn, crushed velvet armchairs occupied the small atrium beyond.

The glass door swung open easily. Ben peered around the corner of desk. No one appeared in sight.

He examined the mailboxes. Each key-locked box contained a small window to view the contents of the cubbyhole inside. Room 516's box contained nothing.

An aroma of gardenias engulfed him as the smoky voice confirmed, "It's been empty for ten days. I checked."

Ben turned. A buxom strawberry redhead dressed in jeans and a dirt-stained, work shirt knotted at the waist eyed him up and down. A smile hovered at the corners of her full mouth.

"And you are?" Ben asked.

"Sophia Nachayev," the woman responded. "Warden of this place."

Sophia's smile broadened as she offered him a freckled, bony right hand.

Ben shook it. Her grip was firm, manlike.

"I apologize for the inquisition," Sophia added. "We are supposed to be careful whom we admit."

Sophia's hazel eyes sparkled. Ben felt his resolve of purpose ebbing.

"So, you think you have lost your daughter?" Sophia asked.

"Not yet," Ben replied. "But I'd prefer to confirm that my misgivings are just in my head."

Ben glanced at the handle of the garden shears poking out of one front pants pocket. The antenna of a two-way radio protruded from the other.

"What's that for?" Ben asked and pointed at the radio.

"Coordinating our staff," Sophia responded.

"And the shears?" Ben asked.

"Trimming the bushes," Sophia replied.

"Your job description includes maintaining the shrubbery?" Ben asked in surprise.

"Virtually everything when you run the place," Sophia replied with an easy laugh. She pointed past Ben's shoulder. "Your daughter helped me plan the garden out there."

"Who did the planting?" Ben asked.

"Caitline did," Sophia responded. "It was her idea to plant roses with jonquils. I'd never have thought of that combination."

Ben felt totally disarmed. Jonquils were Caitline's favorite, he recalled. She had told him once that you could tell the difference between them and daffodils because daffodils had no fragrance.

"Let us put your fears to rest," Sophia encouraged as she guided Ben by the elbow down the hallway. "Then I will show you the place."

She maneuvered him past the elevator to the stairwell door on the opposite side, opened it, and sprang up the cement steps.

"It's only five flights!" Sophia exclaimed and bounded up the stairwell.

Ben grabbed the railing and followed. He paused on the landing of the third floor and gasped for breath. Sophia maintained the youthful exuberance of her charges despite being twice their age.

He trekked up the remaining two floors and reached for the doorknob. His right hand quivered, his neck and forehead felt flushed. Did he dread what he might find? Or had he grown so far out of shape?

Ben opened the metal fire door. Sophia stood in front of the window at the other end of the hallway and fiddled with the drawstrings of the Venetian blinds. The afternoon sun cast lurid bars across the mahogany stained door opposite. The brass numerals above the peephole read 516.

Sophia spun toward him.

"That wasn't so bad, was it?" Sophia asked.

Ben shook his head.

"Not if you're a mountain goat," Ben replied.

Sophia grinned, grabbed the metal chain around her neck, and withdrew a plastic key card out of her cleavage.

"You need to exercise your heart more often," Sophia advised.

Sophia inserted the card. Nothing happened. She pulled a pocket scanner from her pocket, recalibrated the card, and tried again. The door opened. Lit only by the fading light from the hallway, the nether reaches of the room remained in total darkness. An odor of moldering food lingered in the stale air.

Sophia flicked the light switch beside the doorway. Nothing happened.

Ben stumbled over a pile of clothes on his way to the window. He pulled on the bottom of the drawn shade. Nothing happened. The shade had been taped shut with duct tape.

He ripped the tape from both sides of the frame. The shade sprang up to the roller with a retort like a starter's pistol.

Men and women's clothes lay in scattered heaps on the beige carpet of the empty living room/kitchen. A stack of cardboard boxes from a local pizza delivery, Pisa Pizza, lay on the counter beside the metal sink.

"Where's all the furniture?" Ben asked.

He opened the door nearest to him. A battered mahogany coffee table lay tilted on one end inside. A metal lamp and shade resided in the space under it.

He strode to the partly open doorway on other side of the room and pushed the door inward until it hit the exterior wall. A metal bed frame and mattress occupied the far corner of the otherwise empty bedroom inside. The carpet had been pulled up to reveal the grimy oak floor beneath. Ben opened the closet door. A lime green wool carpet lay rolled up against the back wall.

Ben examined the headboard. The black lacquer finish had rubbed off in equi-distant spots. The footrest contained similar markings.

He scanned the room. Everything resembled the room in Caitline's video.

Ben's heart raced. He sat on the mattress, waiting for his pulse to return to normal while he gazed slowly around the room. The angle from the bed was identical to the one in the video.

He peered at the brick wall behind the metal struts of the headboard. As one of the outside walls of the building, it contained little room for a hidden camera.

"Find anything?" Sophia asked.

"Just what kind of an establishment are you running, Ms. Nechayev?" Ben asked.

"I assure—"

"Stay where you are," Ben ordered.

He lay on the mattress, eyeballed the angle from the door to the bed, and pushed the cot frame away from the corner of the intersecting walls. A one-inch groove had been gouged into the plaster just above bed level. He leaned back and ran his fingertips down the right-hand wall of the corner. A similar groove had been worn into the opposite wall at the same height.

Ben sat up. His fingertips tingled. He rubbed the plaster dust from his hands as Sophia approached the cot.

"Find anything?" Sophia asked.

"Where's Caitline?" Ben replied.

"I don't know," Sophia answered.

"People deface walls and remove entire rooms of furniture from a fifth floor apartment and you tell me you don't know?" Ben asked.

"No," Sophia said as she sat on the bed. "I do not."

"That's a helluva answer for someone in charge," Ben retorted. "You can devise a better one for the police."

Sophia gazed around the room, pitched forward, and enveloped her face with her spidery fingers.

Ben grabbed her shoulders and raised her to a sitting position.

"You're not going to pass out on me now," Ben advised.

"Who is passing out?" Sophia responded. "I am trying to think."

Sophia shrugged out of Ben's grip, scooted against the metal footrest, and covered her face with her hands.

All of Sophia's actions seemed too theatrical for an experienced landlord, Ben thought. Perhaps she wasn't as experienced as she appeared. Or, was her helplessness just for his benefit?

"When was the last time you saw her?" Ben asked.

"Maybe ten days ago," Sophia answered.

"Was her rent paid?" Ben asked.

"In full to the end of the month," Sophia replied.

"Ever see her with anybody?" Ben continued. "Anyone unusual?"

"No, never," Sophia said and lowered her hands. "I never paid much attention."

Ben pitied her. Experienced or not, Sophia's reaction seemed genuine as if no one had ever skipped out on her before.

Someone rapped on the hallway door.

"Open up," a man's voice ordered. "This is the police."

Ben glanced at Sophia.

"Your idea?" Ben asked.

Sophia glanced toward the door. The rapping recurred, this time louder, more insistent.

"Open up!" the policeman insisted.

Ben stood up. Sophia scooted to the other end of the cot.

"We'd better answer it," Ben said as he surveyed the room. "It's not as if we have anything to hide."

Sophia continued to stare at the door.

"Nothing like this has ever happened to me before," Sophia said.

"Ten seconds or we're coming in," the policeman warned.

"This is not the way you greet the police," Ben said.

Sophia stood up and placed her fingertips on each side of her forehead as if she were summoning up all the powers of Thespis.

"Yes, let's do it," Sophia said and strode to the hallway door. "What do you want?"

"This is the police," the policeman responded. "Open up."

"Why are you here?" Sophia asked.

"We were informed that a house of prostitution is operating at this address," the policeman replied.

"Hadn't you better let our guests in?" Ben asked.

"I did not invite them," Sophia said.

Ben turned the knob, and the door flew open. Three uniformed officers burst into the room with their revolvers unholstered. The shortest, a blond woman in her early thirties marched up to Ben.

"Are you Benjamin Hackwell?" the policewoman asked.

"I am," Ben said.

"We have a warrant for your arrest," she replied.

"On what charge?" Ben asked.

"Violation of your restraining order," the policewoman replied. She glanced at her male cohorts who scanned the walls of the living room and blew the air from her cheeks. "You have the right to remain silent. You have the right to…"

Ben ignored her rendition of the Miranda Act and turned toward Sophia who stood in the middle of the room with her hands on her hips studying the two male officers. The taller of the two men fumbled along the wall behind the door.

"There's a switch on the other side of the door," Sophia told them. "But it doesn't operate anything."

The policeman flicked the switch several times, but no lights turned on.

"For Christ's sake. Let me!" Sophia exclaimed. She strode to the protective panel, popped it with her screwdriver, reconnected the wires, and flicked the switch. The recessed ceiling lamp flooded the room with light.

"There," Sophia said and whirled toward the female officer. "Where did you get the idea that prostitutes—"

"Whoa, wait a minute," Ben interrupted. He scanned the policewoman's nameplate pinned above her left shirt pocket. "Ms. Johnson, before you finish reciting my rights, may I ask whether you have reviewed the terms of my restraining order?"

"Of course I have," Johnson replied.

"It stipulates that I not have any physical contact with my daughter," Ben said. "Correct?"

"Yes," Johnson said.

"Do you see her anywhere in this apartment?" Ben asked.

"No," Johnson said.

"Does it appear that anyone's been living here recently?" Ben added.

"No, it doesn't," Johnson admitted.

"Then, technically," Ben replied. "I'm not in violation of my restraining order. Isn't that so?"

"Yes, technically," Johnson admitted and pushed her cap back on her forehead. "Just what are you doing here?"

"The same as you," Ben said. "Trying to learn out what's happened."

Sophia removed Ben's hand from her shoulder.

"Who told you that prostitutes were operating here?" Sophia asked.

"We got a telephone call," Johnson replied.

"Did they identify themselves?" Ben asked.

"They preferred to remain anonymous," Johnson replied.

"Those were their exact words?" Ben said.

"I didn't take the call," Johnson said. "That's how it was reported it to us."

"And on that basis you raided my establishment," Sophia exclaimed. "I thought this was America!"

"This is a country run by the rule of law, Ms. Nechayev," Johnson said.

"You found no prostitutes here," Sophia declared. "But on the word of some idiot off the street you come busting in here like the Mother Empress."

"I won't be intimidated, Ms. Nechayev," Johnson advised.

Ben grabbed Sophia's right arm.

"Just what do you think you're trying to do?" Ben asked in a loud whisper.

"Stand up for my rights," Sophia replied.

"I can't afford to go downtown," Ben urged. "Can't you see other people are involved here?"

"I will not be shoved around by a lady fascist," Sophia replied and shrugged out of Ben's grasp. "This is America, not mother Russia."

"Perhaps you'd better come with us, after all," Johnson sighed. "Both of you."

CHAPTER 7

▼

Ben descended the granite steps of the 31ˢᵗ Street police station several hours later with his leather jacket draped over his shoulder. The freshening night air provided welcome respite from the cramped and stuffy interrogation room.

He reached the sidewalk, inhaled and exhaled twice, and put on his jacket. He'd had enough fresh air. It was still March.

Ben zipped his coat shut and glanced toward the entrance.

They had nothing on which to hold him, but the police had fingerprinted and booked him anyway. It wasn't as if they needed the practice. Several teenage drunks and a couple of preteen graffiti artists got booked during the time it took them to determine that he had not violated his restraining order.

Sophia had not helped. She maintained her anti-totalitarian rap down the elevator, out to the squad car, and all the way to the police station where the two policemen placed them in separate rooms.

Ben didn't know what happened to her after that. He didn't care. If her act got her out of custody, more power to her. He didn't want to be involved with her further.

Ben wondered whether that was what Sophia had wanted. He clenched and unclenched his right hand. What better way to remove an interfering parent than to have the police come and haul him away. And when he protests his innocence and their incompetence, have him arrested.

What did Sophia stand to gain by separating herself from him?

Ben glanced up and down the empty street that fed into Calhoun Square. All he did know for certain was that the police never provided escort service back to the spot where they arrested you.

He stuck his hands in his pockets and started walking. It was eight blocks back to his cycle. He hoped that it still was parked in front of the Grafton.

Why wouldn't it be, he wondered. This was a safe part of town. He had been thinking that before he discovered Caitline's barren apartment. He also had been thinking how protected and safe this area was from theft, mugging, and prostitution.

Ben picked up his pace. What better way to deflect guilt from yourself than to displace it on your accuser?

He saw it now. Sophia had set him up. In the time it took him to mount the stairs she had phoned the police from Caitline's apartment. They knew nothing about his daughter's disappearance before. Now they suspected him. With the restraining order and his record, he would be the prime candidate.

Ben leaned into the turn as he loped around the corner of the uneven sidewalk. He slowed after half a dozen paces, his calfskin boots ill-designed for excursions beyond a quarter mile.

The Grafton was on the far corner of the next block. Once he retrieved his wheels, he could...

Ben halted.

Could what, he asked himself. Begin again? He'd used up the options he knew. His data on Caitline had blown up in his face. He wondered whether Jennifer know more than she had let on. Now was the time to find out.

Ben gazed down the deserted street. The next intersection appeared just as empty. He picked up his pace, sprinted the last half block, and halted in the middle of the intersection.

His cycle was not there.

Ben leaned forward and cupped his knees. His seared lungs refused to let him catch his breath. Glancing up, he reconfirmed that he was not delusional.

He waited until his breathing slowed. A gray, late model Buick sedan beeped next to him. The elderly male driver beeped his horn again.

Ben stepped onto the curb. The Buick resumed its journey up the street.

He checked his pulse. It felt strong, steady. His puffing reaction to climbing five flights of stairs had been an aberration.

Ben gazed around the intersection. None of the houses looked familiar. The brownstone apartment on the corner did not have a metal gate.

Ben turned toward the way he had come. Four blocks over, two blocks down from Calhoun Square. Or, was it two blocks over, four blocks down?

He retraced his steps and halted after half a dozen strides. He'd come that way and had seen nothing. There was no other reason to cover the same ground.

Ben gazed down the street. The houses were mostly two-story stucco family dwellings built in the 1920s and 30s. In the elm-obstructed light of the street lamps, the only distinguishing bit of data seemed to be the landscaping, or lack of it.

He returned to the intersection and turned left toward the next parallel block. If he headed that way, he could check each corner in an arc that encompassed all the likely possibilities where he could have parked.

Ben grimaced and gazed down the street toward the next intersection. The stoplight turned green, and a city bus roared through the intersection. He remembered no stoplights at the intersection where he'd parked. No brownstone apartment buildings here, either.

He glanced at the street signs. They read Fairchild and 32nd He'd parked on 33rd.

A wave of nausea swept over him. Ben rechecked his pulse. It seemed fine. His cheeks remained flushed.

Was he having a senior moment? He'd read somewhere that the first sign of Alzheimer's was misplacing things. He was the right age for that. Next came urinating in the refrigerator followed by a diapered residence at the old folk's home.

He dismissed the thought with a wave of his hand. This was no way to deal with anxiety. He had miscalculated the location of his cycle. That was all.

He glanced across the street. A youth in his early 20s with his Twins baseball cap perched sideways on his full afro waited with his dachshund and red setter on the other side of the street for the light to change.

Should he ask directions?

The light turned green, and the youth herded his dogs across the intersection. The dachshund pulled at his leash, the setter trotted beside his master.

As they approached the curb, the youth angled the dogs toward the park opposite. Both dogs began tugging at their leashes.

He stepped onto the curb, produced a white plastic trash bag from his jean pocket, and untied the foot-long plastic shovel attached to his belt loop. The setter whined; the dachshund yipped.

The youth turned toward Ben.

"Can I help you?" the youth asked.

Ben glanced at the salivating dogs.

"No, thanks," Ben replied. "You've got your hands full."

The dogs wrapped both leashes around the youth's legs in their excitement.

"Scylla! Charybdis!" the youth barked. "Behave!"

The setter sat on her haunches. The dachshund paced back and forth along the curb, her brown eyes focused across the street.

Ben felt the youth's eyes searching his.

"You look lost," the young man said.

"No problem. Really," Ben assured him. "I used to live here."

"Whatever," the youth replied. He jerked the leash and led his salivating hounds across the street.

Ben clenched and unclenched his right hand as he watched them pass through the gate. He didn't recall a park in this neighborhood, either.

He shook his head and crossed the street. This was one misplaced file out of the myriad of details that constituted the data cloud of life. He was employing a logical utility to recover it. It just needed time to work.

Ben found nothing at the next intersection, or the next. He leaned against a street sign, pulled off his boot, and smoothed the sock bunched around the ball of his foot. He kneaded the arch and slipped the boot back over his foot. Despite the chill, he'd broken a sweat. His feet ached, and he was tired, with no sign of his bike.

Ben gazed up at the street sign that read 38th and Emerson. He'd completed half his sweep. Had time and space been altered to keep him from finding the Grafton?

A foolish thought, Ben chided himself. He checked his watch. It showed 11:05 P.M. His watch confirmed that time continued its linear course.

He peered down the street through the canopy of bare elm branches. The next intersection appeared as unpromising as the rest.

Few people stirred in this neighborhood at this time of night. No one would witness his geographical debacle. If he managed so little success finding his cycle, Ben wondered, how could he expect to discover what happened to Caitline?

Ben trudged up the avenue, the blister he had anticipated forming along the ball of his right foot. He unzipped his jacket below his breastbone. His rising fume of body odor underscored his distress.

A bead of perspiration trickled across the right lens of his glasses. His finger flattened the bead to slime. The street light ahead transformed to an Expressionist painting.

Ben unzipped his jacket, pulled out the hem of his T-shirt, and buffed each lens. Extending his arms toward the street lamp, he examined the results. They remained filmy.

He rebuffed the lenses until they reached transparency and perched them on the ridge of his nose. The street lamp no longer appeared like a kaleidoscope. Under it gleamed his Dyna Super Glide Harley.

Ben resisted his urge to run. His blister made forbearance an easy choice.

He limped through the last dozen paces to his motorcycle, gave it a cursory examination, swung his swollen right foot over the seat, and climbed aboard.

Ben gazed around the intersection. Everything seemed still in place. The gate to Caitline's apartment building remained closed, the lobby dark and uninviting.

Should he talk to Sophia again? This time find out what she really knew?

To hell with her, Ben decided.

Ben stepped on the starter. The pain of his blistered foot flared across his instep and radiated up the outside of his calf. He leaned back to let the soreness ebb.

Was this going to be his end result, he wondered. Would all that he gained from this be a sore foot and a null set of missed opportunity, plus the renewed attention of the police?

He owed Caitline more than that.

Ben glanced at the end window on the top floor of the wing closest to him. His daughter's room remained dark, empty. The windows of the apartment next to it were lit, their storms raised to welcome in the chill midnight air.

Everything seemed so normal, Ben thought. He scanned the windows of the rest of the building. Those rooms that were lit had their storm panels raised to the top sill.

He chuckled. Residing in a vintage apartment on this side of town meant an equally vintage furnace to go with it. If Sophia represented the owners, they did not seem to be inclined to modernize the property, except the door locks for a safe and secure building.

Ben stepped on the starter. The pain flared again. He knew that he should go home and treat it. He jabbed at the starter another time. It did not catch. Its hours in the night air had rendered it crankier than he was.

Treatment would be the smart option. All he needed was a boil or two to complete his misery. He jammed on the starter as hard as he dared. The engine coughed. And coughed again. It did not catch.

Ben glanced about the intersection. No cabstands appeared anywhere. He'd have to deal with his cycle in the morning. It would be warmer then, he reasoned. And his cycle would be more responsive in the warmer air.

As Ben turned the front wheel of his bike against the curb, he noticed something moving in the corner of his eye. A lanky silhouette sidestepped down the front steps like a lumbering fiddler crab at the far end of the Grafton's courtyard.

Sophia halted at the bottom, grumbled something in Slavic, and re-gripped the iron handle of her heaping coalscuttle.

Ben crouched into the shadow cast by his bike as she neared the front gate. He did not want to tempt the wrath of feminist anti-socialism a second time.

He heard the scuttle's metal bottom scrape to a stop on the concrete. Hearing nothing further, he limped to the gate wincing from the angry blister inside his boot.

Sophia scooped the top layers of ashes with her hands and tossed them onto the bare dirt of the flowerbed. After several such administrations, she dumped the scuttle onto its side and scattered the pile of remaining ashes around the roots of the dormant rose bushes with her toe. After a hasty signing of the cross, she picked up the empty scuttle and marched to the front steps.

Ben watched her ascend the steps and disappear into the shadows of the foyer. What building superintendent fertilized their flower beds at midnight? Would even the most ardent organic agronomist bless the ashes they spread across their bushes? Sophia struck him as neither superstitious nor nurturing.

He rattled the iron bars of the gate. No give there. He wondered whether he should confront her again, or call the police. All he had to give them were his suspicions that she was concealing evidence. His unsubstantiated accusations would not wear well with the beleaguered officers. Their first reaction would be to wonder what was so incriminating about a harried building manager completing her landscaping duties after hours. Their second would be to re-invoke the strict interpretation of his restraining order.

Ben surveyed the flower plot. A black blob draped in purple braid protruded from the mound of ashes that surrounded the wimpled bush nearest him. Ben's shadow obscured his discerning finer detail. He repositioned himself at the other end of the gate to allow the street lamp to flood the entire entrance.

Ben cupped his hands over his eyes and peered between the bars. His perspective from this angle transformed the blob to the butt of a whip handle; the braid a ragged filigree that looped around the length of its charred haft. Ben pressed his forehead against the bars.

The color of the braid was devil's red.

CHAPTER 8

▼

Ben ran to his cycle and rammed the starter. Hard. The engine chuffed. And huffed. And held.

He raised his arms in triumph. The engine screamed while fiery tendrils of sensation crept back into his foot. The renewed feeling washed over him as the engine steadied and the smoke cleared. Ben sealed the pain in a distant corner of his mind as the soreness subsided.

He wondered whether Caitline had done the same. Had she, too, with each lash of the whip withdrawn to a deeper, safer spot? And when Wilson leveled the gun barrel at her heart...

No more analysis, Ben decided. Sophia and Wilson were connected. The whip handle confirmed it. He had to check Schariah's. He owed Caitline that much.

Ben maneuvered his cycle through the construction sites and clots of pedestrians as he headed downtown. The congestion cleared once he passed the Walker Art Gallery and crossed over the Lowry Hill Tunnel. All he had to contend with there were lines of cars navigating the lane changes to reach their particular arterial to the northern suburbs.

He turned right and stopped under the Interstate 94 overpass. His blister continued to protest. Ben shifted his foot inside his boot and hugged his knee against the manifold to reduce the pressure on it.

The pang in Ben's abdomen signaled his stomach was empty. He had not eaten since noon. Preoccupied by Caitline's fate, he had not considered it.

At the next intersection he turned into the Warehouse district that contained most of the city's gentlemen's clubs along with the few factories that hadn't been converted to apartments. Schariah's occupied a refurbished turn-of-the-century brick warehouse that sprawled an entire block along Washington Avenue.

Ben slowed as he passed the club's fuchsia carpet that stretched to the curb with a matching awning over it. The same awnings loomed above the first-floor windows extending the length of the building to the valet parking lot at the other end. The crystal chandeliers enhanced the impression of refined decadence. Only the unadorned windows of the second and third floors suggested the building's sweatshop history.

Ben drove past the parking lot, turned into the alley, and parked between a black Cadillac SUV and the cement loading dock. A college couple strolled toward the SUV as Ben hobbled up the cobblestone incline to the street.

Ben watched them enter the SUV. In his day, the ogling of bored strippers and inept dancers remained the provinces of leering fraternity pledges and middle-aged truck drivers. Now such activity catered to business executives and couples seeking to improve their sexual techniques. Judging from the intensity of their discussion, the young woman's scrutiny had proven more instructive and alarming than her escort's.

Ben shook his head as he reached the sidewalk. He wondered how many men truly were comfortable with a partner more experienced than they were.

A white stretch limousine disgorged a pair of boisterous couples onto the carpeted runway. Ben followed them inside. While the men bantered with the cashier dressed in a French chambermaid outfit, Ben absorbed the ambiance.

The walls resembled the inside of a Tiffany Easter egg. Gilt arabesques extended across the felt, fuchsia wallpaper. Swarms of cherubs in the frescoed ceiling readied undraped females for the act of love. Cut glass censers on gilded chains dispensed a cloying musk. In the gift alcove beside the cashier's station a brocaded sign encouraged patrons to "Let us host your next business luncheon or social event."

Ben smiled at the petite brunette cashier as she adjusted the renegade sleeve of her outfit that appeared two sizes too small. Her thick eye shadow and ebony lipstick failed to disguise that she couldn't be more than 19 or 20. She returned his smile with her own that revealed her uneven gray teeth.

"Eight dollars, please," the cashier said.

Her accent sounded like Sophia's, perhaps Eastern European, if not Russian.

"Does that include a drink?" Ben asked.

"One drink, two drink minimum per show," the cashier replied.

"How much are the drinks?" Ben continued.

"Eight dollars," she said.

"And how many shows?" Ben asked.

The young woman licked her lips.

"As many as you want," she replied lasciviously and rolled her brown eyes.

Ben handed her the money.

"Enjoy your evening," the cashier said and licked her lips again.

At the other end of the hall, a dusky blonde in similar attire opened the right of two massive mahogany doors set with etched glass windows. Ben stepped through into an amphitheater where three concentric tiers of circular cocktail tables surrounded the square center stage with attendant circular platforms on either side.

A balalaika wailed on tape as a voluptuous redhead wriggled out of her white corset on center stage and placed it on top of the starched lace party dress lying against the brass pole beside her. Two women not so endowed wearing peasant outfits did the same on the adjacent platforms. Wearing gilt g-strings and matching heels, all three women wrapped themselves around their respective poles.

Ben sat at an unoccupied table near the door. He glanced at the performers from time to time as he searched the room for Wilson. Outside of the two neckless youths seated before the farther secondary stage who looked like bouncers dressed in their sharkskin sport coats, he spotted no one that might be in authority.

The women concluded their gyrations, descended their respective platforms, and scattered into the audience. Each selected a man who appeared neither the most attractive nor financially well off. The common denominator seemed to be that none of their targets was alone. While jiggling and swaying before them, the women evaluated the effect of their performance on their companions and the surrounding audience.

"Excuse me, sir," a woman's voice said behind him.

Ben glanced over his right shoulder. A thick-legged cocktail waitress dressed in net stockings and a milky halter-top that revealed the dark nipples of her breasts swayed atop her black spike heels. Her accent was thicker than the cashier's had been.

"What are you having this evening?" the waitress asked.

Ben hesitated. He needed to stay alert.

"Coffee," Ben said.

"Beer and alcohol only," the waitress responded.

"No soda or bottled water?" Ben asked.

"Just beer and mixed drinks," the waitress replied.

"What kind of beer?" Ben asked. He wondered with idle amusement just how long the waitress was willing to pursue her tip.

The waitress rattled off the names of some domestic brands. None appealed to Ben.

"Any wine?" Ben asked.

The waitress' deep set, amber eyes swept the room with impatience.

"Mixed drinks are best," she advised.

"I don't want to get drunk," Ben acknowledged.

The waitress shifted her weight from one foot to the other as though she had been wearing her heels for a long shift.

"Mixed drinks are best bet," the waitress said. "Order one with fruit in it. Make everybody happy."

Ben smiled. He'd tormented her long enough.

"Brandy old-fashioned," Ben ordered. "Got anything to eat with that?"

"Restaurants are on Hennepin Avenue," the waitress said without smiling.

"Not even chips or pretzels?" Ben asked.

The waitress surveyed the room and signaled the men seated at the table beside the stage. One with a shaved, bullet head stood up and sprang up the stairs to them. His aura of Aqua Velva enveloped Ben's table.

"Is there a problem?" the man asked.

Ben's stomach growled at the scent of spearmint from the bouncer's breath. His accent sounded more Russian and better educated.

"No problem," Ben said and shook his head for emphasis. "Just hungry, that's all."

The bouncer's florid face cracked an ingratiating grin.

"I'm sure Yazmin has explained that we don't serve meals at this establishment," he said.

Ben glanced at the foot-sore waitress. She did not look like a Yazmin.

"Yes, she already explained that," Ben replied.

"No problem then. As you said," the bouncer responded and glanced toward Yazmin. "What'd he order?"

"Brandy old-fashioned," Yazmin replied.

"Tell the bartender to put a double order of cherries in it," the bouncer advised and grinned at Ben. "That should give you enough body sugar. Enjoy your evening."

He started down the carpeted stairs.

"One more thing," Ben said as he watched the young bouncer balance between two of the carpeted steps. He might as well find out how much the help knew. "I'd like to speak with Mr. Wilson."

The bouncer grinned.

"Mr. Wilson is unavailable," he said and resumed his downward trek.

"It's about Caitline Hackwell," Ben said. "She used to work here."

The bouncer halted and glanced at the tables around him. One of the male students had Ben followed inside stuffed a couple of twenties in the main performer's g-string. She began to gyrate her hips inches in front of his nose.

The bouncer retraced his steps.

"You know Miss Caitline?" he asked solicitously.

"I'm her father," Ben explained.

The bouncer frowned.

"Mr. Wilson may have the time," the bouncer replied with a thicker accent. "I will check."

Ben sat back and watched the redhead sway before the student. She lowered her arms, cupped them behind his head, and guided it forward until his nose rested in the deep hollow between her breasts. His cohort ordered another round of drinks. Their dates whispered between themselves.

Yazmin arrived with Ben's drink and a glass of water and set them on doilies beside his elbow. The mound of cherries and orange slices left a shallow pool of liquor at the bottom of the six-ounce tumbler.

Ben popped a cherry into his mouth and crushed it with his back teeth. Brandy spurted against the roof of his mouth and trickled down his throat.

He coughed several times and rinsed his throat from the water glass. He ground the cherry into a fine mash between his teeth and swallowed. A flush rose up his neck and into his cheeks. The sensation recalled his first bite into his alcoholic Aunt Doris' fruitcakes years ago.

Ben munched several of the orange slices. Each was engorged with liquor. Thinning the drinks did not appear to be how this establishment made its money.

Below, the redhead withdrew the young man's face from her bosom and pinched his cheeks. She tousled his spiked black hair, moved to his companion, and shimmied before him. Two more twenties in her g-string reinitiated the sinuous sway of her torso.

"Mr. Hackwell?" a man's voice asked with a Russian accent that sounded as refined and overripe as the drinks.

Ben turned sideways in his chair. Beside the bouncer stood a taut, wiry man with pomaded, wavy black hair and pencil-thin sideburns that plunged to the corners of his jaw. Neither the aura of his magnolia cologne nor the sheen of his gold brocade tuxedo could disguise the pockmarked face of Caitline's virtual executioner.

"You're Wilson?" Ben asked with contempt.

"Yes," Wilson said.

"And you own this place," Ben said.

"I have that distinction," Wilson replied. "What do you think of it?"

"What do you care?" Ben retorted. He did not appreciate the man's easy familiarity with him.

Wilson gazed around the room.

"You disapprove," Wilson observed.

"Mostly of your tuxedo," Ben replied as he scanned the brocade in Wilson's jacket.

Wilson chuckled and glanced at his lapels.

"It is a bit much, isn't it," Wilson agreed. "In a business such as this one you're expected to make, what do they say, a certain statement." He gazed toward the dancer bumping and grinding at the table below and sighed. "Maybe it's not still too late to move back into wrestling."

Ben scowled. Dammit, he thought. He would have preferred that Wilson's personality be as distasteful as his tuxedo.

"I'm here about Caitline," Ben said.

Wilson's brows furrowed.

"And your relationship with her is what?" Wilson asked.

"Her father," Ben said with authority. He glanced toward the bouncer standing beside Wilson. "I expect your goon told you that."

"We do not use that term here, do we, Pyotr?" Wilson admonished with a grin. "Mr. Hackwell, meet Pyotr Petrov. Pyotr, this is Caitline's father."

Petrov's stolid expression did not change after Wilson's introductions.

"Where is Caitline?" Ben asked.

Wilson's hawk-like eyes swept the room.

"Your guess is as good as mine," Wilson replied. His gaze fixed on Ben's. "Perhaps better."

Ben sat back in his chair. He wondered how far Wilson was prepared to go with his evasions.

"Why should that be?" Ben asked. "You were her employer."

"And you her estranged father," Wilson replied as his eyes returned to the vermilion-haired dancer below. "Caitline told me how it was between you and your wife."

Ben sat erect. First, Hoot, now Wilson. Why would Caitline confide in either of these men?

"You look surprised," Wilson observed. "Don't be. It's common in most professions for its employees to become lovers."

"This is hardly a profession," Ben replied. He dismissed Wilson's second assertion.

"What would you call it?" Wilson replied and glanced toward Ben.

"I think you know," Ben said evenly.

"I don't know. You tell me," Wilson demanded. "Do you know that over half of the women I employ have a college education? That most of them make at least five times what they could make doing something else? That we take in more in a week than you make in a year?"

He'd struck a nerve, Ben thought. Press on it and see how much heat Wilson can take. He'd reveal where Caitline is in the process.

"So you make a lot of money. So what?" Ben replied. He gazed at the dancer gyrating below. "How many of them actually see any of it?"

"More than I'd care to admit," Wilson replied with a good-humored grin. He glanced toward Petrov. "Just ask my accountant."

Ben folded his arms across his chest.

"And what's he going to tell me?" Ben replied. "What a struggling businessman you are? How much you're exploited by the government?"

Wilson smiled again.

"Maybe I am," Wilson said and turned toward Petrov. "What do you think, Pyotr? What are the figures? When you throw in health insurance, sick leave, and the rest of it, maybe I am the one who is exploited."

Petrov kept his eyes on the women below and folded his massive arms across his chest.

"It adds up," Petrov acknowledged.

This train of questioning was getting him nowhere, Ben decided. He grasped the edge of the table with both hands.

"You can't tell me these women enjoy using their bodies this way," Ben exclaimed.

"Some do, some don't," Wilson said with a shrug. "Some don't have any choice."

"What choice?" Ben replied. "You force them into it."

"Everybody has choices," Wilson responded and turned toward Ben. "What caused you to come here tonight? Was that not a choice?"

"I came here for my daughter," Ben declared.

"Ah, yes, the outraged parent," Wilson scoffed. "Here to avenge the horrible wrong she has suffered working for someone like me."

"There's no choice in that," Ben admonished.

"But you waited how long to find out?" Wilson asked. "A year? And when you came here, did you go right to my office or bring the police with you? No, you decided to take in the show first. Have a drink or two, take in the sights, make yourself at home."

Wilson's pale tongue flicked around his lips.

"I was worried when Pyotr first told me you were here," Wilson admitted. "But when I approached your table you looked comfortable. And I thought to myself is this the behavior of an outraged father? He looks like someone quite comfortable with what we do."

Wilson leaned forward and leered.

"Maybe, in fact," Wilson suggested. "He enjoys it?"

Ben sprang forward. His leap died in mid-air. Petrov seized Ben's shoulders and locked Ben's arms behind his back.

Wilson straightened his cummerbund and scanned the audience.

"Sorry for the disturbance, folks," Wilson apologized. "Some of our patrons get more, how do you say, turned on by Vera's performance than is good for them."

Wilson grinned and beckoned toward the flame-haired dancer.

"You can see why!" Wilson exclaimed. "Have a drink on us and enjoy the rest of the show."

Vera nodded and resumed shimmying. Several heads that had turned in Ben's direction swiveled back toward Vera and the other performers. Wilson turned toward Petrov.

"Take him to my office," Wilson ordered.

Petrov maneuvered Ben up the stairs and through the mahogany doors. His toes scraped the top of the shag carpet as they turned down a side hallway and headed toward a panel door at the end.

They entered an unpretentious office that smelled of stale smoke and unwashed socks. An old-fashioned calculator, spools of tape, and a royal blue ceramic vase occupied the blotter in the center of the square oak desk.

Petrov pulled a worn, wood frame chair away from the wall, shoved it before the desk, and deposited Ben into it.

"Sit," Petrov ordered.

Ben rose. Petrov shoved him back in his seat. Ben tried again with the same result. On Ben's third attempt, Petrov seized Ben's right wrist, spun him back upon the chair, locked Ben's ring finger between his fists, and pulled.

Ben slumped against the back of the chair and cradled his throbbing hand.

"Depending how you behave I dislocate another," Petrov warned and unbuttoned his sport coat. "Or I use this."

Ben glimpsed the sheath of a Polish hunting knife attached to Petrov's belt before he re-buttoned his jacket.

"It is your choice," Petrov advised.

He crossed his arms and stood behind the chair. Wilson rounded the desk, set the calculator off to the side, and plunked into the chair. He scanned Ben's face.

"Thank you for participating in our floor show," Wilson acknowledged.

Ben winced from the pain of his dislocated finger and tried to remember more of the interrogation techniques he had learned as part of his Intelligence training. Since Wilson felt he had the upper hand, it would easier for Ben to keep Wilson talking. He had to if he wanted to learn anything more about Caitline.

"You didn't leave me much choice," Ben said through gritted teeth.

Wilson produced a gilt cigarette case from inside his tuxedo and pulled a tan, flattened oval cigarette from inside it.

"Our audience always appreciates when one of them gets over-heated," Wilson explained. "They feel they are part of something exciting. It is good for business."

Wilson tamped the cigarette on the edge of the desk, opened the center drawer, and pulled out a Cheapo lighter. Lighting the cigarette, he took a draw, and sat back.

Ben decided it was time to nudge Wilson out of his comfort zone.

"Look, if you're going to bring charges, call the police," Ben demanded and squirmed in his chair. "Or tell me where Caitline is."

Wilson exhaled and studied the smoke ring he'd created.

"You misunderstand, Mr. Hackwell," Wilson replied. "You are free to go."

"Why?" Ben retorted. "Afraid what the police might find?"

"Not particularly," Wilson said.

"Given your connections, I might be," Ben advised.

"Really?" Wilson remarked as he blew another smoke ring. "Such as?"

"Chechnya has a reputation as a pipeline for drugs and prostitution," Ben observed.

Wilson appeared unfazed by Ben's remark. He glanced toward Petrov.

"Would you escort Mr. Hackwell to the front door?" Wilson asked.

"Don't patronize me," Ben demanded. "I know Caitline worked here. I saw the video."

"What video?" Wilson asked. His agate eyes latched onto Ben's in sudden alarm. "What video do you mean?"

Ben had struck a nerve. He had to press his advantage.

"The one where you kill her," Ben responded.

"Is that what this is all about?" Wilson chuckled. His confident grin revealed the gap between his front teeth as he sat back in his chair. "That piece of play-acting?"

"Don't act coy," Ben insisted.

"For the record," Wilson said. "I never killed anyone."

"Just tortured and whipped them instead," Ben suggested.

Wilson took another drag and executed a French inhale.

"The only thing I recall was Caitline asking me to perform in a videotape she was doing for her media arts class," Wilson replied with a smile. "She told me I'd make a good character actor."

He leered at Ben.

"I had to strip for that one," Wilson confided.

"For the torture scenes, I suppose," Ben replied.

"For the love scenes," Wilson replied and rolled his eyes. "Caitline got quite animated for those."

Ben glanced at the bouncer, clenched his injured right fist, and winced.

"She could never love you," Ben declared.

"You think that impossible?" Wilson responded as he tamped out his cigarette in the plastic ashtray and stood up. "I learned long ago never to argue with the father of a woman in my employ. I told you that you were free to go."

Wilson rounded the desk.

"All we did is a little harmless play acting one weekend for one of her classes," Wilson explained.

"And an affair grew out of it?" Ben asked.

"Yes," Wilson admitted as he opened the door to the hallway.

"But you don't know where she is now," Ben said.

"No," Wilson answered.

Wilson contributed this information because he felt he still had the upper hand, Ben thought. He needed to play along until he could trip Wilson up.

"How long since you saw her last?" Ben asked.

"What would you say, Pyotr?" Wilson replied and turned toward Petrov. "A month? Six weeks?"

Petrov shrugged.

"That's bullshit and you know it," Ben retorted.

Wilson widened the opening. Ben stood up and massaged his injured finger.

"Strong arm tactics and deceit don't play very well over here in the States," Ben said as he strode to the doorway. "Was Caitline ever one of your dancers?"

"For a time," Wilson said. "She was not very good at it."

If Caitline had not been a good dancer, Ben wondered, why had Wilson sent her to Hoot?

"What did she do for you, then?" Ben asked.

"She answered our ad for a Web site designer," Wilson explained.

"Interesting," Ben observed. Wilson's answer seemed reasonable. Ben had one last ploy in his arsenal. "But not very convincing."

"Why is that?" Wilson asked.

"Because the Web is where I saw her video," Ben replied and scanned Wilson's face for a reaction. "That doesn't interest you?"

"Should it?" Wilson asked.

"You're the one everyone on the Internet sees torturing a teenage girl for 50 dollars a pop," Ben replied.

"Paying for sexual titillation over the Internet is not a crime in this country," Wilson observed.

"Sex acts performed by a missing girl who used to be employed at your strip club?" Ben asked.

"Those acts were between consenting adults," Wilson declared. "There was nothing illegal about them."

He had Wilson now, Ben thought.

"An underage, missing girl," Ben added with emphasis on "underage." "If the authorities learned about that, they would come down on you and your establishment like a house of bricks."

"Let them come," Wilson retorted. "Let them check our records. Your daughter's signed employment application stated that she was 18 when she started to work for us."

He grinned again.

"I have done nothing illegal," Wilson declared.

"Maybe so," Ben acknowledged, frustrated by Wilson's self-assurance. "Then why did Sophia Nechayev burn and bury a whip like the one you used in the video last night?"

Wilson's eyes narrowed to slits.

"Good night, Mr. Hackwell," Wilson said and shut the door with a firm click. Ben marched down the hallway, grinned at the hostess, and strolled into the early March morning.

CHAPTER 9

▼

Ben's sense of triumph did not last long. The pain in his hand and in his foot had rekindled by the time he reached the alleyway. He removed his boot and massaged the inner arch with his good hand.

What had he accomplished? Wilson had baited him into the role of sex-starved hothead. If the police had come a dozen witnesses could attest to his violent behavior.

More important, he had divulged the one byte of information that Wilson did not have. Power was not in what you knew, but in what your opponent thought you knew. Now that Wilson knew Ben had witnessed the destruction of possible evidence, he would take steps to cover it up. He also would retaliate.

Ben eased his boot back on. The pain in both extremities remained, but at a tolerable level.

He hobbled to his cycle. Puncturing Wilson's sang froid had provided his one consolation during their discussion. Wilson's discomfiture over Ben's knowledge about the whip had been revealing and scary.

Ben turned the ignition key. The engine coughed, ejected a thin stream of white smoke, and turned over. Ben watched the smoke dissipate. He knew that even the greatest fabrication contained a kernel of truth, but he didn't know how much it did in Wilson's story. He did know that Caitline had Internet training. He'd taught her to learn the rudiments of PERL (Practical Extraction and Resource Language) scripting language. But, of all the jobs Caitline could have chosen, why had she decided to work as a Web manager for a sex club? And then be shot in one of its videos?

Ben shook his head in frustration. All the data he had uncovered revealed more null sets of information. What caused an attractive, normal girl like Caitline to get involved with a sex purveyor like Wilson? Was it peer pressure? The media?

Or lack of family. Girls needed fathers in their lives. They needed someone to look up to. Jennifer had taken away that role away from him.

Ben shook his head. It was time he stormed the dragon's den. Jennifer damn well could restore to him what she had taken.

Ben popped the clutch, and his cycle bucked and roared up the cobble incline. He turned onto Hennepin Avenue and headed toward Loring Park where Jennifer would be poring over legal briefs as she always did before she went to bed.

Loring Park's bean-shaped lagoon was located several blocks east of St. Mary's Basilica. He crossed one of the lagoon's Venetian style bridges and drove past a series of some of the most expensive apartment complexes and condos in the Twin Cities whose proximity to downtown commanded New York Park Avenue quality prices.

Ben stopped in front of a brownstone high-rise with the street number embossed in foot-high white letters on the forest green awning and searched for a place to park. Foreign cars and SUVs crammed the curbsides for the full extent of the block.

Guiding his cycle between a cream-colored Volvo and a black Durango, he parked it on the sidewalk, strode up to the plate glass entrance, and peered into the atrium. A stolid doorman with iron-gray dreadlocks under his gold-braided green cap sat behind a counter and examined a resident's list.

Ben rapped on the glass. The doorman turned toward an intercom mounted on the wall beside the counter.

"The Montague does not accept unauthorized visitors between the hours of midnight and six A. M.," the doorman announced in a clipped British accent.

"I'm expected," Ben replied and grinned. "Could you buzz Ms. Roloson and inform her I've returned?"

The doorman cocked his left eyebrow.

"If you live here, sir," the doorman asked. "Why not use your apartment key?"

Ben produced his key ring from his pocket, ready for a game of cat and mouse with this gatekeeper.

"I left it in my other set of keys," Ben answered.

The doorman set his list on the counter.

"Why haven't I seen you here before?" the doorman asked.

"Perhaps you're new here?" Ben replied.

"Nine years here in this position next month," the doorman stated and pursed his lips. "I'm instructed not to permit access beyond a certain hour. As you are not on my list of permitted visitors, I suggest that you make other arrangements for the rest of the evening and take your business up with Ms. Roloson in the morning."

Ben massaged his neck with his uninjured hand and sighed. Penetrating Jennifer's human firewall was proving as tiresome as she had intended it to be when she moved here.

"You acknowledge that I'm Mr. Hackwell?" Ben asked.

"Certainly," the doorman said. "It is not my position to question your identity."

"Is it your position to prevent my communicating with my wife?" Ben replied.

The doorman's smile disappeared.

"No sir," the doorman answered evenly. "It is not."

"May I speak to her then?" Ben asked.

"You may contact her any way that you like," the doorman stated.

Ben glanced toward the phone beside the doorman's elbow.

"Let me call her," Ben requested.

"Let me repeat," the doorman said. "I am instructed not to permit access beyond a certain hour."

"Then notify her I'm here," Ben replied.

"The occupants of this complex prefer not to be disturbed beyond a certain time," the doorman repeated.

It was time to play his trump card, Ben decided.

"Even if I tell you that a young woman's life may be at stake?" Ben asked.

The doorman shot Ben a dubious look and produced a flat cellular phone from the inside pocket of his blazer. He drummed three numbers on its cramped number pad, sat back in his chair, and waited.

Ben glanced up the street. No one moved about at this hour, especially since the temperature drop had turned the mist into snow pellets.

He pulled the zipper of his jacket up to his collar. The pain had subsided in his injured ring finger. Ben shifted his weight from one foot to the other to stay warm, and stamped his feet on the stoop to restore the circulation in his cranky right foot.

The doorman's brows knitted.

"Ms. Roloson re-informed me that she receives no visitors at this hour," the doorman declared and glared at Ben.

"Did you tell her that our daughter's involved?" Ben asked.

The doorman drew erect in his chair.

"I did mention it, sir," the doorman replied.

"And that didn't concern her?" Ben asked.

"Apparently not," the doorman said.

"Wouldn't it concern you?" Ben replied.

"It's not my nature nor my position to pass judgment," the doorman said as he picked up his list. "Good evening, sir."

Ben scanned the front windows. None of them appeared to be lit. He rapped on the glass door.

The doorman did not look up.

Ben rapped harder.

The doorman sighed.

"Yes?" the doorman said.

"Is there a pay phone nearby?" Ben asked.

The doorman thought for a moment.

"You could try the pizzeria down the street," the doorman responded. "They might be open."

"Could you call…"

Ben watched the doorman stretch his arms, stand up, and head toward the elevators. As Ben watched him stroll out of sight, it recalled anew the effectiveness of Jennifer's restraining order. Every fresh instance reconfirmed Ben's pariah status and cracked the scab that never seemed to heal.

He stared toward the glow at other end of the street and wondered whether the light indicated a thriving establishment about ready to close its last orders.

Ben descended the steps. He was cold, tired, and still hungry. He decided that a slice of double pepperoni in a busy establishment could assuage all three for a while. As for his cycle, he had to choose between leaving it, or spending 15 minutes finding another place to park.

He pulled his collar up around his neck and started off. A stiff breeze between buildings shoved him off stride. Dry snow scattered in waves to the opposite curb as he regained his balance.

Ben scanned the other end of the block. Its data set remained the same as before, cold, dark, and slumberous. He decided that "Just up the street" must be code that doormen used to rid their buildings of undesirables.

The cesium lamps along Hennepin Avenue transformed the roiling clouds to the color of a deep thigh bruise. A black van obscured the one or two store lights that glowed in the dark at the end of the street as it pulled out from the alley and disappeared down the street. The fogged store windows suggested activity inside both buildings. The proprietor of the bakery on the left must have decided to get an early start baking the morning's donuts. The red neon sign on Ben's right proclaimed "Luigi's Pisa Pizza. Buy it By the Slice."

Ben opened its plate glass door, and the aroma of rising dough and melting mozzarella billowed out. The tiny room contained three square tables with red and white checked tablecloths and a counter with an open cash register. Behind the counter bobbed the top of a chef's hat.

Ben stepped inside and gazed over the counter. Under the hat an agitated Asian man stood on an overturned crate and shoved two extra-large pizzas into the upper giant wall oven. He wiped his hands on his apron, turned toward the counter, and waggled his floury arms.

"No more pizza tonight," the pizza maker cried. He grabbed a giant wood paddle and turned back to the ovens. Ben asked if he had a pay phone.

"In back. In back," the pizza maker responded.

He opened the door of the lower oven, scooped out two medium pepperoni pizzas, pivoted, and deposited them onto the counter. Their golden brown crusts bubbled and oozed like oversized bronze coins fresh from the mint. The aroma of the mozzarella and oregano short-circuited Ben's efforts at self-control.

"Can I have a slice?" Ben asked in anticipation.

"No way," the pizza maker said. "These are for order."

"And those in the oven?" Ben asked hopefully.

"Last order," the pizza maker said. "We close now."

He bustled around the counter, wiped his hands and arms with a sauce-stained towel, and spun the deadbolt latch on the door.

"Can I make a call?" Ben asked in irritation.

"Five minutes," the maker replied with harried resignation. "Make quick!"

Ben strode toward the cooler that stood against the back wall. A dial pay phone hung on the opposite wall. A metal binder resided in the slot under the phone. Half the pages in the binder were torn out including the R section. H through N remained.

Ben sighed. His stomach growled.

The baker drew the shades and extended his thumb, middle, and index finger.

"Three minutes," he announced and scurried back into the galley.

Ben couldn't remember Jennifer's new number. He wondered dully whether that was because he couldn't, or wouldn't.

He opened the blue business pages in back, ran his finger down the M's, and found the Montague listed in the right-hand column. Ben produced some coins from his trouser pocket, jammed them into the slot, and spun the dial. He heard the last two pizzas clatter onto the counter behind him as doorman announced in the phone's earpiece, "This is the Montague."

Four chops rang out from the countertop. Four more followed.

"This is Detective…" Ben began and cleared his throat. He needed to disguise his voice to fool the doorman and wrapped his hand across the receiver.

"Excuse me," Ben apologized, coughed, and continued in a lower voice. "This is Detective Mann of the Hennepin County bureau of missing persons. Is there a Ms. Roloson at this address?"

"Yes," the doorman said uncertainly.

"May I speak to her, please?" Ben asked.

"We ordinarily do not disturb our clientele at this hour, sir," the doorman reported.

"This is official business," Ben said. He felt a tug on his coat sleeve. The baker held up his index finger.

"Is it not a little late for official police business?" the doorman asked.

"Yes, it is," Ben replied. "But, I received official notification ten minutes ago. If it has been determined that the person involved truly is missing, I'm honor bound to act upon this information as soon after the notification as possible."

"I see," the doorman said.

Ben felt another tug on his shoulder.

"You go now," the pizza baker ordered.

Ben fanned out the fingers of his right hand.

"Just five more minutes?" Ben asked.

The pizza baker grabbed his mop and bucket.

"Hello?" Jennifer inquired. Her voice sounded as if she'd argued a big case.

"This is Inspector Mann of—" Ben said.

"Benjamin?" Jennifer interrupted.

"Madam, I—" Ben continued.

"Your calls used to be more creative, Benny," Jennifer observed.

An ember turned over inside Ben's chest. She never called him that unless she were tired or…

"Look," Jennifer declared. "If this is about Caitline disappearing again, I'll hang up right now."

"Why haven't you already?" Ben replied. "I have no other reason to call."

"I thought maybe—" Jennifer responded.

"Maybe what?" Ben interrupted. He imagined Jennifer running her hand through her raven hair scented with almonds from the shampoo she always used.

Combined with her musky female scent wafting up from under the bodice of her nightgown...

"Maybe what?" Ben repeated, leaving his thought unfinished.

The pizza baker tugged Ben's coat sleeve and pointed at his watch.

"Two minutes," the baker warned. "Or I call police!"

"Where are you?" Jennifer asked in alarm.

"Some pizza joint down the street," Ben replied.

"Luigi's?" Jennifer asked.

"Yeah," Ben confirmed. He glanced toward the neon sign. "Pisa Pizza."

The pizza baker stood with his mop handle poised for action across his chest.

"Out!" the baker ordered. "Now!"

Ben raised his right index finger to ward the pizza maker off.

"You must be worried as I am, or you wouldn't still be on the phone" Ben reasoned and leaned closer to the receiver. "This is not the time to raise barriers between us."

"She's never been gone this long before," Jennifer whimpered. She sounded as if she was speaking into her receiver from across the room, Ben thought.

"You have no idea where she is?" Ben asked.

"No," Jennifer said in a small voice.

"You go now, please," the pizza baker pleaded.

Ben stared at the defiant little man and wondered how he could make him understand.

"The daughter of the lady on the other end is missing," Ben said and extended the receiver toward the pizza maker. "One minute more, OK? Then I'll leave. I promise."

Ben turned toward the phone. To get Jennifer on his side, he needed to enlist her help.

"Did Caitline have a PC?" Ben asked.

"What?" Jennifer replied.

"Did Caitline ever send you e-mail?" Ben asked, changing the nature of his question.

"A couple of times," Jennifer responded.

"Good," Ben confirmed. "Did you get her address?"

"Somewhere," Jennifer said.

"Get me her address and I can get her account number," Ben said. "Maybe it's still open."

"What will that do?" Jennifer asked.

Ben ignored her question. Explaining would give Jennifer time to change her mind.

"Can you do that?" Ben urged.

"OK," Jennifer said.

Jennifer hung up. Ben hung up and rubbed his hands. It was a start. He spun on his heel and halted beside the counter. Neither his foot nor his hand felt as sore.

"You go now?" the pizza baker asked. He stood resolute beside the cash register, knuckles white around the mop handle. "Will you go now?"

Ben pointed toward the delivery box the countertop.

"What's that?" Ben asked.

"Pepperoni pizza," the pizza baker replied. "The delivery man did not deliver to the people who ordered it."

Ben pulled out his wallet and asked, "How much?"

The pizza baker deposited the box in Ben's hands.

"On house," The baker declared and opened the door. "You go. I close now."

"You're sure I can't pay for it?" Ben asked.

"On house!" the pizza baker insisted. "On house!"

The pizza baker pushed Ben out the door. Ben caught his balance on the stoop. The door lock clicked behind him, the shade dropped, and the establishment went dark.

He pulled out a slice, stuck it into his mouth until the tip collided with his upper palette, raised his lower jaw, and let the mozzarella spurt against the roof of his mouth. Sticking his prize under his arm, Ben turned down the street in satisfaction as the wintry wind whipped at his back.

CHAPTER 10

▼

Ben had devoured four of the six slices before he reached his cycle. He wiped his handkerchief across his mouth, folded the carton in two, and stuck it in his saddlebag. He turned the ignition key. Nothing happened. He jiggled the ignition switch and tried again. The engine fired and caught.

His luck must be changing, Ben decided. He opened the throttle, pivoted on his rear tire, and sped down the street.

He had won Jennifer to his side, if only a little while he reminded himself. Jennifer never cried or got angry, except when it involved her relationship with him. Given her response over the phone, she must be worried sick.

Ben's chest constricted at the thought. Jennifer needed him after all.

He pulled into his driveway, clicked the garage door opener, and sped inside. After a quick rubdown of both fenders, he entered his apartment and initiated his Internet mailbox protocol.

Ben tapped the playback button on his phone. His caller identification displayed one new number: Jennifer's.

"Benjamin, this is Jennifer," Jennifer's message said. "The only address Caitline gave me is Caitline@geocities.com."

His answering machine whirred for five seconds.

"Phone me if you find something," Jennifer said finally. "Anything. OK?"

Another five-second pause followed.

"Good luck," Jennifer added.

The warmth in Ben's chest radiated to his extremities. Jennifer did need him, he decided. After everything that had happened between them, it felt…

Good. His assessment felt that simple and true.

Ben keyed in the address Jennifer had given him. After 30 seconds a message window popped up with "There was no response." He tried again with the same result. He tried different extensions. He truncated the address. He ran a validity check. The message reappeared each time.

Ben slumped against the back of his chair. Some security expert, he scoffed. Even given an address, he could not uncover a clue to his daughter's existence.

He stretched his arms and clenched his hands. The pain in his right ring finger had subsided to a dull ache, he realized. He also realized that after ten months Jennifer had called on him to do something for her besides sending a support check. She was relying upon him.

The warm, pleasant sensation reinvaded Ben's limbs. He luxuriated in it for a moment and stood up. Recalling his researches with Hoot, Ben knew that moving around sometimes fostered a new approach.

He went out into the hall and checked his mailbox. A sheaf of envelopes stuck out of his mail slot. Leafing through them, he found two bills, one refinance advertisement, and a letter from the Department of Employee Relations.

Dear Mr. Hackwell,

As a follow-up to an internal report on the incident of March 23rd at Professional Health Delivery, please be advised of a hearing scheduled for March 27 at 2 P.M. in Room 203 of the IDS Building where your employment status will be reevaluated. You may bring legal representation if you wish. Should you decide to wave such counsel…

Ben shredded the letter in disgust. He had as much chance of winning that hearing as he did smiting the moon with one of his leftover pizza slices. He hurled the shreds against the door and reentered his apartment. His watch read after three.

He felt tired, alone. What did time mean to a man with no job, no family, and no prospects? Yet, Jennifer was beginning to believe him, he reminded himself. It was a matter of time before he collected enough data to convince everyone, including the police.

If he was right, and if Caitline were dead, Ben reasoned, what would he do then? Then those responsible would get what was coming to them. It was as simple as that.

Ben lay on top of his unmade bed. When in doubt, recharge your batteries, he remembered from his Special Forces training. Whether your mission involved military intelligence or computer research, you never knew when you might get to sleep again.

The sun was emerging through leaden clouds when Ben awoke. The inside of his mouth tasted brackish, furry like the inside of a used pair of wool socks. He dangled his feet over the edge of his rumpled bed and clenched his hands. The puffy fingers felt as compliant and detached as a handful of sausages. The puffiness was a side effect from the salt in last night's pizza.

Pizza, the breakfast of champions, Ben recalled with a chuckle. Hoot still believed it, judging by the stack of pizza cartons that Ben saw stacked in Hoot's kitchen. He needed to reestablish contact with Hoot despite their differences. Hoot had been the last one to actually see Caitline alive. He also knew that he needed something to eat. Ben lumbered to the refrigerator and glowered at the solitary box of air freshener on the top shelf. He couldn't remember the last time he'd bothered to shop for groceries.

He recalled the two pizza slices that remained in his saddlebags. Swabbing his furry tongue against the roof of his mouth, he wondered whether it was time for more hair from the same dog.

Ben retrieved the cardboard box and tossed it on the wood coffee table. He grabbed the telephone from the kitchen and dialed Hoot's number. His cell phone buzzed on the other end of the line while Ben grabbed the larger of the remaining slices, folded it in two, and stuck the wad into his mouth.

Ben chewed three times and swallowed. The masticated pulp slid down in one lump. He tossed the remaining slice into the sink, stuck his head under the faucet, and rinsed the furry tang from his mouth. Taste never had mattered that much to him before. On their first ARPNET project, Ben recalled that he and Hoot had cranked out two weeks of data streams on cigarettes, Mountain Dew, and a giant pepperoni pizza.

Hoot's phone continued to buzz. Either he had neglected to switch it to voice mail or he refused to answer. From previous experience, Ben knew the latter option was more likely. Judging from Hoot's involvement with Caitline, Ben determined that he needed to call on Hoot in person.

Ben slipped into his boots, grabbed his jacket, and roared out of his garage a moment later. When he arrived at Hoot's house a half-hour later, the copper Bronco was not there. Ben dismounted and checked the side door to the garage. It was locked.

He strode up the front sidewalk and tried the breezeway door. It also was locked.

Ben mounted the front steps and studied the bronze horse head attached to door. A ring through its mouth served as a knocker. He tapped the ring against door twice and received no answer.

Ben slammed the knocker against the doorplate as hard as he could. His effort produced the same result as if he been scratching the hull inside a submarine. If Hoot were in his study, he'd never hear it.

Ben pounded the door with his fist. The house maintained its tomblike silence.

He gazed the length of the porch. No windows had been built into the left side of the house. To his right, the drapes of the front picture window remained closed.

Ben descended the front steps and scanned the houses on either side. Tucked toward the rear of their one-acre lots, these suburban homes were spaced too far apart for the neighbors to notice someone prowling around Hoot's property.

Ben rounded the far corner of the house. A double storm window provided the only light on the home's north side. He treaded the muddy lawn and discovered that its drapes had been drawn tight. The frames surrounding the screens were cracked and broken, their split and pliant jambs needed caulking.

Ben rapped on the frame three times and received no response. He pounded his fist against the frame until the lower right corner popped away from the jamb. His knocking should have been loud enough to spark Hoot's attention, Ben thought, if Hoot were in the room.

He peered toward the far corner of the building. The narrow path around it appeared to contain enough grass for him to maintain his traction. Slipping twice, Ben reached the corner to find the marshy culvert that drained the neighborhood. Three windows occupied the western side.

The curtains on the two nearest windows were drawn. It seemed odd, Ben thought as he scratched his chin. Even Hoot needed light once in a while. And air.

The far window was set in the back of the garage. Ben recalled that in an earlier age when car owners tinkered on their vehicles, the garage windows permitted the ventilation and light that an amateur repairman needed to do his work. If Hoot was anywhere in the house, that's where he'd be.

Ben trekked to the window of the attached garage. The curtains had not been drawn in some time. Caked in cobwebs, their bottom halves rested upon cardboard boxes, electronic equipment, and computer appliances. The jumble testified to Hoot's personal mantra: "Yesterday's hardware may be the guts of tomorrow's inspiration."

Ben squatted and peered up through the window. The jumble extended all the way to the ceiling of the garage. No Bronco appeared to be in there.

A copper glint flashed against the lower half of the grimy pane.

Ben cupped his hands over his eyes. A glossy patch of reddish-brown extended toward the ceiling. He shifted to his right. The sloping outline of the Bronco's roof materialized beneath the jutting edges of three computer keyboards.

Someone had rammed the truck into the pile and buried it. Ben knew that Hoot never would do that to any vehicle, particularly his own.

Ben slogged the way he had come and scanned the 1950s style rambler hidden behind the arbor vitae next door. His watch read 1:30. The rambler's inhabitants wouldn't be home for hours.

Ben stole to the bedroom window and glanced in both directions. Breaking in would take this game to a new level, Ben knew. What credibility he had with Jennifer and the law would be shreds if they found out. Hoot could be at any of a number of places without taking his Bronco, but he wouldn't have buried his Bronco in his garage.

Something more sinister was going on than simply a missing girl in a video, Ben decided. Hoot had been the last person who admitted that he'd seen Caitline alive. He also was the only other person besides Ben who could connect the buried whip to Caitline's disappearance.

Ben pounded on the loosened frame of the storm window. It popped free after two blows. He checked the lock of the inside window. It had been turned inward and did not give. Nor did the window's unyielding frame. Ben searched his pockets for something to pierce the paint seal. After running his thumb along the edge of his credit card, Ben decided they were too pliable. He pulled out his key ring and ran his thumb along the jagged edge of his cycle key. It seemed sturdy enough. Ben ran the point of the key the entire length of the jamb. Brittle little pieces of paint broke off here and there.

Ben brushed the shards from the sill and heaved against the jamb. Half the length of the jamb gave way. He pressed the point of his cycle key along the painted interface between the jamb and inner window frame and tried again. The window did not budge.

Ben sawed the key against the patch that remained most stubborn. A large flake sheared away. Several smaller shards followed it.

Ben scored the remaining paint seal and heaved again. Again it refused to give. Ben maintained the pressure just hard enough to prevent the glass from shattering in his face as sweat beaded on his forehead and his fingers felt about to give way.

The paint ripped apart like the tattered seam of a sport coat.

Ben scored the fissure, wiped the filings from the sill, and pushed upward. This time the frame offered Ben no resistance. Hoot could send the bill to him later.

He pushed the musty drapes aside and grabbed both ends of the window jamb. Ben leaped upward, slid down the sill, and stopped, his belt buckle caught the eyelet screw that held the storm window in place.

Ben's feet dangled inches above ground, unable to grab a foothold. He scrabbled against the wall like a manic bicyclist and captured a toehold on the foundation. Puffing and grunting, he wriggled forward until his belt buckle snapped free of the eyelet and his upper torso entered the room. Scrabbling for something to grab onto, Ben spread his fingers against the baseboard and pushed. Using the interior wall for leverage, he wriggled his hips until he tumbled into the room.

The air in the room was dusty, stale. Ben sneezed. No one burst in at the sound. No anxious footsteps echoed in the hall.

Ben checked his mode of access. The storm window remained upright beside the window frame. He maneuvered the window beneath the sill and pulled it through the opening. After setting the storm window against the exterior wall, Ben closed the inside pane, and rounded Hoot's desk. A giant, black larva sprawled across the haptic keyboard. A hundred wires radiated from it to the foot well.

The hairs on the back of Ben's neck tingled as he brushed his fingertips along the dorsal section. The surface felt slick and dry like Hoot's mesh condom.

A concealed zipper ran down the front the body suit. Two electrodes entered the eye sockets. Another formed the mouth.

Ben lifted the hood. An odor of vomit wafted out. He placed his fingertips on the jugular artery. He did not feel a pulse. A pallid tongue lolled out of Hoot's scorched mouth.

Ben let the fabric snap back. The monitor displayed a standard star field screen saver set at maximum warp to some parallel universe.

Ben tapped the Enter key. The screen flashed enormous blood red letters.

WHAT HAPPENS WHEN THE HURT
NEVER GOES AWAY?

An arrow-pierced heart replaced the message. Virtual droplets descended to the bottom of the screen and pooled until the background transformed to crimson. The screen went blank and the hurtling star field returned.

Ben grabbed Hoot's shoulder. His death appeared to have been quick, painless. Unexpected.

Ben shook his head. A hundred sensors didn't carry enough voltage to electrocute a man. Hoot knew that.

Suicide?

If Hoot had intended to kill himself, Ben wondered, why would he bury the Bronco in his garage?

Ben touched the monitor. The bleeding heart icon returned. He brushed his fingers against the screen. All of its input had been redirected into the suit.

Ben shoved Hoot's arms off the keyboard. He noticed no sign of rigor mortis. The monitor flashed and rolled, and a set of creamy female shoulders appeared.

Ben nudged Hoot's right arm. The image shifted to the bodice of a black lace bustier with scarlet ribbons, its top three buttons undone. The curve of the woman's right breast heaved against the fabric in rhythm with her breathing.

He touched Hoot's right temple. The monitor image shivered and cleared.

He nudged the side of Hoot's head. The image panned across the woman's bodice and returned to its original setting. He pushed Hoot's head sideways until it nestled in the crook of his left arm. The outline of the woman's right biceps and forearm appeared.

Ben tilted Hoot's head backward. The image scanned the woman's collarbone, traveled up her throat, and halted under the curve of her chin.

He laid Hoot's head on his shoulder. A black mask appeared. Scarlet stitching outlined the frowning eyes and mouth. Strawberry bangs framed the top and sides.

Were her eyes mauve?

He studied the area around the desk. Hoot's head did not align with the monitor. The coaster impressions in the carpet revealed the chair had rolled six inches left.

Ben restored the chair to its original position. The monitor image returned to the woman's open bodice.

He repositioned Hoot's head on top of his left arm. The image rolled and stabilized on the woman's right wrist, her fingers clutching the handle of a black leather whip with devil's red trim, lash lying coiled upon the floor.

She had not held a whip before.

Ben scanned the keyboard and spotted Hoot's left thumb and index finger curled around a one-inch vertical lever. He pushed the lever forward. The image flashed

PLEASE CREDIT $49.95 TO YOUR
HURT
ACCOUNT

Ben rotated the stick left. The image flickered and held. He moved the lever right and received the same response. He rotated it 360 degrees. A freeze frame image stabilized. The masked woman sat on the edge of a cot and stared straight into the camera until the hurtling star field reappeared.

Ben rotated the miniature joystick again. The woman removed her mask and laid it upon the bed.

The woman was Caitline.

CHAPTER 11

▼

Ben's left leg buckled. His arms flailed, scrabbled for a handhold, any handhold.

No, not this, Ben thought and recoiled in horror. Yet, he knew it must be true. The data was right there on the screen. Caitline was the focus of Hoot's pornographic fantasies. Ben's stomach knotted at the realization. The dim room started to spin around him. He wanted to faint, but his outrage and his training wouldn't let him.

What had possessed Hoot to do it? Why had Caitline complied?

The moment passed. Ben steadied himself upon Gibson's shoulder and focused upon the onrushing stars. It was obvious that Hoot thought so little of their friendship that he could use Ben's only daughter to advance his experiments. The only way Caitline could do such a thing was if she had been forced. If that were true, the video was real and Caitline was dead. If Caitline was dead...

Ben repressed the thought as his anguish surged through him again. He wondered what the real relationship was between Hoot and Wilson. They were not the adversaries Hoot had indicated. Had they conspired together in Hoot's scheme? Were they partners?

So many unanswered questions, Ben thought. He knew that Hoot seldom second-guessed himself. He never expressed remorse or shame, either. If not for any of those motives, Ben reasoned, why did Hoot endure the pain a lash provided? Could it have been just to promote the reality of his interface?

There was a bigger question that Ben could avoid no longer. Why had Caitline provided it?

His queasiness returned. A tear trickled down Ben's cheek despite his anger. Hoot never would tell. Never again would Ben have to listen to Hoot's ideas, share his bromides, or suffer his biases. Ben squeezed his dead friend's shoulder. Nor would anyone else. Perhaps that's why he felt so bereft.

Ben's palm felt warm and damp. He brushed the sensation away. The dampness returned on top and underneath his fingertips.

He palpated the area surrounding the nearby sensor. It felt moist, sticky. Ben sniffed the blackened tip of his finger. It smelled like blood.

He pulled back the collar of Hoot's body suit. New welts interspersed the scabbed minefield that comprised Hoot's back and shoulders.

Ben let the fabric snap into place. Something about the data in the room did not feel right. Would Hoot flagellate himself to death? Wasn't self-inflicted pain supposed to build to a climax like any other sexual arousal?

Hoot was too good an engineer, Ben decided. He was too good and too careful in his predilections for an accident like that to happen. Hoot overindulged only when it came to his work, and pizza.

Who stood to gain most by Hoot's death? Ben wondered. Wilson was the obvious choice. Did he have the technical expertise? Ben doubted it. Who else had?

Caitline? Ben thrilled at the idea of her being alive, however remote the possibility. But, if Caitline were alive, why would she murder her father's best friend?

Ben grimaced. Right now, Caitline's computer image constituted her sole existence. And computer images didn't bury Broncos.

The obvious candidate was himself, Ben realized. Who would be a better candidate than the outraged father? Who had a better motive? With his technical knowledge and his fingerprints everywhere, the police would arrest him as the prime suspect just as quickly as they had hauled him in at the Grafton.

Ben clenched his hands. Nobody suspected anything yet.

He wiped his fingers on the body suit, shoved the chair against the desk, and paused. Eliminating the incriminating evidence would be a fruitless task, Ben reasoned. He had touched too many things since he crawled inside this mausoleum to remove all the evidence.

He needed to compile what data he could and keep quiet as long as possible. The real killer would expose himself in the interim.

Ben returned to the computer monitor. Hoot's actions before his murder might reveal something. Ben pushed Hoot's corpse aside and clicked the Enter key.

Hoot's Internet account appeared. The History section listed five addresses in his HURT account, the last accessed six hours ago. Clicking its Web address produced an information box requesting his credit card number.

Ben clicked the Enter key. Nothing happened. Despite Hoot's prodigious memory, Ben knew that Hoot would not key in all 16 digits in his credit number every time. He would cut and paste it from somewhere else, or run a macro to insert it each time he needed it.

Ben clicked on the Program file, clicked on the expansion icon, and scrolled down the list. A host of applications appeared on the screen, but none contained a name that could be associated with a credit card mnemonic.

If Hoot had embedded his card number in the programming code of the site address' initiation sequence, the file would open automatically. Since it did not, it must be buried somewhere else.

Ben surveyed the room. Where would Hoot keep his identification?

He strode to the doorway and flicked the light switch. The hallway remained as dim as the master bedroom. Ben searched the walls on both sides as he strode to the bathroom, fumbled around the doorjamb, and flipped the switch. The sudden increase in wattage blinded him like the blaze from the noonday sun.

Ben rubbed the afterimages from his eyes and returned down the hallway. A white doorknob indicated a second doorway that opened onto a small bedroom painted in flat white latex. A metal bed frame stood in the opposite corner. The bottom half of a string of stenciled letters stuck out from under the folded sheet. They read:

PROPERTY
U.S. ARMY
BLACKHAWK

Ben released the sheet and ran his fingertips along the top of the headboard. It was dust-free.

He surveyed the wall opposite. Despite finding an uneven crease that ran from floor to ceiling, he could not find a handle. The flat white expanse extended to the adjoining walls. Even the carpet was slate white.

Ben struck his fist against the wall. The closet door yawned. Two pair of khaki cotton pants hung from separate hangers on the closet bar. A pair of spit-shined combat boots lay on the floor beneath them. In the corner a pivot arm extended to a hydraulic mechanism attached to the bottom of the door.

Ben struck the wall again. The closet door slid shut.

He reopened the closet and searched the pockets of the nearest pair of pants. They were empty. A black leather wallet dropped out of the front pocket of the second pair. Its leather felt stiff, unused. A photograph of Kate Jackson occupied the license window, an American Express card the side opposite. Its expiration date: 12/25/06

Ben withdrew the card, reentered the master bedroom, and stared at the ciliated larva slumped across the desk. Inside that sheath a brilliant man died trying to perfect his vision of touch connectivity. Ben brushed away another tear. Hoot had been his friend, whatever the nature of the man's involvement with his daughter.

Ben knew that Hoot never would let sentiment cloud his judgment. Nor should he. He pulled up the financial request panel onscreen and keyed in the numbers from Hoot's credit card. A sequence of asterisks appeared.

Ben clicked Submit. An hourglass icon flashed, the monitor donged. Weeping twin hearts appeared at the center of the screen. Their lash-filled eyes brimmed, burst, and deluged the screen with virtual tears.

Another panel appeared to inform him that his account was no longer active.

The weeping hearts reappeared and disintegrated.

FARE WELL!

The star field returned and plunged into hyperspace.

Ben closed the screen saver. Hoot's account had been shut off at the other end, he decided. Whoever operated the HURT site knew something had happened at this Internet Protocol address and had pulled the plug. Ben knew that responsibility usually fell to the account manager.

He opened the Cookies accounts and found anyuser@hurtful.com followed by a string of four digit numbers running across the top line. IP addresses tended to be grouped into blocks of two to eight digits that identified nodes and sub-nodes like city and street names in a postal mail address.

Ben ran the cursor along the top of the information screen, copied the address code, and pasted it into the address line. Black squares interrupted the number sequence at irregular intervals. Assuming that the squares stood for periods within the sequence, Ben reasoned, the first 16 identified the main node of the address that would identify the server on which the HURT account operated.

He cut the remaining digits in the address and pressed the Enter key. After five seconds, the software flashed "Waiting for response from host."

The screen returned to the onrushing stars.

Ben pressed the Enter key and watched the second hand of his wristwatch tick off 20 seconds. Given Hoot's direct service line, Ben decided that business must be good at the site, especially so early in the afternoon.

The hourglass reconverted to an arrow. "No response from host" appeared.

Ben tried again, but the same message appeared within 20 seconds. He tried a third time. After ten watch ticks, the screen flashed and rolled. Twin pierced hearts appeared in the center, filled the screen, and disintegrated.

> You have entered a secure site.
> Please enter your name, password, and secure ID number.

Ben scanned the three information boxes and keyed in eight garbage characters followed by Hoot's last name, a string of letters, and a string of numbers. The software responded:

> Your validation check failed. Please try again.

The site's security protocol worked fast. Ben tried different sequences of numbers. The program took twice as long to produce the same result each time.

Ben mulled the results. The security software employed a random number generator that controlled the numbers and the duration allowed for their input. If he knew Hoot's password, he needed to input it within the time frame allotted by the number generator. With such a sophisticated program, that would be difficult to accomplish without a matching chronometer.

What commercial provider had the means to employ such software?

Ben clicked the View selection from the Menu bar and opened Source. A single line of code ran across the top of the panel, <Enabling Java! IDref="Schariah/ ua.com">

What now? Ben wondered. After hacking with the computer for 10 minutes he had learned more about the black box that was Hoot's inner life than he had in their 30 years of friendship.

What was Hoot's relation to Caitline, Ben asked himself. Was she his dream girl? His dominatrix? She was his connection to HURTFUL, surely. Was she his partner?

Ben's chest tightened. Someone maintained the site at the other end. Someone transmitted the pain Hoot needed. Someone needed to pull the plug, someone with the knowledge to do so. Was that someone Caitline?

He wondered how he felt about that. How did he feel about Caitline's involvement with a man three times her age? How did he feel about the pain and humiliation she facilitated to Hoot and to others? How did he feel about the money she made from it?

Ben clenched and unclenched his fist. He had so many questions and so few answers. All he knew for sure was a Web address that may or may not be associated with Wilson's strip club. And that Caitline once had set up Wilson's Web page.

Ben shook his head. Schariah might be the domain name for a 100 Web sites. Would Wilson be so foolish as to affiliate his club with such a prominent site name?

He needed someone to investigate Web domains, copyright, and intellectual property rights, Ben decided. He needed someone familiar with contracts and licenses. He needed a lawyer like Jennifer.

The back of Ben's neck tingled. Of course, Jennifer, he realized. It felt as inevitable as the impact from a thrown custard pie.

Would she do it for him? Of course not, he decided. She'd do it for Caitline. Was it worth going down that road again?

Ben gazed at the sensor wires converging at the computer ports and followed them back to their host. It would have to be, for now.

He stretched his fingers towards the ceiling. The cramped and aching muscles screamed as if they had been released after spending a month in a tiger cage.

He wiped his handkerchief across the keyboard and glanced toward the window. No need to return the way he had arrived. His cycle remained parked in the driveway.

Ben sidestepped the host of sensor wires and hesitated. Should he return the room to the manner he had found it?

It wouldn't matter to the police one way or the other, he decided. Someone had been here. The buried Bronco indicated as much. Nor would it matter much to Hoot to any more.

It mattered only to him.

Ben nudged the reboot button with the knuckle of his right index finger. The computer processing unit lit up and its software proceeded through the initiation sequence. The screen rolled and flashed as Ben retreated to the doorway. The sound card emitted an accompanying crescendo to the desktop that appeared onscreen. The star field reappeared and resumed its headlong surge through hyperspace.

CHAPTER 12

▼

A wintry gust pummeled the daffodils to the ground as Ben descended the front steps. The mid-afternoon sun glimmered behind a line of North Dakota snow clouds scudding toward the zenith.

Should he investigate the buried Bronco?

Ben climbed onto his cycle. Let the police do their job.

As Ben headed down the street, the deserted front yards he passed failed to quell his feeling that someone lurked behind a curtain with a running camcorder. He pulled his cell phone from his jacket pocket, but the red light in the corner indicated the batteries were low. He stuck the phone back in his pocket and focused on the road ahead. He'd call the police as soon as he reached Jennifer's office. All he had was a feeling that Caitline might be alive. Without more hard data on her whereabouts, a feeling wouldn't convince the police or Jennifer.

Jennifer's office building remained as quiet and solemn as the first time. Ben's work boots thudded on the polished wooden steps of the stairwell to the second floor. The waiting area of Jennifer's office was empty.

Ben peered into the kitchen alcove. Azeb poured water into a paper funnel resting atop a glass coffee maker.

He cleared his throat. Azeb glanced up and smiled shyly.

"Good afternoon, Mr. Hackwell," Azeb said.

"Doesn't anyone do business in person anymore?" Ben asked with a smile.

"There is plenty of business for us," Azeb replied. "People are always doing something they regret later on. Then they call us."

"Someone like me?" Ben asked.

"Never one like you," Azeb replied. Her smile broadened.

Encouraged by the warmth of Azeb's reception, Ben glanced toward Jennifer's office.

"Is she in?" Ben asked.

"She was on the Internet earlier," Azeb responded. "I shall see."

Azeb set the decanter on the counter and strolled past him with a lingering fragrance of sandalwood. She tapped on Jennifer's office, stuck her head inside, and turned toward Ben.

"Ms. Roloson says to come in," Azeb announced.

Ben followed the rust-red Turkish rug to the Plexiglas workstation where Jennifer sat sideways behind her desk hunched over the keyboard. He cleared his throat.

"Could you give me another moment, Benny?" Jennifer asked. Her uncertain smile revealed worry lines around her eyes. "I need to get this last point on our template."

"Sure," Ben agreed.

Hearing her pet name for him had caught Ben off guard. He fiddled with her Rolodex as he studied her new haircut. Its anthracite flip was more stylish than her old pageboy style, he decided, but he missed its telltale iron gray streak in the crown.

After 30 seconds Jennifer raised her hands from the keyboard and flashed him an intoxicating smile.

"You don't know how glad I am to get that document out of the way," Jennifer exclaimed.

Ben grimaced as he thought of all the legal documents he'd waited for Jennifer to finish in the past.

"And here I thought you'd be waiting breathlessly beside the phone for my call," Ben quipped.

Jennifer pointed toward the beige phone at the opposite corner of her desk.

"My phone's right where it always is," Jennifer said brightly. "Like I am."

"You don't seem terribly concerned about what I've got to tell you," Ben observed.

"You haven't told me anything yet," Jennifer replied with a smile as she crossed her legs. "Did you find Caitline?"

"No," Ben replied.

"Do you know where she is?" Jennifer asked.

"No," Ben repeated.

"Do you know if she's all right?" Jennifer persisted despite her increasing exasperation.

"It depends on what you mean by all right," Ben said.

"What do you mean?" Jennifer asked with an emphasis on "you."

"She's a hooker in an electronic brothel," Ben responded. He decided that Jennifer should learn the truth just as he did. "At least a virtual image of her is."

"That's not possible," Jennifer replied. She swiveled her chair and stared out the window at the busy street. "I don't believe it."

"Believe it," Ben declared. "Caitline is a dominatrix on a Web site devoted to humiliating its customers. It's probably the most sophisticated and advanced sex site I've ever seen with interactive video combined with real-time physical sensation."

"You sound proud," Jennifer observed.

"Not very," Ben replied. "Not when a man like Hoot loses his life over it."

Jennifer spun back toward Ben.

"Hoot?" Jennifer exclaimed. "What does he have to do with this?"

"I found him dead at his desk," Ben replied. "He was all hooked up to the Web site I told you about, literally plugged in through an animatronic suit. And there was Caitline onscreen delivering the voltage that—"

"Enough," Jennifer's interrupted. Her cobalt eyes blazed. "You don't expect me to believe this?"

Ben retreated a step. Why did Jennifer doubt him when she had asked him to find out what had happened to Caitline?

"You know I wouldn't tell you something like this unless it were true," Ben replied.

"Perhaps," Jennifer said.

"Perhaps?" Ben retorted, frustrated by the doubt that registered on Jennifer's face. "How can you doubt it?"

Jennifer stood up and moved toward the window.

"With everything that's happened..." Jennifer's voice cracked. She covered her face with her hands. "I don't know what to believe."

Ben stepped forward, eager to reclaim his role, any role in Jennifer's life. He just wanted to bring everything back to the way it used to be.

"What's happened, Jenn?" Ben whispered as he touched her shoulder. "Tell me."

"Don't touch me," Jennifer warned and twisted away. "You've no right ever to touch me again!"

"I just want to help," Ben implored.

"Is that what you were thinking while you were beating me?" Jennifer asked as she backed against the corner of her workstation. "You thought you were helping Caitline and me?"

Ben dropped his hand to his side.

"It was only two slaps," Ben murmured.

"From a Special Forces officer," Jennifer replied. "With combat training."

"Ex-Special Forces," Ben corrected. His hand felt inert, numb, like the rest of him. "I never used the training."

Jennifer raised her hand toward her jaw.

"It was hard to tell the difference," Jennifer observed.

"I was weak," Ben admitted. To Jennifer it must have seemed like he had pummeled her from one side of the room to the other, he realized. "I felt helpless. I lost control."

"So you struck out at the one who made you feel that way," Jennifer scoffed. "How often have I heard that defense in court?"

"I never meant to hurt you," Ben replied.

"How can I be certain of that any more?" Jennifer responded as her eyes focused on her handbag beside her desk phone. "How do I know that you won't strike me again?"

"You have to trust all of the data," Ben replied. He wondered what Jennifer had in her handbag that could distract her from their conversation. "If you trust what you know about me, you also know I wouldn't do it again."

"And Caitline?" Jennifer asked as she eyed Ben. "Who is she supposed to trust?"

"What do you mean?" Ben asked.

"Is Caitline supposed to trust you after your attack?" Jennifer retorted. "It's hardly any wonder you can't find her."

"Are you blaming me for Caitline's disappearance?" Ben asked in disbelief.

"Do you have a better explanation why she's acting out like this?" Jennifer said, regaining her composure. She straightened her skirt. "Azeb will show you out."

Nothing had changed between them, Ben realized. Jennifer blamed him for everything that had happened. Her trump card was to make him responsible for Caitline's disappearance just as Hoot had blamed him for Caitline's acting out. With nothing left to lose, he might as well to go for broke. His first priority was to find out what Jennifer had concealed in her purse.

"The Caitline I saw had augmented breasts," Ben said as he edged toward the far end of Jennifer's desk.

"So?" Jennifer remarked.

"Where'd she get them?" Ben asked.

"How should I know?" Jennifer replied coolly. "Check your Preferences feature next time."

Ben studied Jennifer's face. Now that she had recovered her self-control, she seemed disinterested.

"You seem awfully determined to dismiss everything I've told you," Ben said.

"What are you saying?" Jennifer replied.

"A mother usually is more worried about her daughter's whereabouts," Ben replied.

"You're blaming me for her disappearance?" Jennifer retorted. She hurled the papers onto the desktop, strode to the door, and flung it open. "MRS. ANOURI!"

She bellowed her secretary's name a second time.

Azeb stepped into the middle of the outer office.

"Yes?" Azeb said.

"Please show this 'gentleman' to the door," Jennifer ordered. "If he's not out of the office in one minute, call the police."

Azeb beckoned toward Ben with a sweep of her right arm. Jennifer sidestepped around Ben into the reception area. Ben jumped in front of her.

"You don't have to play a part in this, Azeb," Jennifer cried. "Just call the police."

"Am I not already playing a part?" Azeb responded.

Jennifer glared at her. Azeb retreated to her desk and started dialing.

"The police will be here in five minutes," Azeb announced as she hung up the phone receiver.

Ben eyed his ex-wife who returned his regard like a cornered cat. More than reproach or resentment lurked in her eyes. Something he had never seen before, something inchoate, terrified.

"Are we replaying our last court session?" Ben asked. "Are you fixing something now like you did then. I'm guilty whether I committed a crime or not."

"You haven't much time," Azeb urged. "I suggest you leave."

Ben turned toward Azeb. As a one-woman jury, he had to make her see his side.

"Lawyers like Jennifer feel the only way to insure criminal behavior won't recur is to eliminate the circumstances that caused it in the first place," Ben explained. "Remove the possibility that it can ever happen again. Put it out of harm's way, so to speak."

Azeb set the receiver in its cradle.

"Have you not destroyed each other enough?" she asked.

"You misunderstand, Azeb," Jennifer said as she embraced Azeb's hands in her own. "I admire Benjamin's concern. I'd expect nothing less from a devoted father. I wish I'd seen more of it when we were married."

"You are right, Ms. Roloson," Azeb replied and released herself from Jennifer's grip. "Though perhaps he feels now he has no other choice."

Someone thumped twice on the top panel of the hallway door.

"This is the police," a male voice called through the door.

Two uniformed police officers strode into the receptionist's area, scanned the interior, thumbs on the hammers of their unbuttoned pistols, and marched to the doorway of Jennifer's office.

The male officer, tall and slim, with a gray mustache, introduced himself as Officer Loring. He smiled, turned toward his female partner, and introduced her as Officer Tannen. His russet-haired cohort nodded.

"We understand there's been a domestic disturbance," Loring said.

Jennifer nodded. Loring turned toward Ben.

"Is this the gentleman that's causing the disturbance?" Loring asked.

Jennifer nodded again. But when Tannen grabbed Ben's arm, Jennifer stayed her wrist.

"You have a confession to make, don't you, Benjamin?" Jennifer said.

Ben scanned his ex-wife's face. Her sapphire eyes betrayed nothing. Was this another test, Ben wondered, or a final humiliation? Perhaps it was both.

"I found a dead man this afternoon," Ben said. "His name was William Gibson, a friend of mine."

Tannen pulled a notepad from her shirt pocket. Loring asked where.

"In his house," Ben replied.

"How did you get in?" Loring asked.

"I broke in," Ben said.

"Why?" Loring asked.

"I knocked," Ben said. "Hoot didn't answer. Something felt wrong. All the doors were locked. So I climbed in through an unlocked window."

"And?" Loring asked.

"And I found him dead at his desk," Ben added. "Electrocuted, I think."

"Why didn't you report it?" Loring said.

Ben shook his head. All of his answers sounded improbable.

"The batteries went out on my cell phone," Ben explained.

The male officer scrutinized the faces of Jennifer and Azeb.

"That address is 20 miles away," Loring observed. "You couldn't have phoned from his house? Or somewhere in between?"

Ben glanced at Jennifer and decided that his family concerns did not fall under the category of police business.

"I was in shock, I guess," Ben replied.

"You guess," Loring retorted and grabbed Ben's shoulder. "You'd better come with us.

CHAPTER 13

▼

"Just a minute!" Jennifer said and stepped between the two officers. "What charges are you bringing against him?"

"Violating his restraining order, for one," Loring replied. "Leaving a potential crime scene for another."

"Does it appear that he's bothering me?" Jennifer asked.

The two police officers exchanged glances.

"You were involved in some kind of confrontation when we came in," Loring replied, perplexed by Jennifer's change of attitude.

Jennifer placed her hands on her hips in indignation.

"We were discussing our daughter," she replied. "There are always disagreements between the best of parents about that."

"There's still his leaving the crime scene," Loring asserted.

"Have you determined probable cause?" Jennifer asked. "At this point it's simply been reported that a body was found."

Jennifer returned to her desk.

"I suggest you send some people to check it out," Jennifer advised.

Loring glanced at Ben with skepticism.

"What about him?" Loring asked.

"He's not going anywhere," Jennifer responded.

"How do we know that?" Tannen asked.

"You have his address," Jennifer replied. "And you have my assurance as a member of the Hennepin County criminal justice system that he will keep himself available for any questions you might have."

Jennifer glanced toward Ben for confirmation.

"Isn't that right, Benjamin?" she asked.

Ben nodded without conviction. He knew this was Jennifer's turf. He also knew he had few other options.

"Anything else?" Jennifer asked.

"We'll check out the report," Loring replied as he leveled his gaze on Jennifer. "This isn't proper procedure, counselor, and you know it."

"Would you like some coffee for the road?" Jennifer asked in her best hostess manner and turned toward Azeb. "Make sure these officers have a cup of cappuccino before they leave."

Azeb preceded the officers out of the office and shut the door behind them. When the lock clicked in the jamb, Ben turned toward his ex-wife. He was as perplexed as the police officers at Jennifer's attitude shift.

"Anything else I can do for you, counselor?" Ben asked. "Fix the lights, scrub the floors? Virus-check your hard drive?"

"A simple thank you would suffice," Jennifer replied.

Ben bowed from the waist.

"I'd like to express my thanks in a way that's more substantial," Ben said. "Not everyone could get rid of those officers with such skill."

Jennifer spun toward her keyboard.

"You can find your own way out," she said.

Ben edged forward and peered into Jennifer's black leather handbag. It contained a set of car keys, a compact, a travel-sized box of Kleenex, and a foot-long black flashlight. Nothing appeared threatening or lethal in there. He removed the flashlight. Despite its length, its weight surprised him.

"What are these?" Ben asked and pointed at the twin knobs located side by side on the lens. "Recharge posts?"

"Would you leave my things alone, please?" Jennifer asked as she clicked the left button of her mouse. A wheat field replaced the rapacious Godzilla on her desktop. "Just put it back."

"What is this, Jenn?" Ben persisted.

Jennifer ran a hand through her hair in exasperation.

"A stun gun, if you must know," Jennifer replied.

"A stun gun," Ben repeated in surprise. "Why do you need that?"

"I like to feel safe," Jennifer replied.

"Has the deacon been making inappropriate advances?" Ben asked with a grin as he turned on the flashlight portion of the gun. "I hope."

Ben gazed at the spot of light cast on the opposite wall. He savored the prospect of disabling his main competition.

Jennifer screwed up her face in disgust.

"He's been a perfect gentleman," Jennifer replied and reached for the gun.

Ben seized her wrist. Jennifer never did anything without a reason.

"Why, Jenn?" Ben demanded.

"The police are still in the building, you know," Jennifer warned.

Ben released his fingers. He knew Jennifer always kept her cool during their arguments.

"You've kept your grip," Jennifer remarked as she massaged her wrist with her other hand. "I'll say that."

"You do everything for a reason," Ben insisted. "This time's no different."

"I like to feel safe," Jennifer repeated with a shrug. "Is there anything wrong in that?"

Ben studied Jennifer's face, but it betrayed nothing. Hers was a logical reply. Though stun guns were illegal, he knew many women had purchased them over the Internet for self-defense.

"I guess not," Ben acknowledged and returned the gun to Jennifer's handbag. "Thinking of using it on me?"

Jennifer flashed Ben a tight smile.

"It had occurred to me," Jennifer admitted.

Ben grimaced. Jennifer's reconfirmation of their relationship made her behavior all the more perplexing.

"Look, you had me where you wanted me with the police," Ben said. "With this second incident I'd have been out of your hair for good. Why did you call them off?"

"I don't know exactly," Jennifer mused. "You were willing to sacrifice yourself, I guess. Your story was total bullshit, but you were committed to it. That impressed me enough to think there was something to it."

Ben chuckled ruefully. It was going to take a lot to regain Jennifer's trust.

"I should be thanking you for the vote of confidence, I suppose," Ben said.

"Put it in writing," Jennifer advised as she scanned a ledger beside her keyboard. She pointed toward the in basket and resumed keying in data. "Just leave it in there. I'll get to it eventually."

"Did you mean what you said to the police officers?" Ben asked as he studied the spreadsheet software converting the dollar figures into foreign currency. The large exchange differential indicated a third world currency. "I'm talking about our differences in raising our daughter."

"I said it, didn't I?" Jennifer replied.

"Then I still need to know," Ben said.

"About what?" Jennifer asked.

"About the implants," Ben replied. "Did you buy them for her?"

"Breasts! Breasts! Breasts!" Jennifer cried. "Is that all men ever think about?"

Ben smiled at her outburst. It was a small consolation, but he had gotten a passionate reaction out of her.

"Sometimes I think about feet," Ben acknowledged and stared at the leg well of her desk. "And legs."

Ben's gaze drifted upward. He recalled their first nighttime stroll along the Potomac years ago, and their first kiss.

"And thighs," he added and his eyes skipped to her throat. "Shoulders are nice."

His gaze halted at the tongue curled behind Jennifer's partly open mouth.

"And lips," Ben said.

He glanced upward. Jennifer's sapphire eyes studied his.

"And?" Jennifer asked.

"And why you'd want to change any of that," Ben said.

"You're a man," Jennifer responded. "You wouldn't understand."

"Try me," Ben encouraged.

Jennifer stared out the window and ran a hand through her hair. A whiff of her Obsession floated past Ben's nostrils.

"When you just can't stand things any more," Jennifer said, "getting something like a new hairdo makes you feel better."

"Change yourself instead of the situation, you mean," Ben said.

Jennifer turned back to Ben. The wariness had returned to her face.

"Some things you can't change," Jennifer declared.

Ben ignored the accusation implicit in her statement.

"So you change a body part that doesn't need it," Ben said.

"That's a matter of opinion," Jennifer replied. "Everything can be improved."

Ben flicked his thumbnail against the side of her Rolodex. Jennifer's pursuit of perfection always had been a flash point between them, Ben recalled. For Jennifer the world was in a state of perpetual improvement, no matter how ill-advised the decision or ill-prepared the forces were in promoting that improvement.

"Is that what you told Caitline?" Ben asked. "Did you fill her head with more tales of how everything from women's body parts to human rights are destined to get better and better?"

"What's wrong with that?" Jennifer asked.

"Because it doesn't happen that way in the real world," Ben said.

"It happens," Jennifer argued. "The opportunities are there, if you're prepared."

"As simple as ABC, isn't that your tagline?" Ben retorted. "Was your Women Across Boundaries Cooperative prepared for the atrocities in Kosovo? Or the rapes in Rwanda?"

"Perhaps not," Jennifer admitted. "We've learned a lot since then."

"A lot of good men died protecting you during the learning curve," Ben replied.

"Not all us decide to disengage just because our efforts don't turn out like we expected," Jennifer replied haughtily. "Some of us stand by our commitments."

Ben recoiled, shocked by Jennifer's statement. Returning with Jennifer to her home state for a new start had formed the basis of his decision to leave Washington.

"I thought you supported my decision to leave the military," Ben said.

"I said I understood why you made it," Jennifer replied. "I never agreed with your reasons behind it."

"Hoot would have seen eye-to-eye with you about that," Ben retorted.

"Don't compare me to that awful man," Jennifer cried with a shudder. "And I don't care how you feel about the aims of our Cooperative. Just get out of here."

Jennifer's admission angered Ben. He rounded her desk in a fury. Despite their differences, his comparing her to Hoot had done more than strike a nerve with Jennifer. He had to know why.

"'That awful man' is the last one to see Caitline alive," Ben declared. "He's also the man with the technology that transformed Caitline into the pneumatic harlot I saw murdered on the Internet. Think there's a connection?"

"Isn't it obvious?" Jennifer replied in alarm.

"Perhaps, perhaps not," Ben replied as he extended his hands in from of his chest. "The Caitline I knew before she got murdered on the Internet didn't have breasts out to here."

"What of it?" Jennifer asked and twisted up her face in disgust.

"Getting a boob job isn't like getting a new hairdo," Ben persisted. "I want to know why you allowed it."

"Can you think of a better use of technology for improving women's self image?" Jennifer countered.

Ben grabbed the back of Jennifer's chair and spun her around.

"Is that what this is all about?" Ben cried. "Women's self image?"

"If you say so," Jennifer said.

"If I say so?" Ben replied and threw up his hands. "Just whose self image are we talking about here?"

Jennifer folded her hands in her lap.

"You know, the one thing I hated throughout our relationship was the sarcasm," Jennifer observed. "That and the superior little smile that went with it."

Ben stepped back. He'd seen Jennifer use this courtroom ploy many times before where she deflected the damaging data onto a related yet irrelevant topic. He wondered how far she was prepared to go with this strategy this time.

"Women's self-image?" Ben taunted. "C'mon."

"I don't know what you're talking about," Jennifer said.

Ben glanced at the sable coat hanging behind the door.

"A liberated woman doesn't wrap herself in furs," Ben observed.

"I have a right to wear anything I want," Jennifer replied.

"Furs of dead animals," Ben said. "Is that the politically correct image for a socially conscious lawyer?"

"I like the feel of it, the warmth," Jennifer replied. "It makes me feel special. Where's the harm in that?"

Ben chuckled and shook his head.

"As long as it feels and looks real, it's OK," Ben said.

"Yes."

"And that's what motivated you to give Caitline implants," Ben said.

"She wanted them," Jennifer said and shrugged. "All her friends were getting them. Why not?"

"What about accepting yourself for who you are?" Ben asked.

Jennifer rounded her desk.

"Young women face challenges enough these days," Jennifer responded. "If having a better body can help overcome them, I'm all for it." She placed her hands on her hips in a gesture of defiance. "What do you want that will make you go away?"

"Specifically?" Ben asked.

"Yes, specifically," Jennifer replied and gritted her teeth. "I specifically want you out of here."

Ben hesitated. Jennifer's answers sounded reasonable, but their logic didn't satisfy him. What was she offering him? Why was she offering it now? Did it have anything to do with Hoot's interface?

"I want a court order allowing me to examine Hoot's hard drive," Ben demanded.

"You didn't do that while you were there?" Jennifer exclaimed.

"I broke in," Ben explained. "There wasn't a lot of time for that sort of thing. Now that you've sent the police out there, I'll need a court order to inspect Hoot's data files."

"Why?" Jennifer demanded.

"Our daughter's life is at stake here," Ben declared as he studied Jennifer's suddenly resolute eyes. "You said you believed me before. If that was true—"

"You'll have it within the hour," Jennifer declared and tapped the keypad of her cellular phone. "Anything else?"

Ben shook his head.

Jennifer spun back to her spreadsheet and pulled up an e-mail template. After several cranks and groans, her printer started grinding out the body of her missive.

Ben closed her office door, reeling at all that he had learned. He'd won the round, but he didn't feel exultant. Jennifer's replies had opened more questions than answers.

He glanced at his knuckles. Both fists had drained of color in his effort to maintain his self-control. Ben clenched and unclenched his fingers several times. Their ruddy color returned along with his reawakened sense of their attachment.

Ben peered into the alcove. The coffeepot had disappeared.

"Did the police get all of the coffee?" Ben asked.

"No, no!" Azeb cried with concern. "For you I will make a new pot."

She bustled past Ben into the alcove. The clangor of rinsing pots and grinding beans disabled his perception of Azeb's body scent.

Ben crossed the waiting room, plopped into the vinyl couch that ran along the outside wall, and sifted through the data. Azeb emerged from the alcove carrying a steaming white clay mug in her right hand and set it atop the law journal on the glass coffee table before him.

Azeb folded her arms across her chest.

"Aren't you going to drink it?" Azeb asked.

"Maybe I'll just inhale until it's gone," Ben replied with a smile.

"As you wish," Azeb chuckled and sashayed to her desk. The wall clock above her desk ticked off the seconds as Ben raised the mug to his lips. Its rising vapor singed his nostrils as he sipped the warm nectar, let it linger on his tongue, and course down his throat.

He wondered why Jennifer had capitulated. His role as her operative could not be that important to her. What was she afraid he might find out about Caitline? How was Caitline's breast surgery involved?

Ben drained his cup, strode to Azeb's desk, and cleared his throat.

Azeb closed the file on which she was working and spun toward him.

"You are finished," Azeb observed. "Would you care for a refill?"

Ben shook his head and asked what he should do with the empty.

"Just place it in the sink," Azeb replied.

"I wouldn't have asked," Ben said as he set his cup beside the drain in the sink, "but it seemed to me the alcove might be off limits."

"We appreciate your concern," Azeb said. "Especially from such a one like you."

"What do you mean?" Ben asked.

"You are no respecter of limits, sir," Azeb cautioned.

Ben shook his head. The whole world seemed to be his critic today.

"Who told you that?" Ben asked.

"I observed it," Azeb replied with a smile.

Ben chuckled. He had one friend in the citadel, he decided.

"In that case," he said. "What do you know about Ms. Roloson's sable coat?"

Azeb covered her mouth with her left hand.

"I shouldn't tell you this," she said in a lower voice. "But it is fake."

"I know that," Ben replied.

"It was given to her by Mr. Rykert," Azeb added. "Did you know that?"

Ben studied her face. It contained the earnestness of someone swapping conspiracy theories on the Kennedy assassination.

"Why are you telling me this?" Ben asked.

"I thought it might interest you," Azeb said.

"It might," Ben replied. "If I was trying to win her back."

"Are you not?" Azeb declared.

"I'm trying to find out what happened to my daughter," Ben declared.

"Her daughter, too," Azeb observed. "Children are the rose buds of our existence, each possessed with their own capacity for delight or despair."

The FAX machine clicked and buzzed. Azeb pulled the top sheet out of its paper tray, scanned it, and laid it on the corner of her desk.

"This is the document you requested," Azeb said. "Go now. Learn what you must learn."

Ben scanned the document that proved to be a standard legal writ requesting equal access to evidence.

"Hardly carte blanche," Ben muttered and stuck it in the back pocket of his jeans. "It'll get me in if no one examines it."

He opened the outer office door and paused.

"Do you think I'll find Caitline?" he asked.

Azeb's face clouded.

"If she wishes to be found."

CHAPTER 14

▼

Ben crossed the hallway to the stairwell. He and Jennifer always had disagreed on fundamentals. Her subsidizing Caitline's cosmetic surgery constituted the latest flash point in the charge cloud that constituted their parental relationship. The writ Jennifer had supplied him legitimized his actions as her operative, but Ben knew that it also could be revoked at her discretion.

He peered down the empty stairwell. An "official" agent need not take the back stairs, he decided. Instead, he strode to the elevator, descended to the atrium, and bounded down the front steps to his cycle. When the engine roared to life, he throttled back until he felt it humming between his legs, and gazed down University Avenue at the paired cells of muzzy red and white that streamed toward the horizon in opposite directions. The underside of an advancing storm front that glowered a dull copper above the speeding lights reminded Ben of Hoot's Bronco.

A wave of anguish washed over him. Hoot was dead. If Caitline had caused it, what transformed an intelligent girl into a death-dealing dominatrix by remote control?

Ben glanced toward the light in the law office window and decided that Caitline's behavior was Jennifer's fault. Giving Caitline money instead of love, cosmetic enhancement, rather than guidance could result only in her acting out. If he had been around, Hoot's murder never would have happened.

But he had not been around, and Caitline had electrocuted his best friend because of it.

Ben wiped a tear from his cheek frustrated by his sense of impotence. Hoot never would have tolerated such sentiment.

Had Caitline disappeared because she murdered Hoot?

That seemed the obvious solution, but Ben shook his head. Caitline had been killed, too. Rather, a virtual image of her had been, to be strictly accurate. Jennifer had granted him the legal means to determine which interpretation of the data was true as a minor concession in their struggle for parental supremacy.

All his questions devolved to why, Ben decided. Why had Jennifer continued to let him be involved at all?

Unless he discovered harder data, Ben had only his previous knowledge about Caitline and his determination to know the truth to go on. He opened the throttle, and his cycle plunged forward. In his new capacity as family detective, he determined to learn why. Or die trying.

Ben sped west on University Avenue until he reached the exit ramp onto Interstate-35 West that split Minneapolis in two. Within minutes, he was weaving in and out of those onrushing streams of automobile lights towards Hoot's house. He turned off onto Highway 5 and sped up the boulevard where the enormous homes on both sides yawned, swallowed a Bronco or Ranger whole, and resumed their dream-like repose.

Ben passed a Hennepin county police car parked on the front edge of Hoot's lawn. A gray Plymouth Intrepid and a blue Audi were parked in the driveway. Flapping yellow tape wrapped the downspout at one end, spanned the garage door, extended over the jonquil beds to a pole on the front porch, continued to the far corner of the house, and snaked around the downspout.

Ben parked behind the unmarked sedan. He ducked under the yellow tape and peered inside the garage window where the Bronco remained buried in its cardboard sarcophagus.

He opened the front door and scanned the living room. A tawny pane of light reflected off the hallway wall that led to the bedrooms. Ben stepped across the threshold toward the hallway and heard the murmur of voices inside Hoot's bedroom. With law enforcement agents all around, he decided it was best to make his presence known.

"Hello?" Ben called as he took another step forward. "Anyone here?"

A tall police officer with a blond mustache emerged from the bedroom. The name on his badge read Olafson.

"This is a crime scene area, sir," Olafson advised. "Authorized personnel only."

"I was a friend of the deceased," Ben replied.

Olafson raised his bushy eyebrows in sudden interest.

"Who are you?" Olafson asked.

"Benjamin Hackwell," Ben replied and produced his driver's license for verification. He wondered whether or not to show Olafson his writ right away. His interrogation training told him to wait. "I reported the death."

Olafson steered Ben by the arm into the kitchen where a lean, short man with tawny hair that curled to salt behind his ears was stripping the filter of a Camels cigarette. The ragged seams in his navy blue suit coat matched the folds of his face. The embossed black letters on the identification tag hanging from his coat pocket read: BERGSTROM, WALTER Detective

Bergstrom flushed the cigarette strands down the sink and turned toward Olafson.

"Who's this?" Bergstrom asked with a trace of Nordic burr.

"Benjamin Hackwell," Olafson replied. "The guy who reported Gibson's death."

"You're Hackwell?" Bergstrom asked as he pulled a packet of cigarettes and a steel lighter from his hip pocket. "What're you doing here?"

"I thought I might be able to help," Ben said.

"Just a conscientious citizen, huh?" Bergstrom remarked as he cupped the cigarette in his sallow fingers and lit it. "Help how?"

"I thought I could provide some details, maybe give you a time frame." Ben replied with a shrug. He didn't want to appear diffident or afraid. "He was my friend, OK?"

Bergstrom's amber eyes pierced to the back of Ben's skull.

"OK," Bergstrom replied and inhaled deeply. "What time did you find Gibson?"

"Early afternoon," Ben answered, unnerved by the sensation of Bergstrom's penetrating stare. "Around one, I think."

"Was he alive then?" Bergstrom asked. A gray fume shot from the corner of his mouth like engine exhaust.

"No," Ben said and grimaced. "Of course not."

"Touch anything?" Bergstrom continued.

"As little as possible," Ben replied. "I knew the police would want to go over everything."

"Yet you waited two hours to call them?" Bergstrom asked.

"The batteries went out on my cell phone," Ben explained.

Bergstrom took an another draw from his cigarette.

"Why not call from here?" Bergstrom asked.

"And implicate myself by adding my prints?" Ben replied.

"If they're just on the phone, that's understandable," Bergstrom said as he tamped out his cigarette butt on the metal drain. "Us getting the tip as a result of a domestic dispute, that's implicative."

"I was in shock, I guess," Ben said.

"But not so as to forget about fingerprints," Bergstrom replied. "Or see a lawyer."

Ben knew his actions seemed suspicious. He needed a reasonable explanation.

"She's my ex-wife," Ben explained. "OK?"

"That's why you drove twenty miles," Bergstrom retorted. "To use her phone?"

"I had to see her about our daughter," Ben said.

"After you'd broken into a dead man's home?" Bergstrom asked.

"My daughter's important to me," Ben declared.

Bergstrom focused his disconcerting stare on Ben again.

"Was she the cause of your dispute with Gibson?" Bergstrom asked.

"There was no dispute," Ben answered and clenched his fist. Angered by the implication of Bergstrom's suggestion, Ben knew that when the police, military or civilian, found a suspect, they sunk their teeth in and shook. Any lead that fell out resembling the truth they worried to death until it proved otherwise. "Look, you are going to find more of my prints in the study."

"Why?" Bergstrom asked.

"Hoot had shown me this new software device he was working on," Ben replied.

"When?" Bergstrom said.

"A while back." Ben responded and shrugged. He wanted to appear obliging yet noncommittal. "He even offered me a job."

"Why?" Bergstrom asked.

"I'm a security agent for internal and external information systems," Ben explained. "Hoot wanted a firewall to protect his."

"Isn't that unusual for somebody's personal computer?" Bergstrom wondered.

"Not particularly," Ben replied. "Everybody's afraid more and more that somebody will hack into their system these days." Ben peered into Bergstrom's leonine eyes. He could not tell how much Bergstrom knew about computers or the Internet. "Shouldn't I have?"

"Depends on the software," Bergstrom said. "What was it for?"

"Touch screen interfaces," Ben responded.

Bergstrom's face remained blank.

"Like on an ATM?" Ben added.

"Did Gibson ever mention a military application?" Bergstrom asked.

"It was mostly computers and cycles with Hoot," Ben answered. "And pizza."

"Hoot?" Bergstrom asked.

"A nickname he picked up in Special Forces," Ben replied and turned toward the bedroom. "Have you removed his body?"

"Just another minute," Bergstrom said. Ben spotted Bergstrom's fingers tightening their grip on the underside of the kitchen counter. "Did you know Gibson worked for the government?"

Ben halted. Like any good interrogator, Bergstrom revealed data on a need-to-know basis.

"We both did, years ago," Ben said cautiously. "Military intelligence."

"You left the military?" Bergstrom asked and his leathery face clouded. "When?"

"About twelve years ago," Ben answered and wondered what his military training had to do with Hoot's death. "Why?"

"I'll ask the questions," Bergstrom said.

"I had 20 years in already," Ben explained. "My wife wanted a more secure life for our family," Ben added. "Is there a reason you're asking me this?"

"Your friend never did," Bergstrom said. His facial expression did not change.

"Ridiculous," Ben retorted. "Hoot took a job with Honeywell a year after I left, came out here when his mother died, then went on his own a few years after that."

"You're sure of that?" Bergstrom asked as he glanced over Ben's shoulder. "His associates are in the bedroom now, downloading his hard drive."

Ben followed Bergstrom's gaze. Had Hoot still been living the life? That would explain his Spartan lifestyle and his secrecy, with no excess data to give him away. It also explained Hoot's knowledge about Wilson. If Hoot's interface had a military application, was that the reason why he was killed?

Bergstrom cleared his throat.

"And you say he never once mentioned the military to you?" Bergstrom asked. Ben nodded.

"Or what he might be working on," Bergstrom concluded. A grim smile worked the corners of his mouth. "Follow me."

Ben followed Bergstrom down the hallway expecting a horde of investigators swarming over the evidence. When he entered the bedroom/study he found Hoot's sheathed body still sprawled across the desk. Beside it a trim, professionally dressed woman in a blue suit with shoulder-length hair the color of frosted wheat watched a diminutive woman in a lab coat prod the joystick of Gibson's computer with white-gloved fingers. Behind them a male agent in a gray trench coat kneeled in front of the window and scanned the carpet.

The monitor displayed a bust shot of Caitline puckering into the camera. The seated woman rotated the control stick, but Caitline's image did not move. She gazed up at the older woman.

"That's all the further it goes," the woman in the lab coat remarked.

"Have you figured how it works?" the older woman asked.

"Not yet," the seated woman replied.

Ben watched the manila-haired woman peer at the image on the monitor. She appeared to be in charge, but he did not see her identification badge. Nor did she seem concerned that he and Bergstrom had entered the room.

"They're not real," the frosty-haired woman declared.

"Of course they're not," the woman in the lab coat agreed.

"Have you identified her yet?" the frosty-haired woman asked.

"She doesn't appear in any of our photo indexes," her subordinate responded and pushed her horn-rim glasses onto her nose. "I fired a query off to Interpol. We should hear soon if they have anything."

"Inform me as soon as they do," the woman in charge ordered and turned toward Bergstrom. "Back from the land of nicotine. What did you do with the butt?"

"Field-stripped it and flushed it down the sink," Bergstrom replied.

If the frosty-haired woman was satisfied at Bergstrom's answer, she didn't show it. She scanned Ben and knitted her eyebrows.

"Who's this?" she asked.

"His name's Hackwell," Bergstrom replied. "He's the one who reported Gibson's death to the police."

"Does the term unauthorized personnel mean anything to you, Detective Bergstrom?" the woman asked. "Or does the Hennepin County police department permit its suspects to return to crime scenes?"

"I haven't declared it a crime scene yet, Agent Stanfeld," Bergstrom replied as he studied Stanfeld's face. "Do you know this man?"

"Not really," Stanfeld replied with a shake of her head. The sprayed ends of Stanfeld's hair followed her head movement with the pliancy of a riot helmet. "One of the state's attorneys on the tobacco lawsuit called herself Mrs. Hackwell."

The back of Ben's neck tingled. During the state's tobacco lawsuit, Jennifer had mentioned that a Food and Drug agent's personal testimony had done much to undermine the industry's case.

"He met with the deceased yesterday afternoon," Bergstrom said.

"And you believe him?" Stanfeld asked.

"Enough to give him a crack at that thing," Bergstrom replied.

"Why?" Stanfeld retorted.

"Because Gibson tried to hire him," Bergstrom responded.

"Who told you that?" Stanfeld asked. "Him, I suppose?"

"Yeah," Bergstrom admitted.

"Great detective work, Bergstrom" Stanfeld hooted. "That insight should secure your promotion to chief."

Stanfeld's chuckle trailed off like the draining of water through basement pipes. Bergstrom's expression did not change.

"Why is he here then?" Bergstrom asked.

"He probably saw the yellow tape and decided to join the party," Stanfeld replied and winked at her colleague. "When in doubt, check the source."

Stanfeld turned toward Ben.

"Why are you here?" she asked.

Ben pointed at the monitor.

"That's my daughter," Ben said.

Ben had expected some display of sympathy because of his revelation, but he didn't find it. Stanfeld turned to Bergstrom.

"How long did you plan to keep this from us?" Stanfeld asked.

"I just heard it myself," Bergstrom replied.

"And you figured it wasn't it important enough to tell the women working the case," Stanfeld said angrily.

"Cut it out," Bergstrom cautioned. His gaze resumed its stalking intensity as he turned toward Ben. "You weren't entirely forthcoming in the kitchen. What else haven't you told us?"

"Very little," Ben said. Given the data he had gleaned from the conversations so far, he doubted that he could trust anyone in the room. "I only found out about Hoot's operation yesterday."

"What operation?" Bergstrom asked.

"Virtual sex," Ben replied. "S and M. Maybe prostitution."

Bergstrom grimaced at Ben's answer.

"Where's your daughter now?" Bergstrom asked.

"I'm not sure of that, either," Ben replied. "She might be dead."

"What makes you think so?" Bergstrom asked.

"She got shot in the video sequence that I saw her in," Ben responded.

Something beeped behind them. Print heads whirred back and forth and stopped.

"Bergstrom!" Stanfeld called and beckoned him to a portable FAX machine lying beside the desk.

Bergstrom returned with a sheet of paper, its corners curled under from the heat of the print heads. The mug shot in the corner was of Caitline. Beside it appeared:

Lara Tarashkova
Height: 5' 11"
Weight: 9.5 stone
Eyes: deep grey
Wanted for shoplifting,
money laundering,
pandering, and
prostitution.

"Is that your daughter?" Bergstrom asked.

Ben nodded. How many Internet identities did his daughter possess?

The male agent in the trench coat sidled up to the desk and conferred with his colleagues. Ben could not see his face or determine the color of his bushy hair.

Stanfeld turned toward Ben.

"Looks like you've got a lot of explaining to do, mister," Stanfeld warned.

"I've told you everything," Ben replied with as much sincerity in his voice as he could muster.

"I think not," Stanfeld replied and opened her fist. In her palm lay a dusty filament of brown leather that she pinned over the scrape mark across Ben's leather jacket. "Looks like we've identified your suspect for you, Bergstrom."

"And his motive?" Bergstrom asked.

"Revenge," Stanfeld said and gestured toward the monitor. "He said the girl was his daughter."

"So?" Bergstrom responded.

"So, the simplest explanation usually is the best," Stanfeld declared.

Bergstrom whirled toward Ben.

"Don't tell me she's right about that," Bergstrom said.

"About Hoot's death or her scientific method?" Ben retorted. He had to prove his innocence right now, or remain the prime suspect in Hoot's death. Ben stepped over to Hoot's body and pulled the back of his spandex collar. The sheath ripped away with a sucking noise like that of plastic wrap torn off a beef-steak. "See those?"

He pointed to the scabbed lacerations on Hoot's back.

"They look like burn marks," Bergstrom replied.

"They're shock marks," Ben corrected.

"What are you saying?" Bergstrom said.

"I'm saying the record of Hoot's experiments resides in those marks," Ben declared.

"How is that possible?" Bergstrom asked.

"Hoot was working on total virtual interaction: taste, touch, emotions, the works," Ben said. "It may be that he succumbed to the rewards his device created. Like an addict, he needed more and more until an overdose killed him. Or—"

"Or what?" Bergstrom interrupted.

"Or, he found a true killer application," Ben concluded.

"What do you mean?" Bergstrom said.

"I mean that Hoot's death was committed deliberately," Ben explained. "Someone used electric shock to kill him. Whether it was done direct or by remote control is why Stanfeld and her friends are here, to find out which."

"You seem to know all about your friend's murder and the motives behind it," Stanfeld observed darkly. "Just as his murderer would."

"Or the people investigating it," Ben retorted.

"Preposterous!" Stanfeld cried. "If what you're suggesting were possible, we certainly wouldn't kill the man who invented it. The only intrigue here is the one perpetrated by the person who stands to gain the most from it."

Stanfeld grabbed Bergstrom's shoulder.

"Why else would he return to the crime scene?" Stanfeld asked. "Ask yourself that, Bergstrom. And who's declaring it a crime in the first place? You said you officially had not declared this a murder. Whoever advocates murder usually stands to gain the most from it."

"If that were true," Bergstrom replied. "Why would he return to the crime scene and explain his crime to the investigators?" Bergstrom removed Stanfeld's hand and studied Ben with what seemed benign interest. "Why did you come back?"

Ben returned Bergstrom's level gaze. He had to trust someone whose involvement seemed the least hostile. Bergstrom looked like his best bet

"To do the same thing they're doing," Ben answered. "Harvest IP addresses. Somebody had to send the transmission that killed Hoot. I wanted to find out if any of those Internet addresses were connected to my daughter."

"What makes you think she has anything to do with this?" Bergstrom asked.

"Look at the monitor," Ben replied and pressed the Enter key before the other female agent could brush his hand away. Caitline's image returned to the screen in the same devouring posture. "It doesn't look like Hoot was playing checkers before he died."

He scanned the faces of the three law enforcement officials surrounding him. He had their attention. Now he had to keep it.

"Look, I know it sounds fantastic," Ben acknowledged. "I hardly believe it myself. But Hoot was a genius with computers. He was working on a system that extended touch screens to their logical conclusion. That's why he's wrapped in that animatronic sheath over there."

"You mean like the aliens in the *Star Wars* movies?" Bergstrom asked.

Ben nodded. Everyone seemed to know the secrets of Hollywood.

"But don't they only send signals?" Bergstrom continued. "Like puppet strings?"

"Look at the number of electrodes," Ben answered. "More than half are receptors."

Bergstrom scanned the forest of wires leading to the twin CPUs in the foot well of the desk and shrugged.

"If what you say is true, why is your daughter's image still onscreen?" Bergstrom asked. "If they were having sex, why didn't the connection break?"

"Image capture, maybe?" Ben suggested.

"Like on tape?" Bergstrom said. "If she's on tape, how does her image respond?"

"Interactive relays?" Ben replied. "I'm spit-balling at this point."

"Did he shout out directions, too?" Stanfeld scoffed.

Ben balled his fists to suppress his rage. Bergstrom grasped Ben's shoulder.

"It does sound fantastic," Bergstrom agreed.

"If I was lying, don't you think I'd come up with something more plausible?" Ben replied.

"The cleverest lie is one so fantastic that there's no way to verify it," Stanfeld declared and turned toward her female cohort. "What do you think, Lockett?"

"I think the basis of Mr. Hackwell's hypothesis is unsound," Lockett said as she readjusted the glasses on her pug nose. "If Mr. Gibson was electrocuted through his Internet connection, why didn't his surge protector stop it? Or blow up?"

"Good point," Ben said. "But high voltage may not have been required to kill him."

"What do you mean?" Lockett asked.

"You saw the burn marks on Hoot's back," Ben said.

"Yes," Lockett said. "But how would the killer know how much voltage to use?"

"He wouldn't!" Stanfeld interjected. "Gibson either electrocuted himself, or someone already knew his condition." Stanfeld studied Ben. "Someone with sufficient knowledge and enough hatred to avenge his daughter."

Ben groaned. Further protest would only fuel Stanfeld's indictment. He reached inside his jacket and handed Jennifer's writ to Bergstrom.

"This allows me access to all evidence found at this crime scene," Ben declared with all the certainty he could add to his voice while Bergstrom and Stanfeld scanned the document.

"On what basis?" Stanfeld asked.

"Why didn't you show this to me before?" Bergstrom said.

"Explain the logic of this situation to me, Bergstrom" Stanfeld interrupted. "If Hackwell here is so innocent, why does he come here with a meaningless legal writ already in hand?"

"I haven't seen your credentials," Ben replied.

Stanfeld's ice blue eyes glittered as she produced a wallet-sized case from her coat pocket. Notarized over an American eagle stood the words: Barbara Stanfeld, Federal Bureau of Investigations.

Stanfeld turned to Bergstrom.

"Now which of us are you going to trust?" she asked.

"What about them?" Ben asked and gestured toward the desk.

Bergstrom extended his left hand toward the agent seated before the computer.

"What's your name again?" Bergstrom asked.

"Agent Lockett," Lockett replied.

"You have a first name, Agent Lockett?" Bergstrom continued.

"Lisa."

"Fine," Bergstrom said. "May we see your credentials, Lisa?"

Lockett flipped open a flat leather case. The embossed letters read: Lisa Lockett, United States Central Intelligence Agency.

"And you?" Bergstrom asked the man in the trench coat who glanced at Stanfeld.

"C'mon, c'mon!" Bergstrom snapped. "We haven't got all day!"

"You better tell him who you are," Stanfeld advised.

"Avery Rykert," the man answered in a resonant baritone. "Federal Securities and Exchange Commission"

CHAPTER 15

▼

"That wasn't so hard, was it?" Bergstrom asked.

Stanfeld stepped between Rykert and Bergstrom.

"If you're done with introductions, could you conduct your investigation outside?" Stanfeld said. "We have business to complete here."

"What's he doing here?" Ben exclaimed in amazement. "Rykert is a church deacon. He has no more right here than I do."

"Are you telling me how to do my job, too?" Bergstrom replied and pulled Ben to the corner of the desk. "Stand here and be quiet until I need you."

He lowered his voice.

"There are enough critics in the room already. I'm getting to it," Bergstrom assured Ben.

Satisfied that Ben would remain quiet for the moment, Bergstrom turned back to Stanfeld.

"What is he doing here?" Bergstrom asked with a nod toward Rykert.

"I called him in on an expert basis," Stanfeld explained. "This isn't my area of expertise."

"You called in a church deacon as an Internet expert?" Ben scoffed.

"Be quiet," Bergstrom warned. "Or I'll call Officer Olafson in to keep you quiet."

Ben folded his arms and leaned against the corner of the desk while he watched Rykert bob between the authority figures in the room. Rykert seemed the kind of man who always managed to affiliate himself with the winning side. It would be interesting to see whether Stanfeld or Bergstrom had the greater authority in the power equation to gain Rykert's allegiance.

"Homeland Security doesn't usually concern itself with the Internet, does it?" Bergstrom asked.

"Not usually," Stanfeld replied. "But this instance contained some unusual features."

"Such as?" Bergstrom asked.

"It involved a former CIA operative," Stanfeld explained. "There's always the possibility of a breach of security when that happens."

"Yours or the government's?" Bergstrom replied.

"Both," Stanfeld said.

Bergstrom turned toward Rykert.

"Are you a church deacon?" Bergstrom asked with a glance toward Ben.

"I am," Rykert answered with pride. "First Evangelical Church of our Lord."

"And your involvement with Agent Stanfeld's operation is?" Bergstrom asked.

"Restraint of trade," Rykert replied.

Bergstrom cocked his eyebrow in surprise.

"You needn't look so startled," Rykert responded. "Just because I have a strong, ongoing relationship with the Lord in my life doesn't preclude me from a secular life as well. In my case the one has nourished the other."

"What do you mean?" Rykert asked.

"As CEO of a dot.com," Rykert replied, "I was in a unique position to encounter and understand those forces that would use the Internet for their own unlawful and immoral ends."

"So you put yourself on the board of SEC," Ben exclaimed.

"I was appointed," Rykert corrected with a smile at Bergstrom.

"That's still a conflict of interest," Ben interjected.

Bergstrom glared at Ben who peered at his shoe tops. Given his precarious position, he knew he had to be more careful and let Bergstrom to handle the questions.

"It would be," Rykert agreed. "If I hadn't put my holdings in a blind trust."

"And in your capacity on the SEC board you do what?" Bergstrom asked.

"We investigate rights infringement and violations of interstate commerce," Rykert replied.

"Such as?" Bergstrom said.

"Pornography, for one," Rykert replied. "Prostitution, for another."

Bergstrom's brow arched higher.

"Gibson was operating a business?" Bergstrom asked.

"That's what all of our departments are trying to find out," Rykert explained with a glance toward Lockett and Stanfeld.

Ben grabbed Rykert's arm.

"You said rights infringement," Ben said. "What rights?"

Rykert wrestled free and straightened the sleeves of his overcoat.

"Don't let this man near me again," Rykert demanded. "He's capable of anything."

"You know each other?" Bergstrom said.

"Only by reputation," Rykert replied.

"How?" Bergstrom asked.

"I've retained his ex-wife on a number of occasions," Rykert said with a sidelong glance toward Ben. "She told me she needed a restraining order to keep him away."

"Gee, Hackwell," Bergstrom retorted. "Everybody seems to love you around here."

Bergstrom returned to Rykert.

"I'm missing something," Bergstrom admitted. "You mentioned rights infringement. What rights?"

"Copy and patent rights," Rykert replied. "If you must know."

"Whose?" Bergstrom asked.

"I'm not at liberty to say," Rykert said.

"But you are at liberty to come to a murder scene at a moment's notice," Bergstrom retorted.

"Agent Stanfeld called and requested my presence," Rykert said, unfazed by the skepticism in Bergstrom's remark.

"On what basis?" Bergstrom asked.

"On the basis of my expertise," Rykert replied.

"Which is?" Bergstrom persisted.

"Broadcast communications," Rykert said.

"What do you know about the Internet?" Bergstrom asked.

"Not a whole lot," Rykert admitted. "My principal area is rights management. Lockett's the technology expert, isn't she, Barbara."

Rykert turned to Stanfeld for confirmation. Stanfeld offered Bergstrom an officious smile. Knowing he would get little additional information from Stanfeld, Bergstrom turned toward Lockett.

"How much success have you had operating the keyboard behind you?" Bergstrom asked.

"I don't see what—" Lockett said.

"Have you made it work or not?" Bergstrom interrupted.

Lockett shook her head.

"Well, then," Bergstrom replied and rubbed his hands together. "We have someone here who claims to have seen it in operation."

Bergstrom turned toward Ben.

"You're a programmer, right?" Bergstrom asked.

"Network security agent," Ben corrected.

"Whatever," Bergstrom replied and beckoned Ben toward the monitor. "You've seen how it works. Step up to the plate and show us."

Stanfeld blocked Ben's path.

"That's government property, Bergstrom," Stanfeld warned.

"So you claim," Bergstrom said. "It's also evidence at a crime scene that neither you nor your computer expert know how to operate."

Bergstrom glanced toward Ben.

"That man does, or he wouldn't be here," Bergstrom said. "Don't you want to see what he knows?"

Stanfeld remained immobile as Ben sidestepped around her. Bergstrom beckoned Lockett to relinquish the terminal. Ben slipped into her vacated seat, pulled the chair forward, and stretched his fingers. He pressed the Enter key. Caitline's image remained frozen on the monitor.

"I tried that," Lockett said.

Ben scanned the keyboard and under the desktop for the reboot button. One green light in the central processing unit blinked in the shadow of the foot well.

"There's no reboot," Lockett added.

Irritated by Lockett's officiousness, Ben examined the maze of plastic filaments that emanated from the processing unit. A black cable extended from the box beyond the back of the desk. He tugged it, and the green light disappeared. As did Caitline's image.

"Now you've got nothing," Stanfeld said. "Satisfied?"

Ben stood up. The desk chair slammed against Lockett's shins.

"Idiot!" Lockett cried.

"Sorry," Ben replied.

Ben sidestepped around Lockett and Rykert, strode to the opposite wall, and restored the plug to its socket. Lockett had reclaimed the chair by the time Ben returned.

"See that?" Lockett said and pointed at a discolored knob on her little toe. "You've reopened the corn and torn my nylons."

Ben gazed at Lockett's ruptured stocking. Few computer nerds and even fewer CIA agents that he'd met worried as much about their clothes.

"What do you think you're accomplishing here?" Stanfeld intervened. "Besides injuring a federal agent."

Ben turned toward Stanfeld. Her show of concern failed to disguise her greater need to control the situation. For the moment, Ben decided that he and Lockett shared a common enemy.

"Sometimes breaking the connection is the only way to clear the buffer," Ben explained and turned toward Lockett for confirmation. "Isn't that so, Agent Lockett?"

"I suppose," Lockett grumped.

"The only way to find out is to turn on the computer, right?" Ben coaxed as he stared into Lockett's peevish face. Perhaps Lockett was not the potential ally he had thought. "Do you want to do the honors?"

Lockett rose from the chair and limped behind it to stand next to Stanfeld.

Ben rebooted Hoot's computer and waited for the initiating file to scroll through its routine. He wiped his palms on the underside of his jeans. He couldn't recall this much emotion ever accompanying a startup sequence for him before.

The brand name of the unit flashed in red letters that faded to an announcement that some files had closed illegally. Ben scanned the double row of icons on Hoot's screensaver. None represented an obvious Internet connection.

He reached beside the keyboard and remembered there was no mouse. He examined the giant roller ball occupied the center of the keyboard and recalled Hoot's comparison in using it, "like a squirrel rolling nuts."

Ben ran his index finger across the ball, and the cursor leaped off the screen. Coaxing the ball with his index and middle fingers, Ben nudged the cursor over the Start button, pressed the Enter key, and retrieved a standard Control Panel menu. He wondered how Hoot got online.

"What now, genius?" Lockett asked.

Ben scanned the control panel and opened the voice activation component.

"Computer on," he ordered.

Nothing happened.

"Start computer," Ben said.

Still nothing happened.

"Talking won't help," Lockett advised. "You don't know the password."

"Maybe it wants you to call it by its pet name," Stanfeld suggested.

Ben spun his chair around and eyed Lockett. It was time for somebody else to fail for a change, Ben decided. It might as well be Lockett.

"Do you have any bright ideas?" Ben asked.

"Reopen the Control Panel and click on the Internet icon," Lockett said.

Ben did as Lockett instructed. The monitor screen flipped, rolled, and turned black. An image of intersecting, pierced twin hearts swelled and filled the screen.

"What's that?" Bergstrom asked.

The information panel at the top of the screen read: HURTFUL.com

"That's the Web site page of the sex site he was involved with," Ben explained. "Hoot must have used it as his home page."

Lockett readjusted the hairpin holding her bun as she leaned forward.

"Looks like he let it run continuously," she said.

"What makes you think that?" Ben asked.

"Voice activation, roller ball cursor, enormous band width, no reboot. All earmarks of a system designed never to shut down," Lockett declared and stood erect. "Check the history. I'll bet there's no record of his going to any other sites."

Ben clicked the History icon. The History pop-up screen was empty.

"What does that prove?" Ben asked.

"Nothing, perhaps" Lockett replied. "Or it indicates the depth of his obsession."

"I don't believe it," Ben said.

"Think about it," Lockett replied. "You said he could barely move his hands. Why activate the same system every time? Why not save yourself the trouble and pain?"

Ben stared at the bleeding hearts. He refused to believe Lockett's conclusion, but he knew she was right. Hoot's invention had replaced his need for companionship. The tendencies toward isolation that computer programming fostered had started a rift between them before Ben left Washington. They had culminated for Hoot in the machine standing before them.

Ben opened the Cookies icon. The rectangular screen contained nothing. The depth of Hoot's attachment to his interface did not prove that he was doing anything illegal with it.

"If Hoot ran this site continuously, why isn't there a record of his transactions?" Ben asked in defense of his friend. He eyed Rykert. "It's hardly the way to run a prostitution ring with no income."

"That's your inference," Rykert replied. "I said nothing about a ring of any kind, did I, Barbara?"

Stanfeld chuckled.

"Are you naive enough to expect an illegal operation to keep a record of its payments for us to find in its hard drive?" Stanfeld asked.

"No," Ben replied. "But I do expect a center of operations to list the IP addresses with whom or what it's doing business."

"So, he operates from a mirror site," Rykert said with a shrug. "Big deal."

"I thought you said you knew nothing about the Internet," Bergstrom interjected.

"I don't," Rykert responded. "Given the man's reputation, I would expect it to be sophisticated."

Lockett pushed her glasses back onto her nose.

"It is curious," Lockett observed as she examined the skein of wires that penetrated Gibson's sheath. "There's a lot of wiring, but hardly enough computing power here to run the kind of operation we're describing."

"What do you mean?" Stanfeld asked.

"Two off-the-shelf CPUs can't handle all the processing that's required," Lockett explained. "Gibson would have needed a small mainframe to handle all the traffic."

Lockett leaned over Ben's shoulder. A whiff of her Lavoris mouthwash tickled his nostrils at the same time he felt the nudge of her full right breast yield against his shoulder blades.

"Try returning to Gibson's home page," Lockett suggested.

Ben keyed in the command, distracted by the blunt feel of Lockett's shoulder holster rubbing against his shoulder. A suit concealed so much, he thought.

The coded home page that popped up to fill the screen contained a simple header:

```
<?php HURTFUL.com
href="bleeding hearts"?>
```

"Just what I suspected," Lockett said. "It's in PHP."

"So what?" Ben replied, irritated by Lockett's familiarity with the coding language. He recalled that PHP had become popular after he had decided to focus on Internet security.

"What's PHP?" Bergstrom asked.

"It stands for Personal Home Page," Lockett explained. "PHP is a form of Perl scripting language. It means we can only see results on the view screen."

"And what does that mean?" Stanfeld asked.

"We can't break into the code," Lockett replied.

"So?" Stanfeld said.

"It means there's no way we can find the server that processes the commands," Ben interjected with grudging respect. "Or my daughter."

The spot remained warm where Lockett had leaned against Ben's shoulder. Aside from Hoot and himself, Ben had encountered few people besides Lockett who relished the deciphering of computer code.

Lockett keyed in a command that brought up a blue screen while she maneuvered her hips around Ben's chair. She bumped against Ben's knees in the process, tripped and grabbed Ben's chair arm.

Ben watched Lockett with amusement while she teetered above his lap trying to regain her balance. Taking pity on Lockett's misguided sense of propriety, Ben nudged her to an upright position.

"Go ahead," Lockett exhorted standing between Ben and the desk. "Bring up the DOS editor."

"What for?" Ben retorted, irritated by Lockett's absorption.

"I want to check the Startup file," Lockett replied, oblivious to the tone of Ben's voice.

Ben reached past Lockett, tapped the keyboard, and produced a file that was scripted in 14 point lavender Courier font.

"Artistic color choice," Ben observed. It was not the type of font color Hoot would have chosen. "What now?"

"Scroll through it," Lockett advised.

Ben searched the keyboard with increasing irritation. He had grown so accustomed to using a mouse that he had forgotten his keyboard commands.

"Try the Tab key," Lockett instructed.

The image moved to the bottom of the script.

"Again," Lockett said.

The image shifted further down into the code.

"Again," she asked.

The image shifted once more.

"Hold it," Lockett said.

Ben's right index finger remained poised in mid-air. He wondered what Lockett expected to find.

"There!" Lockett said and pointed at a one-line string of code at the bottom of the screen.

if $name = HURTFUL.com

"Press the down arrow on the key pad," Lockett ordered. "Just once."

A new screen of code appeared: then?<href= "WEB(W)RIGHTS.com">

Lockett turned toward Stanfeld.

"What's WEB(W)RIGHTS.com?" Lockett asked.

Stanfeld turned toward Rykert.

"That's your company's domain name, isn't it, Avery?" Stanfeld asked.

"My former company," Rykert responded. "I put it in trust, remember?"

"Did your company ever do business with Gibson?" Ben asked.

"Never," Rykert replied.

"You're sure?" Ben asked. Any connection between a pornography site and an Internet trading company would be bad public relations, particularly for a firm whose CEO maintained high visibility as a conservative Christian official. Watching Rykert squirm provided the sole pleasure Ben had derived from his search for Caitline. "They can check."

Rykert returned Ben's insinuating stare.

"Web(W)rights has never done business with Mr. Gibson," Rykert declared.

CHAPTER 16

▼

Bergstrom leaned over Ben's shoulder.

"I hope you've got liability," Bergstrom growled in obvious irritation with Ben's comments. "You've linked one of the most influential men in the Twin Cities to a murder without one shred of evidence."

Ben pointed at the Web address on the monitor.

"Doesn't that constitute evidence?" Ben asked.

"Of a kind," Bergstrom retorted. "The kind that compels judges and lawyers to shut down an investigation."

Rykert was speaking into his cell phone. Bergstrom turned back to Ben.

"Ten gets you one that he's calling them right now," Bergstrom said.

Stanfeld leaned in between Bergstrom and Ben.

"If you're finished here," Stanfeld said. "We'd like to wrap up our end of things."

"What do you have in mind?" Bergstrom asked.

"We need to complete our analysis," Stanfeld replied.

Bergstrom strode up to Rykert and grabbed his cell phone.

"This is Detective Bergstrom," Bergstrom spoke into the phone. "He'll call you back."

Bergstrom snapped Rykert's cell phone shut and deposited it in Rykert's outstretched hand.

"If you think this little power display impresses anyone, you're mistaken," Rykert said. "National security always takes precedence in a case like this."

"In a case like what, Mr. Rykert?" Bergstrom asked with a meaningful glance toward Ben. "You claim innocence, yet you've demonstrated more knowledge of the facts than I have. Is there something else you'd like to tell us?"

"Don't push me, Bergstrom," Rykert warned.

"Don't tell me how to run my investigation," Bergstrom replied.

"Well, run it," Rykert declared.

Bergstrom pointed at Lockett.

"You, in the chair," Bergstrom ordered as he grabbed the chair back and spun Ben around. "Out in the hall."

Bergstrom grabbed Lockett's shoulders and steered her into the vacated chair. He turned toward Stanfeld.

"You," Bergstrom commanded. "Keep an eye on her."

Before Stanfeld could protest, Bergstrom turned back to Rykert.

"Make sure they don't steal anything until I get back," Bergstrom ordered.

Rykert scowled and stuck his hands in his coat pockets. Lockett stuck a storage disk into the CD-ROM slot and brought the diagnostic menu onto the monitor.

"You're letting them download Hoot's hard drive?" Ben cried.

Bergstrom yanked Ben into the hallway. Ben regained his balance and examined his shirt collar. One of its buttons was gone.

Bergstrom produced a pack of Camels and lit one with trembling fingers.

"You're lucky I don't haul your ass down to the station right now," Bergstrom said.

"Why don't you?" Ben replied. "You're obviously on their side."

"Yeah, I am," Bergstrom agreed and took a long draw from his cigarette. "You want to know why? Because I like order, law and order. It's as simple as that."

His exhale rose into the air like a mushroom cloud.

"That's why I'm not letting some wild man off the street jeopardize my investigation," Bergstrom added.

"But you are letting Stanfeld and Rykert remove evidence," Ben replied.

"What evidence? You and Lockett showed me that there wasn't any," Bergstrom said and cocked his right eyebrow. "Unless you're withholding something, too."

Ben shook his head.

"I didn't think so," Bergstrom replied. He glanced toward the bedroom and took another draw as if turning over something in his mind.

"Go on," Bergstrom ordered. "Get out of here."

Ben hesitated. Grateful as he was to be allowed to leave, Ben knew standard police protocol dictated running him to the nearest station for further questioning.

"How do you know I won't just take off?" Ben asked.

"I don't," Bergstrom said.

"Well, then," Ben replied in confusion.

"You still want to find your daughter, don't you?" Bergstrom asked.

"Yes, but—"

"I have a daughter, too," Bergstrom acknowledged. "Just make sure you give Missing Persons all the information you have about her when you get home."

Ben nodded and watched a smile curl the corners of Bergstrom's mouth before he took another deep inhale.

"WEB(W)RIGHTS must own a lot of domain names," Bergstrom mused as he watched another of his billowing exhales rise into the air.

"You think—" Ben began.

"I don't think anything," Bergstrom declared and flipped his cigarette in the sink. "Just go before I change my mind."

Ben glanced toward the open bedroom doorway. He knew of no one other than himself who would come to claim Hoot's body.

"Hoot didn't have any close relatives," Ben began. "There's no one to claim his body."

"I figured as much," Bergstrom said. "I'll take care of his body after the forensic guys do their jobs."

"Thanks," Ben replied. "I appreciate it."

He watched Bergstrom head toward Hoot's bedroom as he tried to determine Bergstrom's motive for releasing him. Was it charity, Ben wondered, or just Bergstrom's way of keeping Ben obligated?

Ben shrugged and opened the front door. A southwest wind buffeted his cheeks. Bending forward until his head reached the level of his belt buckle, he breathed in and let the evening air suffuse his lungs.

Ben straightened and exhaled. The breeze atomized the vapor from his lungs the moment it left his mouth. He inhaled and exhaled again. He felt better.

Ben gazed at the bedroom window. Ragged silhouettes shifted behind the drawn curtains. He supposed that the silhouettes were Lockett and Stanfeld in the process of downloading Hoot's hard drive with Rykert anticipating his ultimate ownership. Despite all of Hoot's efforts, the results of his years of trial and error lay a mouse click from Rykert's disposal. Given what he'd heard and seen of Rykert, no one would get access to Hoot's interface without paying.

Ben peered through the first in the bank of windows that ran across the top half of the garage door. The rear end of the Bronco remained visible. The door refused to budge when Ben tugged its metal handle. He surveyed the dim space above the vehicle. A 1/2 horsepower garage opener hung from the ceiling at the head of the track.

He checked the side door. It had been locked from inside.

Ben stole to the front porch, slid inside, tiptoed to the hallway, and peered into the kitchen. There was no sign of Olafson, or of Bergstrom field-stripping another cigarette like a guilty schoolboy.

Ben crossed the kitchen, fumbled with the breezeway door until it squeaked open, and searched for the single cement step with his toe. Six inches below his right foot he found it, six inches below that his other foot touched the cement floor.

The armoire's bulky outline loomed against the opposite wall. Beside it would be the door to the garage.

Ben shuffled between the mounds of equipment and found the door. He turned the knob silently in its groove, and the door popped forward. He pushed on the handle. The door retreated six inches. Through the opening, a musty odor of discarded cardboard and old dust tickled his nostrils along with something else, something sour and rotting. He stifled a sneeze and pushed again. A toppled pillar of pizza boxes blocked further entry.

Ben slipped through the fissure he'd created. The outline of the buried Bronco loomed in the darkness.

He let the weight of the boxes press the door against the frame. Despite the uncertain lighting, he recognized Pisa Pizza's bitten slice logo embossed across the top. Outside of Starbucks, pizza chains served as the number one business denizen of the suburbs. Hoot was no pizza connoisseur. Why had he ordered his from downtown Minneapolis?

Ben forged a pathway to the passenger side of the vehicle. It was locked. He peered inside. The Bronco's tinted windows prevented seeing anything. He forged another path to the vehicle's rear door. It, too, was locked.

He surveyed the vehicle. The boxes appeared less numerous on the driver's side which indicated they had been stacked in a corner on the passenger side of the garage. The rear license plate read: MINNESOTA SCH 001. The vehicle stood at an angle to the entrance with a good six feet of clearance between the garage door and rear bumper. Someone had driven in very fast and plowed the Bronco into the stack before they could apply the brake, someone out of control.

Ben surveyed the pathway he'd created. The original position of the boxes would have indicated the speed and direction of impact. Ben grimaced. Now he could add destruction of evidence to his growing list of misdemeanors.

He gathered the armful of boxes between himself and the driver's door, stacked them behind the rear fender, and tested the handle. The door popped open. The sprayed scent of a vehicle fresh from the dealership wafted out.

Ben surveyed the interior. The view from its raised, black leather seats resembled that from a stagecoach with similar handling and maneuverability. He flicked on the dome light. No crumbs lay in the seams of the driver's seat, no dust balls rolled on the floor. Even the floor mats retained their pristine, rubbery odor. The Bronco appeared as unused as the inside of Hoot's house.

He scanned the battery of gauges that extended across the dash. A plastic tag dangled at the end of a chrome key chain beside the steering wheel. One side of it was blank; the other contained an empty name and address template.

Ben glanced toward the breezeway door and wondered how long it would be before Bergstrom or one of his assistants came out to inspect.

The door tumblers clicked.

Not long.

Ben turned off the dome light and nudged the parking light switch with the knuckle of his index finger. Twin amber beacons glowed beneath the cardboard cascade across the hood. The gauges in the dash glimmered an eerie electronic green.

He knelt closer. A raspberry filament dangled on top of the steering wheel. He peered at the filament. It was dark on one end.

The breezeway door chuffed open, then closed.

Ben scanned the boxes and knew they wouldn't hold the police out much longer. He noticed the hair strand on the steering wheel shiver and still. He had little time to examine it further.

The door chuffed again. The mound of pizza boxes shivered and advanced six inches.

Ben scrambled to the rear door. The mound of cardboard heaved, crested, and tumbled across the hood of the Bronco.

Ben slipped through the doorway and dashed to his motorcycle. The cold engine sputtered and roared to life. He pivoted on his rear tire and sped down the driveway.

Ben glanced over his shoulder after a half mile. No sirens howled, no avenging posse followed. He almost felt disappointed as he eased back on the accelerator. Was that what he wanted? Being an outlaw would not help him find Caitline.

Caitline must have been physically at the crime scene, he decided. The dangling hair strand confirmed it. Who else dyed their hair raspberry?

Almost anyone in Wilson's employ, Ben realized.

He turned right and climbed the icy entrance ramp onto the beltway. The telltale hair strand had been planted like a calling card for the police to find. It was an old ploy that the CIA used to deflect suspicion by giving local law enforcement agents the most obvious clue. If Stanfeld had planted it, Ben reasoned, why would she do so? If Caitline had not been at Hoot's house, who had delivered the electronic jolt that killed him?

Ben skirted a patch of ice. How could Caitline or someone else kill Hoot if they hadn't been there physically? Lockett had pointed out that Hoot's system contained an insufficient number of capacitors to hold that kind of charge. If the murderer were present physically in the room, there should have been some signs of struggle.

Whoever killed Hoot wanted his death to appear fantastic. Given the data Ben had, you either believed that a digital prostitute electrocuted its clients, or the CIA sacrificed one of their own to protect a potential new weapon. And used the police to cover it up.

Ben shook his head. None of the data he had uncovered so far added up to evidence either way

Even if Hoot failed to recognize the lethal potential of his research, Ben believed Stanfeld when she said that the CIA and the FBI were not in the habit of killing people they could buy out.

Ben sped up Cedar Avenue toward his duplex. He knew that Hoot would never be a lackey for either agency. If he had been, his would not have been such a threadbare operation.

Ben clicked his garage door opener, wheeled his cycle 180 degrees, and backed it into the space between Tyler's Escort and the workbench. He grabbed the chamois hanging from a nail and swabbed the cycle fenders to help him think.

If Hoot had not been killed by the CIA organization itself, who stood to gain from such duplicity? Could it be Stanfeld? Rykert, perhaps?

Wilson.

He seemed the obvious suspect, Ben decided, but no connection existed between he and Hoot outside of Hoot's hiring one of Wilson's dancers to model for Hoot's interface. The other incriminating bit of data was Hoot's runaway Bronco. Whoever drove it into the garage had been physically at Hoot's residence. Whether or not the driver had killed him, a red hair strand had been left on the wheel. What was the connection between the Bronco and one of Wilson's dancers?

The first three letters on Hoot's license plate matched the first three letters of Wilson's strip club, Ben recalled. Was that coincidence, or something more ominous? Ben knew of one way to find out.

He tossed the chamois on the bench, entered the hallway, and unlocked the door to his room. Curled up on the bed, Desdemona yawned and blinked her olive green eyes at him in welcome. Ben scratched under her collar before he sat in front of his computer and erased the only other animated thing in the room, Farah Fawcett's beckoning finger.

Ben brought up his Internet Home page and typed in the address to the state Department of Motor Vehicles. The Minnesota government Web page appeared. He clicked on the link to the Department of Motor Vehicles, scanned the side bar index of subdivisions, and clicked Vehicle Registration.

The next screen listed options and instructions on how to apply for a license. None of the pages mentioned owner identification. Ben knew that state privacy laws prevented anyone outside of government from obtaining that information.

Ben opened his bookmarks file. He could pay $29.95 at a pay-per-use site for the information. Or he could enter the so-called dark Web. He typed in the site address operated by one of Hoot's colleagues whom Ben knew only by his Web identity: Henry Morgan.

Twin red and yellow vipers flicked their tongues while his speakers emitted an electronic hiss. The query panel beneath them requested his user ID and password.

Ben typed in his name and secret identity. A message screen appeared.

HAIL COBRA! THE COMMANDER BIDS YOU WELCOME!

The message dissolved to a Web site filled with images, memorabilia, and a variety of role-playing games devoted to overthrowing COBRA's archnemesis, G.I. JOE. Ben bypassed this and several other screens devoted to TV show trivia. The information he sought resided several levels underneath to prevent search engines and Web filters from stumbling upon it.

He arrived at a screen titled "State Governments" and entered the Minnesota site. After he input the license plate number in the search engine, a PDF photocopy of the registration form appeared. The first line contained the plate number, the second the registrant's name, SCHARIAH. The rest of the data matched that of Hoot's Bronco.

Ben paced the area between the bed and his desk. Why would one of Wilson's vehicles be in Hoot's garage? Wilson was too smooth an operator to leave a vehicle hidden in the victim's garage unless he intended it to look that way. The raspberry hair strand indicated Caitline or someone resembling her with raspberry hair and dark roots had driven the Bronco.

He typed in Schariah's Web address. The name written in white pseudo-Persian script stretched diagonally across a burgundy velvet background while the opening movement of Rimsky-Korsakov's Scheherazade theme wafted from Ben's speakers.

The next screen displayed a dozen thumbnail snapshots of performers dressed as dancing girls with their hair dyed to match the color of their ensembles. Three of them possessed red hair. One hair was fire engine red, one cherry, and the last was indeterminate. It could be raspberry or dark pink, Ben determined, depending on the number of rods in one's eyes, the quality of the photograph, and the acuity of one's browser.

Each thumbnail linked to a page that contained larger pictures of their act, each with fictitious biographies that stoked the male fantasy that each of these women enjoyed copious amounts of impersonal sex in her own titillating way.

Ben examined the three women with red hair. The roots of the women with lighter hair color appeared blond or light brown. The roots of the woman with raspberry hair extended three inches from her scalp. Depending on the date of the photo, the length was too long for the strand residing in Hoot's garage.

He studied three images of the performer taken from below stage level. The camera angle caused her to appear taller, but it failed to disguise her thick waist and peasant ankles, not the dream torso for an exotic dancer.

The center photograph contained a close-up of dancer's face. Crooked, gray teeth protruded between the pouting lips. Ben recognized the Slavic waitress. The caption beneath her close-up billed her as Yazmin, the Arabian Salome.

Ben scratched his chin as he pondered the data. He knew that waitresses were the bottom feeders in the strip club pecking order. What would Yazmin be doing with Wilson's Bronco? He wondered whether she owned a license.

Entering her name in the registration page produced a null result. Ben clicked on the Home page, selected U.S. Government, and entered the site marked Immigration. He entered the same query and received the same result.

Wilson's dancers never would register themselves under their stage names, Ben decided. He returned to Schariah's home page. The menu bar across the top contained six headings including ABOUT THE CLUB. When he ran his cursor over it, a menu screen descended that was the same lavender color as the script on

Hoot's PC. If Caitline had created this site, Ben thought with scant pride, she had scripted it in Java.

The History window explained that the club started in 1978. New management changed the name to Schariah's in 1993. Ben decided that "new management" must refer to Wilson and his henchmen.

The Employment entry listed three more headings, Opportunities, Requirements, and Personnel. Ben clicked on the last. A screen appeared that listed all current employees in descending alphabetical order by last name. Each contained the performer's pertinent statistics as if the data had been imported from a spreadsheet. Some contained postal and e-mail addresses. All of the latter contained the suffix SCHARIAH.com. The prefixes used stage names.

Ben searched for a prefix beginning with Y. Two entries from the bottom he found YAZMIN@SCHARIAH.com. The column beside it read: Zanourri, Yazmin. The address box listed an Elliot Street address that coincided with Sophia's apartment complex.

Most of the other street address entries were empty. Outside of products and services, commercial Web sites seldom revealed personal information.

Ben paused at N. The second entry listed Nechayev, Sophia, but gave no address.

Ben scrolled toward the top. Sophia once had worked for Wilson as a stripper. The empty address box indicated that she no longer did. Yet, he knew that she supervised the apartment building where many of Wilson's strippers lived. Perhaps she had moved beyond stripping for him. Had Caitline done the same?

He halted at the letter H. No Hackwell was listed. The second entry under T showed: Tarashkova, Lara. e-mail LARA@SCHARIAH.com.

Ben clicked on the blue link and received a "No response" message. He tried again with the same result. When he clicked the link of the entry above it, an e-mail screen materialized with the link appearing beside the address line.

Ben scrolled to Zanourri and clicked her e-mail address. The same message box appeared. Sophia's e-mail address produced the same result.

He stared at the message box and tried to determine the implications of his results. The screen contained three Schariah's employees, three addresses, and three null results. The link for the other dancer had worked, so the server must be active, Ben reasoned. Why were these three addresses inoperative?

Ben returned to the COBRA registration page, entered the Federal Government section, and keyed "immigration" into the search engine box. The software returned more than 100 entries. The fourth listed an address with an U.S. gov-

ernment suffix. At its homepage, Ben found another search engine where he
typed in the waitress' name and received:

Name:	Zanourri, Yazmin
Age:	28
Status:	Six-month permit
Place of Departure:	St. Petersburg
Place of Birth:	Afghanistan

He typed in Nechayev, Sophia. The same string of fields and information
appeared. The sole difference was native country: Georgia. The dancer whose
link had worked was from Tajikistan.

Ben grimaced at his discovery. Wilson was an equal opportunity employer all
right. He recruited strippers from everywhere in Central Asia and the Middle
East.

He typed "Tarashkova, Lara" and received:

Name:	Tarashkova, Lara
Age:	32
Status:	Six-month permit
Place of Departure:	St. Petersburg
Place of Birth:	Chechnya

Ben sat back in his chair and contemplated the data. Caitline's Internet identity belonged to an immigrant woman twice as old as she was. What had happened to her?

He compared the women's dates of departure. The permits for the three who
had disappeared had expired within the last six months. None had applied for
extension or renewal.

Ben stroked Desdemona's back. To the immigration service, these women had
stayed their allotted time and returned home. No evidence existed that proved
otherwise. Even their e-mail accounts had been rendered inactive. Yet, he had
seen Zarima and spoken to Sophia within the past 36 hours. And his missing
daughter had acquired the identity of a missing Chechnyan national.

Ben returned to the listings at the Schariah's Web site and selected several
e-mail addresses at random. Each opened a blank e-mail form. He returned to the
Web site home page. He needed to obtain the identity or address of the Web
site's server. He entered the View Source and found:

```
<header>title: SCHARIAH.com </header>
<body>Linux enabled</body>
```

Ben closed the Source screen. The site administrator was his only lead. He wondered whether he should e-mail to complain about their inaccessibility and decided that he would receive an automated response that proved nothing.

He closed the remaining screens and returned to the COBRA Web site. He searched the index on the query page for recent obituaries listing but found no such entry. Both Web pages were Linux enabled.

That Hoot and Morgan used Linux did not surprise him. Its employment for Scariah's Web page did. Linux was not a common server platform. Too many inducements both economic and utilitarian prompted most administrators to use Unix. Only freebooters like Morgan who advocated open access to everything on the Internet employed Linux. Why use Linux when Unix was so much easier?

Unless escaping detection was your primary concern.

Ben entered HURTFUL.com in the address line. His cursor transformed into an hourglass for 30 seconds and produced "No response."

The server administrator had taken the Web sight address off the server. Who stood to gain by disguising their Internet transactions?

Ben paced back and forth in front of his terminal. Who cared what undercover schemes Internet pirates like Morgan and Hoot transacted? So long as they interfered with no one else's activities, nobody.

Unless those activities involved money, he reasoned. Or government security.

Ben keyed in WEB(W)RIGHTS.com. The site that materialized was glossy, yet tastefully done. It even contained a low graphic feature. The ABOUT US page told a history of their representing the rights of business, retail, and entertainment firms.

The Customer Representation page listed five different categories. He scanned the list of clientele under Entertainment. Nothing stood out.

Ben entered the other four categories. No SCHARIAH'S or HURTFUL appeared.

What did he expect, Ben wondered. Did he think he would find a banner that proclaimed their connection? The sound clip testimonials from WEB(W)RIGHTS' satisfied customers celebrated their integrity and devotion to its clients.

The fourth thumbnail contained the photo of a nondescript businesswoman with hair the color and texture of a Brillo pad. The caption read Zarima Melekhov. A balloon message accompanied the audio, "E-mail me for personalized customer satisfaction. Click on the thumbnail."

Ben clicked on it. An e-mail screen appeared with the address line filled in. YAZMIN@SCHARIAH.com

CHAPTER 17

▼

Ben stared at the screen in astonishment. This was his smoking gun. Zarima solicited from Rykert's company Web site. He wondered how much of her earnings went to Web(W)rights. The more important implication, Ben realized, was Rykert's relationship to Wilson.

He scanned the list of entertainers at Schariah's Web site. Lara/Caitline's and Sophia's e-mail addresses appeared there, too. He typed a few garbage characters in Caitline's and sent it. An error message appeared "No such user address."

Ben received the same result with the other two addresses. He clenched his right hand and wondered what to do now that he had found three women who no longer existed virtually.

Ben scanned the code underlying the screen display. Lines of code detailed the length, size, and color of the links, icons, and images of the home page. Beneath that resided the message: Encrypted by KeepItSafe, a copyright product of Web(W)rights.

Ben sat back and examined his options. Without the source code or his random number generator it would be days, even weeks before he cracked the cookies that revealed the company transactions. Professional protection devices discouraged hackers by outlasting them. Any code could be broken, but throwing enough obstacles in a hacker's path rendered cracking less secure sites more cost and time effective.

He stretched his arms above his head and followed the hairline crack in the ceiling joist to where it plunged into the doorjamb. He knew that a security system proved only as strong as its weakest link. And the weak link in most instances turned out to be human.

Ben strode into the hallway and surveyed the foyer around the front door. He scooped up two shreds of the letter announcing his hearing that lay beside the front doorway. They contained everything but the hearing address.

"Hi, Mr. Hackwell," Kim called as she descended the stairway. "Lose something?"

"Nothing critical," Ben replied. His problems were none of Kim's business.

Kim eyed the paper in Ben's hands.

"A letter, huh?" Kim asked as she scanned the stairwell.

"You needn't trouble yourself," Ben responded.

"No, let me help," Kim said as she opened the inner door and found a scrap trapped in the jamb. "Is this it?"

Ben took the crumpled paper from Kim's hand and opened it. It's torn message read:

...in Room 407 of the IDS Building at two P.M.

Brian Davidson
Regional Director,
PHD

"I never thought of looking there," Ben admitted with chagrin. "Thanks."

"No problem," Kim replied, beaming at Ben as she opened the outer door. "Sometimes the wind traps stuff there. Have a good one."

Kim slammed the door behind her.

Ben shook his head in wonderment. Did youth ever encounter a problem that its energy and enthusiasm could not conquer?

He stuck the scraps into his shirt pocket and reentered his room. If he retained Jennifer to represent him at the hearing, he could keep tabs on Rykert and learn more about his operation. It wasn't much, but enough that he could call it a plan.

Ben glanced at his watch. It read 10:30 A.M. He had less than four hours to sweet talk his ex-wife, grab a shower, and find the hearing site. He dialed Jennifer's office number.

"Is Ms. Roloson in?" Ben asked.

"Ah, Mr. Hackwell," Azeb answered. "Good morning."

"Thank you, Azeb," Ben replied, pleased by approval communicated in her greeting. "Is Ms. Roloson available?"

"No, she is not," Azeb replied. "May I take a message?"

"Is she not there?" Ben asked. "Or simply unavailable?"

Azeb chuckled.

"For you it is the latter," Azeb admitted and lowered her voice. "Have you learned anything about your daughter?"

"Some," Ben said. "But I need Jennifer's help if I'm to learn anything further."

"By her lights she has helped you quite a bit already," Azeb said. "If I may say so."

"You may," Ben replied. "Still—"

"Have you anything more to say, sir?" Azeb interrupted.

Azeb's sudden obstinacy puzzled Ben.

"Not if you're unwilling to help," Ben replied.

"You ask a lot of me, too," Azeb said.

Ben grimaced. He never had considered the burden that his search for Caitline might place on others.

"I know that," Ben acknowledged.

"I will see what I can do," Azeb promised.

After two minutes, Ben started counting the seconds on his watch. At three minutes 47 seconds Azeb's voice returned on the phone.

"I am transferring your call to Ms. Roloson," Azeb said.

"This is Jennifer Roloson," Jennifer announced.

"Hi," Ben replied. "It's me."

"So Azeb informed me," Jennifer said.

"Aren't you going to ask how I am?" Ben asked.

"Really—" Jennifer replied.

"OK, OK," Ben apologized. He didn't want his request to get off on the wrong foot. "I'll get to the point. I want to retain your services."

Traffic noise emanated from the other end of the line.

"Did you hear what I said?" Ben asked.

"I can't believe you're serious," Jennifer said.

"Why not?" Ben replied. "You are a lawyer, aren't you?"

Jennifer sighed.

"Is it too late to impress on you AGAIN the restrictions of a restraining order?" Jennifer said wearily.

"You mean those restrictions you ignored in talking to me the last time?" Ben replied.

"That was an exception," Jennifer said.

"You could make another," Ben said.

"I could," Jennifer admitted. "But why would I want to?"

"Listen, I know all the stuff that's between us," Ben argued, trying to put all the contrition he could in his voice. "You haven't asked why I would even consider this. Or what my problem is."

"OK," Jennifer agreed. "Why?"

"Because I need legal representation," Ben replied.

"I figured that much," Jennifer retorted.

Ben decided he had to reveal a little bit of the truth.

"Look, it's a reinstatement hearing, OK?" Ben admitted. "I need representation to keep my job."

"What's the charge?" Jennifer asked.

"Sexual harassment," Ben replied.

"And you expect me to represent you," Jennifer exclaimed. "Are you out of your mind, or just stupid?"

"I like to think neither," Ben replied.

"You make it pretty difficult," Jennifer said.

Ben heard the traffic sounds return on the other end. At least she hadn't hung up, Ben thought.

"What're you thinking?" Jennifer asked.

"I was thinking it might impress the board if I were represented by a female lawyer," Ben replied. He knew he needed a clincher. "Especially if she was my ex-wife."

"I do have a reputation to protect, you know," Jennifer replied. "Along with obligations to my other clients."

It was time to appeal to Jennifer's feminist side, Ben decided.

"Wouldn't it help my case to have a noted feminist lawyer arguing on my behalf?" Ben asked.

"You think my appearance will make that much of an impression?" Jennifer asked with surprise in her voice.

"It can't hurt," Ben argued. Perhaps flattery would convince her, he thought. "You are well thought of for your progressive causes, like the WABC."

Ben heard the street sounds on her end again. Was Jennifer thinking his proposal over, or letting him hang?

"Were you really molesting the woman who made the complaint?" Jennifer asked.

"No more than I do you," Ben replied.

"That's not funny," Jennifer declared. "A wise-ass attitude won't help regardless who represents you."

Ben gritted his teeth. He knew Jennifer was right. He hated to have to admit it to her.

"I'm sorry," Ben apologized.

"Were you molesting this woman?" Jennifer asked.

"I was downloading Caitline's video," Ben explained, relieved that Jennifer had accepted his apology. "She saw me doing it."

"In the office?" Jennifer asked.

"In the foyer," Ben said.

"Smart," Jennifer declared.

"It was the only touch screen monitor I had access to," Ben replied.

"You couldn't have used your monitor at home?" Jennifer asked.

"Not if I wanted to really know what was going on," Ben explained. He needed someone to realize how he had felt. "I had to feel the impact of the bullets to believe it."

Jennifer remained silent.

"I did it before office hours," Ben added. "I figured I'd download it and get out of there, but I never got that far."

"It doesn't sound promising," Jennifer advised. "Have you given any consideration at all as to why I should do this for you?"

It was time for Jennifer to know everything, Ben decided. Whether she represented him at the hearing or not.

"Three women have disappeared, Caitline among them," Ben said. "I need clearance from the board to get into my office to find out if any of them are still alive."

"What time did you say the hearing was?" Jennifer asked.

"Two P.M.," Ben replied.

"Where?" Jennifer asked.

"The IDS Building, fourth floor," Ben said. He wondered if Jennifer's questions resulted from curiosity, or if she was going to help. "You know it?"

"I know it," Jennifer said.

"You'll be there?" Ben asked with relief.

"Just you be there" Jennifer advised. "And look presentable. If possible, act contrite, like it'll never happen again."

Jennifer's dial tone burred in Ben's ear. He felt exultant. Jennifer was going to work on his behalf. The spark was still there.

Slow down, Ben reminded himself. He had much to do before the hearing. Ben ran his body through the shower and rummaged through his closet. Presentable meant suit and tie. His navy blue sport coat lay on the floor in back of the closet. He turned over the right sleeve. A salsa stain ran down the forearm.

He found a folded white shirt in his bottom dresser drawer. Under it lay the bull's head string tie Hoot had given him when he left the service. Ben draped the tie around his neck, grabbed a clean pair of jeans from the top drawer, strapped his leather jacket across his shoulders, and examined his mirror image.

Tiny carnelians gleamed in the bull's eye sockets and in its flaring nostrils.

Ben grinned in satisfaction. He knew that Rykert was not the type likely to wear a string tie. He dampened his fingers, ran them through his hair, and left his apartment.

"Hey, Ben," a quavering contralto voice called from the stairs. "You leavin'?"

Ben's stomach knotted. Despite the familiar tone of Tyler Olsen's inquiry, they were not friends. Tyler eyed him from under his sand-colored dreadlocks. Low-slung cargo pants and a hooded jogging jacket wrapped around his lanky frame completed his yardbird chic outfit.

"What is it?" Ben asked.

"Nah, it looks like you're on your way out," Tyler replied. "It can wait."

"If it just takes a moment," Ben said without feeling the propriety that his words suggested. He knew from previous experience that Tyler's appearance of consideration seldom disguised the underlying sense of immediacy and expectation. The next time the problem (There was always a problem) would be exponentially worse. Tyler would make it so.

"It's the showerhead again," Tyler said. "It still doesn't work."

"I checked it just last week," Ben replied. "It worked fine."

"Then," Tyler emphasized. "The dripping's worse than ever now. I can't sleep."

Ben glanced at his watch. So far, their conversation had gone as he expected.

"I'll take a look after my appointment," Ben promised.

"Uh-uh," Tyler replied. "Have a professional examine it. Get it done right this time."

Tyler's elfin eyes zeroed in on Ben's throat.

"Outrageous tie," Tyler declared and raised his right thumb in approval before he re-climbed the stairs.

Ben gritted his teeth as Tyler entered his room. Was it the implicit criticism, he wondered, or the juvenile smugness behind the remark that bothered him more?

Mykill Miers' album, Cut Throat, thumped the floorboards above Ben's head. He knew the origin of the music was Tyler's room. Since no one else was in the house, Ben entered the garage and climbed onto his cycle. Dealing with the angst of 20-somethings could wait until his return.

He headed downtown and parked in the ramp beneath a mid-size office building located a block away from the Nicollet Mall. From there he took the elevator to the skyway level where an enclosed street overpass connected to the second floor atrium of the IDS Tower.

Ben peered up at the ceiling of the enormous enclosure that spanned an entire city block. PHD's downtown business offices were located somewhere on the fourth floor of the 48 stories above Ben's head. He took the escalator to the fourth floor and scanned the room numbers nearby. Room 401 lay to his left, 402 across the hall. The hallway widened beyond the third duo of opposing office entrances onto a set of double oak doors with 407 carved in art deco numerals above the entrance. Inside it stood a mahogany conference table and an oak podium located on the end nearest to him.

Brian Davidson and his secretary conversed with a balding, gray-haired man seated beside the podium. Ben recognized the man as Hector Bidwell, the head of Personnel. Across from him Jennifer pulled a legal pad out of her briefcase while Rykert draped her faux sable coat across the back of the chair beside her.

Ben rounded the podium end of the table determined to have Rykert involved as little as possible. He grinned at Jennifer.

"Here we are again," Ben said.

Jennifer scowled as she scanned Ben from head to foot.

"All I asked for was a suit and tie," Jennifer exclaimed. "I can't even trust you for that!"

Ben ignored Jennifer's displeasure and glowered at Rykert who seated himself on the other side of her.

"I thought we were going to keep this in the family," Ben replied.

"He is family," Jennifer replied. "My family."

"I don't see a ring," Ben observed.

"Don't let that bother you," Jennifer said and squeezed Rykert's hand.

Rykert smiled up at Ben.

"Jennifer thought I might be able to help," Rykert said.

"Help yourself to what?" Ben retorted as he thought of Rykert's looting of Hoot's interface. Ben couldn't decide whether it was Jennifer and Rykert's display of mutual affection, or their apparent lack of concern over his knowing about it that bothered him more. He turned back to Jennifer.

"Is he my fairy godfather or something?" Ben asked.

"I don't know about that," Jennifer replied. "But, Avery is a computer and communications expert."

"So am I," Ben retorted. "So what?"

"So you might need outside corroboration for your fantastic story," Jennifer answered. "That's what."

Ben folded his arms in annoyance.

"And he just happened to be in the area," Ben said as he eyed Rykert. "Why am I the lucky recipient this time?"

"Because she asked me," Rykert replied.

Ben groaned and plopped into in the chair between Jennifer and the podium. He'd wanted to question Jennifer about Rykert. He had not expected her to use him as an expert witness in Ben's behalf.

"It's two o'clock," Bidwell announced. "Let's have this hearing come to order."

Bidwell stepped behind the podium and glanced toward Davidson.

"Do you have an opening statement, Brian?" Bidwell asked.

Davidson rose to his full height and addressed the other four hearing members as though he were arguing a case for the cameras of Court TV.

"The facts of this matter speak for themselves," Davidson declared. "This most recent incident exemplifies Mr. Hackwell's consistent behavior pattern of disrespect towards women and towards authority."

Bidwell nodded toward Jennifer.

"Despite the feminist reputation of his legal representative, Mr. Hackwell's retention of his ex-wife is a shallow attempt by a desperate man to influence the outcome of this hearing," Bidwell argued. "It only underscores his contempt for our company's personnel policies. If it were up to me I would ask Ms. Roloson to recuse herself from this hearing."

"It isn't up to you," Ben said. "Fortunately."

"This is not a place where such outbursts will be tolerated, Mr. Hackwell," Bidwell warned. "As Mr. Hackwell's representative, Ms. Roloson, please instruct your client to confine his responses to when he is addressed."

"Yes, sir," Jennifer replied and seized Ben's wrist. "It won't happen again."

"I do have the right to legal counsel in this instance, do I not?" Ben asked.

"That is the privilege of any person in matters of this sort," Bidwell replied.

"Then it might be said that Mr. Davidson exceeded his bounds in making such a remark as to how I conduct my defense," Ben said.

"It might," Bidwell agreed reluctantly.

Ben wrested his wrist from his Jennifer's grasp.

"It is my contention that such behavior represents a systematic overreaction to events common to the workplace," Ben declared.

"PHD does not consider sexual harassment common to its workplace," Davidson huffed. "Nor will it tolerate such behavior."

Ben leaned forward and folded his hands on the table. Davidson wanted Ben removed to cover up his criticism of Davidson's questionable decisions. Ordway's complaint had provided the means for Davidson to do it. Ben knew that he had to make his defense forceful and convincing yet controlled and objective for it to be effective.

"Have you examined the nature of the complaint?" Ben asked.

Bidwell adjusted his trifocals and scanned the document.

"It says that you were caught downloading lewd and lascivious materials on company equipment," Bidwell said. "Such an act violates company policy of maintaining a safe and non-threatening workplace environment."

Ben stared at the wrinkles on the top of his fingers. His experience told him that no one was safe in today's world.

"Who felt threatened by it?" Ben asked.

"The complainant, obviously," Bidwell replied.

"Does Ms. Ordway's complaint indicate where this activity occurred?" Ben asked.

"Yes," Bidwell answered. "In the lobby."

"Isn't that considered a public area?" Ben said.

"Generally," Bidwell agreed. "But technically, PHD's responsibility to its staff extends to all parts of the workplace including its public areas."

"Technically, Ms. Ordway wasn't at work," Ben replied. "She was on her way to it when the unsettling event occurred."

Davidson jumped to his feet.

"Sexual harassment is more than just an unsettling event," Davidson declared.

"True," Ben agreed. "But what evidence do you have that there was any intent to harass, sexual or otherwise?"

"We have her statement," Davidson replied.

"Do you have mine?" Ben asked.

"We have all—" Davidson began.

"Sexual harassment does not necessarily require intent," Bidwell interrupted. "It can be quite unintentional."

Ben noted Davidson's discomfiture. He had to demonstrate to the others in the room that the complaint was groundless.

"Besides the fact that what I did was a first-time offense," Ben said. "Do you have any proof as to the lascivious nature of the material in question?"

"We have Ms. Ordway's sworn statement," Davidson replied.

"Do you have any witnesses?" Ben asked.

Davidson peered toward Bidwell for help.

"This line of questioning is completely irrelevant," Davidson protested.

"Do you have anything at all?" Ben declared and rose to his feet. "I believe that even in a hearing of this kind a certain burden of proof is incumbent upon the parties prosecuting the complaint. Isn't that so?"

Ben studied Bidwell's face. Bidwell appeared so controlled that Ben could not determine whether his argument had made any impact at all. He turned toward Jennifer.

"Weigh in here any time, counselor," Ben advised.

"You're making a fool of yourself," Jennifer hissed. "And me."

"As always?" Ben retorted. For the first time, he recognized neither pity nor sympathy in Jennifer's face. Again, he wondered why she was here for him.

"Save me from myself," Ben requested. "Just do it."

Jennifer's eyes blazed with controlled fury. She squeezed Rykert's hand for assurance and stood up.

"My ex-husband, and I must emphasize "ex", is slightly misinformed," Jennifer said. "You do not need to prove intent. Ms. Ordway's complaint is sufficient grounds for disciplinary action."

Ben tugged the hem of Jennifer's jacket.

"Thanks," Ben whispered sarcastically. "For everything."

Jennifer brushed Ben's hand away.

"However, there are extenuating circumstances in this instance that mitigate Mr. Hackwell's behavior," Jennifer argued. "Despite its abhorrence to Ms. Ordway."

"And those are?" Bidwell asked.

"At the time of the incident Mr. Hackwell believed that his daughter, our daughter, Caitline, may have been murdered," Jennifer said.

"Why wasn't this reported to the police?" Bidwell asked.

"He couldn't," Jennifer replied.

"Why not?" Bidwell said.

"Because the murder occurred on a Web site," Jennifer answered.

"Preposterous," Davidson cried and surged to his feet. "This is what I mean, Hector—"

"Sit down, Brian," Bidwell ordered. "I'll determine what's preposterous."

Bidwell waited until Davidson resumed his seat.

"In and of itself, Ms. Roloson, viewing a Web site isn't grounds for dismissal unless the nature of the site is questionable," Bidwell said. "What kind of site was it?"

"It was a sex site, sir," Jennifer replied.

"See?" Davidson said.

"And Mr. Hackwell felt it necessary to view it on a public terminal?" Bidwell asked.

"He didn't care about that," Jennifer said. "He was trying to save our daughter."

For the first time, Bidwell seemed disturbed by the implications of what Jennifer described.

"Why that particular terminal?" Bidwell asked.

"It was a touch screen terminal," Jennifer said. "It allowed Ben to feel the bullets enter her body."

"And you believe him?" Bidwell asked.

"I believe my ex-husband would do anything to save the people he loves," Jennifer declared.

Ben peered at his ex-wife in amazement. If she believed in his motives that strongly, why had she divorced him?

"Including his making up a cock-and-bull story like this one," Davidson scoffed. "And getting you to believe it."

"Be quiet, Brian," Bidwell ordered and turned back to Jennifer.

"Why do you believe it?" Bidwell asked.

"I'm not sure I do," Jennifer replied. "Except he has no reason to make something like this up and expect me to believe it."

Jennifer turned toward Rykert. He smiled at her and rose to his feet.

"Let me add at this point, sir," Rykert interrupted. "That such impressions are possible."

"Who are you?" Bidwell asked. "For the record."

"Former president of Web(W)rights," Rykert declared. "A rights clearinghouse and Internet advisor."

Ben groaned at Rykert's statement of his credentials. He doubted whether Hoot would appreciate Ben's being defended by Hoot's Internet business enemy.

Bidwell picked up a pencil and rotated it with his fingers.

"What is your relationship to Mr. Hackwell?" Bidwell asked.

"None," Rykert replied. "I came to verify that such sense receptions as Mr. Hackwell claims to have experienced are possible. They are a product of what is called haptic technology."

"Are these sense receptions real?" Bidwell asked.

"They're very real," Rykert declared and thumped his fist against the tabletop. "They're as real as the impact of my fist against the wood of this table. What's open to question is whether they signify anything outside the medium in which they are experienced."

"Virtual reality, you mean," Bidwell said.

"Yes," Rykert agreed. "Just because someone sees and feels the impact of a bullet in cyberspace does not mean that the bullets or the situation are real."

"You mean nobody was actually murdered," Bidwell said.

"I mean the bullets heighten the reality of the virtual experience," Rykert responded. "It does not mean the experience has reality outside of the video game or Web site that produces it."

"You mean Mr. Hackwell imagined the scene to be real," Bidwell said.

"Given the programming, he could not be expected to believe anything else," Rykert replied and grinned at Bidwell and Davidson. "And, given that he is a professional Web producer himself, Mr. Hackwell's reaction is a testimony to the workmanship of the site that induced it."

Bidwell's pencil spun faster.

"Interesting," Bidwell commented without looking up.

Davidson leaned toward Bidwell.

"What does this have to do with Ms. Ordway's complaint?" Davidson asked.

"If what Mr. Rykert says is true," Bidwell replied. "It becomes a question of an overactive imagination."

A flush of anger started up Davidson's neck.

"It was a sexual Web site accessed on company property," Davidson protested. "That still constitutes harassment."

"This isn't the military, Hector," Bidwell replied. "If you allow the letter of the law to always dictate policy, you eliminate allowing for human foibles or the need for interpretation. Do that and there goes managerial judgment."

Davidson leaned closer to Davidson.

"Can we afford to take that chance when we're under a state of heightened alert?" Davidson asked in an urgent whisper. "The FBI agent said their intelligence indicated the terrorists could strike anywhere, at anything, just to make a point."

"I don't think that applies in this instance," Bidwell said and stopped rotating his pencil.

"The circumstances don't constitute the basis for dismissal," Bidwell declared with a glance toward Ben. He closed his folder and turned back to Davidson. "I'm sure when you explain the circumstances to Ms. Ordway, she'll understand."

"You're going to let this incident go without any sort of disciplinary action?" Davidson cried in dismay.

Bidwell hesitated. Ben squirmed in his seat. He knew Bidwell felt obligated to placate his subordinate in some fashion.

"How much time has Mr. Hackwell been suspended from his job?" Bidwell asked.

"A week," Davidson said.

"With or without pay?" Bidwell asked.

"Without," Davidson declared.

"Make it a second week," Bidwell decided and turned toward Jennifer. "So long as we all understand that this sort of thing won't happen again."

"It won't," Jennifer promised. "Mr. Hackwell regains immediate access to his office, correct?"

"So long as he works off the clock," Davidson said with a resigned shrug. "We open for business at 8 A.M. sharp."

Bidwell stood up and left the room with a frustrated Bidwell in tow.

Jennifer straightened the hem of her suit. Rykert gathered her coat from the back of the chair beside her and draped it across her shoulders as she leaned down toward Ben.

"Thank you, Benjamin," Jennifer said.

"For what?" Ben replied as he stared at his folded hands. Why was Jennifer acting this way? "Thank you for what?" Ben repeated. "That I'm on Davidson's shit list more than ever? That it's official I'm from Cloudcuckooland?"

"Cloudcuckooland?" Rykert asked.

"Aristophanes, isn't it?" Jennifer asked, as she stood erect. A whiff of her Obsession floated past Ben as she wriggled into her wrap. She turned toward Rykert who slipped his arm around Jennifer's shoulder.

"Ben used to write me poetry a million years ago," Jennifer confided with a chuckle. "If you can believe it."

Jennifer patted Ben's forearm and smiled.

"The ball's in your court now," Jennifer urged. "Just do it."

Ben relaxed his hands. Everything he knew, everything he'd fought for felt as if it was slipping away despite all his efforts.

"You know who owns the site Caitline operates from?" Ben said as Rykert steered Jennifer out the doorway. "Web(W)rights, that's who."

Ben watched them disappear around the corner.

"You're dating an Internet PIMP!" he cried.

CHAPTER 18

▼

A heart-shaped face wrapped in tight blonde curls appeared in the doorway a moment later.

"I'm sorry," the woman apologized. "I didn't know this meeting room was occupied."

"It's not," Ben replied. "I'm finished."

"Our staff meeting's not for ten minutes yet," the woman said as she gave Ben a tolerant smile. "Take your time"

Jennifer's fragrance lingered in the air as if to mock Ben's thwarted expectations. He felt as devastated and alone as he had after his first divorce hearing. What had he expected? Did he think some romantic finish would occur like at the end to the movie *Casablanca*? He had called Rykert out, cried his infamy loud enough for everyone to hear, but Ben's words did not matter to Jennifer any more. Rykert tended to her now; and Jennifer bestowed all her attentions upon him in return.

Ben wandered into the hallway. Staff and executive assistants passed by him preoccupied with their own concerns. As should he be, he reminded himself.

Ben grimaced at the irony in Bidwell's decision. Jennifer had used the testimony of Ben's best friend's business rival to help Ben retain his job. Besides reconfirming that Jennifer was his woman no longer, it underscored that Ben's sole purpose in Jennifer's new life was to find a daughter who no longer existed, a daughter for whom the court had ordered that Ben come no closer than 200 yards. If Ben found his phantom daughter was alive, every bit of data Ben possessed indicated that she had killed his best friend. If he discovered that Caitline was dead, it would confirm that he had been right about her murder, but guilty of being the psychological impetus for it.

Ben balled his fist in frustration as he approached the escalator. No matter what he did or what he uncovered, Jennifer had fixed it so he could derive no pleasure or satisfaction from the discovery. For the first time, he recognized the depth of Jennifer's abhorrence, the lengths she was willing to go to thwart any hope of their reconciliation or his forgiveness. The two blows Ben had thrown in anger had created a rift of fear and recrimination that could never heal for any of them, particularly Caitline. He wished she had never been born to see them.

Ben halted at head of the escalator. What kind of father thought like that?

A bad one.

Only bad fathers used their daughters' deaths to vindicate themselves, Ben realized. By extension, he was a bad husband as well, something that Jennifer had claimed all along. Perhaps Rykert wasn't the bad guy Ben wanted to make him. His attentiveness was a quality Ben decided he should have cultivated long before his marriage came to this impasse.

Ben stepped onto the descending grid of stairs. He expected a surge of righteousness to rise up and vindicate his actions to himself as it always did.

Ben reached bottom, but the surge did not come.

Ben crossed the atrium to the skyway entrance and gazed toward the Pei Building at the north end of Nicollet Mall. Ground fog obscured the concave columns that formed the distinctive colonnade in front of the building.

Jennifer had bestowed one task to him that remained from their previous relationship, Ben thought, to recover their daughter dead or alive. He knew that the path to finding Caitline lay through Rykert, yet he could he not convince Jennifer of that. The Jennifer Ben remembered had been warm and receptive. She may have become fearful and manipulative, but Jennifer was not duplicitous. If he had been a little more attentive and not played the churl at every encounter...

Enough self-recrimination, Ben decided. That got him nowhere. He checked his watch. It read twenty past three. He had time enough to proceed to his office and fire up the number generator before PHD's security crew closed the building for the evening.

He found his cycle in the parking ramp and turned the ignition. The backfire boomed and echoed throughout the concrete confines. On his fifth try the engine caught, and he descended to the frosty street below.

Ben sped down a one-way street to the fork that emptied onto Interstate-94 heading northwest out of the Twin Cities towards Fargo. The air nipped his chin, but he felt no exhilaration, just an urgency to grab the one lifeline that remained to his previous existence before the head office closed for the night.

After 40 minutes of steady driving, Ben spotted the twin towers of PHD head-quarters looming at the end of the gravel access road. He parked in the first open space in the lot and checked his watch that read 4:45. He'd made the trip in good time. He still had over an hour before closing.

The boyish security guard did not look up as Ben strode through the revolving door of the atrium entrance. He crossed the floor to the west elevator, pressed the button, and glanced toward the security station. The guard had not moved. With flat budgets, the security guards seemed to grow younger all the time. Of course, Ben thought, who beside a young, uneducated bachelor could live on PHD's starting salary?

He reached third floor and strode past Mavis Portillo. She did not look up, either.

Ben reached his office door, pulled his pass card out of his wallet, and slid the card through the slot. Nothing happened. He tried the lock again with the same result.

He pulled the handkerchief out of his back pocket, rubbed it across the strip several times, and tried once more. That did not work either.

Ben returned to Mavis who sat before her terminal listening to her head-phones as she keyed in her document. He knew company policy did not allow employees with public contact to listen to music in the office.

Ben sidestepped around Mavis' desk to catch her attention.

"Ms. Portillo?" Ben asked in his most business-like manner.

"Mr. Hackwell," Mavis cried and removed her headphones. "I didn't see you come in."

"Of course," Ben said and presented his malfunctioning pass card. "My pass card doesn't seem to be working."

"It doesn't?" Mavis responded solicitously. She turned toward her desk drawer. "I have some cleaning—"

"I tried that," Ben interrupted.

Mavis reached toward the bulletin board above her head.

"Mr. Davidson sent out a memo last week," Mavis explained. "Didn't you see it?" She giggled and covered her mouth at her mistake. "No, of course not."

Mavis' face grew solemn.

"With the recent upsurge in terrorist activity, Mr. Davids—the management felt it was a good idea to change the locks as a security precaution," Mavis explained. "You of all people should understand that."

Ben grimaced. Because of its government contracts, PHD had been at the highest state of technical alert before the World Trade Towers were bombed. He speculated whether it was a conspiracy, or poor timing that the lock change occurred during his absence.

"What about my getting into my office?" Ben asked.

"Oh, I don't know," Mavis' voice quavered as she scanned both ends of the hallway. "Mr. Davidson's not here."

"You couldn't call security?" Ben suggested.

"Not without his authorization," Mavis answered.

Ben gazed around the room. Under Davidson's management, none of the staff dared to think or act for themselves. He glanced at the headphones wrapped around Mavis' neck.

"Are you authorized to wear those?" Ben asked.

"You won't say anything, will you?" Mavis said in a low voice. She enveloped his right hand with both of hers. Both of them felt chilled.

"There must be some way for me to get into my office," Ben urged as he rested his free hand upon hers.

"Wait here," Mavis replied. She unlocked Davidson's office and returned to Ben a moment later. "Follow me."

Mavis bustled to Ben's office door where she ran a new pass card through the slot.

"There," Mavis announced with a satisfied smile as she beckoned him inside. "You're all set."

"Thanks," Ben said.

"Happy hunting," Mavis called out before she returned down the hall.

Under Davidson's restrictive version of office administration nothing could get done without someone on the staff acting outside formal established procedures. The upshot was that now Ben owed Mavis a favor. Given this latest instance of petty corruption, Ben doubted whether his silence would be enough.

He turned on his computer and a security box appeared onscreen. Ben typed his name and password. The cursor transformed into an hourglass. He wondered whether Davidson had changed the intra-net access codes as well. After 20 seconds came, "Good evening, Benjamin," and he entered his e-mail account. Thirty or so unopened messages appeared in the index. One subject line read,

GIVE A HOOT—DON'T SALUTE!

The address line was blank. Either the message came from a dubious source or it contained advertising nobody would read. Ben opened the message.

Friends and Colleagues,

Our brother in virtuosity, William Gibson, was found dead at his home yesterday evening. Authorities consider it a simple case of self-electrocution.

They claim to have no motive or suspects for the slaying and no parties have claimed responsibility for this act. One anonymous source regarded it as the work of a Chechnyan agent, who works as part of the Al-Qaida network.

To this we say:

BULLSHIT!

The agents of this atrocity are well known. They belong to the world's most powerful network—Korporate Amerika! As virtual brothers in arms you know that over the past ten years they have worked systematically to take away or restrict our rights to an open Internet.

Of these korporations, the most conspicuous and influential is a kompany called Web(W)rights, whose founder and CEO is Avery Rykert. It is well known that he opposed Mr. Gibson's efforts to secure a free and open Internet for everyone. We want to know why he was present at the scene of the crime, why he helped police download evidence from Hoot's computer, and the identity of the spendy redhead who left the house the night before. We also want to know the identity of the bearish man with the ponytail spotted fleeing from the crime scene.

We give Mr. Rykert and his two akomplices 72 hours to come forward and explain their actions. If they do not capitulate by noon on Thursday, we promise a calamity that will shut down the Internet until they come forward with the truth.

Do **NOT** think that we have not the means to do so.

Your brothers and sisters
In virtual solidarity
AFI—Allies for a Free Internet

Was AFI Rykert's accomplice? Ben opened two more messages with blank addresses on his index screen and discovered that AFI's message had spread all over the Internet.

Who were these guys? Ben knew many advocates for an open Internet, but never had heard of this group. It was no surprise that he had felt he was being watched while he was at Hoot's house. He had been. He wondered who the "spendy" redhead was caught leaving Hoot's house the night before. Was it one of Wilson's women? Caitline?

Ben reread the message. They gave the authorities 72 hours to find Hoot's killer. Over a third of the time was gone.

He sneezed as he rummaged through the drawers of his storage cabinet. The dust bunnies inside shivered and scattered to the corners of the top compartment. Ben remembered that Housekeeping's annual cleaning sweep had succumbed to cutbacks in staffing. His search through the bottom drawers met with the same lack of success.

He spotted a six-inch square metal box with the power cord and receptor plug wrapped around it hidden behind some discarded storage discs and a box of magnetic tape. Ben inserted its plugs into their respective sockets, brought the number generator online, and typed WEB(W)WRIGHTS.com in the address line.

Web(W)rights' glitzy home page filled the screen. He returned to the page that listed all of the company clients, selected Lara Tarashkova, and clicked on her thumbnail photograph. After 30 seconds, he received the response: No such user. Please check your Web address or contact the server administrator.

Two more thumbnails produced the same result. Ben scanned the list for another female client and found Svetlana Baispul. When he clicked on her name, twin bleeding hearts emerged at the center of the screen and burst in a crimson explosion.

Welcome to X-STREAMSEX.com!

Ben proceeded to the PIN number window of the Payment screen, set the number generator for an eight-digit sequence, and watched the numbers click off on the readout in the corner of his display screen. Depending on the system's sophistication, cracking the site code could take a few minutes or a few hours.

He glanced at his watch. It was past closing. No sounds emanated from the hallway. The readout screen on the monitor repeated the same numerical sequence.

When Ben pressed Enter, the screen went blank. Twin winking hearts appeared and swelled to bursting.

WELCOME TO HURTFUL.COM

Ben scanned the options. The interactive videos were divided into themes: Western, Roman, Cossack, Arab, and Mystery.

He entered the last one. A snarling, trench-coated detective fired his .38 into the darkness as a voluptuous redhead cowered in the shadows behind him. An information box asked: ARE YOU EXPERIENCED? Each video had four versions: First Timer, Novice, Experienced, and Sophisticated.

Ben studied the clip. The swarthy face under the trilby resembled Wilson's. The redhead behind him could have been Caitline. The video clip was too dark and grainy for him to tell.

He opened the first text box in the Cookies file that contained a long list of computer addresses. Most were written in Cyrillic. Web(W)rights was not among them. The other three boxes contained similar information, most of it also written in Cyrillic.

No wonder that Agent Lockett could not trace the IP addresses, Ben thought. No wonder Hoot had wanted a firewall. He had farmed out the simultaneous processing to third world computers at a tenth or less of what it would cost if he had done it stateside.

Was this why Stanfeld was involved, Ben wondered. Did Stanfeld think Hoot was a traitor? Was this why Hoot was murdered?

Ben shook his head and rejected the possibility. Hoot was no traitor. He was no idiot, either. He never would give his associates any idea of what their comrades were doing.

Ben wondered who had found out. Who stood to gain the most by Hoot's demise? All the data pointed at Rykert.

He wondered how much of this Jennifer knew.

The last information panel in the Cookies file contained 40–50 addresses. The other three contained as many or more. That meant over 200 suspects could have killed Hoot.

Were the three missing sex performers involved? Or were they lures manipulated by the major players?

Ben knew that investigating each Web address could take days. If Hoot had used each simultaneously to process parts of his program, that would be all each one knew about his project. Each worked as an individual cell in a larger matrix.

Ben wondered what to do as he closed all the windows on his monitor. His Farrah Fawcett screensaver image cocked her enticing finger at him. Ben pressed the Enter key and the image disappeared.

Ben contemplated whether that was what happened to the missing women. Had they been snuffed out with the click of a mouse? Or were they alive somewhere?

His e-mail software bonged and a message popped up onscreen: You have mail.

Ben checked his watch. It read 6:00 P.M. He knew from experience that electronic solicitors were as punctual as their telephone counterparts. Some poor devil had sent out his last mailing that advertised a new Internet security system before he went home for the night.

The subject line on his index screen proclaimed, IMPORTANT MESSAGE. The address box read L. Tarashkova. The message read:

> My Dearest Father,
>
> I am alright. Do NOT worry about me. I do not wish to cause further pain for you or for Mother. If you feel that we must talk please put on your earphones and press the audio stream attachment.
>
> Love always
>
> Catiline

No header appeared with the message. Ben reached behind the monitor, placed his headset beside the keyboard, and opened the attachment.

A video clip of Caitline without raspberry hair and sultry makeup appeared. She spoke into the camera in three-quarter profile as if participating in an interview.

Ben turned up the sound knob. The screen went dark. A blue-white arc leaped between the earphones.

Ben coughed and waved the acrid cloud of smoke away. The stench of scorched wood and rubber pervaded the room. He covered his mouth and examined his face and shoulders with his free hand. Everything felt as if it were in its proper place.

He checked his headphones. One earpiece had disintegrated, blue smoke rose from the other. A twelve-inch scorch mark scored the veneer of his desktop.

Davidson burst into the room.

"What the hell happened?" Davidson asked. "You better have a good explanation, Mister."

Ben stared at Davidson in disbelief. Where had Davidson come from? Did Davidson think Ben had caused this?

"Just for the medical record," Ben said. "I am OK."

"Explain why you're here," Davidson demanded.

"I work here," Ben replied. "Remember what Bidwell said at the meeting this afternoon?"

"Past six?" Davidson asked.

"Is that any of your business?" Ben replied.

"I'm responsible for everything that happens in this office," Davidson declared.

"Is it your business to be right outside my door when my headphones explode?" Ben asked.

"I'm not going to argue with you," Davidson said, ignoring Ben's question.

"You're accusing me of this?" Ben asked.

Davidson started dialing his cell phone.

"If you'd just give me a chance to ex—" Ben said.

"SECURITY!" Davidson bellowed into his phone.

Ben disconnected the generator and slid past Davidson into the hallway.

"What are you afraid of?" Ben asked as he backed toward the elevator.

"He's taking the south elevator," Davidson cried into his phone. "Take him when he reaches the ground floor."

"Is it AFI?" Ben shouted. "They sent me a message just before the sparks flew out of my headset."

Davidson charged forward oblivious to Ben's appeals. Ben eluded Davidson's grasp and opened the fire door across from the elevator. Two sets of work boots thumped on the steps above him as clambered down the stairwell. He raced through the atrium into the parking lot, revved his cycle, and spun toward the frontage road.

Ben spotted a black minivan cresting the hill on the frontage road. He squeezed the accelerator and escaped down the frontage road in the same direction as Davidson and the young security guard burst out of PHD's front entrance.

CHAPTER 19

▼

Ben reached River Road and checked his mirror. Nobody followed. He found no sign of the black minivan either.

He pulled onto the gravel shoulder, wrenched off his helmet, gulped in the night air, and coughed until his lungs ached.

AFI had tried to kill him. Like Hoot, he had gotten too close to something they didn't want him or anyone else to know. They were willing to risk the revelation of their remote control weapon to silence him.

It was a tribute in its way, Ben reflected. AFI feared him enough to kill him.

Or was it arrogance, Ben wondered. Was AFI's killer application so powerful that they did not care if anyone knew of its existence? Even feared it? Was that why Davidson was so afraid?

Despite Davidson's paranoia, Ben doubted whether his death was the calamity the AFI e-mail referred to. Another electrocution would occur, Ben decided. His, if he wasn't more careful.

Ben inhaled again. His breathing and pulse continued to race. Given his own close call, Ben acknowledged the effectiveness of the AFI strategy. How much would e-commerce diminish if its users feared their next mouse click could be their last? What did trafficking in souls, virtual or otherwise, matter against the threat of physical annihilation?

He had to stop the Alliance. He had to stop Rykert and his henchmen. He had to rescue Caitline and the others before it was too late.

He had to get a grip, Ben realized. He bent forward and placed his head between his knees. After holding his breath for a count of five, Ben exhaled, and leaned backward until he spotted the curve of the Big Dipper resting above the rim of the horizon.

A chilling possibility prompted Ben to stand erect. What if Caitline were not the helpless victim she appeared in the video clips? What if her involvement was something more sinister?

Ben turned and traced the stars in the Big Dipper's handle. Thickening clouds obscured his view of Polaris.

He asked himself who had appeared in the video that killed Hoot. And who had appeared in all the other videos for Hurtful.com? The incriminating questions piled one upon each other. Who had taken acting lessons? Who had set up Wilson's intranet? And who comprised most of the hackers on the Internet? Teenagers, like Caitline, that's who.

Ben clenched his right hand. Despite all of the data, he knew that Caitline was not one of those frustrated adolescents. He patted the box that protruded from his coat pocket. His number generator would prove it.

Ben thrust his helmet over his head and climbed onto his cycle. With the generator, he knew that he could trace each of the accounts back to their source.

Ben rounded Minneapolis on 494 until he spotted the lights of the Mall of America in the distance, and headed north on Cedar Avenue until he reached his home street. Red and blue lights flashed at the bottom of the hill two blocks beyond. Two police cars had been parked in front of his house. A fire engine stood in the middle of his driveway.

He skirted the knot of onlookers on the sidewalk and parked his cycle on the lawn beside the fire engine. A beefy fireman stripped out of his rubber coat and stuffed it in its locker behind the cab. The black and gold badge on his helmet read Chief Christensen.

"What happened?" Ben asked in bewilderment.

"We're not sure, yet," Christensen replied with a wide grin. A thick wad of gum lodged between his front incisors. With each exhale Christensen spewed a fume of Dentine. "But there's nothing to worry about. Everything's under control."

"What started it?" Ben asked.

"Undetermined origin, at this point," Christensen said. He glanced at Ben's cycle. "Yours?"

Ben nodded.

"Nice bike," Christensen observed and pulled a crisp towel from a storage locker. "You should move it. The owner may not like it being on his lawn."

"I am the owner," Ben said.

"I was wondering when you'd to get around to admitting that," Christensen said with a glance toward the house. "Nice place."

"Goes with the bike," Ben replied. He pondered what Christensen was trying to accomplish with these questions. "Any damage?"

"We managed to confine it to the downstairs living area," Christensen replied as he turned back toward Ben. "The girl was pretty shook up about it"

"Girl?" Ben asked.

"The one living upstairs," Christensen replied. "Kimberly."

"Oh," Ben remarked, relieved that the girl had not been Caitline. "I thought you meant someone else."

"How many girls you got in there?" Christensen retorted.

"Just her," Ben said, aware how strange his response seemed to the fire chief. He glanced toward the house. "Did she phone it in?"

Christensen spat out his gum and thrust his jaw in the direction of the birch tree.

"You have to thank that fellow over there," Christensen replied.

Tyler Olsen gave them a sidelong glance as he adjusted the book bag in his arms. Ben could not decide whether Tyler acted out of modesty or arrogance.

"What time did it start?" Ben asked.

"His call came in at 6:35," Christensen replied.

Ben calculated the time of the fire was half an hour after the AFI attack at PHD. He wiped a sweat bead from his brow and noticed his left hand was quivering.

"Are you all right?" Christensen asked.

"I'm fine," Ben said. He had no time for psychological aftershocks if he was to find Caitline. "Did anybody report anything unusual?"

"Not yet," Christensen acknowledged as he eyed Ben. "Did you have something specific in mind?"

"Nothing in particular," Ben said and stuck his hands in his pockets, certain that Christensen thought Ben's responses were peculiar. "Can we go in?"

"Sure, we're cold, too," Christensen agreed. "We need your help to figure out what started it."

"In a moment," Ben said and strolled toward Tyler who pretended to study the firemen rolling up their hoses. Ben tried to act nonchalant. "The chief tells me you're the one to thank for saving my house."

"You should have had your wiring inspected," Tyler said.

Something moved inside his bag. Two gimlet eyes peered out above the half-drawn zipper. Rudy's head popped out, swiveled in both directions, and returned inside.

Ben shrugged irritably. Graciousness was not Tyler's long suit, Ben realized. That did not exonerate Ben from expressing his gratitude.

"You're right," Ben admitted. He decided to act matter of fact. "Do you think it was electrical?"

"Of course it was," Tyler retorted. "What else stinks like that?"

"You smelled something?" Ben asked.

"Right through the door. Then, phoom," Tyler said as he wriggled his fingers up and out like a mushrooming cloud. "You must have left your TV set turned on."

"Why?" Ben asked.

Tyler faced Ben.

"Kim and I heard voices," Tyler explained.

"Where?" Ben asked.

"In your room," Tyler added.

"Where were you?" Ben asked.

"Out in the hall," Tyler replied. "We both heard them."

"When?" Ben asked in alarm. Could the fire be connected with his near-electrocution at PHD?

"Right before the phoom," Tyler answered.

"You're sure?" Ben declared.

"Of course I'm sure," Tyler responded with annoyance.

"What'd they sound like?" Ben asked.

"I dunno," Tyler said with a shrug. "Voices."

Tyler had opened up to him, Ben realized. He needed to take a different tack if he were to get as much data from Tyler as possible.

"Did you recognize them?" Ben asked.

Tyler shook his head and pondered for a moment.

"One sounded kinda like a woman," Tyler suggested.

Ben paused. He had recovered all that Tyler could contribute regarding what caused the fire, he decided.

"Where's Kim?" Ben asked.

"Back in her room, I guess," Tyler answered.

Ben glanced toward the fire truck. Christensen was not there.

"Have you told the chief this?" Ben asked.

"Not yet," Tyler replied. "I'm saving it for the inquiry."

"Inquiry?" Ben asked in alarm.

"You think you can get away with substandard wiring in an apartment complex?" Tyler demanded.

"There was nothing wrong with the wiring," Ben declared.

"What else would it be?" Tyler scoffed.

"I can't say for sure at this point," Ben replied. There was no way he could tell Tyler about the electrocution. Ben started for his house. "It's what I hope to find out."

"Desdemona's fine," Tyler shouted. "Just in case you're interested."

Ben stopped. He'd forgotten his cat in all the excitement.

"Where is she?" Ben asked.

"Kim's got her," Tyler replied.

Ben proceeded again toward the house.

"You'll hear from my lawyer," Tyler warned. "There're definite consequences for negligence."

Ben glared at Tyler, and shook his head. Why should he make things worse with a stupid response?

"You're gonna fry for this one," Tyler promised.

So much for reaching out to Tyler, Ben thought as he strode through the garage and opened the door to the hallway. The same odor of burnt rubber he had smelled after the shock in his office filled his lungs. He covered his nose and mouth and peered into his apartment's living room. Christensen and a short, nondescript man in street clothes poked through the ash trail that extended from his bed sheets to the blackened monitor on the card table.

He would deal with them after he had talked to Kim, Ben decided. He mounted the staircase and knocked on Kim's apartment door.

"Who is it?" Kim asked.

"Ben Hackwell," Ben replied. "I'd like to ask you about the fire, if you're up to it."

"The door's open," Kim said.

Ben entered the room that smelled of smoke with an underlay of Tide-cleaned sheets. Kim sat on top of the end of her bed and hugged Rex. Desdemona skulked in the corner, and the dog's eager puppy eyes followed her every move. Spotting the open doorway, Desdemona darted behind Ben and scampered into the hallway.

Ben glanced around the room. Outside of a picture of Kim and her parents on her dresser, the room contained few of the frills that Ben recalled had decorated Caitline's bedroom. He advanced toward Kim's bed.

"You look worn out," Ben observed.

"I'm fine," Kim said. She sat upright in response and repositioned Rex in her arms. "Ask away."

Ben sat on the far end of her bed.

"First, let me assure you that the wiring wasn't faulty," Ben said.

"I know," Kim replied. "Tyler can be such a butthead sometimes." She sighed and glanced out the window. "Don't be too hard on him, Mr. Hackwell. I might not have gotten out of there in time without his help."

Ben nodded. Unfortunate as it might be, they both shared an obligation toward Tyler's fastidiousness.

"Tyler said that both of you heard voices before the explosion," Ben said. "Did you recognize them?"

"Why?" Kim asked.

"It might help identify who or what caused it," Ben explained.

"I thought I did, at first," Kim said and closed her eyes. "The woman's voice, in particular, sounded familiar."

She opened her eyes and giggled.

"But, I can't remember where," she exclaimed. "Probably from a TV commercial or something."

"Are you sure?" Ben asked. "It's important."

Kim scrunched her face.

"I remember thinking that it sounded like something I heard fairly recently, but I just can't place it," Kim recalled with a shrug. "Sorry."

"Well, thanks for trying," Ben said and retreated to the door. "If you think of anything…"

"I'll let you know," Kim replied and massaged Rex's deformed paw. "Don't worry about Tyler. His bark's a lot worse than his bite."

Kim grinned.

"His mother refuses to give him any more money," Kim confided. "So he can't afford to sue you."

"That's a relief," Ben replied with a chuckle. "Just don't tell him my ex-wife's a lawyer. She'd do it pro bono."

Kim giggled and covered her mouth.

"Oh," Kim said in disbelief. "You can't mean that."

Ben grimaced. This young woman knew nothing about how the real world operated.

"Sure I can," Ben replied. "In fact, if it wasn't for my daughter, Jennifer'd—"

"That's it!" Kim interrupted and stood up. Rex scrambled to right himself on the bed.

"What's it?" Ben asked.

"That's the voice I heard," Kim declared.

"Jennifer's?" Ben asked, perplexed by Kim's certainty.

"No, your daughter's," Kim replied.

"Do you know her?" Ben asked.

"Not really," Kim replied. She reached for the cell phone on the nightstand beside her bed, pressed the replay button on its side, and extended the receiver toward Ben.

> "Hello, this is Avery Rykert. We tried to reach you at home, but were unsuccessful. Please contact us at your earliest convenience regarding the disposition of your first shipment."

"That's a man's voice," Ben said.

"Ssh. Wait," Kim ordered. "There's more."

The recording hissed.

"See," Kim observed. "The line's still open."

Click. Ben heard his voice mail greeting emerge from the earpiece.

> "You have reached the phone of Benjamin Hackwell. He can't speak with you now, but he will return your call. Please leave your name and number after the beep. Thank you."

The voice mail software shut off, but the line remained open.

> "This is Caitline Hackwell. I'm sorry to have missed your call. In the future, please contact me at 612-555-4800. Thank you."

Ben closed his right hand to a fist. That was Jennifer's office number he realized. Jennifer had known Caitline was alive all along.

"How did you get that call?" Ben exclaimed.

"Our voice mail system makes mistakes sometimes," Kim said and hugged Rex closer to her. "I've been meaning to tell you about it, but you always seemed too busy."

Ben relaxed his grip. The ruddy color returned to his fingers. It discomfited him to know he had been seemed so forbidding that Kim was afraid to approach him with this information.

"Sorry," Ben apologized. "I guess I've been preoccupied."

"That's all right," Kim said and grinned. "I can help you with the setup, if you like."

"Setup?" Ben asked.

"Of the voice mail, silly," Kim explained. She released Rex and bounded to the phone. "It's usually because people don't get the setup options right the first time."

She punched several numbers on the keypad.

"And since they seldom call themselves they never fix it," Kim said as she picked up the receiver and listened. "There. All fixed." She offered Ben the receiver. "Wanna hear it?"

Ben shook his head at his oversight. It surprised him that this young woman he hardly knew had taken the time to correct his answering system. He felt surprised and gratified.

"How long has this been on your phone?" Ben asked as he sat on the edge of Kim's bed.

"About a week or so," Kim said as she sat beside him. "I know I should've told you sooner, but I didn't want to get your daughter in trouble." She hugged her knees against her chest. "Believe me, I've been there."

Ben grimaced. Teenagers and their parents, he thought. The eternal conflict.

"Me, too," Ben replied, trying to encourage her. "I'm sure it's not as bad as you think."

"You don't know my parents," Kim responded. "They're not exactly thrilled with my being here."

"In my house?" Ben asked.

"Here in the Twin Cities," Kim corrected. She leaned forward and peered earnestly into Ben's eyes. "She isn't, is she?"

"What?" Ben asked.

"In trouble," Kim said.

"Not with me," Ben replied.

"She is in trouble, though," Kim confirmed.

Ben peered into Kim's wee face. He wondered how much of his story he should he tell her.

"Let's just say that she's lost," Ben said.

"Lost?" Kim asked.

"Yeah, lost," Ben said with a smile. "And I don't know where to find her."

Kim studied him.

"Oh," Kim said dully and slapped Ben's shoulder with the back of her wrist. "You're teasing."

"No, I wasn't," Ben protested.

"Sure you were," Kim declared. She scrunched herself against the headboard and stared at the rumpled bedcovers at her feet. "Why not? Everybody else does."

"Does what?" Ben asked. He felt totally confused by the direction their conversation had taken.

"Tease," Kim said and pinned Rex against her chest. "Oh, Kim is so cute. She never has a problem with clothes. Or boys. Or parents! Or anything else!"

Her cornflower eyes locked onto Ben's.

"You think it's easy being like this?" Kim asked.

Ben suppressed a smile.

"I suppose not," Ben replied.

"There," Kim exclaimed and pointed at Ben's face. "I saw it."

"What?" Ben asked helplessly.

"That smile," Kim said. "You think I'm cute, too."

"You are," Ben said. Why wouldn't this young woman accept a compliment?

"That's no reason to treat me like a child," Kim replied and stroked Rex's paw. "I'll bet you don't talk to your daughter this way."

Ben winced. He tried to remember when the last time was he had talked to Caitline. It seemed years.

Someone rapped on Kim's hallway door. Christensen stuck his head inside the doorway. The odor of a fresh stick of Dentine reached Ben's nostrils.

"Thought I heard you up here," Christensen said and nodded at Kim. "Good evening, Ms. Jorgenson."

"Good evening, Chief," Kim said.

Ben noticed the color rising in Kim's cheeks. Christensen turned toward Ben.

"We need you downstairs," Christensen urged. "Hurry up."

Christensen left the room. Ben watched Kim scratch Rex's paw as she stared out the window to relieve her embarrassment. The somnolent dog stared into space. Ben stood up, dazed by the whirl of this young woman's feelings.

"We don't talk at all," Ben admitted. "In case you're interested."

Kim said nothing. Ben had not intended his statement to sound patronizing

"Time's wastin'!" Christensen bellowed from the bottom of the staircase.

Rex closed his eyes as Ben headed downstairs. Kim continued to peer into the night.

CHAPTER 20

▼

Ben descended the stairs and paused in the open doorway to his room where Christensen chatted with two police officers who stood in front of Ben's blasted monitor.

"There you are," Christensen said and summoned Ben with a wave of his hand. "This is still your room, you know. What's left of it."

Christensen stopped chewing his gum.

"I want you to take a look at something," he said.

Ben nodded at the two policemen who stepped aside as he approached the remains of his makeshift desk. The badge of the shorter one with the blond, pencil-bar mustache, read Torkelson, who fidgeted with his holster cover. The taller and older of the two, whose badge read Lindbohm, readied his palm pilot. Christensen pointed at the scorched keyboard.

"What do you make of that?" Christensen asked.

Ben examined the cable underneath the card table. Scorch marks followed the electric cord past the surge protector to the floor socket behind the headboard. The damage resembled that done to his office desk, yet he doubted whether he should tell Christensen this.

"Looks like I need a new surge protector," Ben equivocated.

"Yeah," Christensen replied uncertainly. "That's exactly what I thought. What caused this?"

"How should I know?" Ben replied.

"I thought you might have an idea," Christensen answered. His eyes lost their crinkle. "Look, you face four code violations not to mention reckless endangerment. You better have an explanation."

"You wouldn't believe me if I did," Ben replied.

"Try anyway," Christensen insisted.

Ben determined that he might as well try out his theory on the fire marshal. He lost nothing if Christensen refused to believe it.

"What if I told you that foreign agents had developed the means to kill people over the Internet?" Ben suggested.

"You're right, I don't," Christensen replied and with a sidelong glance at the police officers behind him. "Try something else."

"What if I said that the same thing happened at my work PC 30 miles away?" Ben added.

"Another fantasy story doesn't make the first one any more believable," Christensen declared.

"What if they happened within 30 minutes of each other?" Ben asked.

"Coincidence," Christensen said.

"And if I have two witnesses who can corroborate my story?" Ben said. He doubted whether Davidson or Tyler would back him up.

"I wouldn't count on the boy's testimony," Christensen said and chuckled. "Unless it's for the prosecution in a regulatory hearing."

"And Kim?" Ben asked.

"Oh," Christensen said. "You know her name now?"

Ben grimaced. His lack of concern must be evident to everyone.

"What about her?" Christensen asked.

"She heard the same voices Tyler did before the explosion," Ben said.

"Voices?" Christensen replied. "Whose?"

"Of my daughter," Ben explained. "She was in the streaming video on my PC."

"Congratulations," Christensen chided. "Your daughter's on TV."

"Not TV," Ben corrected. He refused to give Christensen the satisfaction of patronizing him. "The Internet."

"So?" Christensen said.

"That's how they deliver their killer jolt," Ben said. "Through the Internet."

Christensen appeared unimpressed.

"They?" Christensen asked. His eyes crinkled with mock perplexity. "Who's they?"

"Foreign nationals," Ben said. He knew Christensen had decided that Ben's story sounded so unbelievable that he could play games with him. "Their cookies are all written in Cyrillic."

"Anyone specific?" Christensen asked.

"Yes," Ben replied. "But I don't have proof."

"And you think these foreign nationals are trying to kill you through the Internet," Christensen said and rolled his eyes. "Any particular reason?"

"Because I know about their haptic interface," Ben declared.

"Ah-ha," Christensen replied. "And this does what?"

Ben explained the simulated sensation created by Hoot's haptic interface.

"Simulated you say?" Christensen said and placed his right hand on Ben's shoulder. His Dentine mist enveloped them. "But at a low level."

"It's not a simulation any more, obviously," Ben cautioned.

"Obviously," Christensen agreed. "But you weren't here when it happened."

"No, I wasn't," Ben admitted. "Luckily."

"Kind of poor timing on their part," Christensen observed dryly. "Especially if you're supposed to be touching the computer for it to kill you."

"I said you wouldn't believe it," Ben declared and spun out of Christensen's grasp. He had tired of playing this game. "You have a better explanation?"

"Try this on," Christensen suggested. "A computer engineer takes in renters to supplement his income. He cuts a few corners along the way, like doing his own wiring. All of a sudden, whoom, we're called in on a two alarm fire."

"Two alarm?" Ben asked in surprise.

"Yeah," Christensen said.

"Who called it in?" Ben asked.

Christensen shrugged and glanced toward the policemen.

"Where did those calls come from again?" Christensen asked.

"One from this address, the other from across town," Lindbohm replied.

"Did you get a name with the second one?" Ben asked.

"It came from a gentlemen's club, Schariah's," Lindbohm said. "The caller said she knew you."

Ben shrugged. He knew no one at Schariah's besides Wilson and Petrov. He was not eager to renew the acquaintance with either of them.

"Did she identify herself?" Ben asked.

"Yeah," Lindbohm replied. "But when we called back for confirmation the owner said he had no one with that name."

"What name?" Ben said.

"Zarima Melekhov," Lindbohm answered. "Do you know this woman?"

Ben shook his head. That was the Web(W)right identity of the waitress at Schariah's, he realized. Why had she called in the alarm? How had she known?

Ben turned toward the doorway.

"Not so fast," Christensen ordered. He grabbed Ben's arm and spun him around. "There's still the matter of the fire in this building, a building that you're responsible for."

"You don't understand," Ben said.

"We're trying," Christensen said. "But you haven't given us many straight answers."

"Everything I told you is the truth," Ben insisted.

"Why don't I believe that?" Christensen asked as he tightened his grip. "Is it because everything I said makes more sense?"

Using a half-forgotten judo move, Ben spun out of Christensen's grasp, but Lindbohm blocked Ben's path to the door. He heard the click of handcuffs as Torkelson snapped them around Ben's left wrist. Christensen wrapped his arms around Ben's shoulders as Torkelson snapped on the other cuff.

Ben rocked backward and heaved Christensen over his shoulder. Lindbohm tackled him around the knees.

"Let him go," Bergstrom ordered.

Lindbohm released Ben's knees.

"We were holding him for you, sir," Lindbohm explained as he stood erect. "Until you arrived."

"I see," Bergstrom said as he peered at Torkelson's badge. "Remove those cuffs, Torkelson."

"Just a minute," Christensen said and scrambled to his feet. "This man is responsible for half a dozen fire safety violations, not to mention reckless endangerment, and you're letting him go?"

"It looks that way," Bergstrom said.

"I don't care what you're working on," Christensen said while his jaws worked overtime. "Your authority doesn't cut it at a fire scene."

"It doesn't have to," Stanfeld announced as she parted the two police officers standing in the doorway and flipped open her worn leather wallet. FBI gleamed in gold letters at the top of her identification card. "It's a national security matter now."

"You mean this joker's telling the truth?" Christensen said in astonishment.

"You know what you need to know to make your report," Stanfeld replied. "We'll keep you informed if there are more developments."

"This isn't the way Homeland Security is supposed to work, you know," Christensen said. "There's supposed to be cooperation between agencies."

"I think it best for everyone if you just get on with it," Bergstrom advised. His gaze hardened on Christensen. "Don't you?"

Christensen swallowed his gum, opened another pack, and disappeared into the hallway. Bergstrom ordered the two policemen out into the hall.

Lindbohm handed Bergstrom his palm pilot.

"Everything's in here in case you need it," Lindbohm said.

Bergstrom closed the door behind them and slipped the pilot into his pocket.

Ben sat on the folding chair in front of his monitor. His luck seemed to be holding. His first set of inquisitors had been replaced by another set that was much worse.

"OK," Ben asked. "When do you guys break out the rubber hoses?"

"Oh, no. Nothing like that," Bergstrom equivocated and winked at Stanfeld. "We only use rubber hoses for gardening, don't we, Barbara?"

Stanfeld grunted as Bergstrom strolled to Ben's bed.

"May I?" Bergstrom asked.

Ben grimaced. He wondered at their sudden change of attitude. Perhaps Bergstrom and Stanfeld thought he knew something they did not. He decided to play along and find out.

"Be my guest," Ben said and extended his right arm toward the charred bed.

Bergstrom sat on the edge of Ben's bed furthest from the scorch marks. Ben glanced toward the hallway, then at Stanfeld.

"Where's Agent Lockett?" Ben asked.

"Back at headquarters," Stanfeld replied. "What do you care?"

Despite Lockett's antagonism, Ben smiled at his recollection of her rubbing against his shoulder.

"You two were working together at Hoot's place," Ben replied. "I thought you might have brought her along to examine my computer."

"That burned out piece of crap?" Stanfeld retorted. Her chuckle ended in a slushy cough. "She's very good, but she's no miracle worker."

"We're more interested in what you know about Sophia Nechayev," Bergstrom said as he pulled a pack of Camels from his coat pocket. He cocked his right brow at Stanfeld who folded her arms across her chest. Bergstrom turned toward Ben.

"OK?" Bergstrom asked.

Ben shrugged. Cigarette smoke could not make the room smell any worse.

"I'm trying to quit if that makes you feel better," Bergstrom apologized. His first inhale shot from his nostrils like motor exhaust through twin tail pipes. "So what do you know about her?"

"Very little," Ben equivocated, certain they knew much more about her than he did. The detail about the whip handle he'd keep to himself. "Outside of her being lousy backup during a police raid."

"Yeah, we heard about that," Bergstrom said as he studied the smoke cloud hovering against the ceiling. "Tell us about it."

"There's nothing more to tell," Ben replied.

"Let us decide," Stanfeld advised as she grabbed the nearest chair from the dinette table and straddled it. "Why were you with her in the first place?"

Ben summarized the incident at the Grafton up through the police raid.

"She was probably just as glad to get away from me," Ben concluded.

Stanfeld and Bergstrom exchanged knowing glances.

"You didn't phone the police?" Bergstrom asked.

"Why would I?" Ben asked.

"And she didn't, either?" Bergstrom said.

"Not that I know of," Ben replied. He wondered where Bergstrom was going with this line of questions. "But she could have."

"When?" Bergstrom asked.

"During the time we climbed the stairs," Ben said.

"Why didn't she use the elevator?" Bergstrom continued.

"She said she always takes the stairs," Ben responded.

"Isn't she the fitness freak," Bergstrom retorted.

"There's a new invention you may have heard of," Stanfeld said. "The cellular phone? Most building managers use them nowadays."

"She may have had one in her front pocket," Ben recalled and shook his head. "I didn't think much of it then, but it looked like a two-way radio. She could have called during the time it took for me to catch up with her."

Ben scanned their faces. His speculations had produced no effect.

"Do you know who Sophia Nechayev is?" Stanfeld asked.

"Should I?" Ben replied.

"She majored in telecommunications at the University of Moscow, then went underground and joined some slicer group called the Allies for a Free Internet."

AFI, Ben thought. They had sent the e-mail before he almost was electrocuted. He noticed Stanfeld watching his reaction. Ben shook his head.

"What about high energy radio frequencies?" Stanfeld asked. "Ever hear of those?"

"Sure," Ben replied and nodded. "HERFs are part of the electromagnetic pulse spectrum that enables nuclear explosions to knock out electrical systems."

"Organized crime in Russia uses HERF guns to knock out the computer systems of its enemies," Stanfeld said.

"What of it?" Ben asked.

"Your friend Gibson did research on them before he left the Defense Advanced Research Projects Agency," Stanfeld explained. "Did you know that?"

Ben stared at his aching fist. That Sophia had proven to be more than a building superintendent did not surprise him. That Hoot was involved did.

"What has this got to do with my daughter?" Ben asked.

"Geez!" Stanfeld retorted. "Virtual sex, Russian mobsters, and killer applications. Wasn't it you who pointed out this connection in the first place?

Ben turned toward Bergstrom who scrutinized Ben's reactions through his self-produced smoke clouds. Which one was going to start playing the good cop?

"I thought you were investigating Hoot's murder," Ben said.

"We won't decide on that officially until the coroner's report," Bergstrom replied. He crushed the lit end of his cigarette between his fingers and tossed the butt into the sink. "But we are willing to hear you make more connections, off the record."

"How should I know?" Ben asked. "I already told you everything."

"Why don't I buy that?" Stanfeld said. "You're the common denominator in all these Internet electrocutions. Outside of Nechayev, you're the only one who has knowledge enough to do it."

"Why don't you talk to her?" Ben asked.

"We're working on it," Stanfeld replied.

Stanfeld's reply meant they were having trouble finding her, Ben figured. They should be keeping tabs on Rykert.

"You might as well talk to Rykert while you're at it," Ben said. "He was at Hoot's house, too."

"Rykert's clean," Bergstrom replied. "Despite his dating your ex-wife."

"He is?" Ben retorted. "Have you checked his company, Web(W)rights?"

Bergstrom nodded.

"Have you checked its Web site?" Ben asked.

Neither agent responded. Ben decided it was time to inject new data into Bergstrom and Stanfeld's detection files.

"Did you know that the intellectual property rights Rykert's company represents are mostly those of entertainers?" Ben asked. "And that three-quarters of them are men's club performers, most of them from Schariah's Club?"

Stanfeld's eyes betrayed her surprise. She stood up.

"How do you know that?" Stanfeld asked.

"From the cookie addresses," Ben replied.

"That doesn't mean anything," Stanfeld argued as she planted her right foot on the seat of her chair. "Lockett said the programming script Gibson used had no cookies associated with them. Hell, the links you found could lead anywhere!"

"It's a guess," Ben admitted. "But most of the cookies leading from Schariah's performers are written in Cyrillic."

"Wouldn't a Russian be likely to use his own language in his programming?" Stanfeld asked.

"Maybe, but Wilson's Chechnyan. He could know Arabic, too," Ben said as he shifted in his chair. "He said that my daughter set up his Web site before she disappeared."

"So he's a liar. So what?" Stanfeld replied and emitted another throaty chuckle. "Hardly surprising behavior from a sex club owner and God knows what else."

Ben glanced at Bergstrom.

"My daughter doesn't know Cyrillic or Arabic," Ben said.

Bergstrom pulled another cigarette from his pack.

"What's that supposed to mean?" Bergstrom asked.

"It means that someone else wrote the programming scripts for Wilson's Web site," Ben replied. "The same person who programmed Wilson's Web site also scripted the distributed programming for the haptic interface connection."

Bergstrom exhaled a smoke ring.

"You mean Gibson," Bergstrom said.

"Possibly," Ben replied.

"He's dead," Stanfeld observed.

"Very true," Ben agreed. "Yet his virtual sex service continues to run."

Ben pointed toward his burnt-out PC.

"You can see the result," Ben added. "The condition of my PC is just like Hoot's now."

Bergstrom blew a second smoke ring and watched it hover in the air. Stanfeld watched Bergstrom with increasing irritation. Ben crossed his legs and cupped his hands around his right knee. He'd pricked their balloon. He had to float another theory as valid.

"Who was Gibson fighting a rights battle with to keep an open Internet?" Ben asked.

Stanfeld and Bergstrom exchanged blank stares.

"You worked with him earlier today," Ben hinted.

"Are you saying Rykert?" Stanfeld replied. "That's impossible!"

"Why else is the AFI up in arms?" Ben asked.

Bergstrom and Stanfeld said nothing.

"Allies for a Free Internet?" Ben asked. "You mentioned them a moment ago." Neither agent responded.

"Do you know about their threat to shut down the Internet if Hoot's murderer isn't arrested?" Ben asked, groaning at their lack of insight. Both agents appeared dumber than he thought. "Do either of you ever pay attention to the Web?"

"No, wise guy. You tell us." Stanfeld replied with glance at Bergstrom. Her ice-blue eyes leveled onto Ben's. "That's what we're here for."

"AFI thinks Rykert did it," Ben said.

"Why?" Stanfeld asked.

"Because his company has cornered rights to every domain name on the planet," Ben replied.

"So?" Stanfeld said.

"That would eliminate distributed computing," Ben answered and sat back to observe the agents' reactions. When neither agent said anything, Ben added. "Let me connect the dots. Hoot's network relies on the free and open access to thousands, perhaps millions of Web addresses. Rykert's company owns the rights to billions. Statistically, Rykert probably owns the rights to most of the addresses of the members in Hoot's network. As a member of the SEC Rykert's in a position to enforce intellectual property right laws including those on the Internet. By enforcing those laws he would cut or eliminate the profits thousands of these little guys could make off of utilizing the spare memory in their PCs."

Stanfeld retreated to her chair. Bergstrom took another drag from his cigarette.

"You think somebody from the AFI would kill for that?" Bergstrom asked.

"Maybe not just for that," Ben replied. "If the energy of millions of these relays could be funneled onto one Web address simultaneously, it would provide power enough to kill whoever was using the site at the time."

Ben eyed Stanfeld.

"Isn't that why you were downloading Hoot's IP addresses?" Ben asked.

"Something like that," Stanfeld admitted.

"Wouldn't Gibson's surge protector prevent such an attack?" Bergstrom asked.

"Commercial surge protectors work within a relatively narrow range of tolerances, Ben replied. "They're not designed to stop anything. They just break the connection when the voltage goes above a certain tolerance like a circuit breaker."

"You're saying that Gibson killed himself," Bergstrom concluded.

"Not necessarily," Ben replied. "Even industrial surge protectors can't stop an enormous spike in voltage. A charge like that in a lightning bolt can leap across the junction in a surge protector and short the whole system. That's why they advise you to unplug your PC during an electrical storm."

Ben turned to Stanfeld for confirmation.

"Isn't that right, Agent Stanfeld?" Ben asked.

Stanfeld grunted something inaudible.

"Even if your wild speculations were true, Homeland Security would warn everybody about the danger," Stanfeld replied and chuckled dismissively. "It probably would result in a market for better quality surge protectors."

Ben smiled at Stanfeld's discomfiture. It indicated that he was on the right track. It suggested something else as well.

"That's the genius of Hoot's haptic interface Web site," Ben reflected. "The users of his Web suit would be the ones with the greatest exposure and least likelihood of turning their computers off, or of listening to government warnings."

"Some genius," Stanfeld scoffed. "Putting millions of American lives at risk, even if they are perverts."

"Let's stay on track," Bergstrom interrupted. "You think this someone is Rykert."

"He's the prime candidate," Ben declared.

"Any particular reason why?" Stanfeld asked.

"Hoot told me Rykert and his company have tried to derail his distributed computing network for years," Ben said.

"Why couldn't it be Wilson?" Bergstrom asked.

"Why jeopardize an entire prostitution network to eliminate the creator of one money source?" Ben responded. "Wilson's too smart a businessman for that."

"And Rykert isn't?" Stanfeld scoffed.

"If someone like Wilson benefits directly from Hoot's network, Web(W)right's association fades into the background," Ben explained. "You guys take out Wilson, and Rykert's performed a community service and relieved himself of a headache later on."

"What's in this arrangement for Wilson?" Stanfeld asked.

"Besides his Internet income, it provides the perfect cover for a guy on the inside to deflect things," Ben replied. He scanned the unimpressed faces of the two enforcement officers. "Rykert's already convinced you Hoot's death was an accident."

"Sounds a little thin to me," Bergstrom decided as he peered at the ceiling. "Especially for a pillar of the community. What do you think, Barbara?"

"You're asking me?" Stanfeld responded in surprise. She turned toward Ben and tapped her index finger against the side of her aquiline nose. "It doesn't smell right. I say we go with what we've got right here, the person with the obvious motive."

Bergstrom leveled his gaze on Ben.

"Hate's a pretty powerful emotion," Bergstrom declared.

"There's no one to hate," Ben replied.

"Oh?" Bergstrom asked.

"The person I could hate is already dead," Ben said.

"And jealousy?" Bergstrom added.

"I wasn't jealous of Hoot," Ben replied. "Just the opposite."

"I wasn't talking professionally," Bergstrom corrected.

Ben knew Bergstrom referred to Hoot's relationship with Caitline.

"Don't be ridiculous," Ben retorted.

Bergstrom's feral eyes widened like a lens before the snapshot. His pupils seemed to engulf the room before he clapped his hands on his knees and stood up.

"OK, then," Bergstrom concluded as he tossed the rest of his cigarette in the sink. "Let's go, Barbara."

"What?" Stanfeld asked in amazement.

"Let's go," Bergstrom declared.

"Are you serious?" Stanfeld said.

"We've got all we're going to get here," Bergstrom said and opened the hallway door. "Let's go."

"How much more do you need for an arrest?" Stanfeld exclaimed. "We could haul him in right now just for criminal neglect and for leaving a crime scene. And who knows what else behind all his Internet babble!"

Bergstrom shrugged and beckoned Ben to the door with a wave of his hand.

"Maybe we do need a trip downtown just to clear the air," Bergstrom decided.

"Finally!" Stanfeld said.

"C'mon," Bergstrom ordered. His arm sweep was more peremptory this time. The wall phone burbled in its cradle.

"Should I answer it?" Ben asked.

"You want to run him in now?" Bergstrom asked, glancing toward Stanfeld. "Or give him one last call?"

Stanfeld shrugged. Ben removed the receiver.

"Hello?" Ben asked.

"Are you alone?" the caller asked. It was a woman's voice with a thick Eastern European accent.

"Who is this?" Ben asked.

"Zarima Melekhov," the called replied. "The one you call Yazmin."

It was the waitress who had phoned in the fire, Ben realized. He attempted to keep the urgency out of his voice.

"I've got company at the moment," Ben said.

"Can you not get rid of them?" Zarima asked.

Ben grimaced. He had to find a ploy that got rid of Stanfeld and Bergstrom. Would Zarima know enough to play along?

"It offends me that your organization would call me at this time of night," Ben declared.

Bergstrom lit another cigarette. Stanfeld stomped into the hall. Ben lowered his voice.

"What makes you think we have anything to discuss?" Ben asked.

"That depends," Zarima replied.

"On what?" Ben asked.

"How bad you want to see your Caitline," Zarima replied. "I know where she is."

CHAPTER 21

▼

Ben hesitated. He wondered if this another wild goose chase. Or did Zarima know something? How could he know for sure?

"What makes you think I'm looking for her?" Ben asked.

"A man does not get his finger dislocated unless it is for a good reason," Zarima replied.

"How do you know about that?" Ben asked in surprise.

"I see things not meant to be seen," Zarima replied.

"What things?" Ben asked.

"Things that could get someone in trouble if the police knew about them," Zarima said.

Ben glanced about the room in frustration. Zarima's vagueness was growing tiresome. If she knew anything, her forthrightness needed a jumpstart.

"If you want to talk to the authorities, they're right outside," Ben said. "They might be quite interested to review the current status of your citizenship."

The other end of the line was silent.

"Are you there?" Ben asked.

"Yes," Zarima replied.

"You still want to talk?" Ben asked.

"Not if you are going to behave like that," Zarima declared.

She sounded hurt, Ben thought, though she was the one who possessed the critical data.

"How about if we start from zero?" Ben suggested and glanced toward the door. Little seemed to be happening out in the hallway. "I'm still interested in finding my daughter. Do you want to tell me where she is?"

"Not when you threaten me with police," Zarima replied. "How can I be sure I can trust you?"

Ben gritted his teeth. Given the spot he was in, Ben decided he needed a display of faith to discover where Caitline was.

"OK," Ben agreed. "I'll get rid of the police and meet you at Schariah's."

"No," Zarima said. "Not there."

"Where, then?" Ben asked.

"At my apartment building," Zarima said.

"The Grafton?" Ben replied. With Sophia lurking in the building, that site seemed as dangerous as Schariah's. He was in no position to argue. " When?"

"In one hour," Zarima said and hung up.

Ben returned the receiver to its cradle and stepped into the hall. Bergstrom peered at the smoke ring he had created while Stanfeld paced back and forth. The two police officers waited for instructions.

"Well?" Bergstrom asked.

"Some of those phone solicitors won't take no for an answer," Ben declared.

"There's a number to call to stop that," Bergstrom advised.

Stanfeld stopped pacing.

"Do you boys think we could finish this tonight?" Stanfeld asked.

"Are we done here?" Ben asked and pulled his keys from his pocket.

Bergstrom crushed the end of his cigarette between his thumb and index finger.

"Yeah," he said. "Lock it up."

Bergstrom brushed past Stanfeld and headed toward the front door. Stanfeld and the policemen watched Ben stick his key in the lock. Ben wondered what to do.

"How long are we going to be at the station?" Ben asked.

"Who knows?" Stanfeld replied and gave Ben a frosty smile. "Maybe a lifetime in your case."

"I just wanted to know when I could call my lawyer," Ben said.

"You'll have time for that," Stanfeld assured him.

"Am I being charged with anything?" Ben asked.

"We have 24 hours to come up with the details," Stanfeld replied.

Ben returned his keys to his pants pocket. His pulse thudded in his ears.

"I'm not coming," Ben declared.

"Get going," Stanfeld warned. The sour acid odor had returned on her breath.

"Then read me my rights," Ben said.

"Hurry up and lock your door," Stanfeld ordered.

Bergstrom parted the two policemen standing on either side of Stanfeld.

"What the hell's going on?" Bergstrom asked. "I thought we were going downtown."

"We are," Stanfeld replied.

"What's the holdup?" Bergstrom demanded.

"He wants his rights read to him," Stanfeld replied and pointed at Ben.

Bergstrom scanned the determined faces of the three officers and turned toward Ben.

"I thought you had agreed to come with us," Bergstrom said.

"I haven't agreed with anything so far," Ben replied.

"Don't play word games with me," Bergstrom warned. "Let's go."

"Read me my rights!" Ben demanded.

"OK, smart guy," Bergstrom retorted. "You have—"

"What's the charge?" Ben interrupted as he turned the doorknob. When the door receded into the room, he pulled it close to the jamb. His vision appeared fuzzy at the edges as if he were about to faint. "Do you have a writ?"

"What?" Bergstrom asked.

"This is a duplex apartment complex. You're standing in a public thoroughfare," Ben said as he nudged the door back inside his room. "If you're going to charge me, you need a warrant for my arrest."

Ben slid inside the doorway, clicked the deadbolt, and leaned against the door panel. His heartbeat thudded in his ears. Had those years of listening to Jennifer's recitations of legal statutes finally paid off?

A muffled exchange emanated from the other side followed by two measured raps against the top panel.

"Open up," Bergstrom ordered.

Ben resisted the urge to respond.

"You're charged with resisting arrest," Stanfeld began and proceeded through every word of the Miranda speech as if she were reciting in front of an academy training class. "In a few minutes Sergeant Torkelson will return with the document you requested. Wouldn't it be better if you changed your mind and cooperated?"

Ben glanced around the room. They'd break down the door the moment Torkelson returned with the FAX-ed writ.

He pulled the telephone receiver from its cradle, stole into the bathroom, and pressed the speed dial button. The dial signal buzzed twice on the other end.

"Hello?" Jennifer answered in a groggy voice.

"This is Benjamin," Ben whispered.

"Who?" Jennifer asked.

"Your ex-husband. Benjamin," Ben answered.

"Is it about Caitline?" Jennifer asked. "Have you found her?"

"Not exactly, but I know where she is," Ben said and fought to keep the urgency out of his voice. He wondered how long Jennifer would pretend not to know about Caitline. "I need your help."

"Is she in trouble?" Jennifer asked.

"I don't know for sure," Ben replied.

"You're the one in trouble," Jennifer declared. "Aren't you?"

Ben said nothing.

"AREN'T YOU?" Jennifer cried.

"Yes, I'm in trouble," Ben admitted with a sigh. He decided that capitulating might work this time. Jennifer might help if she thought her agent needed it. "I need your help. The sooner the better."

"Who with?" Jennifer asked.

"The police," Ben said.

"Again?" Jennifer groaned. "What can I do?"

"You can get me a writ to countermand my arrest," Ben explained.

"For what?" Jennifer asked.

"Resisting arrest," Ben answered.

"And you expect—" Jennifer said.

"Zarima called," Ben interrupted.

"Who?" Jennifer said.

"Zarima Melekhov, a waitress who works for Wilson," Ben said. He wondered how long Jennifer would continue to stonewall him. "She says she knows where Caitline is."

"Why didn't she just tell you?" Jennifer asked.

"She said she needs my help," Ben replied.

"And you believe her?" Jennifer asked in dismay.

"She's an illegal alien," Ben explained. "She doesn't want to be shipped back."

"Trust the authorities," Jennifer urged. "Let them help you for once."

More voices sounded in the hallway as shadows flickered back and forth under the door. Ben knew he did not have much time.

"I'm sure that's good advice," Ben agreed. "But not this time."

Ben stepped into the bathtub, heaved the lower half of the window upward, and scanned the length of the house on both sides. Torkelson maintained a vigil beside the downspout at the far end.

Ben rechecked his hallway door. No shadows showed underneath the door. He rummaged through the folders on his desk until he found his address book, opened it to J, and thumbed the seven numbers into the keypad.

"This is Kim," Kim answered.

"Kim, this is Ben Hackwell," Ben replied.

"Hi," Kim said.

"I need your help," Ben said.

Kim did not respond. Ben did not expect that she would be eager to help him.

"I'm sorry if you thought I was teasing before," Ben apologized. "I certainly didn't intend for you to take it that way."

"That's OK," Kim sighed. "I guess I shouldn't be so sensitive about it."

"I should think more before I speak," Ben admitted. He glanced around the room trying to think what he should say next. "I really need your help."

"Does it involve the men downstairs?" Kim asked.

"I'm afraid so," Ben said.

"I'm sorry, Mr. Hackwell," Kim declared. "But I really don't think I should."

Ben hesitated. He knew it was better if Kim didn't get involved. He also knew he was desperate. What argument could prompt a young woman to help a middle-aged man evade the police?

"I don't have much time," Ben said. "I thought my daughter was dead until I heard her on your answering machine. Now I need to meet a woman who knows where Caitline is."

"Can't the police help you with that?" Kim asked.

"Not this time," Ben said.

"She's in trouble with them?" Kim asked as the realization entered her voice. "Gee, I don't know."

"I'm not asking you to do anything illegal," Ben coaxed. "I just want you to go downstairs and ask them what's going on. I'll take care of the rest."

"Wouldn't that be complicity?" Kim asked.

"Not if I don't tell you what I'm going to do," Ben replied.

"I'd still be helping you to escape," Kim said.

"You don't know that. If I were, would I tell you my intentions?" Ben equivocated. How much could he ask of this girl? "Of course, I could be tricking you."

"How can I know for sure?" Kim asked.

"You can't," Ben declared. "You just have to trust from the data you have about me that I'm doing the right thing."

"OK," Kim sighed. "What do you want me to do?"

"What I asked," Ben said.

"When?" Kim asked.

"I'm not going to tell you," Ben replied. Not telling Kim placed the responsibility for Ben's actions on his shoulders alone. "Sooner rather than later."

Ben hung up. The shadows moved back and forth under the door again. If Kim were an obedient daughter, he figured that she'd fulfill her role in the next few minutes.

Ben grabbed the charred bed sheets and heaped them on the floor beside his PC. He scattered some loose papers over the sheets, strode to the kitchen cabinet, and withdrew a box of wooden matches. Where one electrical fire had occurred, a second could also, or appear to.

He struck a match and held the flame up to the corner of a sheet of paper he pulled from the printer tray. When the lower half ignited, he tossed it onto the pile, and dipped the corners of two other paper sheets into the flame.

The paper sheets burned to ashes; the cotton ones failed to ignite.

Damn fire-retardant, Ben thought. A match fire wouldn't be convincing anyway. It produced the wrong odor.

Voices emanated from the hallway stairs. Ben wondered if they signaled the beginning of Kim's distraction.

Ben opened the front panel of his processor, exposed the hard drive, and unscrewed one white and two green wires with his thumbnail. Crossing all three would fry the disc. And the data within it, Ben realized.

Two loud raps rattled Ben's front door.

He had no time left. Ben pulled the wires over the edge of the bedclothes and crossed the three copper ends. A blue spark spurted between his fingertips.

Ben shot backward, crashed against his wooden desktop, and tumbled into the foot well. He sat upright. A thin gray cloud rose like incense from the sheets at his feet. The acrid odor of electric discharge permeated the air. Ben rubbed the base of his skull. A dull, tingling sensation traveled up each of his fingertips.

Splinters showered the carpet. The hallway door burst open.

"HE DID IT AGAIN!" Bergstrom cried as he crossed the room in two strides, grabbed Ben by the elbow, and jerked him to his feet. "You damn fool. You could have caused cardiac arrest."

He shoved Ben into Stanfeld's arms.

"Here," Bergstrom ordered. "Cuff him."

Ben bumped against Stanfeld's thigh. The two of them slammed their shins against the bed frame while Stanfeld fumbled for her handcuffs.

With a loud snarl Desdemona leaped from under the bed between them and scurried into the hallway. Ben spun from Stanfeld's grasp, rammed his shoulder into Torkelson's chest, and heaved the officer against the hallway door. Ben eluded Torkelson's frenzied grasp, slipped through the doorway, and slammed the door shut.

Ben held the door against the jamb. He knew his strength would not hold for long against the strength of three determined law enforcement officers. He tugged back and forth against their efforts. On their third attempt, Ben pulled the door shut, then released the knob, and dashed out the front entrance.

Leaping aboard his cycle, Ben cranked the engine as a powerful set of hands grasped the hem of his jacket. Ben swiped them away as the engine roared to life, but Bergstrom regained his hold. Ben braced himself with his right leg, pivoted the cycle 180 degrees, and felt Bergstrom's fingers drain away as his centrifugal force sent him staggering toward the overhanging birch tree. He collided against its trunk with a sickening thump.

Ben glanced back at the intersection. No cars followed. Stanfeld already must have sent out the call on police radio.

He sped through the intersection and turned into the alley. If he reached the other end, Ben decided that he could escape the first wave of squad cars sealing off the area.

His cycle bucked and roared through the ice ponds that dotted the alleyway. Sirens yowled in the distance signaling their enclosure. He braked his cycle at the far end and peered up and down the street. There was no sign of them yet.

He turned right at the top of the hill. Two squad cars at the bottom blocked the street in front of the park. Two more approached from opposite directions.

Ben sped toward the blockade, turned into the park entrance, and sped down the path onto a cul-de-sac that connected with the cross-town street beyond.

A siren screamed on the path behind him.

Ben opened the throttle. Slipping and sliding, he reached the cul-de-sac where his tires grabbed the dry cement and his cycle pitched forward. Ben regained his balance, turned right at the intersection, and left at the next block. Zigzagging with every block, he reached another cross-town street and turned left.

The squad car careened around the corner half a block behind. Ben shot up another alleyway. The car's siren screamed as the car whizzed past him toward the other end of the block.

Ben doubled back and turned left. When he reached Hiawatha Boulevard, he turned left again. Opening the throttle as wide as it would go, he maneuvered in and around cars until he reached the Cedar Street down ramp. At the bottom, he sped down Franklin Street toward the Uptown.

The siren wails disappeared by the time he crossed over I-35. It had been just 45 minutes from the time he spotted the fire engine in front of his home and 20 from when he spun Bergstrom into the tree. He couldn't elude the police forever, Ben realized. Would finding Caitline be enough to satisfy them?

Ben parked his cycle at the corner opposite the Grafton. The brownstone appeared dark, somnolent, as any respectable girls' apartment should on a workday night. He wondered how many of these "respectable" women acted as cover. How many of them were prostitutes?

Ben shook his head, convinced that Caitline was not one of them. Caitline was headstrong, rebellious, and independent. She'd never allow herself to be used by anybody. He'd taught her that.

He flicked the intercom switch and received no response. He rattled the gate, and it swung open.

Ben stole to the front door. Every window was dark. In a panic, he wondered whether Zarima had told him the wrong address. He doubted it. Still, the hairs on the back of his neck prickled. Could this be a trap?

A squat, female figure appeared at the top of the entrance. Zarima's hair glinted raspberry under the overhead light as she turned her head in both directions, descended the steps, and grabbed Ben's elbow.

"Did anyone follow you?" Zarima whispered.

"Not that I know of," Ben replied. A whiff of garlic assaulted Ben's nostrils. He shivered in the dark, grateful that he did not have to look at Zarima's teeth. "Where's Caitline?"

"I will tell you as soon as we are inside," Zarima replied.

She wrapped her hands around his forearm and escorted him up the steps. Her thick fingers felt cold as a pair of ice tongs around his wrist as she closed the door behind them. The inside felt no warmer than her hands.

"Can't you turn on the heat?" Ben asked.

"We must not attract attention," Zarima said.

"What about Sophia?" Ben asked. "Where's she?"

"Not here, I assure you," Zarima said.

"Are you worried about the police?" Ben asked.

"Wilson," Zarima said. She pulled aside the drawn chintz curtain and peered into the courtyard. "Pyotr and his men might be outside. We cannot be too careful."

Ben had tired of Zarima's prevarication.

"Where's Caitline?" Ben demanded.

"She is fine," Zarima answered.

"Where is she?" Ben repeated.

"I will tell you as soon as I am safe," Zarima said.

Zarima knew nothing, Ben decided. What could have prompted her to call him about Caitline in the first place?

"Tell me now," Ben demanded.

"Guarantee my safety first," Zarima pleaded.

"Why?" Ben asked.

"I told you," Zarima said. "Wilson."

"Wilson," Ben retorted and feigned indifference. "What do I care about him?"

"He has your daughter," Zarima replied.

Ben thought as much.

"Where?" Ben asked.

"Guarantee my safety, and I will tell you," Zarima said.

"Why should I believe you know anything?" Ben asked.

"You have no choice. She is the only one who can save you and I am the only one who knows where she is," Zarima said. Her muscular fingers clutched his shoulder. "If you do not trust me, you have nothing."

"I have that now," Ben replied. "You will have to offer me something better."

"Hope?" Zarima asked.

"That's all?" Ben retorted. "I've been running on those fumes for days."

Zarima returned to the window and rubbed her hands over each other as she peered outside. Her narrow shoulders trembled.

Ben rested his left hand upon her shoulder. What could terrify this self-reliant woman so? Or was this another trick in her arsenal?

"What makes you think I can protect you?" Ben cajoled.

"You have influence," Zarima declared. "I have seen it."

Ben resisted the impulse to laugh.

"I don't have much sway with anyone right now," Ben replied.

"You're an American. You do not realize the power that you have," Zarima said and let the curtain drop. "If I tried to turn myself in, they would deport me back to Chechnya."

She glanced toward the window.

"It is Wilson or deportation," Zarima declared. "Either way is a death sentence."

Despite Zarima's equivocation, Ben felt pity for her.

"What can I do?" Ben asked.

"Vouch for me," Zarima urged. "Tell them I helped you. That I want to stay in this country."

Ben hesitated. Could her fate really depend on such slim hope?

"Not until you tell me where Caitline is," Ben insisted.

Zarima groaned in despair.

"She is alive. That is all I know," Zarima admitted.

Ben started for the door.

"I do not know for how long," Zarima added.

Ben paused. He sensed another ploy.

"What do you mean?" Ben asked.

"I mean the rest of us have all been killed," Zarima said. "One by one."

"Rest of us?" Ben said.

"The women at the Club," Zarima said. "Schariah's."

"Yes," Ben replied. "I saw the disappearances on the Web site."

"It was not supposed to happen that way," Zarima said.

"What do you mean?" Ben asked.

"We were supposed to disappear with new identities," Zarima explained. "But Tascha, Anitra, Oxana, and Hormuz, and last night, Ivanova, all are dead."

"Who killed them?" Ben said.

"Who do you suppose?" Zarima asked rhetorically as she pulled aside the curtain and peered into the dark. "I do not want to be next."

Ben opened and closed his fist.

"Can you prove Wilson did it?" Ben asked.

"How can you prove murder if the victim does not exist?" Zarima said.

"What do you mean?" Ben asked in alarm. Caitline had disappeared, too.

"I, we, all of us, have no papers, nothing. We are easy to dispose of," Zarima said in despair and let the curtain fall back. "All we had were our bodies to get out."

"And Wilson supplied the means," Ben said.

"Yes," Zarima answered. "From one hell hole into another."

"Which hell hole?" Ben asked.

"Iraq, Afghanistan, Georgia, all over," Zarima said and spat on the floor. "They are all the same if you are a woman."

Ben strode to the curtain and peered into the darkness. He wondered what ghastly phantoms Zarima saw out there. Or were they all in her head? He had to find out which if he ever was going to find Caitline.

"Why bring you over here if only to kill you off later?" Ben asked.

"Once they got us on video we were expendable," Zarima replied. "Wilson could make 20 times as much for our bodies on the Internet as he could at the club. So he got rid of us."

"They?" Ben said and let the curtain drop. "Who's they?"

"Your daughter," Zarima replied. "And the monster she slept with."

"Wilson?" Ben asked.

"No, that slug of a man," Zarima said and screwed up her mouth in distaste. "Gibson."

"You're lying," Ben cried and grabbed Zarima's shoulder. "Hoot would never do that."

"Why should I lie? Everyone knew it," Zarima replied and turned to face Ben. "If I were going to lie, would I tell the person I wanted to protect me that his daughter was involved?"

Ben peered into Zarima's eyes. She returned his gaze without wavering. It was true. Caitline was a prostitute, a madam with resources and market worldwide.

He started toward the door. He thought his search would disprove the obvious, but each step had reconfirmed it with murder as the topper.

"Where are you going?" Zarima called.

"To the police," Ben said.

"What about me?" Zarima asked.

"I'll tell them everything. It's me they want. And my daughter," Ben said as he turned the deadbolt lock. "They'll protect you."

Zarima seized Ben's wrist.

"What makes you so sure?" she asked fearfully.

"Why shouldn't they?" Ben asked and scanned Zarima's face. The fear in it was palpable. What else did she know? "You sounded so confident a moment ago," Ben said. "What data are you withholding?"

Zarima released Ben's wrist and retreated. Ben pressed his advantage.

"How were those women killed, Zarima? Did it come through the wires?" Ben asked and scanned the shadowy room. "Is that why everything's dark? So nothing electrical can spark a fire?"

Zarima retreated another step. Her eyes bulged with terror.

"Why do you keep looking outside?" Ben asked as he seized her wrists. " What do you expect to see? Who is it, Zarima?"

"He said to wait and hold you here," Zarima answered. "That he would come right after you arrived."

"Who told you?" Ben said and shook her hard. "Who?"

Two raps sounded against the door. Ben motioned to Zarima to open it. She turned the knob and opened the door six inches.

A tall man bundled up in a trench coat and felt hat slipped inside. His bushy hair exploded from under his hat the moment he removed it.

It was Avery Rykert.

CHAPTER 22

▼

Ben released Zarima. That Rykert was behind Zarima's charade did not surprise him. His only surprise would be how Rykert would rationalize his involvement.

"Where's Caitline?" Ben asked.

Rykert shook his head, started to open his overcoat, and grinned at them.

"Not very warm in here, is it?" Rykert said.

"The furnace is not reliable," Zarima replied. "When sometimes I turn the heat, the air starts to smell."

"It's because the pipes haven't been drained in a long time," Rykert replied. "Turn the heat up while we're here."

Zarima scurried down the hall.

"Where's Caitline?" Ben reiterated.

"You have every right to be concerned," Rykert agreed and furrowed his bushy brows. "We're doing our best to set her free, but these negotiations take time."

Ben heard the radiator rattle as the furnace came on. The musty odor of stagnant heating water soon followed. Rykert sidled around the coffee table and sat in the overstuffed easy chair beside the empty fireplace.

"Ah, that's better," Rykert said and draped his overcoat across his knees. "You understand."

"Hardly," Ben replied. He resisted his urge to slug him only because he needed Rykert's information first. The slugging could come later, a prospect Ben savored on a multitude of levels. "What the hell's going on? Who are you negotiating with?"

"I'm not sure I can tell you that," Rykert replied. "It's classified information."

"Who are you to withhold classified information?" Ben argued.

"Very well," Rykert said. He pressed his palms together and peered at Ben over the top of his joined fingertips. "I can tell you this much. Your daughter's involved with some very dangerous people."

Ben clenched his fist. He wondered why Rykert was trying to scare him. Or was he trying to piss Ben off? If so, Rykert was succeeding.

"Is Caitline all right?" Ben asked.

"As far as we know," Rykert replied.

"We?" Ben asked. "Who's we?"

"I'm afraid I can't tell you that," Rykert replied. "It might jeopardize the negotiations."

"Convenient," Ben retorted and scanned the darkened room. Rykert intended to stonewall him about Caitline's whereabouts. "Does Jennifer know about this?"

"Of course," Rykert answered.

Ben grimaced. Rykert acted so smug about Jennifer's involvement.

"Since when?" Ben asked.

"Since Caitline was kidnapped," Rykert replied.

"Kidnapped?" Ben exclaimed. "Is that what you think happened?"

"Of course," Rykert said and screwed up his mouth. "What else would it be?"

Ben groaned. Rykert confirmed that Jennifer knew Caitline had been kidnapped before Ben brought up her disappearance. Why had she pretended otherwise?

"So that's why Stanfeld's involved," Ben declared.

"The FBI normally is the body that handles kidnapping cases like this," Rykert observed.

"And the CIA?" Ben asked.

"Stanfeld brought them in when she found out who we were negotiating with," Rykert explained.

"Just who are you negotiating with?" Ben asked.

"Friends of Gibson," Rykert answered.

Ben gestured impatiently.

"Hoot had many friends," Ben said. "I was one of them."

"I know," Rykert said.

The tone of Rykert's response made Ben's association with Hoot sound incriminating.

"Be more specific," Ben urged.

"Hoot's associates," Rykert said. "The people who participated in his distributed processing network."

"You mean AFI?" Ben replied. "They claim they want a free Internet, not murder over it."

"I'm speaking of Al-Qaida," Rykert declared. "More specifically, the Wahhabis."

Ben plumped into the chair across from Rykert in shock. He recalled from his briefings in Desert Storm that the Wahhabis were a radical Saudi Muslim sect allied with a bunch of nationalist groups including the Chechnyan rebels. The Putin government blamed them for bombings in Moscow and elsewhere over the past ten years. Caitline's involvement with such a sect took her endangerment to a new level.

"You think they have the expertise to operate over the Internet?" Ben asked.

"Bin-Ladin has supported all kinds of initiatives of mass destruction," Rykert replied.

"There were no Arab IPO addresses on Hoot's computer," Ben said.

"Pooh," Rykert said and dismissed Ben's objection with a wave of his hand. "How do you know? The sub-processing could be done anywhere.

Besides, you don't need computers with a lot of processing power, just a lot of them. Your friend, Gibson, provided the means through his network."

"Is that the crap you're feeding Stanfeld and Bergstrom?" Ben retorted. "Hoot would never betray his country."

"Intentional or not it amounts to the same thing," Rykert replied. "He knew the type of people he was involved with."

"Gangsters, perhaps," Ben suggested. "But not terrorists."

"What else do they have in Chechnya?" Rykert retorted. "I've been there. I've seen them."

Ben sat up in surprise. If Rykert had founded Web(W)rights, when had he found the time to visit that godforsaken part of Asia?

"How long ago?" Ben asked.

"In '92 during my missionary work before the first Russian invasion," Rykert said. "Nothing is sacred to them. They blow up houses, murder people on the street, defecate in the churches."

Rykert leaned forward.

"We're dealing with people who'll stop at nothing to get what they want," Rykert declared.

Ben recoiled at the tone of Rykert's rhetoric.

"And what is that?" Ben asked.

"Destruction of the American way of life," Rykert answered.

Ben suppressed an inadvertent giggle. He hadn't heard that reply since he left the military.

"You're kidding," Ben said. A study of Rykert's face showed that he was not. "How can Chechnyan terrorists affect our way of life?"

"Read the papers," Rykert said. "What's happened to Caitline happens there all the time."

Ben shook his head. The data he had about Caitline indicated many things. All of it was conflicting.

"If Caitline has been kidnapped, how does that threaten our national security?" Ben asked.

"How much evidence do you need?" Rykert asked. "They've learned to export their violence over the Internet. Gibson's death confirms it." Rykert leaned forward with an expression of concern. "All I'm saying is that we need to show solidarity at this point."

"And ignore the truth?" Ben replied.

"What truth?" Rykert asked.

"Where Web(W)rights gets its income," Ben said.

Rykert appeared startled by Ben's response. He repositioned his coat across his knees in an effort to recover his composure.

"If we're to get Caitline back," Rykert said. "Yes."

Ben stood at the foot of Rykert's chair.

"And maintain the status quo," Ben replied clenching his fist. "We both know who benefits from that."

"Maybe that's the difference between us," Rykert said as he edged back in his chair. "What we're willing to sacrifice."

Zarima reentered the room.

"Are you ready to go?" Zarima asked.

Ben's fingernails dug into the meat of his palms. Where did this virtual pimp get off telling him how Caitline felt? He wondered if that was that how Jennifer had characterized him, sanctimonious and unfeeling?

"Let us get out of here," Zarima demanded. "The sooner the better."

Ben relaxed his fingers. Rykert ordered Zarima to get her clothes as he put on his coat. Zarima opened the hall closet, grabbed a battered knapsack from its peg, and draped a Russian field jacket across her shoulders.

Ben turned his palm upwards. Blood oozed from the corner of the half-moon puncture in the flesh beneath the thumb. He sucked the wound dry as he followed Rykert and Zarima to the front door. Zarima turned, spotted Ben spitting blood into the flower garden, and examined Ben's hand. She glared at Rykert.

"He cannot leave with this," Zarima declared,

She drew Ben back inside, knelt on one knee, and opened her knapsack. Pushing aside a battered Gideon's Bible, she produced a rusty tin kit with a Red Cross painted on the top. Zarima unscrewed the top of a brown vial, pulled Ben's injured hand toward her, turned his palm upwards, and poised the vial opening over the wound.

"This is going to hurt," Zarima warned.

"There's no time for this," Rykert admonished.

Zarima dribbled the brown oily contents onto Ben's hand.

Ben winced. Zarima was right. It did hurt, a lot.

Zarima stretched a Band-Aid across Ben's wound, restored the bottle to its container, and returned the tin to her gym bag.

"The first rule after any enemy encounter," Zarima said to Rykert as she stood up. "Treat the wounded."

"I'm not your enemy," Rykert said.

"How do I know that?" Zarima retorted. "Everyone can be your enemy at some point. It just takes the right circumstances."

She draped her bag over her left shoulder and marched through the front doorway. Ben followed. Zarima walked with an easy sway to her hips as if she could maintain the pace for miles.

When they reached the gate, Zarima held it open for the men to pass. After they had passed through, she pulled a metal key from a side pocket in her bag and cranked it in the lock.

"Why bother?" Ben asked. "Do you ever expect to return here again?"

"It is always best to take care of one's home no matter how long or far away you go," Zarima replied. "You may wish to return to it later."

Ben said nothing. He wondered whether he had ever felt that way about his home, or his family. He watched Rykert escort her toward his blue Audi parked down the street.

"Where are you taking her?" Ben asked.

"Police headquarters for starters," Rykert replied. "Bergstrom and Stanfeld will want to ask her a few questions before they spirit her to a safe house."

Ben started toward his motorcycle.

"Where do you think you're going?" Rykert called.

"Not with you," Ben said.

"I think you might reconsider," Rykert replied as he reached into his coat pocket.

"Pulling a gun won't change my mind," Ben admonished.

Rykert pulled his key ring from his pocket and unlocked the front passenger door of the Audi.

"I didn't think I had to," Rykert said as he returned his door opener to his pocket. "From where I stand I don't think you have many choices as a rational human being."

"Who wants to be rational?" Ben asked.

"Jennifer said you'd respond with something like that," Rykert replied. "Really, Hackwell, you have no other options."

"What makes you think so?" Ben asked.

"Where are you going to go?" Rykert asked. "The police have your home staked out. You can't leave the city. All the squad cars have your description. It's just a matter of time before they pick you up."

"I'll think of something," Ben declared.

"I'm sure," Rykert replied.

Rykert guided Zarima into the front seat, closed the door behind her, and rounded the car.

"Bergstrom told me to tell you he'd do all he can for you if you came in of your own accord," Rykert said. "If the police pick you up he can't promise you anything."

Ben shook his head. He knew he was supposed to be impressed by Rykert's connections with the authorities.

"I prefer the latter," Ben replied.

"Have you considered what Caitline might prefer?" Rykert asked.

Ben watched Rykert slide inside and his Audi glide down the block. He returned to his cycle and started it up. What Caitline might prefer, Ben thought. Rykert sounded so superior. Who knew what any teenage girl thought? Or wanted?

Ben rested his elbow on the handle grip. He wanted to believe that Caitline's behavior defied any simple explanation like acting out. But so much of the data he had uncovered about her indicated the opposite.

Ben shook his head. He had wanted to be a good father. How was he supposed to trust Jennifer or Rykert or anyone else when every bit of data he had about them revealed the flaw in their motives?

He recalled that he had told Kim the same thing just hours ago. Why had Kim trusted him? Why would he alone know what Caitline wanted?

Call it paternal love, call it what you will, Ben thought. He knew that Caitline wanted to be saved by him.

Ben headed toward Uptown. He recalled the security expert's axiom: When in doubt, think like the hacker trying to break into your system. If he couldn't think like a Wahhabi, he needed to consult one, or someone who knew about them.

He slowed his cycle and scanned the sidewalks for a pay phone. Why hadn't he purchased new batteries for his cell phone when he had the chance?

Ben stopped at the intersection of Hennepin and Lake. Its streets were deserted, its shops and restaurants dark. All of its revelers, students, and street people had gone home.

Ben cranked the accelerator. At least they had homes to which they could return; some with friends or loved ones. All he had at his house was an eight-year-old stray cat and whichever guard cop had been lowest in the pecking order.

Several blocks beyond he passed an all night restaurant. Through the window, Ben watched an African-American waitress pour coffee for her only customer. He pulled into the parking lot and strode into the building. The odor of industrial strength cleanser overlaid the aromas from a dozen assorted meals. A Hispanic washboy mopped the floor between the men's room and the kitchen.

A wall phone hung beside a stack of children's booster seats in the annex. Ben grabbed the receiver, checked under the shelf for a phonebook, and found nothing. He turned toward the counter and asked the waitress who produced a pristine tome from under the counter.

Ben scanned the listings under Anouri. They extended across two pages.

Concentrate Ben, he told himself. Where might she live?

The Ethiopians had immigrated to the Twin Cities in stages after their civil war ripped the country apart. First their leaders came, then their extended families. Azeb was a recent immigrant who had started working for Jennifer within the last year. It seemed unlikely she could have accumulated enough money to move to the suburbs in that time.

He ran down the list of addresses and eliminated all of those outside the University area. That left seven possibilities. Three of those employed a first initial rather than a first name that suggested a potential female occupant.

Ben keyed in the first number and heard it buzz four times on the other end before Azeb's voice advised in hesitant English to leave a message at the beep.

"Azeb, pick up," Ben urged.

He repeated his request. The tape continued to whir in the background.

"Please, Azeb," Ben implored. "Answer the phone."

The tape clicked and stopped.

"Is Azeb there?" Ben asked. He heard a click followed by the buzz of a dial tone. Ben redialed the number and listened to the four unanswered rings. Her voice mail message came on followed by the beep.

"Azeb, you know who this is," Ben said. "Please answer your phone."

He received no response. Ben figured that the tape would last about a minute before it played out. He had just one ploy left.

"I know that Caitline is alive," Ben said. "You're the only one who can help me."

He heard the receiver lift off its hook.

"This is Mrs. Anouri," Azeb answered.

"Thank god," Ben said.

"Yes," Azeb replied. Her voice sounded official, aloof. "How can I help you?"

Ben hesitated. He did not want to confide too much in her to scare her off.

"I need to contact the religious elders in your community," Ben said. "Could you give me a name and phone number to call?"

He heard rustling as if she were pulling on a housecoat followed by the crunch of metal box springs.

"Forgive me, Mr. Hackwell," Azeb apologized. "But I do not have such information readily available, especially at two in the morning."

"I realize that," Ben replied. "But this is important."

"So you say," Azeb replied. "And how can an imam help you?"

"I need to find out all I can about the Wahhabis," Ben replied.

"Who?" Azeb asked.

"The Wahhabis," Ben repeated.

"There are no Wahhabis in Ethiopia," Azeb said.

"I know," Ben replied. "They're an extremist Islamic sect in Saudi Arabia and Chechnya."

"Why ask one of our leaders about them if they live in another country?" Azeb asked.

"Because the Wahhabis are Muslim," Ben explained. "And they are holding Caitline. I thought one of your leaders might give me insight into how they might act in such a situation."

The other end remained silent. Even the bedsprings did not squeak.

"Are you going to help me?" Ben asked.

"Shh," Azeb said. "I am thinking."

"What are you thinking?" Ben asked politely.

"I am thinking how such an intelligent man could be so offensive," Azeb declared.

"Offensive?" Ben said in surprise.

"Yes, offensive," Azeb declared, her voice rising. "We are a peace-loving people who have tried to live among our American friends as best we can despite many cultural differences. And you think that with a phone call you can find out something about a violent people none of us have ever heard of just because they are Muslim!"

Ben felt abashed. Azeb never had raised her voice to him before.

"I'm sorry. I didn't mean to offend you," Ben replied. He knew he had to be more respectful. "It's just that you're my only link to the Muslim community."

"I do not know anything about the Wahhabis," Azeb declared.

Ben hesitated. Azeb was evading the larger issue.

"What do you know, Azeb?" Ben asked.

"You are making things very difficult for me," Azeb said.

"I do not mean to," Ben replied.

Azeb sighed.

"I know only that Ms. Roloson has had many conversations with Mr. Rykert and a man named Wilson," Azeb confided.

"And?" Ben asked.

"And that they distressed her deeply," Azeb added.

"How do you know that?" Ben replied.

"Because she said so," Azeb said. "I am not supposed to listen in, but I heard her say many times how the things they discussed were hurtful to her."

"Hurtful?" Ben asked, surprised. "Are you sure that is the word she used?"

"Yes," Azeb declared. "Many times."

"Think carefully, Azeb," Ben said. "Did you ever hear Jennifer say HURTFUL.com?"

"She may have," Azeb confirmed after a pause. "Yes, I think she did."

Ben felt exultant. And bereft. No wonder Jennifer was so interested in his involvement, and so reluctant to promote it.

"Mr. Hackwell," Azeb said.

"Yes?" Ben replied.

"You will not tell Ms. Roloson that I told you?" Azeb asked.

"Of course not," Ben declared.

"Many thank you's," Azeb replied. She sounded relieved. "Ms. Roloson has been so kind that I did not wish to add to her misery when her hurt is so great."

"I don't think—" Ben began.

"Even as her once husband I am sure that you understand," Azeb interrupted.

"What?" Ben asked.

"That you are the cause of all this hurt," Azeb said.

Ben felt chagrined. And angry. He had considered Azeb to be on his side.

"Do you honestly think that Jennifer cares at all about me?" Ben retorted.

"Where once there is love…" Azeb began.

"Go on," Ben encouraged.

"Your daughter is representative of that," Azeb said.

"And the Chechnyans are doing all they can to destroy it," Ben replied.

"Are you sure that it is they who are doing the destroying?" Azeb asked.

Ben felt the warning hairs rising on the back of his neck. Was Azeb going to blame him for Caitline's behavior, too?

"What are you getting at?" Ben asked.

"When the parents fight, it is usually the children that suffer," Azeb said. "I am sure that you know this."

"But I'm the one who's trying to save her," Ben protested.

"Do you not think that Ms. Roloson would say the same thing?" Azeb replied.

"We've been all over that!" Ben cried. "You were there. You've seen us."

"I have witnessed two people tearing at each other," Azeb said.

"But—" Ben began.

"Ask yourself what your motives are," Azeb declared. "Are you trying to find your daughter just to save her? Or are you trying to win her back? And beat your wife in the process."

"I'm doing it for Caitline's benefit alone," Ben declared.

"And what if she should decide that it benefits her most to stay with Ms. Roloson?" Azeb asked.

Ben hesitated. He had not thought beyond his goal of finding his daughter.

"What right do you have to question my motives?" Ben huffed. "I'm her father!"

"Of course. I have heard Ms. Roloson say much the same thing," Azeb retorted. "But a loving parent does what is best for the child."

"And what's best for Caitline is to keep her away from me like I'm some kind of animal?" Ben retorted. "I'm not the one permitting her to alter her appearance. We might not even be searching for her if Jennifer hadn't put her in harm's way."

"I am afraid I do not understand," Azeb said.

"Maybe Caitline wouldn't have attracted a thug like Wilson if she looked like a normal 16 year old," Ben declared.

"That I cannot say," Azeb replied. "I do know that Ms. Caitline is a very attractive girl."

Ben was not mollified by Azeb's compliment.

"The best breasts money can buy I'm sure," Ben muttered.

"Mr. Hackwell," Azeb declared. "That is no way to speak of any woman, particularly if she is your daughter."

Ben felt abashed. Once again, he had managed to offend the only person who was willing and able to help him. He felt angry, too. He was not a diplomat.

"I'm sorry if what I said offended you," Ben apologized. "It was a statement born of frustration. But sometimes the data we have to work with can be seen as offensive."

"What data?" Azeb asked.

Ben hesitated. He did not want to alienate his lone confidant further.

"The data regarding the exaggerated proportions of Caitline's body," Ben said as delicately as he could.

"I have only seen your daughter a few times," Azeb said. "I saw nothing out of the ordinary about Ms. Caitline's body."

"When was the last time you saw her?" Ben asked.

"Several months ago," Azeb admitted. "Last fall, I think."

"And she didn't look unnatural to you?" Ben asked.

"In what way?" Azeb asked.

"That she had been physically augmented," Ben explained. "That her appearance had been enhanced."

"I saw nothing like you describe," Azeb replied. "At the time all I saw was that she seemed to be very excited about working with Mr. Rykert for her mother's cooperative."

"The WABC?" Ben asked in surprise.

"Yes," Azeb confirmed. "She was very passionate about helping women from other countries such as myself come to the United States."

Ben felt stunned by Azeb's revelation. Jennifer's story about Caitline's breast implants had been a total fabrication. Why?

"You never heard anything about Jennifer needing money?" Ben replied in disbelief. "Or about Caitline's surgery?"

"Never," Azeb said. "Ms. Roloson did talk a great deal about the difficulties they had in getting some of us out."

Azeb lowered her voice.

"There was some money involved in that," Azeb confided. "For bribes, I think." Azeb sighed. "Some of our people are more involved with material possessions than they should be."

Ben felt helpless, empty. Why had all of this information been kept from him?

"Why didn't you tell me this before?" Ben asked.

"Ms. Roloson asked me not to tell anyone," Azeb replied.

"Is that why Caitline was kidnapped?" Ben asked.

"That I do not know," Azeb replied. "But, I do know that Ms. Roloson has done everything in her power to get her back."

"In what way?" Ben retorted. "What is she doing besides issuing writs?"

"She is negotiating with her daughter's captors," Azeb answered.

"Through Rykert?" Ben scoffed. "That Wall Street reject knows only how to get more money."

"He is indeed helping," Azeb said. "He has offered to trade for Ms. Caitline's release."

"Trade what?" Ben hooted. "Virtual air?"

"His company," Azeb responded. "The one you call Web(W)rights."

CHAPTER 23

▼

"You're joking," Ben said.

"I would not joke about a thing like that," Azeb said.

Ben dropped the receiver. When Rykert had said he was ready to sacrifice, Ben did not think that Rykert meant his company. Ben possessed nothing to top that.

"Mr. Hackwell," Azeb asked. "Are you there?"

Ben picked up the receiver.

"I'm here," Ben said.

"I thought I had lost you," Azeb replied.

"You're sure he was referring to his company?" Ben asked.

"Many times I heard him say he would offer the Web rights to bring Caitline back," Azeb replied.

"That's not the same thing as his company," Ben said.

"And why not?" Azeb asked.

"They just sound the same," Ben replied.

"I do not understand," Azeb said.

"His company name has an extra W in front of the R," Ben explained. He realized that spelling the word would not help Azeb understand the distinction. Ben summoned his seldom-accessed data files from college. "It's what we call a homonym in English."

"Why would Mr. Rykert offer something that is not his to give?" Azeb asked.

"That's a good question," Ben replied.

"Are you saying Mr. Rykert is a bad man?" Azeb asked.

"No," Ben said. As much as Ben wanted to believe otherwise, the data Azeb had given him had complicated his perception of Rykert.

"I am glad. He and Ms. Caitline helped bring me and my family to America," Azeb explained. "I owe them many debts."

Ben hesitated. He wondered what proof he had that would convince Azeb of Rykert's complicity without alienating her entirely.

"Why would the Wahhabis want his company?" Ben asked.

"That I do not know," Azeb replied.

Ben decided that he needed to put his questions another way.

"Why offer them the Internet rights when they have no respect or need for them?" Ben asked.

"Again, I do not know," Azeb said. "I do know that I would not hurt Ms. Roloson if there were 100 Wahhabis and I knew everything about them!"

Ben heard her receiver slam into its cradle followed by the drone of the open phone connection. He hung up and stared into deserted dining room. For the first time, he appreciated what having people skills meant.

"Are you here for takeout?" the waitress asked Ben as she totaled up the night's receipts at the cash register.

"No," Ben replied. He noted the raspberry birthmark running up her neck and the underside of her jaw. Ben shook his head for emphasis and slid into the nearby booth. "Coffee, black."

"The dining room's closed," the waitress said and pointed up at the sunburst wall clock. "It's after closing time."

"I thought this was an all-night restaurant," Ben replied.

"It used to be, but business didn't warrant it," the waitress replied as her hazel eyes measured Ben. She placed her hands on her hips. "Too much trouble."

"Where can I get something to eat?" Ben asked.

"How should I know this time of night?" the waitress replied and lifted the receiver off its hook. "C'mon, be a good guy and don't make trouble."

Ben knew that the waitress would call the police if he argued with her further. He started toward the exit.

"Doesn't a guy like you have a home to go to?" the waitress called out as she lowered the receiver.

Ben spotted the crinkle in her eyes that he hadn't noticed before.

"What makes you think so?" Ben asked.

A guarded smile darted across the waitress' face.

"You seem like a decent enough guy," the waitress said.

"Thanks," Ben replied and stepped into the vestibule. He zipped up his jacket as he contemplated his options. He could not think of many.

"Here," the waitress said as she handed Ben a 16 ounce paper cup topped with three packets each of powdered cream and sugar on its cardboard cover along with two plastic stirring rods. "It's extra black," she added with a smile that revealed her gold front tooth. "For the road."

Ben reached for his wallet.

"It's on the house," the waitress declared.

Ben heard the door lock snap and watched the waitress bustle into the kitchen. He hadn't noticed whether she wore a nametag. Ben strode to his motorcycle, started the engine, and raised the cup to his lips. The first sip had that burnt taste of coffee that had been sitting too long on the warmer.

He emptied all six packets into the cup, stirred until he felt certain the ingredients had blended, and sipped again. The warm liquid coursed down the walls of his empty stomach. It tasted hot, sweet, and lumpy, but better than before.

Ben took another swallow and wondered why the waitress had bothered to give him coffee when she already had chased him out the door. He wrapped his hands around the cup and sipped again. Whatever her motives, Ben thought, the coffee she had given him had refortified his thinking.

He leaned against his handlebars. His conversation with Azeb had revealed two bits of data whose implications he had not yet fully processed. One, that Caitline's disappearance was more than simple adolescent acting out. That's why Jennifer had tried to hide it from him with her tale about Caitline's breast implants. Two, that Rykert had upped the ante. Rather than just find Caitline, Ben realized now that he had to win her back. With the help of the FBI, Rykert and Jennifer were employing all the conventional means of ransoming Caitline with little success. What would a group of terrorists do with the Web rights to Hoot's network anyway? If terrorists wanted something, they just took it. Ben had learned that lesson in Mogadishu.

To defeat Wilson and the Wahhabis Ben decided that he needed to employ a less conventional approach. He needed a killer application to destroy the Web site itself, some Trojan Horse or Red 8 virus to penetrate and render the site inoperative. All of his security information was located at his office or at home that were off limits to him now. Nor did he have access to the Internet. Where could he get that?

Ben took another sip and felt the warmth surge in his veins. He swirled the dregs and stared at the vortex. He wondered who besides the waitress would take the chance on helping him.

Kim, Ben realized. Not only had she helped him evade the police, but she also had a personal computer. He remembered seeing it on her desk when he visited her room. He knew that her PC was a mid-model Dell, but at least he could get Internet access if she was willing to do it.

Ben's next problem was where to set it up. The police guard would be posted at his house until the manhunt produced results.

Ben downed the dregs of his coffee. He'd worry about where once he got Kim's commitment. To obtain that he needed access to another phone.

Ben tossed the cup toward the trash container and sped down the street. He found a telephone stand in the parking lot of an all-night convenience store four blocks east on Lake Street. The booth's phone binder was eviscerated, but a concentration of memory and will enabled Ben to elicit Kim's phone number from his memory banks.

Kim's phone rang five times before its software transferred to voice mail.

> "Hi, this is Kim. I'm not here right now, but please leave a message at the beep and I'll get back to you as soon as I can. Have a wonderful day."

Ben counted the seconds. After seven, he heard a beep.

"Hello, Kim," Ben said. "This is Benjamin. Ben. Your landlord?"

The sound of the tape machine's broken connection blared in Ben's ear.

"This is Kim," Kim said.

"Hi," Ben replied.

"Hi," Kim answered.

"You're not mad at me?" Ben asked.

"Should I be?" Kim asked.

"You seemed pretty reluctant to help me earlier," Ben said.

"Oh, that," Kim replied.

Ben ignored the casualness of Kim's reply, grateful to speak to someone who sympathized with his situation.

"I wouldn't have put you in such a spot unless I really needed your help," Ben explained.

"I know that," Kim answered.

Ben hesitated. He felt reluctant to enlist Kim's help again. Yet, he had no one else he felt he could trust.

"Listen," Ben said. "I need your help again."

"I figured that when you called at three in the morning," Kim replied.

"If you'd rather I didn't bother you, just say so," Ben said.

"It's no bother," Kim said.

"Why am I feeling otherwise?" Ben asked.

"It's just me, one of my moods," Kim said and giggled. "What do you want?"

"I need to use your computer," Ben said.

"I can't," Kim replied.

Ben was not surprised by Kim's refusal. He wondered what changed her mind.

"I thought you said you weren't mad at me," Ben said.

"I'm not," Kim replied.

"Then why can't I use it?" Ben asked.

"Duh," Kim retorted. "Because the cops are still at your front door?"

Ben felt ridiculous. Getting Kim's computer past the guards was impossible. He ran down his list of alternatives. Hoot never would have let him forget it if he knew Ben had planned to enter a target and failed to account for all the possibilities involved.

"Hey," Kim said with an amused snicker. "You know who does have a computer available?"

"No," Ben replied irritably.

"I thought you were interested," Kim said.

Ben paused, irritated by his ineptitude. Having already had alienated Azeb, he could not afford to alienate his only other ally.

"OK, OK," Ben said and tried to quell the impatience in his voice. "Who?"

"Tyler's mother," Kim replied.

"Great," Ben retorted. "How is her computer going to help me?"

"It's what you need, isn't it?" Kim answered.

"Yes," Ben admitted.

"And it's away from your apartment?" Kim added.

"Yes," Ben replied. He did not like the direction this conversation was taking. He had to convince Kim that her plan was not a viable alternative. "Tyler's mother is not going to let someone she doesn't even know access her computer."

"You're Tyler's landlord, aren't you?" Kim responded.

"Yes," Ben replied.

"Well?" Kim asked.

"Isn't she going to suspect something?" Ben protested.

"Suspect what?" Kim replied.

"That something's wrong," Ben said.

"Isn't it?" Kim asked.

"But—" Ben protested.

"You don't have to tell her the details," Kim interrupted. "Geez, didn't you ever take Coping with Parents 101?"

Ben felt foolish at the futility of his arguments.

Kim giggled.

"You don't like Tyler very well, do you?" Kim observed.

"Oh, it's not that," Ben equivocated.

"C'mon, admit it," Kim said. "Tyler really bugs you, doesn't he?"

Ben bit his tongue. Their conversation seemed so juvenile, he wished it would end. Yet, he also knew that he had no other allies he could count on.

"Your silence is an admission of guilt," Kim declared and giggled again. "But don't worry. Tyler bugs everybody. He's really a pretty decent guy once you get to know him."

"I'm sure," Ben said without conviction.

"He looks up to you, you know," Kim said.

"What?" Ben asked. Tyler never revealed anything other than his displeasure at any of Ben's actions.

"You're the closest thing to a father he has," Kim declared.

Ben said nothing. Kim's revelation surprised him.

"You're kidding," Ben said.

"Don't tell me you didn't know that," Kim said.

"I didn't," Ben admitted.

"It's true," Kim said and yawned. "I need to get some sleep. When do you want to do this?"

"As soon as possible," Ben said with relief. "Where does Tyler's mother live?"

"Not far from here, maybe half a mile," Kim replied and yawned again. "Somewhere off Lake Street, I think. Don't worry, I'll get the address from Tyler before we meet."

"Where should that be?" Ben asked.

"At the corner on Cedar Avenue?" Kim said. "That should be far enough away."

"Is eight o'clock all right?" Ben asked.

"Make it nine," Kim replied sleepily. "I need my beauty sleep."

"Thanks," Ben said, surprised at the warmth he had instilled in that one word.

"Sounds like a plan," Kim concurred and stifled a dreamy yawn. "And don't worry. Tyler's mother won't even be there. Or Tyler, either, if you're lucky."

Kim's end of the line went dead. Ben envied Kim's ability to return to sleep. Now that he had a plan, all he needed was to lie low for a couple of hours until their appointment. He'd worry about what virus to employ once he accessed the HURTFUL Web site.

Ben pulled an Army blanket from his saddlebags and positioned his cycle beside the wall of the store. Wrapping the blanket around his shoulders, he propped his wrapped-up toolkit on his right shoulder, and nestled his head against the bricks.

A car horn woke him after a fitful few hours. Ben massaged his neck and shoulder as he purchased a roll and coffee and proceeded toward their rendezvous point. He figured that it was better to stay on the move to avoid the police and any informers who might suspect a middle-aged cyclist loitering beside a convenience store.

Ben considered what vulnerabilities he knew about a PHP Web site. There weren't many. Most of the processing occurred away from the point of access. Hoot's distribution network parceled the processing even further. You might shut down one or two nodes, but the rest of the system compensated for the outages.

At five minutes to nine, Ben approached their meeting spot, hoping that Kim would not employ her female prerogative of arriving late. He spotted her sitting on the curb watching traffic, looped his cycle across the street in a big arc, and stopped in front of her.

Kim climbed on behind him.

"Let's get going before someone spots us," Kim urged. "Tyler promised to meet us there."

Ben doubted Tyler would be as prompt. They turned onto Cedar Avenue and reached Tyler's mother's house ten minutes later. No one stood waiting for them in front of the stucco bungalow.

"He promised to meet us here," Kim said.

Ben felt relieved that he would not have to deal with Tyler.

"Was he coming from somewhere?" Ben asked.

"He made the call from here," Kim said.

"Maybe he's inside," Ben suggested.

The door of the three-season porch was unlocked.

"Tyler?" Kim called.

"Mrs. Olsen?" Ben called.

Ben opened the front oak door, and they called Tyler and his mother again.

"He must have stepped out for a moment," Kim decided.

"And left both front doors unlocked?" Ben said.

"We do it all the time at home," Kim replied.

"Not in South Minneapolis, you don't," Ben responded.

Ben entered the small living room rendered tinier by the three oak curio cabinets filled with Swedish flags and Vikings bobble-head dolls. The kitchen countertops were clean, the utensils put away in their bins.

He peered down the hallway, checked the bathroom, and opened the door at the other end. An IBM XC stood on the counter of a roll top writing desk.

Ben sat in the carved oak chair and warm-booted the PC. A "C" prompt appeared in the upper right corner of the screen. He keyed in a DIR prompt, and scanned the index as it rolled past. Keying in a Windows command, he clicked the Netscape icon and waited for its startup file to conclude.

"Oh, good!" Kim exclaimed. "You've got it going!"

"For all the good that does me," Ben complained. "It's a Telnet connection."

"Does that matter?" Kim asked.

"In this case it does," Ben replied. "Telnet operates over the phone lines and employs a password to complete the connection. The only trouble is that I don't know the password."

"That's classified information," Tyler announced as he set a tall paper bag on the dining room table. The cork and neck of a wine bottle peeped above the bag top. "What's he doing here?"

"Using your Mom's computer," Kim replied. "Where were you?"

"Down the street," Tyler answered.

Kim turned back to the monitor. Tyler frowned.

"You said you wanted to use it," Tyler declared.

"I do," Kim replied and beamed a huge smile at Tyler. "I don't remember your putting any restrictions on what I did with it."

"You know he's a fugitive, don't you?" Tyler said. "He set fire to his own house."

"Don't be ridiculous," Kim declared and turned toward Ben for confirmation. "It was an electrical fire, wasn't it, Mr. Hackwell?"

Ben nodded. He had decided not to interfere. He had no currency with Tyler, but he couldn't wait all day for Kim to convince Tyler to give her the password.

"See?" Kim said.

"Hmpf. That doesn't prove anything," Tyler said and folded his arms across his chest. "He's a programmer and electrical engineer. He fixed it to look like an accident."

"What makes you so sure?" Kim asked.

"It's on the AFI Web site," Tyler replied.

"So what?" Kim asked in a huff.

"So, they get their stuff from the horse's mouth," Tyler declared. "Surveillance feeds, inter-department communications, the whole bit. The Feds know all that crap about his daughter is just a cover-up."

"For what?" Kim asked.

"For fixing it to look like she murdered William Gibson," Tyler said as he eyed Ben cynically. "At least he finally fixed something."

Ben had had enough. He needed access to a computer, but not with this much criticism of his motives.

"Look, Tyler, I know we haven't seen eye to eye on a lot of things," Ben said and scratched the back of his head in search of his next move. Criticizing the AFI and its motives would aggravate the animosity between them. Maybe simple forthrightness would work. "I also know we don't like each other very much. For that reason alone I wouldn't come to you for help unless I absolutely had to."

Tyler's face remained a mask.

"But I need your help now," Ben entreated. "You're my only chance to find out whether my daughter's still alive."

"Do you believe him?" Tyler asked Kim.

Kim nodded. Tyler sighed.

"olsensmom01," Tyler said. "Plus the university code following the at sign."

"Thanks," Kim acknowledged while she hugged Tyler and grinned at Ben. "We appreciate it, don't we?"

Ben grunted and concentrated on keying the code into the query box. Having a girl plead on your behalf was humiliating enough, Ben thought, But receiving permission from a person you could barely stand seemed intolerable.

He glanced at Kim as the software went through its verification routine. She watched him expectantly while Tyler remained indifferent to everything Ben did except Kim's reaction to what Ben was doing. Ben wondered if Kim handled everything in her life with evasions and half-truths. Or, was he being too judgmental?

The University home page displayed onscreen.

"Now what?" Tyler asked.

Ben scratched his chin. With this mid-age PC he might be able to do very little. He keyed HURTFUL.com into the address line. The pierced hearts filled the screen with blood.

"Cool," Tyler murmured.

"Ee-yiew," Kim responded. "That's your daughter's Web site?"

"It gets worse," Ben apologized. "You might want to leave the room."

"Don't worry about me," Kim declared.

Ben scanned the Index page options and clicked on View Source. Aside from the title line, the screen showed a gray expanse.

"What now, hotshot?" Tyler asked.

"Shut up, Tyler," Kim ordered and grabbed Ben's shoulder as show of encouragement. "Go ahead, Mr. Hackwell."

Ben felt the intensity of Kim's belief coursing through his shirt. He concentrated on the problem before him. With PCP programming all the operations performed in self-contained programs that ran off site. But, the more complex video, audio, and tactile interfaces might not, Ben thought. He returned to the index and pressed the selection that featured his daughter. The boxes that requested his credit card numbers appeared. He keyed in the information, and the image onscreen flashed to the murky bedroom with a bound Caitline lying on the bed.

"That's your daughter?" Kim gasped.

Ben nodded as Wilson's whip-wielding image stalked into the room. Kim's grip tightened at the first retort. Ben froze the image when Wilson raised his whip again. Kim relaxed her grip on Ben's shoulder. He opened a WordPad file and keyed in a dozen lines of text.

"What's that?" Kim asked.

"Programming language," Ben said.

"I don't recognize it," Tyler said.

"Good," Ben answered. He finished typing, turned, and smiled. "Few people do any more."

"What is it?" Kim asked.

"A little basic FORTRAN," Ben replied.

"What are you going to do with it?" Kim asked.

"I'm going to drop a bomb on AFI's operation," Ben said.

"Hmpf," Tyler scoffed. "How will a few characters of ancient code do that?"

"Watch and learn," Ben said.

Ben rebooted the computer, copied the lines of Fortran text from the computer's Word Pad file, reentered the HURTFUL.com Web site, and selected the same video. When the payment screen popped up, he pasted his text into the payment window.

"That'll keep 'em occupied for a while," Ben exulted. He closed the site with a flourish and waggled his index finger at them. "Don't either of you try this at home."

"Geesh, try what?" Tyler retorted. Kim giggled nervously. "So you inserted some ancient garbage characters in a payment box. So what?"

Ben draped his arm around Kim's shoulders and drew her toward him. He needed her support.

"All the financial networks used to use COBOL," Ben said.

"So?" Tyler replied.

"So, they have to respect FORTRAN because it's a legitimate code," Ben explained. "But the few little bugs I've put in will tie up their software for days. No one will know how to fix it."

"They will eventually," Tyler observed.

"Perhaps," Ben admitted. "But Wilson and his Wahhabi friends are not going to use a weapon that doesn't work every time. Without it there's no sense in their hanging on to Caitline."

"That," Tyler agreed. "Or she becomes expendable."

Ben removed his forearm from Kim's shoulders, aware that Tyler's alternative scenario was a real possibility. Tyler replaced Ben's arm with his own around Kim's shoulders.

"I'm sure your plan is great," Kim encouraged. "I just hope it works."

"Yeah," Ben replied as he shut down the computer. "Me, too."

CHAPTER 24

▼

The young couple left in Tyler's Ford Fiesta with minimal leave-taking a few minutes later. Ben drove to the nearby branch of the public library and read computer magazines to stay awake. Stifling another series of yawns after an hour, he reasoned that should have been enough time for his programming bug to work.

Ben tried to access the site from one of the branch library's pre-Pentium model PCs. Their filtering software responded with the message that his access had been denied. The other terminal responded with the same message. Ben recalled the hullabaloo in the Metro section of the newspaper over restrictions on public access to the Internet. He left the building and drove to his bank's nearest ATM machine. He decided to access the HURTFUL.com site through one of the Internet cafes in the Uptown, but he needed more money than the singles and change in his pocket.

A sheet of paper flapped in the breeze above the money dispenser. The caption beneath the grainy photocopy of his PHD identification photo read:

> Benjamin Franklin Hackwell. Height: 6 foot, 1 inch. Weight: 210 lbs. Eyes: gray, Hair: reddish-blond to gray. Wanted for questioning on charges of kidnapping, conspiracy, and terrorism. If you see him or know of his whereabouts, contact 911 or the police tip line. Do not approach. This man is considered extremely dangerous.

Ben sped off. Stanfeld and Bergstrom had worked fast. His photocopied image was probably over every ATM machine in the Twin Cities. Accessing HURTFUL via a public Internet connection was out. He needed a private line and someone with a vested interest in helping him.

He found another pay phone on Cedar Avenue and dialed Jennifer's home number. Since Rykert had confided their ransom negotiations to Ben, it would seem reasonable for him to inquire about their progress. He'd withhold the news about his virus infestation for the proper moment.

"This is Jennifer Roloson," Jennifer answered.

"This is Benjamin Hackwell, your ex-husband," Ben replied.

"Yes," Jennifer said.

"Have you heard anything about Caitline?" Ben asked.

"Should I have?" Jennifer said.

Ben hesitated. Was Jennifer being coy, or evasive?

"I was wondering about the progress of the negotiations," Ben said.

"I know nothing about any negotiations," Jennifer declared.

Jennifer's response seemed to Ben unlikely.

"Your boyfriend hasn't said anything to you?" Ben persisted.

"I'd prefer that you keep Avery out of our discussions," Jennifer demanded.

"I don't see how I can," Ben responded and chuckled at Jennifer's discomfiture. "He told me last night that you and he were negotiating to get Caitline back."

The staccato of a distant jackhammer sounded through the other end of the line.

"Jennifer, are you still there?" Ben asked.

"Yes," Jennifer said.

"What about Rykert?" Ben demanded.

"What about him?" Jennifer replied.

"Is he negotiating Caitline's release or not?" Ben asked.

"Yes," Jennifer replied.

Ben grimaced. Jennifer's admission confirmed his suspicions about her actions.

"You knew Caitline was missing all along, didn't you?" Ben asked.

Jennifer said nothing.

"DIDN'T YOU!" Ben repeated.

"I don't see what this has to do with recovering—" Jennifer said.

"You don't?" Ben cried. "When you knew all along that Caitline was involved with terrorists?"

"I only learned they were terrorists when you got involved," Jennifer explained. "Until then I thought we were dealing simply with kidnappers."

"Glad I could clear that up for you," Ben retorted with regret. The more he data he uncovered, it seemed the more was left for him to find. "Is that why you decided to represent me at my hearing?"

"You are her father," Jennifer replied. "And two investigators are always better than one."

Ben clenched his fist to control his fury. Confirming that his role as Jennifer's agent was all he meant to her stirred the ashes of his anger.

"What has Rykert told you?" Ben asked.

"That the negotiations were still proceeding," Jennifer responded.

"That's all?" Ben asked.

"That and that he's offered them his company in exchange for Caitline," Jennifer replied.

He had recovered all this information from his phone call to Azeb. He wondered what Jennifer's take was on it.

"What good are rights to a bunch of terrorists?" Ben asked. "You know as well as I do the government will invalidate the domain names as soon as Rykert tells them."

"It's the gesture," Jennifer replied.

Ben dug his fingernails under Zarima's bandage to sidetrack his increasing frustration. The pain was significant, but tolerable.

"Why do you believe Rykert?" Ben asked.

"If you can't guess," Jennifer replied. "I can't begin to tell you."

"That's no answer," Ben exclaimed.

"He's there when I need him," Jennifer said.

"And I'm not?" Ben retorted.

Jennifer remained silent. Ben stared dumbly at the receiver, furious at the sense of his own impotence. He decided that a show of contrition might convince her to help him.

"I need to check the HURTFUL interface," Ben said. "You're the only one who can help."

"Why?" Jennifer asked.

"I don't have access to a computer to check it myself," Ben replied.

The sound of the drill filled the other end of the line.

"Are you going to help me or not?" Ben asked.

Ben heard the click of the closed connection. He looked out the booth and stared at the shoppers entering and leaving the K-Mart behind his booth. For a while he thought he had penetrated Jennifer's defenses. For a while he thought they had reconnected. For a while he thought that searching for their daughter had reunited them. He discovered instead that he had so betrayed Jennifer's trust that the only third parties she trusted now were pimps and frauds.

Ben flung open the phone booth door. Who else would let him use their computer? Kim was at class. Tyler? Without Kim he'd hardly allow Ben to use his mother's PC again.

He glanced toward an Internet café across the street. With his photo plastered above every free or public pay terminal accessing a site like HURTFUL insured a response from the authorities.

Ben paused and reconsidered. Perhaps the authorities were what he needed.

He re-entered the phone booth and dialed 911. When an official male voice asked him to state the nature of his call, Ben requested the local number of the FBI and was transferred to its voice mail system to endure a list of options to the final request that he stay on the line.

"This is the Federal Bureau of Investigations," a cultivated, female voice responded. "How may we help you?"

"I would like to speak with Agent Barbara Stanfeld," Ben said.

"One moment," the operator said.

A string of connections linked him to Stanfeld's phone where it burred six times before the operator asked if he wanted to access her voice mail.

"I haven't time," Ben replied. "Is Agent Lockett available?"

"Who?" the operator asked.

"Agent Lisa Lockett," Ben repeated.

"Sir, there is no one—"

"She's a CIA agent," Ben interrupted. "She is liaisoning with Agent Stanfeld on a case in Eden Prairie."

"Sir," the operator responded. "I don't believe Agent Lockett is available."

Ben grinned. He'd confirmed that the FBI was collaborating with the CIA.

"Tell her that Avery Rykert wishes to speak with her," Ben requested.

More clicks followed.

"This is Agent Lockett," Lockett answered.

"Hello," Ben replied. "This is Avery Ry—"

"Mr. Hackwell?" Lockett interrupted. "Is that you?"

"Yes," Ben admitted, regretting that his skills at impersonation had diminished so greatly. "I need your help."

"What makes you think I want to help you?" Lockett asked.

"You don't," Ben said. He saw no reason to prevaricate now. "I need yours."

"By all rights I shouldn't even be speaking to you," Lockett replied. "Why me?"

"I need your expertise," Ben replied.

"My expertise," Lockett said in surprise. "You didn't seem to appreciate my expertise the last time we met."

"Sorry," Ben said. He had apologized to so many people already, why not another, he reasoned. "I need your computer."

"Why?" Lockett asked.

"You may have heard I don't have access to my own," Ben said dryly.

"I was aware of that," Lockett acknowledged.

"And, given my current circumstances," Ben added. "I don't have access to any others."

"And you thought that I would let you use mine?" Lockett retorted.

"Yes," Ben replied.

"That's a bold request for someone on the run," Lockett observed.

Ben decided he was beyond debating whether he acted out of audacity or desperation.

"Look, Ms. Lockett," Ben said. "I know you started tracing this call the moment you figured out who was on the other end of the line. I also know I should be a thousand miles away by now, but my daughter's in trouble and I need someone to allow me access to a computer to determine if I can find her."

"You think you can just walk into an FBI building and access their computers?" Lockett replied in disbelief.

"No," Ben corrected. "I need someone to check a Web site on theirs."

"What's in it for us?" Lockett asked.

"Preventing a major Internet shutdown," Ben replied. He decided to personalize his appeal. "And helping a father save his daughter."

"C'mon in," Lockett declared, "And we'll consider it."

Ben hesitated. After working with Stanfeld, he doubted whether he could trust any agent that was part of Homeland Security. He needed to determine if Lockett was someone that he could.

"Do you have children?" Ben asked.

"I have not been fortunate enough to have that opportunity," Lockett replied.

"You have a father, Ms. Lockett?" Ben asked.

"Of course," Lockett responded.

"He cares about you?" Ben asked. He figured that was a certainty. He needed to try something more problematic. "Maybe he even worries about your choice of career?"

"He wanted me to stay a librarian," Lockett responded.

"Why?" Ben asked, surprised by his own curiosity.

"He's my father," Lockett said. "He wanted me to be safe."

Ben chuckled.

"I think both of us know he was right," Ben said.

"Who wants to be safe all the time?" Lockett replied.

"I hear that," Ben said and chuckled. He felt glad that they shared something else in common. "Did he tell you not to go into law enforcement?"

"Most of the time he was pretty supportive," Lockett said.

"Most of the time?" Ben asked.

"Well," Lockett said. "He and Mom had some reservations."

"But, you talked them through," Ben replied.

"It was my decision, actually," Lockett declared.

"And here you are," Ben said. "A full-fledged federal agent."

"Yes," Lockett agreed and cleared her throat. "What does it have to do with your situation?"

Ben hesitated. He wondered how personal he wanted this conversation with Lockett to be.

"My daughter's made some decisions, mostly bad," Ben said. "And I wasn't there to help her with them."

"You can't always prevent children from making mistakes," Lockett said.

Ben knew what Lockett said was true. Why could he not admit it?

"I wouldn't be in the position I am now if I'd been available to my daughter a little more," Ben declared.

"Even if you had been able," Lockett speculated. "Do you think you could you have changed her mind?"

"Maybe not," Ben admitted. "But if I learn what's happened to her, I might be able to prevent something worse."

Ben heard the squeak of Lockett shifting in her chair. He wondered if she was thinking over what he said. Or, was she confirming the trace of his location.

"Tell me this," Lockett said. "Do you think if the situation was reversed that Caitline would do the same for you?"

"I like to think that she would," Ben replied.

"That doesn't seem likely, given the data you've given us about her," Lockett replied. "You're not even sure whether she's been murdered or not."

Lockett had seen to the core of his dilemma, Ben realized. All the data he had about Caitline was conflicting, much of it contradictory or outright antagonistic toward how he felt.

"Sometimes you have to see beyond the data," Ben reflected. "It's the meta-data. It's your interpretation, how you feel and react toward the data you have that constitutes the reality of the situation."

"That doesn't sound very scientific," Lockett said.

"It isn't," Ben admitted. "But it's all you have to go on sometimes if you truly care about someone."

Ben heard Lockett breathing on her end of the line. He had never thought, much less expressed his actions in this way before. Now his fate was up to someone trained to see that her best course of action was to uphold the law.

"What do you want me to do?" Lockett asked.

"Is your Internet connection on?" Ben asked in relief.

"Yes," Lockett replied.

"Try connecting to HURTFUL.com and see what happens," Ben suggested.

Ben heard the wheels of Lockett's desk chair squeak. After a moment, she announced that she had made the connection.

"What now?" Lockett asked.

"Pick the selection 'Busty redhead gets what she really wants,'" Ben said and heard Lockett's suppressed gasp. "Enter it."

"You want me to charge 50 dollars to my credit card for this—"

"I'll pay you back," Ben promised.

Ben waited for Lockett to key in her credit card number. If the application he had inserted worked, the HURTFUL software would not accept it.

"I'm now witnessing your daughter being whipped," Lockett reported. "With my Bureau account charged for the privilege."

"Your card number went through?" Ben asked in surprise.

"Isn't that to be expected?" Lockett replied.

"The bug I inserted fixed it so it couldn't," Ben said.

"The PHP software Gibson used is designed to allow computer graphic inter-face scripts like Fortran to work in its environment," Lockett explained.

Ben shook his head. He wondered how many Wahhabi terrorists knew PHP. Or how to circumvent the kind of killer virus he'd inserted? Who else was work-ing for them?

"Hmmm. This is interesting," Lockett commented. "They kept the file exten-sions."

"Pretty normal for a Web site," Ben said.

"For payment? At a sex site?" Lockett said. "The idea with PHP is to increase security by reducing the amount of site information."

"Can you trace the extensions back?" Ben asked.

"Just a minute," Lockett said and hummed a Beatles tune Ben could not identify while she keyed in her request. "Got it! It's KeepItSafe."

"That's Web(W)rights' security system," Ben declared.

"You think so?" Lockett asked.

Lockett's response to Ben's conclusion upset his own conviction.

"You don't?" Ben asked.

"Somebody with knowledge of online networks and security is operating the interface your daughter died in," Lockett observed. "Why provide security to a sex site and allow your company to be so easy to trace?"

"Neither KeepItSafe nor Web(W)rights cares about who they provide security to," Ben responded. "Their affiliation with HURTFUL.com proves that."

"Does it?" Lockett asked.

"Rykert doesn't care," Ben declared. "Not if he's offering Web(W)rights to the Wahhabis."

"How did you know that?" Lockett asked.

Ben hesitated. He hadn't expected that question.

"A number of sources," Ben prevaricated. "He told me for one."

"Why do you believe that and not the other?" Lockett asked.

"Other what?" Ben said.

"His other claim that he knows little about the actual workings of the Internet," Lockett replied.

"He doesn't need to if his company's doing the work," Ben replied.

"You're certain of that?" Lockett asked.

Ben was not certain. Lockett had caught him advocating a course of action on the basis of contradictory data. Which data bits should he trust?

"C'mon in" Lockett urged. "We can figure it out together."

Ben hesitated. As attractive as her proposal sounded, it would signal the end of his freedom to find Caitline.

"Lisa," Ben said and paused. "May I call you that?"

Lockett laughed.

"I don't think it violates agency protocol," Lockett advised.

Ben chuckled. It seemed strange to be on a first-name basis with a Homeland Security agent. Yet, their newly won familiarity failed to disguise their opposing viewpoints.

"Everything you've said points the evidence as easily to me as it does to Rykert," Ben said.

"You could prove your innocence better with a computer in front of you," Lisa observed.

"Behind a desk?" Ben asked. "Would you have made those connections without my input?"

"I was doing my job," Lisa declared.

"And that job was to be at your desk waiting for my call?" Ben asked.

"My job was to compile the bits of information collected during this investigation," Lisa replied.

"Who requested that?" Ben asked.

"Agent Stanfeld," Lisa answered dutifully.

"Convenient," Ben responded. "You should ask her why the only person who knows about distributed computing interfaces is doing cleanup work at her desk."

"Not everyone can be out in the field," Lisa replied.

"That's true," Ben agreed. "But given agent Stanfeld's narcissistic need for control, that's why it's essential I stay out here."

A squad car pulled into the parking lot. Ben hung up, returned to his cycle, and stared into the rear view mirror. The squad car glided toward the booth he had abandoned.

He started his cycle and headed toward Uptown. Had Lockett sent the squad car despite their discussion, Ben wondered. If he could not prove the sincerity of his actions to her or to his ex-wife, he could do so to himself.

It took ten minutes to reach the station, another ten to wade through the police bureaucracy to find Bergstrom's office. The desk sergeant pointed to a row of plastic-backed chairs seated against the wall and told him to wait.

Ben sat in the nearest one and folded his hands. He felt composed. Giving himself up offered a cessation of doubt about his motives. Let the Feds find Caitline. Let them uncover Rykert's connection to a terrorist cell. Let them find Hoot's murderer. He was ready for what fate offered him.

"Mr. Hackwell?" the desk sergeant called. "Detective Bergstrom will see you."

Ben marched to the frosted glass door of Bergstrom's office and turned the handle slowly, determined to savor every remaining moment of freedom.

The office inside was small, Spartan, unused except for the several stacks of files on the desktop that surrounded the small clear space on the blotter.

Ben stuck his head inside and sniffed. He did not smell cigarette smoke. He approached the desk and thumbed through the nametags on the files. None pertained to him.

"You've finally decided to turn yourself in," Bergstrom said.

Ben spun around. Bergstrom grinned at him from the doorway.

"Smart move," Bergstrom encouraged. "And the right one."

Ben presented Bergstrom the undersides of his wrists.

"That won't be necessary," Bergstrom said and pressed Ben's arms to his sides. "Since you turned yourself in voluntarily."

Bergstrom sat behind the desk, placed a blank sheet of paper in the center of his blotter, and warned that anything Ben said could be used against him in a court of law.

"I understand," Ben replied without the certainty his response conveyed. He had not considered what crime he wanted to admit to having committed. Over zealousness about protecting his daughter? "What am I being charged with?"

"Nothing formal at this point," Bergstrom replied.

"Then why am I here?" Ben asked.

"Because you're a good citizen?" Bergstrom answered. His face grew serious. "You know that there are any number of felonies we could charge you with. Your cooperation could lessen the charges, or eliminate them altogether."

Ben chuckled. Bergstrom promised the same old bait that every law enforcement agent used, the possibility of exoneration, with him reserving the final decision as to how much Ben's cooperation had been worth. Since punishment was Ben's only certainty in this mess, he wondered why he should make Bergstrom's job easier.

"Have you found out who murdered Hoot?" Ben asked.

"I was expecting you'd tell us," Bergstrom replied.

"You expect me to confess?" Ben asked.

"If you're guilty," Bergstrom said.

"And if I'm not?" Ben asked.

"Then a judge and jury will have to decide," Bergstrom replied.

"So I'm guilty of something either way you slice it," Ben concluded.

"Looks like," Bergstrom agreed.

Ben's feeling of impotence returned.

"Why should I tell you anything?" Ben asked.

"Because you want to find your daughter?" Bergstrom said.

"Why haven't you?" Ben demanded.

"Authorization?" Bergstrom replied and sighed. "This was a federal case long before your daughter was reported being kidnapped."

Ben smiled. That piece of data coincided with Azeb's bit about Caitline.

"How long?" Ben asked.

"The Feds had tapped Wilson's phone and his Web site long before your buddy cozied up to him," Bergstrom admitted.

"You knew about Wilson," Ben cried angrily, "yet you let Hoot and Caitline get involved with him?"

"He hadn't done anything we could arrest him on up to that point," Bergstrom replied. "Nothing we could prosecute successfully anyway."

"He's kidnapped my daughter, maybe murdered her," Ben declared. "What more do you need?"

"A body?" Bergstrom replied. He grimaced and glanced at his PC. "Look. There are many things in this case that don't make sense."

"Such as?" Ben asked.

"Such as the fact that we pulled the plug on Gibson's computer," Bergstrom replied. "Yet the HURTFUL.com Web site continues to operate."

"That's Hoot's distributed computing network," Ben said and smiled at his small triumph. The police had checked out his suggestion. "It operates like a multi-celled organism."

"That should impress me?" Bergstrom asked.

"If you're into open access computing like those guys at AFI, it should," Ben replied.

Bergstrom shrugged.

"Here's another thing," Bergstrom said. "Web(W)rights' stock price continues to rise even though we formally shut down the Web site."

Ben tottered on his feet. Jennifer had lied again. He knew he should not be surprised. Yet he was. Through all their arguments, despite all their differences, Jennifer had never lied to him until now.

"Have you talked to Rykert?" Ben asked.

"Not lately," Bergstrom said.

"Isn't he your expert on this?" Ben asked. He wondered why Rykert wasn't in the room taking notes on Ben's imminent incarceration. "He's the one who's negotiating Caitline's release."

"Who says so?" Bergstrom asked.

"He did," Ben replied. "Last night."

"Did he," Bergstrom said.

The flat tone of Bergstrom's statement indicated that Ben had operated on another false assumption.

"Isn't he liaisoning with you guys?" Ben asked.

"Supposedly," Bergstrom said.

"Then why not talk to him?" Ben persisted.

"He hasn't maintained contact with us," Bergstrom replied.

Ben noticed the sheepish look that crossed Bergstrom's leonine face. He realized that he couldn't locate Rykert either.

"Sounds like you need me," Ben observed.

"I need tangible evidence, not virtual innuendoes," Bergstrom declared and spun the sheet of paper toward Ben with the heel of his hand. "Here's your chance to do yourself a favor. It's the best deal I can offer. And my last one."

Ben ignored Bergstrom's confession sheet.

"Find Rykert," Ben advised.

"Why?" Bergstrom asked.

"He has the connections," Ben said and retreated a step. "He's been working with the FBI and the police all along. He knows a foreign agent with connections to the Wahhabis."

"The Wahhabis?" Bergstrom asked.

"They're the ones holding my daughter," Ben explained.

"Who says so?" Bergstrom asked.

"He did," Ben said and retreated another step. "Last night."

"So, you believe him, too, now. So did we," Bergstrom acknowledged. His face sobered as Ben retreated further. "Don't think that you're going to just walk out of here," he warned. "There are over 30 cops outside and they all know who I'm dealing with."

Ben halted. He knew Bergstrom was right. He'd seen a dozen cops during his search for Bergstrom's office. And he was tired of running. He had to trust someone. Bergstrom's motives processed in parallel with his own more than anyone else's did.

"Have you impounded Hoot's PC?" Ben asked.

"We do our jobs," Bergstrom replied.

"What about the Bronco plowed into the back of Hoot's garage?" Ben countered. "What have you found out about that?"

"What's it to you?" Bergstrom retorted.

"That didn't seem suspicious?" Ben asked.

"Given Gibson's carpal tunnel problem and his driving record," Bergstrom replied. "No."

"There was a hair strand on the steering wheel," Ben explained. "A red one."

"Dyed," Bergstrom murmured. "With Raspberry Silkience."

"So you found it," Ben said.

"Yeah, we know all about it," Bergstrom replied. "We know that it's Caucasian in origin. We also know that it didn't have a hair follicle."

"So?" Ben asked.

"We know that without one it takes weeks for the forensic scientists to check the mitochondrial DNA," Bergstrom replied. His eyes bored into Ben's. "Then they come back and tell us the evidence is inconclusive."

"It didn't appear planted to you?" Ben asked.

"It could have been," Bergstrom admitted in seeming agreement with Ben's suggestion. He folded his hands on the desktop. "It could be actual hair, or it could have come from a wig. Or it could have come from a wig made with real hair."

"Wilson's women have red hair," Ben said.

"They wear wigs too," Bergstrom replied.

"It still points to Wilson," Ben declared.

"And to half the female population," Bergstrom scoffed.

Ben sat back perplexed. He'd hoped the DNA data would implicate someone other than his daughter. Why would anyone plant an inconclusive clue?

Ben glanced upward and saw Bergstrom's feral eyes studying his every action. He realized that he had to regain the offensive to save himself.

"I know a way to find Rykert," Ben suggested.

"That might interest me," Bergstrom admitted. "If I was trying to find him."

"You just said…" Ben paused. Bergstrom held all the cards, or so he thought. "Look, you're getting nowhere with this case."

"Who says?" Bergstrom replied. "I've got the prime suspect right in this room."

"Suspect of what?" Ben retorted. "Without me you wouldn't even know about Hoot's death."

"But, I have got you," Bergstrom declared.

"What good is that?" Ben asked. "If I plead the fifth, it won't be considered an admission of guilt in a court of law."

"There's plenty of evidence—" Bergstrom began.

"Circumstantial and you know it," Ben interrupted. He had to make his last appeal convincing. "All I'm asking is a chance to reenter the HURTFUL Web site."

"You can do that from here," Bergstrom said.

Ben shook his head.

"I need Hoot's interface," Ben replied.

"Why?" Bergstrom asked.

"Because the interface is the heart of Hoot's killer application," Ben replied. "That's why the Wahhabis and Wilson and Homeland Security are interested in it."

"Suppose that's true," Bergstrom suggested and stared above Ben's head. "What good is it if you have to wear a rubber suit to zap somebody?"

"I don't know," Ben admitted. "That's something I need to find out."

"You mentioned Rykert a moment ago" Bergstrom said as he pulled a pack of Camels from his sport coat. "You still figure he fits in somehow?"

"I don't know," Ben replied and watched Bergstrom's first drag blow into the air. "That's another thing I need to find out."

Someone rapped on the outside of Bergstrom's door. A muscular, pimple-faced officer whose badge name read Johnson slipped inside. Bergstrom nodded. Johnson wrapped his fingers around Ben's biceps and steered him toward the door. Ben tried to move his arm. The young officer's grip was polite yet firm.

"Show this man our best accommodations," Bergstrom ordered as he watched another of his exhalations roil the still air. "You have anything else on your shopping list?"

"Yeah," Ben replied. "Find out what's happened to Caitline."

CHAPTER 25

▼

Ben spent an hour in processing and another in a holding cell before Johnson escorted him to an interrogation room void of everything save a table, chair, and mirror on the wall. He waited there for Bergstrom to arrive with the thumbscrews.

When Bergstrom did not come after 15 minutes, Ben moved out of expectant mode and rethought his options. There didn't seem to be many. Bergstrom had his chief suspect in custody. Ben wondered whether he should stonewall the interrogation. At some point Bergstrom would need him to show how he committed Hoot's murder. Meanwhile, the AFI would shut down the Internet. There was less than a day left. Wilson would wait for the event and disappear in the financial chaos that ensued.

And Caitline?

He had failed her again, Ben decided. Despite his best efforts, he remained no closer to learning what had happened to her, let alone rescuing her. Turning himself in had proven an exercise in masochism. All he'd gained was confirmation that his ploy to shut down HURTFUL.com had failed. The opposite seemed to be happening. Web(W)rights flourished, despite his destruction of its primary payment stream.

The door in the far corner opened and Bergstrom strode in carrying a bulky 12 x 14-inch manila folder in his left hand. Johnson followed and adopted an at-ease position beside Ben's chair. Bergstrom's cigarette was gone.

"C'mon," Bergstrom's ordered. His eyes glittered with determination. "Stand up."

"What's that?" Ben asked and pointed at the folder.

"Sergeant Johnson, assist the prisoner to his feet," Bergstrom replied.

Johnson reached under Ben's right armpit and jerked him upward. Ben rubbed the spot where Johnson had grabbed him.

"I planned to cooperate," Ben protested.

"That makes it easier all around, doesn't it?" Bergstrom growled.

The change in Bergstrom's attitude toward him was obvious. Ben guessed the reason lay in the folder Bergstrom clutched to his chest.

"Mind telling me what the file is?" Ben asked.

"Gibson's autopsy report," Bergstrom explained.

"Does it show anything?" Ben asked.

"Not much more than we knew before," Bergstrom acknowledged. "Gibson died between midnight and noon from a rapid depletion of sugar in his muscles."

"Sugar depletion?" Ben said.

"Yeah," Bergstrom replied and squinted at the writing at the bottom of the page. "The forensic pathologist says here that it's the primary indicator associated with receiving a massive dose of electrical current."

"Isn't that basically what I told you before?" Ben said.

"Yeah," Bergstrom retorted. "How about that."

Bergstrom nodded and Johnson grabbed Ben's arm in the same sore spot. It was apparent that Bergstrom now considered Ben's knowledge of events incriminating.

"Where are we going?" Ben asked in alarm.

"To Never Land," Bergstrom replied.

Johnson steered Ben into the hallway where they followed Bergstrom to a metal frame door with a red exit sign above it that opened onto an alley. Bergstrom mounted the cement stairway to the tan brick building opposite.

"Just follow him," Johnson instructed.

Ben scanned the alley and street located fifty feet away from where they stood.

"Don't even think about it," Johnson warned.

Bergstrom opened a metal frame door onto another deserted corridor. Metal doors with four by six inch reinforced glass windows ran down the hallway at ten-foot intervals. Ben recalled seeing such maximum-security detention cells at the Guantanamo Bay military base.

"Straight ahead," Johnson directed as he and snapped the security bolt into place. "Last door on your left."

Bergstrom emerged from the cell halfway down the corridor. A slim, tailored figure with a manila coiffure followed him. The warning hairs on Ben's hairs prickled as he recognized the person under the coiffure was Barbara Stanfeld.

"Inside," Stanfeld directed. "I don't need to tell you we'll be watching."

"And listening," Bergstrom added.

The metal door opened upon a squat figure in prison blues huddled against the wall upon her cot.

"Zarima," Ben gasped.

Zarima's attention remained focused on the brick wall across from her.

"What's this woman doing in a detention cell?" Ben asked as he stepped back into the hallway.

"We're detaining all enemy combatants," Stanfeld replied.

"Enemy combatant?" Ben retorted. "On what charge?"

"We're still considering the exact nature of the charges to be filed," Stanfeld explained.

"Suspicion of terrorism," Bergstrom murmured.

"She's no terrorist," Ben replied with less conviction than he intended.

"Who says so?" Stanfeld retorted.

"Rykert, I should think," Ben replied. "Isn't he the one who brought her in?"

"Yeah," Stanfeld said with a baleful stare at Bergstrom. "We should thank him for that one of these days, when he calls in again."

Ben sensed from Stanfeld's reply that Bergstrom had mishandled the agency's relationship with Rykert. Ben's potential ally was in as dangerous a position as he was.

"What's your evidence?" Ben asked.

"She was identified driving Gibson's Bronco into the garage on the morning in question," Stanfeld replied. "Then a blue Audi belonging to Avery Rykert picked her up."

Ben groaned. He doubted that Zarima was the "spendy redhead" referred to in the AFI memo.

"Are you saying it was Zarima's hair on the steering wheel?" Ben asked.

Stanfeld's eyes narrowed to slits.

"How did you learn about that?" Stanfeld asked.

"I saw it myself," Ben answered. He decided to leave AFI's corroboration out of the discussion. "Do you think she's involved in Hoot's death?"

"She'll do until something better comes along," Stanfeld said.

"Are you serious?" Ben replied.

"Oh, we've had our eye on her for some time," Stanfeld replied and coughed. "She's maintained constant contact with known subversive elements here and abroad."

"You mean Wilson," Ben corrected.

"Among others," Stanfeld replied. "Many of her calls went to Chechnya."

"She has relatives there," Ben explained. "There's nothing subversive in that."

"The money trails point otherwise," Stanfeld said and signaled Johnson to close the cell door. "Her family consists of known Wahhabi militants including some members of Allies for a Free Internet. Ever hear of them?"

"You're kidding," Ben replied.

"We are not," Stanfeld declared. "To show you how serious we are I'll let you in on another little secret."

Stanfeld seemed ready to burst, Ben thought. He glanced at the stone-faced Bergstrom and wondered why he didn't he share his colleague's glee.

"What secret?" Ben asked.

"Want to know who her husband is?" Stanfeld asked. "Or was?"

"I give up," Ben replied.

"Your pal, Gibson," Stanfeld said.

"You are out of your mind," Ben cried in disbelief.

"We check on these things," Stanfeld said. "It's our job."

Stanfeld dominated the room with her assurance like the master of ceremonies at a Friars Club celebrity roast.

"We have Mr. Rykert to thank for that bit of information," Stanfeld added with a another withering glare at Bergstrom. She returned her focus to Ben. "And you. Without your involvement we never would have bothered to run down the connection."

"Gibson used his mother's place as a safe house for illegal aliens for the past 18 months," Bergstrom added.

Ben stood inert by the magnitude of his own folly and ignorance. All those empty Pisa Pizza boxes in the corner, he recalled. No wonder Hoot's house retained its same musty furniture and sense of disuse. A low profile would be less likely to give him away. No neighbors would care or bother to check.

One question remained unanswered, Ben thought.

"Why would Zarima kill her husband?" Ben asked.

"That's for you to find out," Stanfeld replied.

"Me?" Ben retorted. "Why?"

"We need names, addresses," Stanfeld explained. "There must be other cells of unknown agents."

"That's your job," Ben replied.

Stanfeld shook her head. Her immobile frosted wave shimmered under the wire-caged light bulbs.

"You seem to think she's innocent," Stanfeld replied. "If the both of you want to get out of this mess unscathed, you'd better rethink your position. It was your call, remember, that tipped us off."

Ben glanced at the cell door and back at the two law enforcement agents. He knew all it took was one or two phrase changes to make it look like he was connected. If he didn't comply, they'd label him uncooperative and an accomplice.

"Forget it," Ben replied.

Bergstrom grabbed Ben's elbow and pulled him aside.

"WHO's out of their mind now?" Bergstrom said in a harsh whisper. "Does your refusal help anything? I don't like Stanfeld, either. I don't like her methods, or her putting people in detention with no evidence, or her lack of due process. But does your defiance put you any closer to finding your daughter?"

Ben sniffed. Bergstrom's underlying tobacco aura proved overpowering at this range. Yet, Bergstrom's sense of outrage surprised him. Stanfeld had trumped him in an administrative and procedural sense. To find Caitline, Ben realized that he would have to do the same.

"Is this the latest version of good cop-bad cop?" Ben hissed. "One gives an offer you can't refuse and the other convinces you it's the moral thing to do?"

"Suit yourself," Bergstrom replied and released his grip. "But you'll never get a chance at finding your daughter without Stanfeld's help and you know it."

"If you're so eager to help," Ben countered. "Why don't you get me access?"

"Like I told you, it's a national security issue now," Bergstrom said. "Stanfeld's the only one who has legal access to Gibson's interface. You know that."

Ben sighed with resignation. He knew Bergstrom was right.

"Why should I think my cooperation will change her mind?" Ben asked.

"That's the chance you'll have to take," Bergstrom replied.

"Zarima doesn't know anything," Ben declared.

"How can you be sure?" Bergstrom asked.

"Every bit of data associated with her identity has been destroyed," Ben said. "What would the Wahhabis possibly entrust her with?"

"You believe her?" Bergstrom declared and shrugged. "Maybe it's not the Wahhabis."

"You mean Hoot—"

"That's what we want you to find out," Bergstrom said.

Ben examined the bandage covering the cut on his palm while considering what bit of data Hoot would have given her. Was it anything that could help him find Caitline?

Ben squared his shoulders with as much determination as he could muster. Bergstrom nodded toward Stanfeld and Johnson opened Zarima's cell door. Ben stepped inside. Zarima remained huddled on the cot, her eyes focused on an imaginary spot in the wall opposite.

"Zarima?" Ben said. "I'm here to help you."

Zarima did not move. Ben remained unsure how to bring her out of her shell.

"I'm sorry about your husband," Ben said. "Hoot was my best friend."

Zarima continued to stare straight ahead.

"You've got to believe me," Ben urged. "You better trust somebody if you want to get out of here."

Zarima turned toward Ben. Her sloe eyes were filled with disdain.

"What makes you think I want to?" Zarima asked.

"You want to stay in jail?" Ben replied.

"Of course," Zarima replied and flashed Ben a malicious grin. "That is best thing for my cause, is it not? The longer I stay, the better chance my comrades have of getting away."

"Comrades?" Ben asked.

"You know, the Wahhabis," Zarima replied and chuckled. "The cause I would do anything for, no questions asked. Die, if I had to."

She glanced at the door behind Ben and her face grew serious.

"That is what all of you believe?" Zarima said with the certainty of a foregone conclusion.

Ben said nothing. He did not know what to believe.

"Not all of us in Chechnya are Wahhabi," Zarima added as she wrapped her arms around her legs. "Those that are don't agree with everything the imams tell us."

Zarima's reply reminded Ben of the military's botched Mogadishu rescue. His disagreement with Hoot over the on-the-ground decisions had precipitated the fissure in their relationship.

Now that Ben had gotten Zarima to talk, he had to find out as much useful data as he could to save both of them.

"When you're caught in the middle of a revolution, it's hard to know what to do," Ben sympathized. "Or which side to follow."

"Revolution?" Zarima snorted with disdain. "Who said anything about revolution?"

"That is what the Wahhabis are fighting for?" Ben asked. "Freedom for Chechnya?"

"Hmpf. When will Chechnya ever be free?" Zarima murmured. "When roses bloom in the snow."

"Look, I can't imagine what you had to do to get here," Ben said. "Just as you didn't understand what you were getting into when you married Hoot."

"It was a marriage of convenience," Zarima whispered. "I was already lost."

"Lost?" Ben said. He felt out of his depth in dealing with this woman's phantoms.

"I needed a way to stay in this country," Zarima explained. "So why not marry a foreigner?"

Ben shook his head in bewilderment. If Zarima was Hoot's wife, it was no wonder that Zarima regarded Caitline so bitterly.

"Whose idea was it?" Ben asked.

"Your Mr. Gibson's," Zarima answered bitterly. "And Mr. Rykert's."

"They worked together?" Ben said in surprise.

"Mr. Rykert performed the ceremony," Zarima said and pursed her mouth. "He said it would protect me."

Ben grimaced. From one hellhole to another, Zarima had said. The INS treated the foreign spouses of such marriages like carriers of the plague. Deportation was the usual result.

"Did you get a certificate?" Ben asked.

Zarima gazed at Ben in perplexity.

"A wedding certificate," Ben explained. "A piece of paper that proves you were married."

Zarima shrugged.

"Your Mr. Rykert took care of that," Zarima said.

"He's not my Mr. Rykert," Ben replied.

"He goes everywhere with your woman," Zarima observed.

"Jennifer is not my woman," Ben corrected. "She's my ex-wife."

"That I did not know," Zarima said and shook her head. "A thousand apologies. I meant Lara. The one you call Caitline." Her eyes glinted with malice. "She is your daughter, is she not?"

Ben stood mute, conflicted. How many times had he said 'you're kidding' in the last 24 hours? Zarima confirmed that his daughter was still alive, but involved in what? How much could he trust what Zarima told him?

"When did you see them together?" Ben asked.

"Several times," Zarima replied. "Last night, most recently."

"Why didn't you tell me this before?" Ben demanded.

"I did tell you before," Zarima replied. "At the apartment."

"You said she was safe," Ben replied.

"Yes, safe in the arms of her protectors," Zarima snapped.

"Who?" Ben asked.

"The ones who killed the rest of us," Zarima replied. "Wilson and Rykert."

Ben reeled at Zarima's statement.

"You said Rykert had helped you marry Hoot to protect you," Ben said. "Wasn't he bringing you here to protect you after Hoot's death?"

"I thought so, too," Zarima spat as she glanced around her cell. "I'll tell you another thing."

Ben saw the malice return in Zarima's eyes.

"Your daughter is as bad as the rest of them," Zarima said. "Maybe worse."

"What do you mean?" Ben asked in dread of what he was about to hear.

"She knows the ways of the machine that gives them their power," Zarima replied. "She runs it for them."

Ben could not decide whether to believe Zarima or not.

"Did you tell Bergstrom or Stanfeld this?" Ben asked.

Zarima shook her head.

"It did not seem to matter," Zarima added with a smile as if she were laying down her trump card. "They already knew."

Ben resisted his urge to shake her.

"Knew?" Ben exclaimed. "Knew how?"

Zarima glanced toward the center of the ceiling. A tiny red bulb in the fire monitor mounted beside the flat overhead light flashed every two seconds.

"They showed me the video," Zarima replied.

"What video?" Ben demanded.

Zarima remained mute. Ben grabbed her shoulders.

"You're lying," Ben cried.

Zarima resumed staring at the imaginary spot on the opposite wall.

Ben released her shoulders and stepped back. Zarima's totemic silence indicated that he'd get nothing more from her. She trusted no one or anything. Why should she?

He glanced toward the flashing bulb and wondered what reason Zarima had for lying to him. Outside of spite for Caitline's relationship with Hoot, what could she hope to gain by telling Ben such a story? He glanced around the room. Given her circumstances, spite was all Zarima had, and the jealousy to motivate it.

Ben rapped on the cell door. It cranked open. Johnson stood in the fissure he'd created. Stanfeld and Bergstrom stood behind him.

Ben slipped through the opening.

"Is it true?" Ben asked.

"Is what true?" Stanfeld replied.

"Cut it out," Ben said. "You heard what Zarima told me."

"She saw a surveillance tape," Bergstrom explained and checked Stanfeld's face as if seeking her permission. "We wanted to get her reaction."

"You got one," Ben declared. "Are you saying Caitline wasn't kidnapped?"

"It looks that way," Bergstrom said.

"I don't believe it," Ben declared.

"We don't just make this stuff up," Stanfeld said.

Ben scanned the implacable faces of the two investigators. He cared about his daughter, right or wrong. He felt as Zarima must feel. They both had nothing to lose.

"I want to see it," Ben said.

"See what?" Stanfeld replied.

"Don't play dumb," Ben retorted. "The video Zarima saw."

"That's government property," Stanfeld declared.

"Great," Ben replied. "You people have been parceling out just enough data to lead me along until I found something useful. Well, no more."

"You'd be obstructing a federal investigation," Stanfeld warned.

"So what?" Ben said. "You've got enough evidence already on me for that."

Bergstrom whispered in Stanfeld's ear. Stanfeld's obstinacy disappeared.

"OK. He gets what he deserves," Stanfeld said. She handed a brass key to Bergstrom and waggled her index finger at him. "Fifteen minutes. No more."

Bergstrom grabbed Ben's arm and led him back down the corridor to a flight of cement stairs where they descended to another corridor. Bergstrom unlocked the first door on the left with Stanfeld's key, flicked a light switch, and beckoned Ben to enter the silent, dust-free office with an oversize monitor seated atop the metal desk.

"Take a seat," Bergstrom ordered.

Bergstrom opened the top drawer of a metal filing cabinet. After clacking through the plastic jewel cases, he produced a single plastic disc.

"Here," Bergstrom said and tossed the disc on the blotter. "It's all yours."

"Thanks," Ben replied, surprised at the warmth he slipped into one word.

"Don't thank me yet," Bergstrom advised. He pressed a button above the monitor screen, and it flickered to life. "You might not appreciate what you're about to see."

"I've already seen her whipped and shot," Ben replied. "What could be worse?"

"Depends on your point of view," Bergstrom said as he opened the disc drive and plopped the disc onto the tray. "Saddle up."

Ben wiped his sweaty palms on the tops of his pants legs. Seldom had he anticipated a disc load-up as much as this one. He steeled his nerves for the data that lie ahead.

Interlocked bleeding hearts appeared in the center of the desktop and swelled to bursting. The screen glowed crimson with the dripping discharge of virtual blood before yielding to the same barren bedroom scene Ben had witnessed before.

"I've seen this already," Ben said.

"Just wait," Bergstrom advised.

The perspective rotated 180 degrees to focus on the metal frame cot and the bound, buxom woman lying supine upon it. Caitline propped herself on her right elbow as the camera advanced into the room, her body trembling as her image increased in size. A swarthy left hand reached up from offscreen, propped the butt end of a bullwhip under Caitline's chin, and raised her to sitting position on the cot.

Caitline spat, and the screen went dark. Ben recalled Wilson's pale tongue licking her spittle from around his mouth. She fell back against the mattress. The focus shifted to her thighs. The lash of the whip hurtled down the right side of the screen. A single drop oozed from Caitline's trembling left thigh. The lash rose outside the screen and arced down again. A second crease appeared. Ben recalled its retort on Gibson's speakers and the moist, trembling feel of Caitline's skin.

"Enough," Ben declared.

"Hold on," Bergstrom said.

The image froze. A gray information panel materialized onscreen.

ARE YOU MAN ENOUGH FOR WHAT'S NEXT?
FINISH THE JOB!
For only $49.95!
Use your Visa or Master card.

"Is this what you wanted?" Ben asked. "To confirm for me that my daughter's a whore?"

"Keep watching," Bergstrom advised.

The information screened disintegrated. A smaller, sky-blue triangle replaced it.

RESTORE PARADISE ON EARTH!
THE SELECT WILL SHARE ALLAH'S BENEVOLENCE!
Alluha Akbar!

"The last sentence is Arabic for "God is great!" Bergstrom murmured.

"I know," Ben said and watched the frozen image disappear. "What does it mean?"

"It's a recruitment video," Bergstrom replied.

"Recruitment," Ben said. "For what?"

"To join the Wahhabis," Bergstrom answered.

"Why?" Ben asked, reeling in anticipation at Bergstrom's answer.

"Isn't it obvious?" Bergstrom replied. "Your daughter's a true believer."

CHAPTER 26

▼

"Impossible," Ben said though he did not recognize the sound of his voice. The full implication of Bergstrom's statement dawned on him. "Caitline's no terrorist."

"It doesn't appear that way," Bergstrom replied. "Near as we can figure it, these have been sent out on the Internet for the past six months. She worked for Wilson over a year before that."

"She just set up a Web site," Ben argued.

"And then disappeared," Bergstrom replied.

"They eliminated her," Ben said.

"Did they?" Bergstrom asked. "Or was that what they wanted everyone to think?"

"But—"

"But nothing," Bergstrom thundered. "The Web site continues to operate. Wilson has known connections to the Wahhabis. You helped show us those connections."

Ben stared at the blank screen. He felt spent, empty. Zarima had told the truth, Ben realized, but hadn't he suspected it all along? Standard computer trouble-shooting procedure dictated that when you strip the extraneous data away, everything left should point to the correct conclusion no matter how fantastic it may seem. When a police official confirms your suspicions as fact, it does not make accepting the truth any easier.

"What about Rykert?" Ben asked. "Wasn't he working with you guys?"

"Stanfeld brought him in as a liaison," Bergstrom replied. "We had no idea at the time he was dirty."

"Didn't he bring in Zarima?" Ben persisted.

"Yeah," Bergstrom said. "Then he disappeared."

"That doesn't necessarily mean he's working for the Wahhabis," Ben said.

"At this point it doesn't mean he isn't," Bergstrom replied.

Ben considered the possibilities. Though he disliked Rykert for his relationship with Jennifer, he never regarded him as a potential traitor. His jingoistic defense at the Grafton of the American way of life indicated the opposite.

"He told me he was negotiating Caitline's release," Ben said. "I thought through you."

"Not any more," Bergstrom replied and grasped Ben's shoulder. "Look, in 24 hours the AFI is going to shut down the entire Net. They can do it. We know that."

"So what?" Ben said and shrugged. "You'll have it running again in a few hours."

"Think of the disruption it'll cause," Bergstrom retorted.

"I doubt it," Ben replied. "Outside of an increase in profits for some surge protector companies."

"And the precedent." Bergstrom asked.

"Precedent?" Ben said.

"You think these people will stop there," Bergstrom declared and rolled his eyes. "Especially with a killer application like Gibson's in their hands?"

"What's that to me?" Ben retorted.

"Endgame. Wahhabis win," Bergstrom replied. "You want that?"

"AFI, al-Qaida, the Wahhabis," Ben replied. "What's the difference?"

"To your daughter, a lot," Bergstrom answered. "The charges would be a lot less severe if the Internet weren't shut down."

"Are you serious?" Ben asked and peered into Bergstrom's leonine eyes. Of course, Bergstrom was. It seemed only Ben had reservations. "I should let you guys use my daughter as a scapegoat to appease some lunatic fringe group?"

"And save the Internet, not to mention Western economy," Bergstrom replied. His fingers drummed an irregular beat along the top of the desk chair. "She's already an accomplice. An aider and abettor to the enemy. Stanfeld will make sure the Justice Department sees it that way."

He glanced at Ben.

"You want to add espionage to her list?" Bergstrom asked. "That's punishable by death, you know."

Ben stared at the blank screen. Espionage charges did not matter to someone already dead, he thought. The Caitline that he knew was dead to him regardless whether they found and convicted her.

"There's also the matter of your friend, Hoot," Bergstrom added.

"What about him?" Ben asked.

"You could rehabilitate his reputation," Bergstrom replied.

Bergstrom produced a large black bundle wrapped in clear plastic from the closet. Setting the bundle on the desk, he removed three strands of masking tape binding the plastic seam together. The filament segments of Hoot's body suit unfolded and its rubber appendages extended outward. Bergstrom shook one end and held it at arm's length. The segments snapped into place with the toe ends dangling on the floor.

"No way," Ben declared.

"Just hear me out," Bergstrom urged. "We still don't know how or to whom the payments are made."

"I'm sure you'll figure it out," Ben said and headed to the door. "Good luck."

"We need somebody with technical expertise," Bergstrom replied.

Ben halted at the door. Bergstrom was pressing Ben much too hard for a simple experiment. Did Bergstrom think he could ingratiate himself with Stanfeld by convincing Ben to test Hoot's haptic interface suit? He turned and faced Bergstrom.

"Nobody in this entire building knows how to run a computer?" Ben scoffed.

"We need somebody who knows how to evade encrypted security systems," Bergstrom replied.

"What about Lisa?" Ben asked.

"Who?" Bergstrom replied.

"Lisa Lockett?" Ben replied. "The CIA computer expert who you let download Hoot's hard drive?"

"Oh, her," Bergstrom replied with a dismissive wave of his hand. "This requires a knowledge of haptic interfaces."

Ben shrugged and reached for the doorknob.

"Don't tell me your computer forensic people haven't already been testing this," Ben said.

"They couldn't get to first base with it," Bergstrom replied with a wry grin at his unintended sexual reference. "Look. We need your programming expertise. OK?"

"Not OK," Ben replied. "You've got enough evidence on Wilson already. Why not just raid his place and arrest him?"

"We don't know how he does it," Bergstrom acknowledged. "And he's a naturalized U.S. citizen. Without a better knowledge of Hoot's suit, none of the charges against him would stick. We need to draw a complete picture in court."

Ben groaned at the prospect of an entire sting operation held up on a detail of citizenship. He wanted to help nail Wilson, but using his patriotism and fear for his family angered him.

"You want me to risk electrocution to fish for a missing piece of metadata?" Ben asked.

"It's not dangerous," Bergstrom replied.

"Hoot's death would suggest otherwise," Ben replied.

"You said the deadly voltage came from sources outside Gibson's PC," Bergstrom said. He set the suit on the desktop and smiled.

"Don't tell me you're not intrigued," Bergstrom coaxed.

"Not enough to get killed for it," Ben replied.

"I wasn't thinking of the technical aspect," Bergstrom said.

Ben studied the lascivious crinkle around Bergstrom's eyes. He, too, regarded Ben's quest as incestuous, Ben thought with disappointment.

"You're worse than my ex-wife," Ben declared. "It's a bad selling job if you think offering me a chance to have sex with my daughter will change my mind."

"Really," Bergstrom replied while his fingers drummed the power switch. "Your actions suggest otherwise. The very fact you're still standing here corroborates that."

"I thought it was because I'm in the basement of a police department building with a hundred cops between me and the outside," Ben said.

"That, too," Bergstrom admitted.

"Isn't there another way to get the information you want?" Ben asked and dropped his hand from the doorknob. "What about the other women on Rykert's guest list?"

"Your daughter's video is the only recruitment portal," Bergstrom replied.

"If you think that I'm going to have sex with Caitline," Ben said. "You are out of your mind."

"It's virtual, isn't it?" Bergstrom said and shrugged. "What does it matter?"

"It matters to me," Ben replied.

"So, refuse," Bergstrom said and beckoned toward the door. "Go ahead, leave."

Ben studied Bergstrom's eyes and wondered what he was offering him. Was this some kind of test?

"What'll that get me?" Ben retorted. "There still are cops all around."

"If you really feel the way you say you do," Bergstrom replied. "The cops won't matter."

Ben felt the sweat bead inside his palms. He realized that his compliance indicated that he lusted after his daughter. His refusal condemned him as a traitor to his country. Either way he acted on this charge cloud of emotions, he lost.

"I care about my daughter," Ben declared in a low voice. "Despite what you, my ex-wife, or anyone else thinks."

"Show me," Bergstrom said.

Ben snatched the suit from Bergstrom's hand, stepped into the leggings, and stuck his arms into the sleeves. Designed for Hoot's girth, the suit sloughed across Ben's chest. The lightness of the material surprised him. Wouldn't its latex composition minimize conductivity to the skin?

"Aren't you going to remove your clothes?" Bergstrom asked.

"What for?" Ben replied.

"This is an experimental run," Bergstrom said as he searched his pockets for his ubiquitous pack of cigarettes. "Don't you want to experience the full effect?" He asked and winked. "For scientific purposes?"

"I'm fine," Ben responded.

"How are we going to know the full effect on anyone who uses it if your clothes impede the sensation?" Bergstrom asked.

"Then you do it," Ben declared and started to peel the shoulder section from his arms.

"Keep your shirt on," Bergstrom replied. "We'll do it your way."

Ben slipped back into the arms and fastened the Velcro strips across his chest down to his crotch. The electrodes and their attendant cloud of filaments that stretched to the processors impeded his range of motion. He waddled like a porcupine to the desk and sat before the monitor.

Ben tensed before the screen as Bergstrom rebooted the PC and placed the disc into its retractable seat. He wondered how many times in the past that Hoot had done the same thing. And how many times had Hoot done it with Caitline's image on the screen before him?

"Any last instructions?" Ben asked, repressing the thought.

"Keep track of the payment sequence and your sensations along the way," Bergstrom said. "I'll track your activities from outside."

"You make it sound like I'm exploring a new planet," Ben said.

"Aren't you?" Bergstrom asked as he pressed Enter. "Don't enjoy yourself too much."

Ben readjusted his goggles and peered at the monitor. Twin bleeding hearts materialized in the center of his vision, engorged with blood, and burst. The blood-splattered screen was replaced by a view of the metal cot in the barren room.

Ben nudged the joystick. The doorjamb at the edges of his vision melted away while the image of his helpless daughter on the cot grew larger. He nudged the stick again and felt the simulated alternating impact of a wood floor against the balls of his feet.

The mixed sensations matched his initial response to the flight simulations he'd taken during advanced Army training: giddy, disorienting, and disturbingly real.

He approached the cot, and Caitline propped herself upright on her right elbow. Her storm cloud eyes appeared luminous, her lips parted with excitement or fear. Ben couldn't tell which.

Ben's palms sweated. From the increased electrical contact, he decided.

Caitline's image retained its cowering pose. Ben raised his right arm as Wilson had. The lash soared across the upper right corner of his vision. The simulated tactility of polished leather pressed along the length of the love line of his right palm.

Caitline's eyes followed the end of the lash. Her body trembled.

Ben lowered his arm. Caitline returned to her same suppliant pose.

Preprogrammed, Ben realized. He simulated a step backward. Caitline resumed her supine position on the cot.

Ben nudged the joystick sideways. Caitline did not move. He retreated another step. Her image remained inert.

Muffled speech emanated from outside his latex hood. Ben shook his head and pointed at his right ear. Caitline's image did not change.

"What're you doing?" Bergstrom asked. His muffled voice sounded remote, otherworldly, as if he were shouting down the air tube of a diving bell.

"Seeing how interactive the programming is," Ben shouted.

"Don't waste time," Bergstrom advised.

Ben hesitated. Why hurry? They both knew what happened next.

He raised his arm again. Caitline cowered expectantly, waiting for the whip to descend. Ben reminded himself that it was just her image onscreen. He studied her eyes, full of fear. Or longing.

And dropped his arm.

He saw the lash flash past the edge of his vision, felt the shudder of her body as the lash lacerated her flesh, felt the tremor of the impact up his wrist and forearm. The handle slipped and twisted in his sweaty grip.

Caitline's eyes widened. The tip of her tongue lurked behind her teeth in anticipation of the next strike.

Ben struck again. Another oozing welt appeared. The sensation of another body shudder coursed through his fingertips.

He struck a third time, intoxicated at the license of his sensations, his lust for blood, and the sense of his own depravity.

Ben attempted a fourth blow, but the information rectangle that he and Bergstrom had witnessed before appeared in the center of his vision.

Ben halted. His pulse raced, his breath ran short. Caitline awaited another lash, or the death destined by the programming. It depended on the depravity of the participant, Ben realized.

He pressed Continue. Another box popped up with two information spaces. One requested a check mark beside his choice of credit card; the other his card number.

He keyed the data into the assigned slots. The rectangle disappeared.

THANK YOU!

The golden afterglow lingered while the smooth hard curve of a .38 revolver handle replaced the feel of a leather whip handle in his hand. His index finger poised around the polished steel trigger. It seemed so easy to squeeze off a shot, one, two, three, four.

Hell, empty the chamber, Ben decided. Put the fuckin' bitch out of her misery.

Six shots exploded in Ben's ears. Twin hearts swelled, burst to overflowing.

Ben flinched and wiped the imaginary splatter from his eyes.

GOOD BEY FOREVER.

Caitline no longer existed. She had been exterminated. Obliterated.

Ben blinked.

CONGRATULATIONS!

HOW DOES IT FEEL?

The question disappeared. It must be a looped sequence, Ben decided. Another took its place.

RELOAD?

YES!   NO!   EXIT

Ben's index finger twitched. He'd killed once. Did he want a second helping?

He pressed NO. Nothing happened. He tried again, and received no response.

The image returned him to the doorway, facing the occupied bed. It was either defective programming, or a sand trap loop.

Ben grabbed the underside of his hood and tore it from his head.

"Why are you stopping?" Bergstrom asked.

"Isn't that enough?" Ben replied. He knelt forward and gulped two giant lungfuls of air. "You got what you wanted."

"Got what?" Bergstrom asked.

"That," Ben said and pointed at the monitor. "You saw how it works."

"Saw what?" Bergstrom replied.

Ben grew impatient. Bergstrom need not be so obtuse.

"Me killing my daughter," Ben said.

"I saw nothing," Bergstrom declared.

"I'm not doing it again," Ben replied.

"Do what?" Bergstrom asked and switched off the monitor. "All I saw was a video game, not a very good one."

"You didn't see the payment screens?" Ben asked. "Or hear gun shots?"

"All I saw was you entering a room and standing over a bed," Bergstrom replied.

"I killed my own daughter," Ben exclaimed. "I felt the jerk of the revolver six times."

Bergstrom squatted beside Ben. His feral eyes penetrated Ben's own.

"I tell you nothing happened," Bergstrom said. "Whatever you experienced inside the suit did not show up on the monitor." His paw-like hand encompassed Ben's knee. "Trust me."

Ben stared at the blank screen. How could Bergstrom not have seen it?

He examined his ciliated hands. His palms felt dry, warmed by their latex encasement. A prick here, a reaction there, these constituted the basis of simple stimulus-response programming. A moment ago he'd whipped and killed his own daughter. Simulated or not, his emotions and feelings felt genuine.

Ben stripped the gloves from his hands and laid them on the desktop. He rose to his feet and stripped the latex skin from his chest.

"What do you think you're doing?" Bergstrom asked.

"Quitting," Ben replied as he stepped out of the leggings, and handed the latex skin to Bergstrom. "You were right. The cops don't matter."

Bergstrom set the suit on the desktop.

"You're not going anywhere," Bergstrom said. He grabbed Ben's shoulders and shook Ben ever so slightly. "You think a phony guilt show is enough to get you out of this? Not while I've got four unsolved murders!"

"Six. Zarima updated the count," Ben corrected as he removed Bergstrom's hands. The lingering aura of stale cigarette smoke enveloped them like a shawl. "What's it to me?"

"Yours is the only attempt that failed," Bergstrom replied. "I want to know why."

Ben backed away. Bergstrom had lied to him again. Ben knotted his fists to regain control. He was not surprised any more. More accurately, Bergstrom had kept certain data from him. One question remained. How much?

"I told you what happened," Ben said.

"I saw nothing," Bergstrom repeated.

"You can't always believe what you see," Ben advised.

"And less of what you hear," Bergstrom retorted.

"You ought to know," Ben declared.

"All right," Bergstrom said as he fingered one of the contacts where the filament entered the hood. "We knew going in that Gibson's body suit operated two ways. It acts both as a receiver and as a transmitter. What we didn't know was how individualized Gibson had made it."

"What do you mean?" Ben asked.

"Each user gets a different stimulus depending on their response to the situation," Bergstrom said.

"And?" Ben asked.

"Those who react most strongly engage in the most vivid scenarios. Those who don't experience very little," Bergstrom explained as he sat on the edge of the desk. "Stanfeld had no reaction at all."

"That figures," Ben muttered.

"Don't get too uppity," Bergstrom advised. "Nobody else who tried got through the payment screens like you did."

"Great," Ben said sarcastically. "I like being the highest achiever."

"One of our guys did get that far," Bergstrom cautioned. "He's a marksman on the SWAT team. But, the popup windows wouldn't take his card numbers. Only yours got through." Bergstrom studied the tips of his shoes. "Why do you suppose that is?"

A flush shot up Ben's neck. The answer seemed obvious.

"Because I killed her," Ben said.

"So did he. Quicker than you did," Bergstrom replied and grasped the desk edge on each side of his hips. "He had nothing to lose. She meant nothing to him."

"But, I killed her," Ben protested. He stared at Bergstrom, incredulous. What could be the purpose? "I wanted to."

Bergstrom shrugged.

"Who doesn't want to kill their kids at some point in their lives," Bergstrom replied.

"This was different. I meant it," Ben declared and turned away. "I really did."

"You were supposed to. But what really happened?" Bergstrom asked and placed his hand on Ben's shoulder. "You say you killed her, but I saw nothing."

"You don't believe me?" Ben asked.

"I do," Bergstrom replied and nodded his head for emphasis. "But, ask yourself. Why the discrepancy?"

Ben peered into Bergstrom's stolid gaze. Where was this inquiry leading?

"Faulty programming, I guess," Ben suggested.

"You guess. Lives are at stake here," Bergstrom replied. "You're the only one alive who knows."

Ben spun away, trying to make sense of it. He recalled the instant the gun entered his hand, the sensation of the trigger against his finger, the retort and impact of the gun firing. Six times over.

Had he actually squeezed the trigger? Or had the programming done it for him?

He glanced at Bergstrom, desperate for answers. Any answers.

If it was the programming, Ben pondered what that indicated. Why couldn't Bergstrom witness the result?

Six times the gun fired, Ben recalled, but he couldn't recall squeezing the trigger any of those times. Was the sequence prearranged? Or was it a mistake in programming, like the spelling of Goodbye, so sloppy, and so careless…

The hallway door burst open.

"Put away your toys, boys," Stanfeld ordered as she marched into the room followed by a phalanx of FBI agents. "Time's up."

CHAPTER 27

▼

Ben retreated to the center of the room. Two more policemen stood guard in the hall. He did not know whether he should be outraged, or flattered by the attention.

"What's the meaning of this?" Bergstrom asked.

"I allotted you 15 minutes," Stanfeld said. "And gave you an extra five, plenty of time to get results." She cocked her translucent right eyebrow. "And?"

"Inconclusive," Bergstrom replied and glanced toward Ben. "He claims to have gotten past the payment window, but nothing showed onscreen."

"So much for theory," Stanfeld replied turned toward her nearest aide-de-camp. "Show this gentleman one of our best cells and keep him there until we're ready to move him."

"This is ridiculous," Bergstrom protested. "You have nothing to hold him on."

"Don't I?" Stanfeld said and coughed in irritation. "Leaving the scene of a murder, attempted arson, consorting with enemy agents—what more do you need to merit a jail cell here?"

"We don't know for sure that he's associated with them," Bergstrom said.

"One's his daughter, for Pete's sake," Stanfeld retorted.

"That should be enough to give us pause," Bergstrom replied. "Would he spend this much time and effort to locate her if he actually was involved with them?"

"That's your theory," Stanfeld said. "You've had enough time to prove it."

"And I said it was inconclusive," Bergstrom replied.

"Bah!" Stanfeld cried and sliced her palm through the air. "You could do it a 100 times and get the same results."

"You're that sure," Bergstrom said with a doubtful glance toward Ben. "What do you think?"

"Who cares what he thinks?" Stanfeld interjected.

"He's the expert among all of us," Bergstrom declared and faced Ben.

"What do you think?" Bergstrom repeated.

Ben shifted on his feet. Outside of knowing his fate hung in the balance, he had no idea what he thought.

He studied Stanfeld, then Bergstrom. The former appeared obdurate, the other seemed equally insistent. He wondered why Bergstrom championed him now. All the data pointed otherwise.

"You're both right," Ben said as he wondered where to go with his next statement. "Given all you've seen and heard, I should be locked up. I know I'd do it."

He stared into Bergstrom's leonine face and rubbed his neck in perplexity. A grudging sense of gratitude welled within him.

"Still, the metadata feels all wrong," Ben declared. "I shouldn't be able to access the Wahhabi recruitment site, yet I can. Just as it shouldn't be possible to shoot enough voltage over the Internet to kill a man or start a fire, yet both things happened."

He turned toward Bergstrom.

"Nor should I fire six slugs into my daughter's body without once feeling the pull of the trigger," Ben added.

"Her virtual body," Bergstrom corrected.

"True," Ben agreed. "But I shouldn't see good-bye misspelled, either."

"What are you suggesting?" Bergstrom asked.

"Something's wrong. It seems almost intentional," Ben said with a helpless shrug. "If I didn't know better, I'd say Hoot was still alive."

"Ridiculous," Stanfeld said. "You call yourself a security expert?"

She glared at Bergstrom.

"Or you a detective," Stanfeld added. "Inhaling this man's virtual mumbo-jumbo as God's truth."

"Would Gibson make errors like that?" Bergstrom asked.

"Probably not," Ben agreed. His next statement pained him. "But Caitline might."

"What do you mean?" Bergstrom asked.

"Zarima said that Caitline understood the machine," Ben replied. "Who would be better at providing us a warning signal?"

"You think she's trying to contact you?" Bergstrom replied.

"Why not?" Ben said. "Somebody's been sending me warning messages all along."

"This has gone far enough," Stanfeld declared and motioned to the two agents behind her. "Take Hackwell into custody."

"Hold it," Bergstrom ordered.

Bergstrom's peremptory glare froze the two men in place. He turned it onto Stanfeld. Each official's stare suspended the other like opposing magnetic fields.

"He's using you," Stanfeld declared. "Can't you see that? He's so desperate he's willing to sell the idea his teenage daughter could pull this whole thing off. And then send him messages to warn him about it."

"It's possible that his daughter might feel guilty about her involvement," Bergstrom suggested.

"Preposterous," Stanfeld replied. "Conscious or not, she'd still be guilty of treason."

"This is still a homicide investigation that involves citizens of my jurisdiction," Bergstrom replied.

"Who are in up to their necks in hostile terrorist actions," Stanfeld said.

"We have no direct evidence of that," Bergstrom said.

"What more evidence do you need?" Stanfeld asked.

"Something more than guilt by association," Bergstrom replied. "They're U.S. citizens."

"When they attack other American citizens they give up that right," Stanfeld said.

"That's for a judge to decide," Bergstrom said and drew himself erect.

"Under the FISA Act we don't need to obtain a warrant," Stanfeld countered.

"Only for someone who doesn't qualify as a U.S. citizen," Bergstrom replied. "Until you produce a warrant with specific charges, this man's right to freedom remains the same as any other citizen's."

Stanfeld spun on her heel and stormed out of the room. Her two associates followed.

Shaking with suppressed rage, Bergstrom pulled a half-used pack of cigarettes from the desk drawer and returned to the desk chair. He struck a match on the top of the monitor, fumbled a cigarette into his mouth, lit it, and shot a jet of smoke into the stagnant air.

"Thanks," Ben said as he sidled behind the monitor. "I appreciate it."

"Don't shit all over yourself," Bergstrom replied. "My ass was already in a sling. Once Stanfeld gets a warrant, she'll butcher it."

Ben fingered the computer cable. So much for expressing gratitude for Bergstrom's protection, he thought.

"It'll be your ass, too, of course," Bergstrom said as he expelled another roiling billow.

"What do you mean?" Ben asked.

"Don't play stupid," Bergstrom replied. "Unless you produce something more solid than some feeling about mangled data, you and your daughter will go down."

Ben stared at the empty screen. All this time searching for Caitline, he thought he had been saving her skin. Their fates were linked now with death perhaps the best possible outcome. He reproved himself for the thought.

"Did you mean what you said?" Bergstrom asked.

"About what?" Ben asked.

"About your daughter being behind all this," Bergstrom said.

"Yes," Ben replied with little conviction. Zarima and the video confirmed Caitline's involvement. All the data pointed to her guilt, yet part of him clung to the possibility of Caitline's innocence. Was that why he chose to interpret the messages as warnings? "I said it was possible."

"That endorsement sounds like it's on life support," Bergstrom observed. He took another drag and sighed. "But who could blame you?"

Bergstrom dashed his half-smoked cigarette on the rim of the wastebasket and stood up.

"Any ideas how to prove it?" Bergstrom asked.

Ben drummed his fingers on the space bar of the keyboard as he contemplated their options. He thought of the money transactions Azeb had mentioned earlier.

"You haven't been able to trace the money in these transactions," Ben said.

"So?" Bergstrom asked.

"So, the domain names of the missing women still belong to Web(W)rights," Ben added.

"So what?" Bergstrom replied.

"Rykert and Wilson may have been using the domain names to set up bank accounts in the names of the missing women," Ben said. "That way they could transfer funds without calling attention to themselves."

"That's speculation," Bergstrom declared.

"Perhaps," Ben replied. "But if Rykert and Wilson were operating the Web site together, isn't it likely that Rykert went to meet Wilson?"

Bergstrom cocked a skeptical eyebrow.

"You said he was negotiating with the Wahhabis," Bergstrom replied.

"That's just what he told me," Ben said. "I think it was to get his share of the profits."

"When he could just transfer the money?" Bergstrom replied. "Why would he risk it?"

"The easiest way to circumvent technological detection is payment in cash," Ben said.

"Where did you hear that?" Bergstrom snorted.

"Special Forces," Ben replied. "We did it all the time in Somalia. Hoot knew it, too."

"Nonsense," Bergstrom said as he resumed his seat on the edge of the desk. "You're beginning to push me into Stanfeld's corner with your conspiracy theories."

"Think about it," Ben urged.

"I am," Bergstrom replied as he eyed Ben up and down. "Your friend's death begins to look more and more like a simple case of jealousy and revenge to me."

Ben clenched his fist.

"There's one way to find out," Ben said.

"Such as?" Bergstrom replied.

"You have Schariah's staked out, don't you?" Ben asked.

"We do our jobs," Bergstrom retorted. "Like the woman said."

"So it should be easy to go in there and find out," Ben declared.

"You expect me to jeopardize a federal surveillance operation on the notion of a potential accomplice?" Bergstrom asked. "I'm not crazy, or suicidal."

Ben fingered the lead socket into Hoot's sensory hood as he considered his options. The only way to convince Bergstrom of the plausibility of his assertion was to plant an appeal to Bergstrom's professional vanity.

"You said yourself your ass was grass," Ben replied. "What have you got to lose?"

"You're serious," Bergstrom muttered. "From a few bits of missing evidence you've fabricated this whole twisted fantasy about your daughter. And now you expect me to go along and jeopardize a criminal investigation to prove it?"

Ben said nothing. He had to give the virus he had planted a chance to work. He had no other arguments he could use.

"You've got balls. I'll admit that," Bergstrom said. He stared at his polished shoe tips dangling above the floor as if turning Ben's suggestion in his mind.

"What the hell," Bergstrom decided and jumped off the desk. "Let's go."

He strode to the doorway, peered in both directions, and beckoned Ben.

"C'mon," Bergstrom urged. "Too late for cold feet now."

Caught off guard by Bergstrom's sudden enthusiasm, Ben struggled to catch up as he followed Bergstrom down to the other end of the hallway and through the Emergency exit. Shielding his eyes from the late afternoon sun, he saw that the door opened onto a cement platform at the bottom of a ramp.

Bergstrom strode up the ramp and swung around the metal railing at the top. Ben scampered after him and spotted Bergstrom striding toward an unmarked, brown sedan in the center of the station parking lot. Ben had just enough time to slide onto the passenger side before Bergstrom backed out of the stall and sped out of the lot. He turned off the two-way radio, guided the sedan through a series of amber lights, and turned onto the access ramp that led toward the Warehouse district.

Ben sat back in his seat. Hold on, Caitline, he thought despite himself. The cavalry's coming to get you.

He glanced at Bergstrom. It felt odd to have a cohort, especially one connected to the power structure that for so long had enforced keeping he and Caitline apart.

Ben peered at the warehouses speeding past and wondered if Caitline had been held hostage in one of those all along. Or, had she been directing the weapon that electrocuted Hoot? Whatever the outcome, at last he'd know.

Bergstrom slowed the car and rolled through the intersection. Schariah's appeared as somnolent and empty as every other building in this part of the city.

"Where's the surveillance?" Ben asked.

"They're here," Bergstrom said. He turned the switch of the two-way radio and waited for the static to abate. "Team one, are you there?"

"Team one here," a deep male voice replied.

"Team two, you there?" Bergstrom asked.

"Team two here," a female voice reported.

"Anything happening?" Bergstrom asked.

"Nothing here," team one replied.

"All quiet," the team two voice said.

Bergstrom pulled into the alley halfway down the street and parked in the lot behind Schariah's.

"I've got us here," Bergstrom said as he shut off the engine. "What now?"

"You're asking me?" Ben asked.

"This was your idea," Bergstrom replied.

Ben scanned the upper stories of the building. If Caitline were here physically, she'd be held in one of those upstairs rooms.

"We go in," Ben decided.

"That's it?" Bergstrom asked.

"As far as Wilson's concerned I'm still the frustrated father searching for his daughter," Ben replied. "Which I am."

"How do you explain me?" Bergstrom asked.

"I don't," Ben replied. He eyed Bergstrom's identification card dangling from the breast pocket of his suit. "Get rid of the badge."

Bergstrom stuck the card inside his sport coat and got out of the car. Ben glanced toward the alley entrance.

"You're sure your men won't interfere?" Bergstrom asked.

"Nobody's getting away, if that's what you're thinking," Ben replied.

"I wasn't," Bergstrom retorted.

Ben started up the alley. He knew what Bergstrom meant. His appearance of trust was just that, appearance. Ben glanced toward the man following him and felt grateful that Bergstrom had let him come this far. Appearances would have to do for now, Ben decided, until he found Caitline.

Bergstrom rounded the corner as Ben paused to catch his breath. His face and arms were sweating. He hoped they were due to excitement, not advancing age.

"Special Forces, huh?" Bergstrom hooted as he headed toward the entrance. "C'mon, let's see what you're made of."

Ben blew the air from his cheeks and fell in behind Bergstrom's prowling gait. The incident recalled Ben's frustration from his early days of army training. Hoot had badgered him all the way through boot camp so he could graduate and get into intelligence school.

They reached the entrance just as Petrov unlocked the plate glass doors. The cut-glass chandeliers flickered to life above his head as he returned down the hall-way.

Ben cupped his hand over his eyes and pressed his face against the glass. Petrov spread his black leather ledger atop the cashier station. Nobody in a French maid's outfit occupied the gift alcove or stood beside the walnut doors.

He slipped inside the door. The hallway was quiet, tomblike. A panel of after-noon sun slanted across the left-hand wall. He paused in front of the trio of gilt cherubs. The gilt paint on the derrieres of two of them had chipped and cracked.

Bergstrom checked the wall opposite. Dry wall showed through the marks in the fuchsia wallpaper.

Ben sniffed. The cloying scent of incense failed to disguise an underlying odor of cigar smoke.

They proceeded to the cashier station where Petrov restocked the souvenirs seated in the display case. He turned and scanned both of them.

"Can I help you, gentlemen?" Petrov asked.

"I'm here for my daughter," Ben declared.

"We've already told you she's not here any more," Petrov replied.

"Nor anyone else it appears," Bergstrom observed.

Petrov glared at Bergstrom.

"You guys ought to know," Petrov replied.

"Where's Wilson?" Ben asked.

"Out," Petrov replied.

Bergstrom tapped Petrov's shoulder.

"Could you be more specific?" Bergstrom asked.

"On business," Petrov added.

"What kind of business?" Bergstrom asked.

"He's the boss. He doesn't have to tell me more than that," Petrov replied and grinned. "Now, if you'll excuse me."

Petrov strolled down the intersecting hallway.

"Hold it," Bergstrom ordered. "We'd like to look around."

"Sure, go ahead," Petrov said. He halted in the doorway to Wilson's office and faced them with an officious smile. "So long as you have a warrant."

"It doesn't have to come to that now, does it?" Bergstrom growled.

"It shouldn't, should it?" Petrov agreed and shook his bullet head. "Ordinarily, I would not mind. Nor would Mr. Wilson. But with him gone, I cannot take the responsibility."

Petrov grinned again.

"Unless you make it official," Petrov added.

"I can have one in five minutes," Bergstrom said.

"Take your time," Petrov urged. "We are citizens. We have nothing to hide."

Ben clenched his hands. He knew Petrov was stalling. He agreed with everything that Bergstrom said because the big move already had occurred. The marks on the wall said as much.

Someone moved inside Wilson's office. A moment later Vera slipped out the doorway and started down the hall. She was wearing a strawberry wig.

Ben grabbed her elbow. Vera did not struggle. Her asymmetrical face did not appear nearly so attractive at close range.

"Where'd you get that?" Ben asked.

"What?" Vera replied.

"That wig," Ben said.

Vera glanced at Petrov and squared her shoulders.

"In closet," she replied.

"Leave her alone," Petrov warned. "We have dozens of wigs that our girls use."

"Not like that one," Ben said.

Ben sniffed. The delicate fragrance of fresh flowers wafted up from her aura of tobacco. He tightened his grip on Vera's arm and elbowed Wilson's office door open.

Petrov advanced toward the door.

"We're just inspecting the merchandise," Bergstrom declared and barred the entrance with his left arm. "We'll put it on the warrant if you want."

Ben pulled Vera inside and sniffed. The tobacco odor surrounded her head and hair. He turned and sniffed again. The fragrance of flowers pervaded Wilson's office. The azure vase on Wilson's desk contained a mixed bouquet of snow-white roses and buttery jonquils.

Ben released his grip, approached the desk, and extracted two jonquils from the vase. The stems were of different lengths, their bottoms torn and jagged. That indicated they had been freshly cut.

He slid the shorter stem between his thumb and index finger. The soil that adhered to it felt gritty, yet brittle like ash residue.

He knew that roses could come from any floral shop. Fresh cut jonquils came from gardens. Or flower beds.

Ben examined the vase. A mound of tooth-shaped pebbles covered the ash underneath. He turned toward Vera.

"Where'd you get those?" Ben asked.

"I picked them," Vera replied.

"Where?" Ben asked. He knew they came from the Grafton apartment's flowerbeds.

"It is a free country," Vera protested and retreated toward the door. "I do not have to tell you."

Ben seized her right arm and pulled her augmented body against his. Above her halo of competing scents was the terror that registered in her caramel eyes.

"You don't have to be afraid," Ben urged. "We'll protect you. Just tell me where Caitline is."

"Let me go," Vera demanded as she squirmed against Ben's chest.

"Just tell me." Ben urged.

"Let me go!" Vera cried.

Vera pummeled her fists against Ben's neck and shoulders. The doorway flew open. Petrov seized Ben's shoulder.

Ben spun from Petrov's grasp, pulled Vera's face to his own, and kissed her long and hard on the lips.

Bergstrom pulled the three of them apart.

"Get him out of here," Petrov demanded. "This is not Russia. We have rights!"

"What kind of pervert are you?" Bergstrom asked as he grabbed Ben's elbow and shoved him into the hall. "Are you trying to ruin everything?"

Ben wiped Vera's taste from his mouth. The sensation resembled mouthing the edge of an ashtray.

"Get him out of here," Petrov reiterated and shook his fist at both of them. "This is a place of business. We know our rights."

Ben grimaced. At this distance, he knew that Petrov's fist shaking was for effect and for the agents listening outside.

"Let's go," Ben said.

"Go?" Bergstrom replied. "Where do you think you're going?"

"To get Caitline," Ben said. "I know where she is."

CHAPTER 28

▼

Ben reached the front entrance before Bergstrom spun him around.

"You're not going any place," Bergstrom ordered.

Ben glanced down the hall. Petrov shook his fist at them.

"Good," Ben whispered. "Keep it up. Run me out to the street."

"Gladly," Bergstrom replied.

Bergstrom twisted Ben's wrist, thrust it behind his back, and maneuvered him onto the pavement. Ben scanned the street as Bergstrom steered him toward the alley. The cars remained parked where they had been, the sidewalk empty, Bergstrom's surveillance still invisible. Only the angle of the sun had changed. That and Ben's conviction he knew where Caitline was. That made all the difference.

"You can let go now," Ben advised when they reached the corner.

Bergstrom increased his leverage as they advanced toward the car.

"Any reason I should?" Bergstrom asked.

"I know where Caitline is," Ben repeated.

"So you say," Bergstrom said.

"No, really," Ben pleaded. "I do."

"Shut up," Bergstrom ordered.

They halted beside the passenger door. Bergstrom produced a pair of handcuffs from his coat pocket and slapped them around Ben's wrists.

"Behave yourself and you can sit up front like a normal citizen," Bergstrom advised. "If not, I'll slam you in the back seat like any other felon."

"She's at the Grafton apartment building," Ben said as he shifted his forearms back and forth to relieve the pressure of the steel rubbing against his wrists. "That's where the jonquils came from."

"Jonquils, huh?" Bergstrom retorted.

"In the vase on Wilson's desk," Ben replied. "Didn't you see them?"

"I must have missed 'em during your love scene with the stripper," Bergstrom growled. "What of it?"

Ben realized his performance had appeared too convincing.

"The pebbles in the vase come from the same place the jonquils do," Ben explained. "The flower beds at the Grafton Apartments."

"So?" Bergstrom asked.

"They're teeth," Ben declared.

Bergstrom's face remained blank. Ben knew he had exhausted Bergstrom's patience, yet they were very close to finding Caitline.

"Of the strippers who disappeared," Ben entreated. "Wilson burned them in the furnace and Sophia buried the remains in the flower beds."

Bergstrom remained unimpressed.

"Save it for the competency hearing," Bergstrom advised. "Your insane story will play better there."

"That's why Zarima said the air smelled so bad when the furnace came on," Ben added in desperation.

Ben's exhortations produced no effect. Bergstrom produced an electronic key ring, unlocked the door, and shoved Ben inside. He re-locked the doors, crossed to the driver's side, unlocked them long enough to get in, and re-locked them again. He drove up the cobblestone incline and turned left when he reached the street. At the next intersection, he turned left again.

"Where are we going?" Ben asked in alarm.

"Back to the station," Bergstrom said.

"The station," Ben exclaimed. "When I told you where Caitline is? Don't you want to find her?"

Bergstrom glared at Ben in angry disbelief.

"Do you?" Bergstrom retorted.

"Of course," Ben replied.

"Why don't I believe that?" Bergstrom asked. "Is it because you jeopardized an entire surveillance operation, or because you played me for a fool with my superiors? Or, maybe it's because you attacked a woman given the first opportunity."

"I had to," Ben said. "I didn't want to."

"Oh," Bergstrom retorted and grimaced. "That makes it OK."

Bergstrom focused on the car ahead. He drove with the ferocity of a madman. Ben knew that apologizing would not convince Bergstrom to change his mind.

"Vera's one of them," Ben insisted.

"Yeah," Bergstrom agreed sarcastically. "One who will go right to Stanfeld and the police board and cry assault."

"But Petrov won't tell Wilson to clear out," Ben explained. "He just thinks I couldn't control myself."

"Oh," Bergstrom snorted as he speeded through an intersection. "And you're saying that your attack back there was all part of your plan."

"I had to do something to keep them from thinking I'd made the connection," Ben replied.

"Great idea," Bergstrom said with mock approval.

Bergstrom steered the car around the corner of another intersection. The Uptown precinct house lay a few blocks ahead.

"Don't you want to find out whether she's there or not?" Ben asked.

The set of Bergstrom's jaw indicated he had moved beyond caring. Ben stared at the homes and office buildings whizzing past. In a few moments, he'd return to the station without hope of release. In a few hours, the AFI would shut down the Internet. Who knew what Stanfeld would do to prevent it? Or, what Wilson had plotted in anticipation?

He glanced at Bergstrom. The flange of the electronic key bulged in Bergstrom's coat pocket; his seatbelt remained unbuckled.

Ben slid the key of his seat belt into its buckle. When the tumblers clicked, he yanked on the steering wheel. Bergstrom slapped Ben's head and attempted to straighten the wheel. Ben grabbed the bulge in Bergstrom's coat pocket and thumbed it three times.

When Ben's door popped open, he snapped open his seat belt and lunged toward the opening. Bergstrom wrapped his arm around Ben's neck and crushed it against his chest. Ben yanked on the steering wheel. His forehead slammed against the dashboard, bounced off the seat, and hung suspended over a widening fan of gas on the pavement.

Ben tumbled out of the car. Darkness clouded his vision. He shook his head, rocked onto his heels, and staggered to his feet.

The front end of Bergstrom's car lay twisted around the bumper of a black Escalade. Bergstrom groaned, raised his battered head, and turned it in Ben's direction before his forehead thudded onto the steering wheel.

Ben surveyed the area and wondered if he had time to retrieve the key. An elderly woman carrying a bag of groceries gawked at him from the supermarket parking lot across the street. A college student pointed in his direction and jabbered into his cell phone. The police would arrive in another minute.

He scuttled to the sidewalk, stood erect, and started walking in the opposite direction. Remember your training, Ben reminded himself. Keep cool. Resist the urge to run. Blend in.

Averting his face and arms from oncoming pedestrians, Ben crossed the bank parking lot at the corner and hurried down a side street. At the next corner, he turned right, then left at the following intersection. He knew he had to put as much distance as possible between himself and the accident scene.

Ben zigzagged three more blocks and headed north. At the second intersection he turned right and spotted the iron fence in front of the Grafton apartment building.

He slowed his pace and assessed his situation. He had no one else to turn to. Bloodied and handcuffed, he'd managed to alienate, injure, and abandon his only ally. Ben paused as a white Mazda drove past, then he crossed the street and peered through the bars of the gate.

The security light illuminated the main entrance. Young girls moved back and forth in their rooms studying or conversing with their friends. Everything appeared as normal as it did the first night, Ben thought. How could anything sinister be happening here?

Ben scanned the flowerbed inside the gate. The ragged curve in the far corner suggested something had been removed. In the uncertain light, he could be sure of nothing.

He shook the gate. It held fast.

What now, Ben wondered. No one was going to open the gate for him. The wall appeared to be too high to climb, especially for someone who was handcuffed. What other way could he get inside?

Ben examined the intercom box and flicked the Reply switch. A muffled burst of static indicated the box remained functional. He glanced up and down the street. No one approached in either direction. He toggled the switch several times.

"Pizza man," Ben announced.

He received no response. Ben repeated his announcement with the same result. He needed to be more specific to make his ruse work.

"Luigi's," Ben said. "Luigi's Pisa Pizza."

Ben glanced up the street. What the hell, he decided. You're already on the run and standing in front the headquarters of your enemy. You might as well turn up the intensity.

"Look," Ben bellowed in his best imitation of the aggrieved working man. "I gotta pizza here. You want it or not?"

Ben peered toward the alley and pondered the possibilities. Every old brownstone had a back entrance. And a coal chute.

The intercom buzzed and went silent.

"Pisa Pizza?" Ben repeated.

"We are no longer accepting deliveries at this address," a female voice responded. "Please leave."

The voice sounded like Sophia's, Ben decided.

"I got a pizza here," Ben groused. "You want it or not?"

"Nobody here ordered pizza," Sophia replied.

"Look. I got pizza for delivery at this address," Ben declared. "Two Supremos with extra cheese."

Ben's stomach growled. He fancied he could smell their mozzarella aroma. "And a Dago Burger with a large order of fries," Ben added to complete his hunger fantasy.

"We didn't order it," Sophia replied.

"Are you gonna pay or what?" Ben demanded.

Static and a series of mutterings emanated from the box.

"Sir, there must be some mistake," a resonant male voice replied, "No one has contacted your establishment from this address."

Ben recognized Rykert's voice. He had forgotten his voice sounded so vibrant.

"Well," Ben argued. "I got a bill for $27.95 that says different."

"Please leave the premises immediately," Rykert asked. "Or we shall call the authorities."

"Go ahead," Ben agreed. He tried crossing his arms to embellish his sense of outrage. Bergstrom's handcuffs prevented it. "It's a public sidewalk. I'm not moving until I receive full compensation."

Ben pondered what could clinch his projection of insolence.

"And a gratuity," Ben added.

"Benjamin?" Jennifer inquired. "Is that you?"

Ben hesitated. He had hoped that Jennifer was not there. She would be the only one who could see through his voice impressions. Should he acknowledge his identity? Or play out his charade as long as possible?

"If it is you, I suggest that you leave immediately," Jennifer advised. "None of us can be held accountable for the consequences if you don't."

Jennifer's advice sounded like a veiled threat, Ben decided.

"I want to speak to Caitline," Ben demanded and grabbed the bars. "Let me speak to Caitline."

Ben shook the gate door until stars danced before his eyes. He clutched his knees, gulped a lungful of air, and resumed his Samson imitation. He paused to regain his equilibrium. Some of the bolts had loosened in their concrete moorings. He redoubled his efforts.

"Mr. Hackwell," the resonant voice called behind him.

Ben turned. Rykert stood behind him flanked by Petrov.

"Neither of us wish to cause a disturbance in this public thoroughfare, do we?" Rykert said. "Not with so much at stake."

Petrov extended his hand toward the alleyway.

"If you'll come this way, please," Petrov suggested.

"And if I don't?" Ben replied.

Petrov plucked the chain connecting Ben's cuffs.

"I don't see your having a lot of choice in the matter," Petrov said.

Ben winced at the added pressure on his wrists. He fell behind Rykert with Petrov following as though they might be escorting him to his favorite seat at Schariah's. He knew the show of decorum was for whoever might be watching them from the street.

Rykert turned left at the alley and plodded up the unlit path until it connected with a short sidewalk leading to a wooden door in the center of the back wall of the building.

Ben spotted a black minivan parked beside the downspout. The last three digits of the license plate were visible under the alley light. They read 002. A square outline at the base of the wall in front of the van suggested the location of a coal chute. Ben knew this would be useful information should he and Caitline be able to make their escape.

He readjusted his cuffs. Being able was the operative phrase.

Petrov unlocked the door. Once Ben and Rykert had entered, Petrov re-locked it and proceeded down the bare-bulbed hallway toward the building's west wing.

Ben groaned. He realized he had no escape without a key, or a short stick of dynamite.

They proceeded to a fire door located just beyond the hallway intersection.

"Down there," Petrov ordered as he opened the door and beckoned toward the stairwell. "In the basement."

Ben peered over the steel railing. The stairwell ended a one flight down.

"Where's Caitline?" Ben asked.

"You'll find out," Petrov promised.

They descended the stairs, turned right, and proceeded to another fire door at the end of the hallway. As Petrov unlocked it, Ben noticed the door clasp of the coal chute beside it. The door to the furnace room stood across from it.

Ben nudged the door with his shoulder. The scuttle Sophia had used to sprinkle ashes on the flower beds lay in front of a mulching machine that stood beside an ancient, cast iron furnace. A rack of lawn and garden implements hung on the wall behind it.

He sniffed. The air smelled rank, stale sweat mixed with something else. It stank of something dank, fetid. Visceral.

Petrov shoved Ben into the hallway that ran under the west wing. Rykert opened the first doorway on the left, one of the two whose blinds had been drawn shut.

"In here," Rykert directed and nodded toward the dim interior. "You haven't much time."

Ben waited until his eyes adjusted to the dim interior. A bank of computer terminals ranged along the top of a folding table situated in front of the bank of windows. Four metal folding chairs stood in front of them, the middle two occupied by Wilson and a lanky youth with cropped, curly blond hair dressed in a plain brown hijab and jeans who was keying in data.

"Mr. Hackwell," Wilson greeted him and grinned. "If anyone could find our little band, I expected it would be you."

The person at the keyboard continued to type.

"Caitline?" Ben said.

The youth's slender fingers drummed the keyboard with a closing arpeggio.

"Are you OK?" Ben asked.

"Never better," Caitline replied as she swiveled around and flashed Ben an ingratiating grin that so much resembled her mother's. "And certainly better than you are."

CHAPTER 29

▼

"I thought you were dead," Ben said, relieved that Caitline was alive, yet irritated by the banality of his remark. After all this time and effort, Ben reflected, couldn't he think of something better to say?

"Obviously not," Caitline replied.

Caitline gave Wilson an affectionate glance reserved for couples who had been intimate a long time. Ben recalled exchanging such looks with Jennifer eons ago. A wave of repressed anger washed through him.

"What's going on?" Ben demanded.

"Isn't it obvious?" Caitline replied as she extended her arms above her head and emitted an ear-splitting yawn. "I'm running an e-business from home."

"It's not so obvious to me," Ben replied. "I've spent the last three days evading the police, fearing if you were alive or dead, and you sat here playing games?"

"Hardly games," Caitline said and rose to her feet. "I can assure you of that."

"What would you call it?" Ben retorted. "*I Spy?*"

"What would you know about it?" Caitline replied. "Or anything else I do? Or ever did?"

Ben stared at the lettering on the T-shirt that Caitline wore under her hijab. The sentence, "I GOT MORE ENEMIES THAN FRIENDS" was printed in block letters across her less-than-ample bust. Jennifer's money had not gone for breast implants Ben realized. He felt his face flush.

"I'm learning," Ben said.

"A little late for that," Caitline said with a glance at Ben's handcuffs. "Isn't it?"

Caitline flounced onto her chair, turned toward the middle monitor, and resumed keying in programming code.

She typed fast, Ben thought with empty pride. She scarcely made a mistake. He clenched his manacled hands in frustration. Caitline's actions and recriminations spoke to all the discussions they should have had and never did.

Ben glanced toward Wilson who regarded him with a mixture of amatory triumph and possessive vigilance. Caitline was his woman now.

Ben approached her chair and spotted a tiny glass vase of jonquils between her keyboard and the processing units, a gentle reminder of the spring waiting to be born.

"I tried, Caitline," Ben said. The fragrance of the jonquils mingled with the antiseptic odor of Caitline's shampoo. "Your mother…"

"You leave Jennifer out of this," Caitline barked. "At least she helped."

Ben recoiled at the ferocity in Caitline's reply. He needed to get her to talk, to reveal what had caused this disaster to happen.

"Helped?" Ben asked. "Helped how?"

"With this," Caitline replied. She extended her arms to encompass the array of terminals. "Now go away," Caitline ordered.

"What—" Ben replied.

"You are disturbing the lady," Wilson interrupted as he slid between Ben and Caitline. "With so many things yet for her to do."

Ben backed away, knowing Wilson fully was in charge. Wilson was a pimp, a thug, and who knew what else, yet Caitline loved him. Ben realized that. What did Caitline see in Wilson?

He grimaced as he watched Wilson slide his arm around Caitline's shoulders. Every father thought that about their daughters' suitors, Ben reflected. How was it different in Caitline's case? Ben resisted using the word "lover" despite all the data to the contrary.

Caitline took Wilson's hand and rubbed it against her cheek.

"I'm tired, Scott," Caitline said.

"As are we all," Wilson replied.

"Can't this last upload wait until tomorrow?" Caitline asked.

"Not if you care about our cause," Wilson replied as he massaged Caitline's shoulders. "And me."

Ben recognized Wilson's ploy. Confuse the cause with the victim's affections and play one against the other until they do what you want. Ben glanced at the metal door to the furnace room. Perhaps he still could drive a wedge between them.

"You spent Jennifer's money wisely, I see," Ben observed. "At least it didn't go for a boob job."

"Boob job?" Wilson asked.

"Isn't that what you told Jennifer?" Ben replied.

"Is that what she told you?" Caitline fumed. "Mother, come out here! This instant!"

Jennifer entered from the adjoining room. Her hair appeared in disarray. Her eyes hollow from lack of sleep. Ben marveled at Jennifer's transformation as Rykert closed the door behind them.

"Is that what you told Daddy?" Caitline asked. "That I used the money for a set of boobs?"

"It seemed the best explanation at the time," Jennifer replied in a small voice as she rubbed her right hand over the knuckles of the other. "I thought you wanted everything kept secret."

"Not like that," Caitline replied. "It wasn't as if he didn't already suspect."

"Well…" Jennifer replied.

"Are you ashamed of what I've done?" Caitline asked.

"No. Not exactly," Jennifer hedged.

Caitline approached Jennifer like a cat stalking a mouse. In all their years together and apart, Ben had never seen Jennifer cower before anyone like this before.

"Wasn't it your idea to get the oppressed women out of the Middle East?" Caitline asked.

"Yes," Jennifer admitted.

"And weren't you the one who agreed on the idea to give them new identities?" Caitline added.

Jennifer nodded.

"And didn't you tell me never to be afraid to do the right thing?" Caitline said.

"Of course. Perhaps. I don't know!" Jennifer replied. "This whole thing has gotten so out of control."

"Are you saying it's not right?" Caitline argued.

Jennifer's haggard eyes sought support from each of the men's in turn. Ben turned away. Despite his anger, he found no comfort in Jennifer's humiliation. She had taken control of Caitline's life. It had resulted in this less than stellar outcome.

"Why are you so weak-kneed now?" Caitline taunted. "Are you afraid?"

Caitline slapped her mother's cheek. Hard.

"Coward," Caitline cried.

Caitline's second blow sent Jennifer to the floor. Caitline raised her hand a third time before Wilson stayed her arm.

"She is your mother," Wilson admonished.

Caitline dropped her hand at her side. Ben winced at the red welt shaped like a ragged palm print spreading across Jennifer's right cheek. He was grateful that Wilson had stopped Caitline's onslaught, grateful and ashamed. Hadn't he done the same thing as Caitline, he recalled. Caitline's two blows reenacted those that culminated in his divorce.

"Caitline," Ben said.

Caitline turned toward him. Ben spotted the controlled rage that prowled below the surface of Caitline's tempestuous eyes.

"What 'right' thing?" Ben asked.

"Haven't you figured it out by now?" Caitline retorted.

Ben shook his head. Obtuseness seemed his best course of action.

"Some troubleshooter," Caitline scoffed and placed her hands on her hips. "I'm a terrorist."

She peered down at Jennifer.

"It's what I am, Mother," Caitline declared. "Why not admit it?"

Ben's stomach tightened. Everything he had hoped would not happen, everything Stanfeld and Bergstrom had predicted had come to pass. Finding Caitline dead would have been preferable, Ben thought. The only unanswered question left seemed laughable in its insignificance.

"Why?" Ben asked.

No one heard him.

"WHY?" Ben demanded. "I have a right to know."

"What right?" Caitline declared. She focused on Ben. "What right do you have?"

"The right of a father," Ben replied.

"Ha," Caitline scoffed. "You gave that up that right long ago."

"I tried," Ben entreated. "I tried being part of your life. Only Jennifer…"

"Don't blame Jennifer," Caitline interrupted. "That's just your excuse." Caitline's gaze swept the room like a lawyer's evaluating her effect on the jury. "You abandoned us long before Mother's divorce made it official."

Ben turned away. He refused to believe the truth of what he was hearing. Each of Caitline's accusations stoked Ben's shame at being separated from her. Her ending up with someone like Wilson was the end result.

"Don't act so hurt," Caitline added. "All those nights when you were alone before the terminal? I knew it wasn't work. I realized where your true affections lay."

"That was investigation," Ben replied and winced as soon as he said it. His answer sounded like an excuse to him, too. "Relaxation after a hard day."

"Instead of a cocktail, right?" Caitline hooted.

"It's like those guys who play video games to relieve tension," Ben said. "The pictures, those women, they all meant nothing to me."

"About as much as your family seemed to," Caitline jeered.

"That's not true," Ben replied and turned toward Jennifer for corroboration. Jennifer turned away. "It had been over between your mother and I for some time. I just wouldn't admit it."

"So you retreated into porn?" Caitline scoffed. "At least an affair would have been understandable. And less humiliating."

"I was so angry," Ben said. He clenched his fists as he recalled the whirl of events and emotions that led up to his divorce and its aftermath. "I had given up my career for your mother and followed her out to what to me seemed the middle of nowhere. I had to start all over with no prospects, no reputation. Nothing."

Caitline clucked in mock sympathy.

"You felt abandoned, betrayed," Caitline concluded. "And after 17 years of marriage you attacked Jennifer because of that."

"No. Maybe," Ben admitted. Most of what Caitline said was true, but not all of it. His family had not abandoned him, Ben realized. He had withdrawn from them. The divorce and Jennifer's restraining order compounded his feeling of powerlessness and isolation.

Ben returned Caitline's accusing stare.

"I always cared about its effect on you," Ben said.

"Really," Caitline replied. Her eyes widened with mock astonishment. "Which effect on me bothered you more, that of the divorce or of the voyeurism?"

"The divorce, of course," Ben replied. "The others were just images on a screen, for Crissakes!"

"Like I am?" Caitline asked with a smile. She pressed the Enter key of the nearest keyboard. "That's why you're here, isn't it? Like Sir Lancelot to rescue me?"

Caitline's pouting, pneumatic alter ego materialized on all three monitors.

"It's all right if you prefer me this way. Most men do," Caitline said. She pressed the Enter key again. The image froze. "Less hypocritical, anyway."

Ben stared at Caitline as if seeing her for the first time. The Caitline Ben had known and loved as a girl had been murdered by this beautiful, vengeful harpy who retaliated against the world for her feelings of fear and abandonment.

He saw the parallel to himself. Ben had felt powerless. Caitline had followed his example and turned to technology as a substitute. Internet pornography had given him full control, or a simulation of it. Hoot's haptic interface was the logical extension of that feeling of power.

Ben glanced at Wilson who eyed his protégé with increasing unease. Wilson had a human bomb on his hands, Ben decided. With Caitline's knowledge and her neuroses, it was a matter of time before she released that anger against someone, somewhere. Wilson's hope was to channel that fear and animosity onto the Internet before it exploded on him.

"Is that what this is all about?" Ben retorted. He was determined to stop the family cycle of recrimination and revenge, but he knew had to tread carefully. "Hypocrisy?"

"That's one way to put it," Caitline replied. "Unlike you and Jennifer, I see the world as it is and do something about it."

"Such as?" Ben asked.

"Such as the WABC," Caitline replied. "Rather than talk about changing women's lives like my mother, I took that organization and made it live up to its potential."

Ben pressed his fingernails into his palms. The pain helped him control his anger.

"By doing what?" Ben asked.

"By bringing women out of places where they have no rights, no jobs, and no future and bringing them to the United States," Caitline boasted.

"What did that accomplish?" Ben asked.

"It gave them a better life," Caitline replied. "It gave them the freedom and power to choose how to live their lives."

"By working at Wilson's strip club?" Ben replied. "That's neither free nor empowering."

Caitline glanced at Wilson who flashed a smile of encouragement. Caitline's assurance stemmed from Wilson's continuous reinforcement, Ben thought.

"Why not?" Caitline retorted. "Why not get something back from the very people who have oppressed you?"

"Is that how Wilson justified it?" Ben replied. "As female empowerment?"

"It's better than resigning your commission over a difference of opinion," Caitline replied. "And playing with Internet hotties the rest of your life."

Ben dug his nails deeper into his palms. For Caitline, Ben realized, he and Hoot were one and the same.

"You can't equate men's viewing nude photographs with what you're doing," Ben declared. "Or with Hoot's interface."

"Why not?" Caitline asked. "It's simply a matter of degree."

"Murdering people over the Internet is not a matter of degree," Ben countered.

Caitline raised her eyebrows in surprise.

"Who said we murdered anyone?" Caitline said.

Ben smiled grimly. For the first time, one of his replies to Caitline's merciless logic stream had thrown her off balance.

"What about those four dancers?" Ben said.

"We helped them disappear from their pursuers," Caitline replied. "There's a difference."

"How?" Ben retorted. "By killing them?"

"Nobody was killed," Caitline said. She glanced at Wilson for corroboration. "We erased all the data associated with their old identities and gave them new ones."

"Oh?" Ben replied. He ignored Caitline and peered at Wilson. "And where are they now?"

"Safe," Wilson replied. "I can assure you."

Ben spun toward his daughter.

"Is that what he told you?" Ben said. He pointed toward the furnace room. "And what do you suppose goes on in there?"

"Heating," Caitline said.

"Quite a lot of it according to Zarima," Ben replied. "So much so she said the building stank." He glanced toward Rykert for confirmation. "Isn't that so?"

Rykert grunted in acknowledgement. Ben moved toward the doorway and sniffed.

"It smells right now," Ben said and beckoned Caitline toward the door. "Go ahead. Take a whiff."

Caitline shifted in her chair.

"These old heating systems…" Caitline said.

Ben saw the doubt creeping into Caitline's face. He needed more data to convince her. He stepped over to the computer terminals.

"How do you account for these?" Ben asked and scooped a handful of pebbles from the vase. "Or the mulching machine beside the furnace? Or Sophia's nocturnal gardening?"

Wilson stepped between them.

"Ms. Nechayev's supervisory duties unfortunately do not allow her to indulge in her favorite past time," Wilson explained. "Except at night."

"Oh?" Ben retorted. His argument must seem more convincing now that Wilson had decided to intervene. "How do you know anything about her duties?"

"We have an understanding," Wilson replied. "Some of my employees stay here."

"Some?" Ben remarked and felt a rising surge of confidence that Caitline was seeing Wilson for the thug he was. "How many is that?"

"I'm not sure," Wilson replied and glanced toward Petrov. "I'd have to ask Pyotr to check our records."

"Go ahead, check them," Ben replied. "Check with Sophia, too, while you're at it. I'm sure her count is down from last time."

Ben turned to Caitline.

"And check how often she hauls the ashes out to the flowerbeds," Ben added.

"Is it every full moon? Or only when one of the dancers leaves your employ?"

Caitline sprang to her feet.

"Ridiculous," Caitline declared. "We gave them new identities."

"I felt the ashes, Caitline," Ben replied. "And the whip handle."

"We killed no one," Caitline said.

"What about Hoot?" Ben asked.

"What about him?" Caitline replied.

"He died watching your snuff scene," Ben said.

Caitline wrapped her arm around Wilson's elbow for reinforcement.

"Mr. Gibson was like you," Caitline declared. "A victim of his own excesses."

"You don't die from your excesses," Ben replied. "Unless there's a surge of electric current involved."

"Is that what you think?" Caitline retorted. "Mr. Gibson was a sex addict, plain and simple."

"Like me, you mean," Ben said.

Caitline nodded.

"He kept perfecting his system, increasing the stimulation," Caitline explained.

"Until it killed him," Ben said as he adjusted his handcuffs. "With your help."

"Until his heart gave out," Caitline corrected.

"I saw the burn marks," Ben said.

"All over his back, right?" Caitline replied. "Arms and legs, too?"

Ben nodded.

"All evidence of his addiction," Caitline declared.

"Like all Westerners," Wilson added.

"What?" Ben said, caught off guard by Wilson's remark. "What did you say?"

"Like all Westerners," Wilson reiterated. "He was a slave to his vices."

"Hoot had the fewest vices of anyone I know," Ben replied.

Wilson looked at Ben and shook his head in sympathy.

"It must be difficult to feel that way," Wilson declared.

"What way?" Ben asked.

"It must be difficult to feel, how do you say it?" Wilson asked and turned to Caitline. "Oh, yes, to get some of your own?"

Ben smiled at his hard won success. He had gotten Wilson talking in place of Caitline. He had to keep Wilson talking to discover a weakness he could use to escape.

"What are you talking about?" Ben asked.

"It must be difficult for you to understand," Wilson said. "It was for us."

"Understand what?" Ben replied.

"How it feels to have your women violated, your men humbled, your country torn and humiliated," Wilson declared as he drew Caitline closer to him. "In a few minutes your country and most of Western Europe will be forced to shut down their Internet systems."

Ben scanned the faces in the room.

"So what?" Ben replied with as much assurance as he could inject into his rebuttal. "They'll have it back up again in a few minutes. A few hours at most."

"Will they, Mr. Hackwell?" Wilson asked. "When your FBI and NSA have solid evidence that a terrorist faction here in your country is using it to kill consumers?"

"You can't be serious," Ben replied.

"Why not?" Wilson said. "When word comes out as it surely will, how many groups will demand that it be shut down?"

"Your killer application will end with it," Ben declared. "Along with your virtual sex business."

"People will fulfill their needs elsewhere," Wilson asserted. "You know how addictive it can be."

"Not if you don't have the haptic interface suit to go with it," Ben replied.

"Hmpf," Wilson snorted. "Sensors and spandex are available to any third world tailor at a tenth of the price."

"Sweatshop, you mean," Ben prodded.

"Whatever's cheapest," Wilson acknowledged and rolled his eyes. "The police power of the United States does not extend everywhere, especially over the Internet. Some of the best sex sites are located overseas, you know. America cannot eliminate all of them. We secured the domain rights for the rest."

Ben gritted his teeth. Was that the "sacrifice" Rykert meant?

"So Web(W)rights was behind this the whole time," Ben said.

"No, No," Rykert objected and rose to his feet. "That wasn't our intention at all."

"Just good business practice?" Ben replied. " Corner the haptic sex market before it takes off?"

Petrov moved sideways to stand next to Rykert who eased into the folding chair next to Jennifer's.

"Something like that," Rykert admitted.

"And you thought you could negotiate with these guys?" Ben said. "As if they were just another dot.com?"

"We felt we had to do something," Rykert explained as he folded Jennifer's hands in his own. "The data identity exchange for the WABC had spun beyond our control."

"Is that all you think this is?" Ben replied. "Spin management?"

"Quid pro quo," Rykert said and shook his head. "I thought allowing them the use of my company would satisfy them."

"Obviously not," Ben said.

Ben turned away. Such ignorance, such lack of foresight, he thought. No wonder Wilson regarded Americans as corrupt. What better examples did he have?

Ben glanced at Caitline. Or her, either, Ben realized.

Ben tugged futilely against his handcuffs. In frustration, he spun toward the computer terminals to find some means of incapacitating them. He spotted the dentate pebbles in Caitline's vase of jonquils and knew what final application of Hoot's device Wilson had in store for them.

"Do not despair," Wilson urged as he laid his hand on Ben's shoulder. "You cannot blame us for being the better capitalists. We have had decades to learn from your example. It is simple business tactics, really. You create the need, insure a monopoly, and exploit it to death."

"All a part of the business, huh?" Ben replied and shrugged out of Wilson's grasp. "I never played the game that way."

"Perhaps not. Only you know your own motives for certain," Wilson agreed. "But our efforts never could have succeeded so well without your considerable participation."

"What do you mean?" Ben asked.

"We needed a test subject for our recruitment portal," Wilson replied. "Caitline knew that you would search for her, though your persistence surprised even her." He glanced toward Caitline for confirmation. "Did it not?"

Caitline shrugged and nestled her head upon his shoulder.

Ben peered into Caitline's clouded face. The messages that Ben had thought were warnings had been intended as lures to test the strength of the Wahhabi recruitment video. He wondered whether some connection, some familial spark still lurked behind those angry mauve eyes.

"I thought you were lost," Ben implored. "That your messages meant you needed my help."

"Your help," Caitline sniffed. A tear trickled down her cheek. Caitline wiped it away in vexation

"Sometimes I get a little sloppy when I'm tired," Caitline explained.

"You always did," Ben replied. "That's how I knew that it was you sending the messages."

"You did?" Caitline asked in a small, surprised voice.

"Yeah," Ben replied. He glanced toward Jennifer. It was no wonder that Jennifer had decided to hide the truth about their daughter from him. Despite the wisdom of her decisions, Ben realized that Jennifer had done what she thought best. "It's a parent thing."

"Both of us underestimated the power of your attachment," Wilson said. "It is a tribute to you as a father."

Ben groaned. Did his executioner have to be gracious as well?

The hallway door burst open. Sophia Nechayev stood in the doorway dressed in combat fatigues and holding an AK-74 at the ready position across her chest.

"Wilson," Sophia called in an urgent whisper. "The FBI has surrounded the building."

CHAPTER 30

▼

Sophia strode to the window and nudged the drape aside with the nose of her rifle.

"They are everywhere outside," Sophia said. "See for yourself."

"Looks like I drew more attention than you bargained for," Ben said. "I am an escaped felon."

Ben exposed his manacled wrists as corroboration.

"Be still," Wilson warned.

"Now it begins," Caitline murmured. "As you said."

Wilson patted Caitline's arm and peered past the end of Sophia's rifle barrel.

"I see nothing," Wilson said. "Are you certain?"

"YOU IN THE BUILDING," Stanfeld announced. Her amplified voice rattled the bricks in the plaster. "COME OUT WITH YOUR HANDS IN THE AIR!"

"Are our preparations all in order?" Wilson asked.

Sophia nodded. An auburn tress fell down her cheek. Ben watched Sophia return the renegade strand to the loose bun under her beret. He wondered if Sophia had been the "spendy redhead" reported in the AFI memo.

"Caitline," Ben asked. He had to clarify one thing for his peace of mind before he died. "How long since you cut your hair?"

"Does it matter?" Caitline replied.

"It does to me," Ben replied.

"Five, six weeks," Caitline replied.

Ben clenched his fists in triumph. Caitline's hair would have been too short to grow back in the given time frame to have murdered Hoot.

"YOU HAVE ONE MINUTE," Stanfeld announced.

Wilson turned toward the hallway door where Petrov stood guard.

"Take them into the other room," Wilson ordered. "Make sure they are comfortable."

"In there," Petrov ordered and motioned toward the furnace room. "All of you."

Ben started toward the furnace room door. Before they were incinerated, he had to confirm the identity of Hoot's murderer.

"Sophia," Ben asked. "Ever driven a van or SUV?"

Sophia shrugged.

"I have driven many vehicles," Sophia replied.

"How about a Ford Bronco?" Ben asked.

Sophia shook her head. Despite Sophia's denial, Ben knew she was the most likely suspect in Hoot's murder.

"They can do wonderful things with DNA testing," Ben suggested. "A flake of skin can convict someone. Think what they can do with a strand of hair."

Sophia ignored Ben's comment and nudged his shoulder with the rifle barrel.

"Get going," Sophia ordered.

Ben turned toward Wilson for confirmation.

"That's how Sophia did it to Hoot," Ben asked. "Isn't it?"

Wilson pointed toward the doorway.

"You will follow Petrov, please," Wilson said.

Ben pointed at the two-way radio dangling from Sophia's belt.

"She offed them with that," Ben declared. "And with amplification equipment that's probably in the black van out back."

Petrov grabbed Ben's shoulder and shoved him toward the door.

Ben stumbled, regained his balance, and turned toward Caitline.

"Her HERF gun made them all look like electrocutions," Ben said as he gestured toward Sophia with his manacled hands. "My death would have made eight. The ashes of the other five are out front in the flowerbeds."

"I never killed Gibson," Sophia declared.

"That still leaves the other six," Ben replied.

Caitline broke from Wilson's embrace. Her wild eyes searched Ben's face.

"What are you saying?" Caitline demanded.

"You haven't killed anyone," Ben said as he peered into Caitline's defiant, troubled eyes. "Not yet anyway."

If concern or empathy entered Caitline's eyes, Ben could not spot it.

"Just so you know," Ben added and shrugged. "Nobody's going to get out of this alive. You realize that."

"Freedom comes at a high price," Wilson replied. "Your daughter accepts that."

Ben knew they had only moments before the authorities began their assault. When it came, it would be bloody and unrelenting.

"She may," Ben replied. "I don't."

"WE'RE COMING IN," Stanfeld declared.

Ben lunged toward the nearest window. He had one ploy left in his arsenal that might save all of them

"I'M COMING OUT," Ben cried and pulled aside the curtain. "YOU HEAR ME? I'M COMING OUT!"

Petrov pulled him from the window and slammed his pistol butt against Ben's temple. Ben crashed to the floor, fighting to remain conscious. He blinked several times to wipe the sparks from his vision.

"That was foolish," Wilson admonished. "Yelling will not enable you to escape."

"Who's the fool? I've bought you time," Ben replied in a groggy haze and stumbled to his feet. "Hear that? Not a sound."

"So?" Sophia scoffed.

"They're confused," Ben argued. "As far as they know I'm the only one here."

"And?" Wilson asked.

"And you can escape while they make my capture," Ben replied.

"There will still be people in back of the building," Petrov warned.

Ben glanced at Caitline who gazed at him in stupefaction. He felt glad that his offer perplexed her.

"I'll make sure I get everyone's attention when I come out," Ben promised.

All heads turned toward Wilson who remained skeptical.

"WE'RE WAITING, HACKWELL," Stanfeld barked.

"See? They're expecting me," Ben said and turned to Wilson. "It's your call."

Wilson eyed Rykert and Jennifer standing in the doorway.

"What about them?" Wilson asked.

Ben hesitated. He had not calculated the full ramifications of this delaying tactic. Whatever ploy he used to keep them alive was better than marching to their incineration, Ben decided.

"Keep them as hostages," Ben answered. "If this doesn't work, you've lost nothing."

"That's so like you!" Jennifer surged to her feet. "Save your skin at the expense of everyone else."

Rykert pulled on Jennifer's sleeve.

"Look at the matter rationally. It buys time." Rykert said in an urgent whisper. He lowered his voice further. "It keeps us alive."

"30 SECONDS," Stanfeld announced.

"And what happens if he succeeds?" Jennifer asked after Stanfeld's announcement. She pushed Rykert away. "We become expendable, as if we weren't already."

Jennifer scanned the faces in the room.

"I know all of you think that I'm a terrible mother and a worse human being," Jennifer declared. "But I'm not the one who's abandoning you."

Jennifer leveled her gaze on Ben.

"This is low, Benjamin," Jennifer declared. "Even for you."

Ben saw the terror and disgust warring on Jennifer's face. Poised on the edge of oblivion, her antagonism toward Ben remained her lifeline. He marveled and pitied anyone who could hate so much.

"Well, Wilson?" Ben asked. "What's it going to be?"

"THIS IS AGENT LOCKETT," Lisa announced over the bullhorn. " ALL COMPANIES THAT DO BUSINESS ON THE INTERNET HAVE COMPLIED WITH OUR REQUEST THAT THEY SHUT DOWN THEIR OPERATIONS. EVERYONE IN THE BASEMENT PLEASE COME OUT OF THE BUILDING"

"It's over, Wilson," Ben advised. Lisa's announcement had eliminated his ploy. Homeland Security knew that more people than Ben were hiding in the basement. "Homeland Security has removed your threat to the Internet."

"We have others," Wilson replied and turned toward Petrov. "We will go with our alternative plan. Take these people into the furnace room."

Jennifer reached inside her blouse. Pulling out her stun gun, she lunged toward Ben who deflected her thrust with his forearms. He pivoted, seized her wrist, and scrabbled for her stun gun. Poised across Ben's outstretched hip, Jennifer pummeled his head and shoulders with her free hand.

Ben heard the safety snap of Sophia's Kalashnikov as he seized Jennifer's wrist.

"I wouldn't advise shooting anyone," Ben advised. "If they hear a shot outside, Stanfeld's men will storm the building."

Jennifer dropped the stun gun into Ben's hands.

"Take it," Jennifer urged. "It's our only chance."

Jennifer's suggestion was suicidal, Ben decided. Negotiating was the only way to prevent a bloodbath.

Petrov crouched into an attack stance on the other side of the room. Ben spun to face him, and an odor of bleach wafted up from his feet. A heap of glossy black hair lay beside Ben's boots. Raspberry flakes dotted the top of Jennifer's scalp. At once Ben knew the identity of the spendy redhead.

"Why did you kill Hoot?" Ben demanded.

"You know why," Jennifer replied.

Ben shook his head in ignorance.

"AIDS," Jennifer declared. "Gibson had infected Caitline."

Jennifer grabbed the stun gun from Ben's hand, planted her right foot, and thrust her other knee upward. Ben staggered, and Jennifer plunged the gun's electrodes into Ben's shoulder.

Ben dropped to the floor. His right side hiccuped like a broken windup toy. Sophia's legs straddled his head and stretched to infinity above him. Jennifer shifted the stun gun to her other hand and backed away from Sophia toward the opposite wall.

"No," Caitline protested.

Jennifer stood on sudden tiptoe, her lips a startled O of protest. The crimsoned beak of Petrov's commando knife peeped between the second and third button of her work shirt. The mahogany blotch radiated outward on Jennifer's shirt before Petrov placed Jennifer on the cot like a mother laying her child down for a nap.

Petrov spun toward Rykert. In terror, Rykert backed up into Sophia's waiting bayonet. Rykert squealed, squirmed, and kicked free into Petrov's bear hug. Petrov plunged his blade deep into Rykert's chest, and he collapsed onto the floor beside the cot with a groan.

Wilson straddled Ben whose spasms had subsided, but his agony had not.

"Get up," Wilson ordered.

Ben struggled onto one knee as Caitline knelt beside Jennifer's body lying on the cot. Bergstrom had said that hate was a powerful emotion, Ben remembered. All of his energies, all his searching for Caitline had come down to discovering she had received a fatal virus from his best friend.

"Foolish woman," Wilson said as Caitline straightened an errant strand on her mother's forehead. He retrieved the discarded stun gun. "What could she hope to accomplish with this?"

"Wasn't Hoot's murder enough?" Ben replied and scanned Caitline's face. The turmoil in Caitline's eyes had disappeared.

"How long have you known about your illness?" Ben asked.

"I don't know," Caitline replied from somewhere far away. "Forever, it seems."

"I didn't mean for it to end this way," Ben said. "You've got to believe that."

"I know," Caitline replied.

Petrov hoisted Ben to his feet.

"Get going," Wilson ordered.

"WE'RE COMING IN," Lisa said.

Caitline sprang to her feet and faced Wilson.

"Are you afraid to face our enemies?" Caitline asked.

"Not when we don't have to," Wilson replied.

"How much of what my father said is true?" Caitline asked.

"What he says is irrelevant," Wilson replied.

Caitline leaped to the computer console and pressed a button on the keyboard.

"There," Caitline cried. "The interface program has been erased."

Caitline turned toward Wilson.

"How many women did you kill? Caitline asked.

"Did you not think we would make backups?" Wilson replied.

"Tell me," Caitline demanded as she picked up flower vase. "Or I'll destroy Gibson's entire network."

Wilson folded his arms in defiance. Caitline emptied the contents of the flower vase onto the central computer. A cloud of steam billowed upward before Sophia slammed the stock of her Kalashnikov into Caitline's back. Caitline staggered forward, regained her balance, and flung the vase at Sophia's head. In the moment it took for Sophia to duck, Caitline seized the rifle barrel. Sophia's first burst spattered across the wall behind the computer terminals. Wilson and Petrov scuttled into the hallway; Ben dived to the floor while chunks of plaster rained upon his head.

Sophia's second burst ripped through the computer bank as she and Caitline pirouetted across the room. They collided against the doorsill and tumbled into the furnace room where a third discharge strafed the floor inches in front of Ben's face.

Ben got to his knees and scrambled behind the door, as the two women fought for control of Sophia's rifle. Sophia wrested it from Caitline's grip and slammed the butt against Caitline's temple. After Caitline's head thudded against the floor, Sophia positioned the muzzle inches in front of Caitline's nose.

"Enough," Wilson ordered and grabbed the Kalashnikov. "Get to the chute."

"What about you?" Sophia asked.

"Don't worry about me," Wilson replied and pecked her cheek.

Sophia disappeared across the hallway.

"So often we rehearsed this, my dear," Wilson said as he centered the muzzle between Caitline's eyes. "This one's the take."

Ben leapt for Wilson's knees. The Kalashnikov's retort exploded in Ben's ears. Wilson slammed into the opposite wall, recovered his balance, and fired again. Twin missiles strafed Ben's back as he rolled across the floor into Wilson's knees. Ben seized the rifle butt, and Wilson rammed it downward.

The butt glanced off Ben's jaw. Cement dust splattered onto his cheek. He kicked upward, but Wilson refused to let go. Clawing, tugging, scratching for control, the two men rolled to the doorway.

"Hands up," Stanfeld ordered and advanced into the room. Lisa and a half dozen agents followed Stanfeld inside. Stanfeld strafed the floor in front of the two men with her handgun. "Hands up, I said."

Ben and Wilson struggled to their knees. The rifle remained locked in equipoise between them.

"Release the weapon," Stanfeld ordered. "Both of you."

Ben felt Wilson's grip intensify. He felt his own grip failing. Ben summoned the strength to match his adversary's.

"Let go," Stanfeld warned. "Or both of you get it."

No remorse showed in Stanfeld's eyes. Pity, either, Ben decided. Wilson's face revealed the same lack of emotion.

Ben glanced toward Caitline who rose to a kneeling position. He relinquished his grip, and the butt slid through his hands. Wilson wrapped his arm around Ben's neck and propped the muzzle under his broken jaw.

"Out of the way," Wilson ordered.

"You're surrounded," Stanfeld replied. "You have no moves left."

"You think that?" Wilson cried.

The explosion sent everyone sprawling onto the floor. A billow of smoke and dust surged out of the computer room. Choking and coughing, Ben scrambled to his feet, but Wilson already was standing with the rifle barrel pointed at Ben's chest.

"The vengeance of Allah," Wilson said as the dust cloud engulfed his legs. He zeroed the muzzle on Ben's heart. "Again I find myself in your debt."

"Enough to let me go?" Ben asked.

"Enough to make it quick," Wilson replied.

Ben spotted Caitline rising to all fours before the bank of computer terminals. Ben knocked the gun barrel aside. Wilson's burst strafed the computer terminals as Ben thrust his shoulder into Wilson's chest. Wilson's second burst peppered the wall as Ben heaved him forward like a blocking sled toward Caitline's outstretched body. Wilson tripped over Caitline's back, firing wildly as he grabbed Ben's handcuffs. Together they plunged onto the sparking mass of cable and wire.

Computer equipment rained on Ben's arms and head. Somewhere the rifle continued to fire. Ben seized Wilson's other wrist as Wilson jabbed Jennifer's stun gun into Ben's side. Blue sparks, roiling agony, and the stench of electrified flesh ushered Ben's descent into oblivion.

CHAPTER 31

▼

Chartreuse flashes flickered across the ceiling to the beep of the monitors. Unknown voices interspersed the beeps.

"Extreme loss of blood," a female voice said.

"Penetration of the left ventricle," said a second, raspier female voice.

"Third degree burns of the head and upper torso," the first voice said.

"Puncture wounds to the left lung and kidney," announced the other.

The voices grew fainter.

"Did the other man make it?" the first voice asked.

"I think not," the other replied.

Ben tried to speak. Great, heavy drains clogged his nose and throat.

"What a shame," the first voice said.

"Stronger heart in this one," said the other.

Supple fingers raised Ben's head.

"The next 48 hours will tell," the second voice replied.

The strong fingers lowered Ben's head to embrace the coolness of the pillow.

*   *   *   *

The beeps had the regularity of a metronome set at beginners pace. A scent of primrose vied with an odor of disinfectant. Ben felt warm, supple fingers encompassing his right hand.

"Will he be all right?" Lisa asked.

"That's hard to say," Bergstrom replied.

Lisa's grip intensified. To Ben it felt feverish.

"You should return to your room," Bergstrom advised.

Ben tried to speak. The plastic tubes prevented it.

"For both our sakes," Bergstrom added.

Ben opened his eyes. A blob sat beside the bed, a taller blob at its foot.

"Can you see me?" Lisa asked.

Ben willed his eyes to focus. Lisa's blob leaned over him, the right side of its face adorned with a lop-sided, snowy turban.

Ben attempted to nod. The ever-prowling pain roared up his chest, neck, and out his extremities. He fell back against the pillow.

"I'm staying," Lisa declared.

Ben smiled weakly. Lisa's warm fingers squeezed his.

＊　　　＊　　　＊　　　＊

The beeps maintained a steady staccato. Ben sniffed. The fragrance of fresh flowers filled the room.

Ben opened his eyes. The phalanx of monitors that recorded Ben's every vital sign surrounded his bed. He spotted Bergstrom out in the hallway giving instructions to the youthful police sentry who assumed an at-ease stance outside his intensive care unit window. Bergstrom turned and peered through the window. The shiny remnants of twin lacerations traversed the right side of his forehead.

Ben turned toward the barred window. A flower basket resided on the bed stand behind his IV pole. A trio of creamy jonquils surrounded by a garland of evening primroses and baby's breath nodded toward the afternoon sun.

Ben reached for the three by five card pinned to the basket's foil wrapping. The monitor's staccato beat quickened. His tubes remained unyielding. Furtive pain lashed his chest and rolled out his extremities.

Ben fell back against the pillow in exhaustion. Had Lisa just been a fever dream, he wondered. Ben gritted his teeth, rolled over, and tore the card from its mooring.

> May Allah grant you strength to match your wisdom.
> Get well soon.
>
> Azeb Anouri

Ben let his head fall back against the pillow. He was still alive. What had happened to the others, Ben wondered. Especially Caitline, what had happened to her after he shoved Wilson over her back?

He reread Azeb's note. Now that Jennifer was dead, Azeb would have to find another job. It would be difficult for her to stay in the country now that both her sponsors had been killed.

Ben flipped Azeb's card back on the stand and thought of Jennifer. He had seen many people die without feeling a thing, but Jennifer's death filled him with remorse. If he had interpreted the right data sooner, he might have prevented her death. If he had fought with Jennifer less, he might have understood her more. If he had understood Jennifer more, Caitline never would have wanted to disappear.

He glanced out the window. Two bundled up figures standing on the guard's other side peered back at him. Ben recognized in surprise that they were Tyler and Kim. Kim grinned. She opened and closed her mittened hand to signal her hello. Tyler released his arm around Kim's waist and unzipped his backpack. Twin emerald pinpricks peered from the darkness. Ben chuckled at the sight of Desdemona's head emerging from the sack, scanning the area, and disappearing back inside. It felt good to laugh, Ben decided, and painful. He needed to feel his muscles work again after spending so much time in a morphine-induced state of suspended animation.

Ben's chuckle degenerated into a tortured, wracking cough. When his spasm subsided, Ben knew that pain would be his second companion for a long time.

He beckoned Bergstrom and the young couple inside with a wave of his arm.

Bergstrom nodded to the guard and followed Tyler and Kim through the door. He adopted a loose at-ease stance across the bed from them at Ben's right hand.

"How are you feeling?" Kim asked.

"Never better," Ben gasped.

"You don't sound so well to me," Tyler admonished.

"Nonsense. He'll be up and around in a day or two," Bergstrom assured them and winked. "Right?"

"If you say so," Ben coughed.

"Anybody who survives a car bomb and five shots from a Kalashnikov should be well enough to spend a few minutes with his friends," Bergstrom chided. "Don't you think?"

Ben grunted. He had many questions to ask but little strength to get them out.

"How long have I been here?" Ben asked. The hoarse sound of his voice sounded strange to him.

"Almost three weeks," Bergstrom replied.

"The last thing I remember was wrestling for Sophia's Kalashnikov," Ben said. "What happened to Wilson?"

"He didn't make it," Bergstrom replied. "Wilson fell onto a power cord exposed by the shooting. He died instantly."

Ben felt no remorse. After what he had done to Caitline and the other women, Wilson's demise seemed a fitting conclusion.

"He pulled me onto the computers with him," Ben recalled. "Why didn't I die, too?"

"Apparently his body shielded yours from the electricity," Bergstrom replied. He made a wry face. "You could almost say this was one time he saved your life."

"After several attempts you could almost say he owed me that," Ben retorted with a cough. He waited until the spasm subsided. "And the others? What happened to them?"

"We caught most of the others," Bergstrom replied as he reached inside his coat pocket, peered at the No smoking signs, and dropped his hand to his side. "Nechayev, Petrov, along with the staff at Schariah's, we caught them all. The dancers, in particular, have been most cooperative."

Ben smiled. He hardly doubted that they would be once Wilson was out of the picture.

"Even Vera?" Ben asked.

"Particularly Vera," Bergstrom replied. "She hasn't stopped talking since we brought her in."

Ben brightened at the thought of Vera haranguing the prison guards, then frowned. The data Ben really wanted to know he dreaded to ask.

"What about the Homeland Security agents?" Ben asked. "Were any hurt in the blast?"

"Just Stanfeld," Bergstrom replied. "She broke her arm against the door jamb."

"That's all?" Ben exclaimed.

"That's a funny thing," Bergstrom remarked. "Wilson intended the blast to bring down the entire building, but the shape of the blast brought down an interior wall that prevented the blast cone from extending further."

Bergstrom raised his hands to demonstrate.

"They directed the blast cone toward the furnace like this," Bergstrom said as he put the tips of his hands together to form a V. "And the furnace reinforced the wall behind it like this."

"Detective Bergstrom," Kim interrupted. "I think Ben wants to know what happened to Caitline."

Bergstrom sobered.

"I was waiting for you to ask," Bergstrom acknowledged. "You see…"

"Your daughter's fine," Lisa announced from the doorway. Ben noticed the single head bandage that crossed her left temple as Lisa entered the room and stood at the foot of Ben's bed. "I just spoke with her."

Ben tried to sit up. If Caitline was fine, Ben reasoned, she would physically be beside his bed to speak with him.

"Where is she?" Ben asked in alarm.

"She's here in the hospital," Lisa answered. "She received a head injury similar to mine along with some internal injuries and broken ribs, but she's OK."

"Why can't I see her?" Ben demanded. "I want to speak with her."

"I'm afraid that's impossible at the moment," Lisa replied. "You see…"

Ben noticed his young sentry step away from the window as Stanfeld led a trio of federal agents down the hallway. Stanfeld signaled them to halt with her undamaged arm. The person in the middle of the retinue with her head swathed in bandages broke fee and hurled herself against Ben's window.

"Dad!" Caitline cried.

Ben raised himself on one elbow.

"Caitline!" Ben called back.

Caitline shouted Ben's name again before two of Stanfeld's agents grabbed her handcuffed arms, re-cuffed them behind her back, and positioned her within their phalanx. Bergstrom and Lisa exchanged glances.

"Didn't you tell me Stanfeld chose two P.M. to move her prisoner?" Bergstrom asked.

"Stanfeld demanded that she be moved this afternoon," Lisa apologized. "I didn't know that she intended to take this particular corridor."

"I want to speak with my daughter," Ben demanded.

"Can't you do something?" Kim urged.

"I'll see what we can do," Lisa promised.

She and Bergstrom stepped outside as Caitline's retinue resumed its march down the hall. Icy tentacles grappled Ben's heart as he watched an animated discussion among the three officials. His heart leapt as Caitline's retinue followed Bergstrom and Lisa toward Ben's room.

More heated discussion ensued outside Ben's door. Finally, Lisa and Bergstrom reentered the room followed by Caitline and two of Stanfeld's escorts. Bergstrom and Lisa stood on each side while Caitline approached Ben's bed.

"Hey, Daddy," Caitline's voice quavered. "Are you OK?"

"Never better," Ben joked. This wasn't the time to be flippant, Ben realized. "Now that you're here."

Caitline knelt beside Ben's bed. Ben thought he smelled a whiff of primrose.

"Oh, Dad," Caitline sniffed as she scanned the yards of bandages and his phalanx of monitors. "You look so awful."

Ben smiled. For an instant, Caitline was his little girl again.

"They're only flesh wounds," Ben replied as he wiped the tear from Caitline's cheek. "They'll heal."

Ben cupped Caitline's chin in his hand.

"And you?" Ben asked.

"As well as can be expected," Caitline said. A faint smile curled the corners of her mouth. "Given the circumstances."

"Where are they taking you?" Ben asked.

"They said Guantanamo," Caitline replied.

Ben peered into Caitline's eyes. Their depths seemed still, determined, so much like her mother's that his heart ached.

"Are you afraid?" Ben asked.

"Not any more," Caitline replied.

"We have to go now," Stanfeld said.

Caitline stood up. Her manacled hands grasped Ben's left hand, lingered for a moment, and trailed off his fingertips.

Ben watched Caitline take her place beside Stanfeld's bandaged arm and march out of the room. The tentacles tightened their grip, the monitors beeped their alarms as Ben watched Caitline's retinue return the way they had come until they disappeared around a corner. Why had he rescued her, Ben wondered bitterly, if this was to be the result.

Ben turned to Bergstrom.

"She didn't kill anyone," Ben said. "She helped me stop Wilson from carrying out his threat."

"She's been designated enemy combatant status," Lisa replied.

"Guantanamo is the worst place she could go," Ben cried. "She might be infected with AIDS. What treatment facilities do they have there for that?"

Ben's head fell against the pillow.

"I'll bet nobody's bothered to check," Ben gasped.

"I will," Lisa promised. She leaned forward and kissed Ben's forehead. "I'll make sure that they do."

Another whiff of primrose reached Ben's nostrils. He glanced at the gift flowerpot and rubbed his right thumb and index finger together. Caitline's touch still resided in his tactile memory, he realized, available whenever he needed it.

"Don't worry," Kim assured Ben as she took his hand. "Tyler and I will help."

"I'll do everything I can," Bergstrom promised. "When you're strong enough…"

Ben laid his hand over Kim's and closed his eyes. All of them were unrelated, yet Ben felt part of a family again. With their help, Ben knew that he and Caitline would be together again one day. All of the data just felt right.

THE END

978-0-595-36822-8
0-595-36822-0

Printed in the United States
49180LVS00004B/199-216